The Deal

交易 Jiāo Yì

by David Zen

The Deal is a work of fiction. Any resemblance of its characters to actual persons, living or dead, is unintentional and coincidental. Some well-known persons and many actual places are mentioned in the book, but the events involving them are fictional.

First edition 2014

Published through CompletelyNovel.com

Copyright © Maury Shenk 2014

Cover:
Design © Jan Marshall bookcoverdesign@btinternet.com
Girl with fan © Paulo Pagan | Dreamstime.com
Business meeting © Rawpixel | Fotolia.com
Shanghai skyline © Taiga | Dreamstime.com

ISBN 9781849144568

Printed in the United Kingdom by CPI

For my parents Ian and Sylvia
who taught me to believe in myself

Contents

Note for the Reader

The Deal (Jiāo Yì) is about an international investment deal involving China and the United States. It is meant to be a good story even if you don't have a nose for business.

On use of Chinese

Chinese words in *The Deal* are mostly in italicized *pīn yīn* (the modern way to show the sound of spoken Mandarin Chinese, using the Western alphabet and indicating the four Mandarin tones with symbols above the letters), followed by a translation in square brackets. Chinese characters are shown occasionally for interest. Translations and italics may be omitted where the words should have become familiar to the reader (e.g. *jiāo yì* [the deal]) and for Chinese proper names (e.g. Shanghai). Chinese surnames usually appear before given names (e.g. the owner of the main Chinese property company is Wang Jun and his son is Wang Xu).

I hope you enjoy the story.

David Zen
April 2014

Agreement

交易

1

The End of Beginning
July 13, 2009

*Our lives begin to end the day we become silent
about things that matter*

– Martin Luther King Jr.

As her flight chased the sunset over the East China Sea, the young woman in seat 9A found the lyrics to the Beatles' 'Back in the USSR' looping in her head: *"Flew in from Miami Beach BOAC ... Man, I had a dreadful flight."* The context was not quite right—she was flying in from Los Angeles, and the big China Eastern Airlines Airbus approaching Shanghai Pudong International Airport was a far more advanced beast than the one that had taken the Fab Four to Moscow. It was the terrible weather over the Pacific that had brought the song unbidden to mind. Man, it *had* been a dreadful flight. A few passengers had screamed during some of the worst turbulence. She assumed it was not an omen for what lay ahead of her in China.

The young woman curled a loop of her long black hair around a finger and tugged at it. It was a childhood habit that she had tried hard to break, mostly with success. But on the rare occasions when she was nervous, as almost anyone would have been on today's flight, the habit returned. As the weather calmed, she realized what she was doing, let the hair fall on her shoulder, and looked out the window.

Liú Mò Lì [刘茉莉] was twenty-seven years old, and she was flying home, or at least nearer to home. She had grown up in the coastal city of Tianjin, China's fourth-largest city, some distance north from Shanghai, not far from Beijing. After three years living in the United States, trips back to China were welcome. Diving back into China's ancient language and culture made her feel rooted and proud in a way that she could not easily explain. It was like slipping into a warm bath, profoundly relaxing.

Yet Liu Mo Li had an ambiguous relationship with what China had become as a modern country. Her pride at being Chinese felt very different from the assertive, nationalistic confidence of many of her compatriots now that China was again at the center of the world stage. And for as long as she could remember, she had felt a strong competing pull from *xī fang*—"the West". Since her childhood, she had loved literature, film, and music from America and Europe, like the Beatles song accompanying her into Shanghai. Now, living in Los Angeles, she felt that she fit well into Western culture. It wasn't the loose, easy fit of a native culture, like she felt in China. More like the tailored fit of the black suit with a short skirt that she was wearing on the flight to Shanghai. Like the fit of the English translation of her name that she had grown proud to use—Jasmine Liu.

Jasmine was caught—she had recently realized, in one of her more self-aware moments—between the comforting knowns of China and the tantalizing unknowns of the life she had started to build in the United States. She often felt uncertain and in between, not quite sure where she was going. She half-expected that answers would emerge from the routine of daily life, yet they remained elusive. What was the question anyhow? Why did she always feel that she was only beginning something? She felt a dull ache for clarity, and this trip back to China felt like it might offer an important punctuation, the end of confusion, the end of beginning. She liked that phrase, the "end of beginning".

"Excuse me, sir." A flight attendant in a dark blue uniform and colorful scarf spoke to the man in seat 9B next to her. He was a Westerner, with curly, sand-colored hair, apparently in his mid-thirties, and had been intently studying a spreadsheet on his laptop. "Would you like something to drink before we land?"

The man, Jasmine's boss Richard Gregg, responded in Mandarin Chinese. "*Bú yào, xiè xie.* [I don't want anything, thank you.]"

The flight attendant smiled at his Chinese, and responded in English. "You're welcome. We hope you have recovered from the rough flight." When he did not answer, she turned to Jasmine. "*Nǐ ne?* [And you?]"

"*Yě bú yào, xiè xie.* [I also don't want anything, thank you.]"

As she walked down the aisle, Richard said "I hate it that she speaks to me in English after I spoke to her in Mandarin for the whole flight. They only speak in Mandarin when they think they see a Chinese face. Hell, I'm sure if I were Korean or Japanese without a word of Mandarin, they would just carry on without noticing the lack of comprehension."

"I think they are taught to do that. Or maybe it's just human nature. Anyhow, you shouldn't worry about it. You understand Chinese and China better than almost any other American I have met." Before joining the investment world, Richard had studied Chinese language and literature at university. He spoke excellent Mandarin, and used it to advantage in social and business conversations, and in situations when Chinese speakers did not know they were being overheard.

They had been working together since mid-2008. As the global financial crisis threatened to become a tidal wave, she had been lucky enough to find a job with a small but well-funded California investment fund, San Marino Property Investments. Richard, one of San Marino's younger partners, had a vision that the Chinese property market was the next big opportunity, and jumped quickly at the chance to combine his interest in China with a major deal for San Marino. He had hired Jasmine as a native Chinese analyst to help realize his vision.

The project that they had developed, which Jasmine had come to think of as simply *jiāo yì* [交易, the deal], felt like a natural stepping-stone for her on a path to success that had been charted for her since childhood. Due to China's

5

confusing "one child" policy, she had no brothers or sisters, like many of her generation. Like many modern Chinese parents—treasuring their only child as a "little emperor" or "little empress"—hers had very high expectations of her, augmented by their own success. Jasmine felt lucky that intelligence and common sense had allowed her to make a good start at meeting those expectations ... or at least she hoped those were the main reasons. She knew that jealous female classmates thought she got ahead due to her looks.

Jasmine did have the kind of beauty that often made men turn in the street to watch her, a sort of effortless perfection. She had classically Chinese features, long black hair, and what more than one male friend had called a perfect body—taller than average with long legs, a slim waist, rounded hips, and small, high breasts. She liked these natural endowments, who wouldn't?—and wasn't so hypocritical to deny the advantages it gave her in China's male-dominated, sexist society. Yet she wanted to believe that she didn't exploit those advantages, and that she worked hard enough to deserve success by anyone's measure.

She had attended Beijing's leading Tsinghua University, and then slid naturally into a top job as an analyst at Industrial and Commercial Bank of China in Shanghai. A good job at China's largest bank, usually known as ICBC, was a ticket to success in the rapidly growing Chinese economy.

But after two years of boredom, and frustration at her male colleagues, the call of the West prompted Jasmine to submit an application to Harvard Business School, not really expecting to be accepted. When Harvard's answer was yes, so was Jasmine's, without hesitation. She felt that her move to Boston had been another important beginning, although of what she remained unsure.

When she graduated from Harvard, the job at San Marino had appeared almost miraculously, and seemed an obvious next step once it did. Richard and his partners at San Marino believed that the still-growing financial maelstrom following the Lehman Brothers bankruptcy in September 2008 was a big opportunity for those who still had money to invest. A simple case of "Buy low, sell high," Richard told her. She knew it didn't take a genius to see an opportunity to buy low after the spectacular collapse in asset values, but she did admire the confidence of their conviction that the wheels would not entirely fall off the global economy.

While most of the investment world was dazed and confused, San Marino followed these optimistic instincts—and Richard's vision and experience—towards China. As soon as the Chinese government announced a massive financial stimulus in November 2008 to stabilize the economy, San Marino launched an intense effort to acquire a property portfolio in China. Now, in the summer of 2009, she and Richard were flying to Shanghai to complete *jiāo yì*—a joint venture with the Jiangsu-Zhejiang Property Company. If they were successful, it would be a triumph, a landmark deal for Richard and the firm, and for her.

Jasmine felt quietly confident that this trip would successfully tie up the few remaining loose ends of *jiāo yì*. Of course, in a complicated transaction, things could go wrong right up to the last minute. But they had been careful. Richard was an admirably diligent, demanding investor—a bit socially inept, and sometimes very demanding, but a fair boss. And Jasmine and the team at San Marino had done everything they could to get the details right.

As she gazed out the plane window at the now clear skies, Jasmine considered her conflicting ties to East and West. Was she really flying home, or visiting from a new home? The answer was elusive as ever, but for the time being, this couldn't matter. She had to put these questions to one side and focus on the business challenges in front of her. The rough weather on the flight had not distracted her from anticipation of the next three days, which were the climax of an exhausting, eight-month roller-coaster ride of constant work on *jiāo yì*, and insufficient sleep.

Jasmine turned and glanced over at Richard, re-immersed in his spreadsheet. He took pride in being extremely cautious on details, almost to a fault, alongside the risk-taking—he would say "intelligent risk-taking"—that is mandatory for a

7

successful investor. Jasmine thought, not for the first time, that she was genuinely grateful to have him as a mentor ... perhaps even becoming a friend.

"It's a good portfolio, Jasmine," Richard said, looking up from his computer. "It takes some nerve to do what we're doing, and these are tough times. But my hunch is that, in two years, we'll be very happy we did this deal now."

"You did it, Richard," Jasmine answered. She was proud of her own role in *jiāo yì* and determined to make it a success, but really this was Richard's show. "Thanks again for involving me. It's been an exciting ride."

"No kidding," he responded, glancing out the window. They exchanged a knowing look. "I would have liked less excitement on this flight." Echoing her thoughts from earlier, he continued, after a brief pause. "I certainly hope it's not a sign for what lies ahead of us. You've checked everything, right?"

Jasmine looked at him levelly, accustomed to this sort of question. "The lawyers and I have been through all the details a few times. And we will do it again tomorrow."

Richard's expression loosened, and he nodded. "Thanks, Jasmine. Let's get this across the finish line on Thursday. Then we'll celebrate."

交易

2

Waiting for the Americans

July 13, 2009

You can always count on Americans to do the right thing—
after they've tried everything else

− Winston Churchill

April Wang glanced nervously at her watch as she hummed the first bars of 'April Come She Will' by Simon & Garfunkel, which she thought of as her theme song. Apart from featuring her name, the song combined a sense of adventure and longing with the easy calm typical of Simon and Garfunkel. She hoped that this was a combination of traits that she could share. Although real adventure had not found her yet, and she did not feel calm at the moment. Well … maybe she never felt as calm as her ideal self from the song. "OK, cool it, April. You're on time," she said to herself. "How hard can it be to meet a flight?"

A native of Los Angeles, April had been working in Shanghai for the past year as an intern at the Jiangsu-Zhejiang Property Company. The successful business belonged to her rich uncle Wang Jun, her father's older brother, who had spent twenty years building it from scratch. The previous summer, after graduating from Harvard College, April had decided that now was the time to look for adventure, and that exploring her Chinese roots was a good start.

Uncle Jun kept a warm relationship with her father, although it was a relationship at a distance. The families had crossed borders to visit each other only a handful of times. April had a vague memory of a day on the beach in Los Angeles when she was a small child, playing on the sand with her older cousin Wang Xu, Uncle Jun's son. Despite the distance, the family connection had stayed strong enough for Uncle Jun to take her on enthusiastically as an intern at JZP (as his company was usually known in English) and to install her as a long-term guest in the large family house in Shanghai's French Concession neighborhood. April fit in quickly, getting along well with her uncle's wife Li Hong and Cousin Xu, who was now a hip twenty-eight-year-old.

It also turned out to be a perfect time for April to join JZP. The global financial crisis that had been in its early days when she graduated had created an unexpected opportunity for JZP to join forces with a small, bold, California investment firm called San Marino Property Investments. April quickly assumed a key role in the negotiations, and received an almost immediate promotion to junior researcher, because Uncle Jun apparently felt that this *jiāo yì* required something more than an intern.

Conscious of her own inexperience, April was nervous find herself playing a central role in what was obviously such an important transaction for JZP. Yet it did seem that her ability to deal with the Americans, the *Měiguó rén* as they were referred to at JZP, had made a real contribution so far to the success of the deal.

Now, she was waiting at Pudong International Airport for the small team from San Marino: Mr. Richard Gregg and Ms. Jasmine Liu. Uncle Jun had been unable to make it to the airport because of a meeting outside Shanghai, and had sent his top lieutenant Wu Zhiguo, JZP's Head of Business Development. Uncle Wu, as he insisted that April call him, was a childhood friend of Uncle Jun, a few years older than his boss. They had grown up together in Suzhou, a city in Jiangsu province nearby Shanghai, and had both moved to Shanghai after the Cultural Revolution.

Uncle Wu was looking visibly nervous—more so than usual—alternating between intently scanning the crowd of emerging travelers at International Arrivals and re-checking a sheaf of papers in his hand. Next to him stood one of the JZP's junior staff, who had been designated bag-carrier and was following Uncle Wu's gaze obediently.

April too looked around at the constant bustle of the airport, which was somehow proceeding in nearly complete order. On her arrival from the United States a year earlier, she had expected the airport to reflect a chaotic China, one that remained a developing country. This turned out to be only partly right, in the wrong way. China had been developing so rapidly that practically everything was new, as she had quickly realized at the airport and (more so) when they left it. The airport, which she was now visiting for the second time, was entirely modern, covered with Western-style advertising (in Chinese, of course). In its size and capitalist anonymity, it was very much like LAX airport in Los Angeles, from where she had flown to China.

The Shanghai airport was much more organized than its Los Angeles counterpart, thanks in large part to the not-at-all-Western army of uniformed personnel responsible for keeping that order. April particularly liked the uniformed women officers, almost all short-haired in nearly androgynous dress, but somehow sexy.

"*Xiǎo Wáng*," Uncle Wu said, interrupting her thoughts. He usually called April "Little Wang", a typical but affectionate Chinese way to address a well-liked younger colleague. "We have everything ready, right? Schedule for Mr. Gregg and Miss Liu, driver, hotel? Is there anything that can go wrong?" Uncle Wu was good at his job, but he worried too much about protocol and politeness. April knew that protocol was important in China, but Uncle Wu took it a little too far. She also knew that an American businessman like Richard Gregg probably found Uncle Wu too formal and perhaps slightly annoying. On previous meetings Mr. Gregg had not shown it, though. He, too, was exceedingly polite.

April fought her own nervousness, trying to appear confident. "Uncle Wu, there's always something that can go wrong, but I think we're ready. The schedules are in my bag, six copies. The driver will be waiting for us next to the taxi line. San Marino booked their own hotel, the Peninsula. I checked with the hotel, and they are expecting the Americans for four nights. I think that's the list." She looked down at her hands.

"They can see the sign." April was displaying a laminated paper sign—"San Marino Property Investments, Richard Gregg and Jasmine Liu"—which was almost certainly unnecessary, since everyone had already met.

"*Xiǎo Wáng*, you are always well-prepared. *Wáng lǎo bǎn* must be proud of you—intelligence and business skills seem to run in the family." Uncle Wu always called her Uncle Jun *Wáng lǎo bǎn*—"Boss Wang". It was a term of respect, and in this case also of endearment. April knew that the two had been colleagues and friends for decades, although she had yet to learn how they had met.

"Good looks, too, don't you think?" April said, smiling. Uncle Jun cut a particularly handsome and imposing figure at JZP. And April understood that at age twenty-three, she was quickly becoming rather more than a cute college student. Her smooth, tan skin and thick, black hair were not disadvantages, and people often told her that her firm chin was distinctive. Still, she had never felt entirely sure about her looks, and liked to fish a little for what others thought. Having grown up in LA, it was hard for April not to judge by appearances.

"Let's keep focusing on *jiāo yì*," he answered. "Like you say, things can always go wrong. Let's not let any problem be our fault." Uncle Wu shifted his feet as he looked again at the intermittent stream of emerging passengers.

Prompted by Uncle Wu's comment, April turned her thoughts to the deal. She knew that her work on it had been good, and that apart from small, manageable tasks like this one at the airport, its success or failure was now almost entirely out of her hands. Uncle Wu was right. She was very organized, and had always succeeded at school, and more recently at work. But sometimes people made her nervous—particularly new people. Cousin Xu teased her constantly about how shy she was when meeting his friends.

Right now, for reasons that she could only partly explain, she felt especially nervous about Jasmine Liu. In part, it was because she was unsure whether she could ever equal the cool confidence of the older girl, who hardly seemed to notice her at their first meeting.

Coincidentally, as they found out during that initial encounter, April and Jasmine had attended Harvard at the same time, but had never met there. April had been an undergraduate spending most of her time near Harvard Square, and Jasmine had been across the Charles River at the Business School. Now, April felt oddly surprised that she had not known then that Jasmine was present. Working on *jiāo yì*, April had the impression that Jasmine was an *alter ego* on the other side of the table. April, even after her year working in China, still felt very American. Jasmine was one of "the Americans" on the deal, but was certainly very Chinese. Yes, an *alter ego*. One to whom April feared she could not measure up.

"April, pay attention!" Uncle Wu was waving excitedly at Richard and Jasmine as they walked out of the glass doors that led from the customs area and looked around expectantly. Jasmine noticed the group from JZP, spoke to Richard and pointed, and they both walked over.

"*Nǐ hǎo, Wú xiānsheng, Wáng xiǎojiě.* [Hello, Mr. Wu and Miss Wang.]" Richard said. "Thank you for meeting us. It's really appreciated to have our future partners greet us in person." He smiled at both of them. Jasmine also smiled at Uncle Wu and nodded politely at April.

"Of course, Mr. Gregg. It is the least we could do. I hope that you and Miss Liu had a pleasant flight."

"Actually, our flight wasn't too pleasant," Richard said, including Jasmine with a glance at her. "Some of the worst flying weather I've experienced."

"I am sorry to hear that. We hope the rest of your visit to China will be smoother."

"Well, we made it. And the weather kept me awake to do a complete check of the JV property portfolio. It all looks in order to me. We can go over the documents at our lawyers' offices tomorrow, and then have the closing on Thursday, right?"

"Of course, Mr. Gregg," Uncle Wu repeated. "Everything is in order."

A few days later, thinking back on the arrival of the San Marino team at the airport, April realized that none of them could have had any idea how completely wrong Uncle Wu had been.

交易

3

The Crash

February 23, 2009

Dow Jones Industrial Average closing price:
October 9, 2007—14,165 (peak)
October 14, 2008—9,311
October 15, 2008—8,578
March 9, 2009—6,549 (12-year low)

Five months before the meeting at the airport, unlike most others in the investment world, Richard Gregg was liking the numbers he saw in the *Wall Street Journal*. "Buy low, sell high" is an investment truism, and from the numbers on Monday morning, February 23, 2009, it seemed like an incredibly good time to buy low.

"How much worse do you think things can get?" asked his wife, Julie. "What happens if it all falls apart?" Julie was a striking, petite brunette, thirty-four years old to Richard's thirty-six. They had met at UCLA, where both were studying Chinese literature. She was now sitting next to Richard at the breakfast table in their Craftsman-style house in Pasadena, feeding porridge with strawberries to their two-year-old daughter, Lydia, and looking at the headlines of the *Los Angeles Times*.

"It could get a lot worse," Richard answered, smiling ironically, "but my instinct is that the markets are nearing the bottom. This is *my* first experience with a market panic, but it's happened many times before, and things always turn around."

"How do we know that this time isn't Armageddon?" Julie smiled too, betraying that she was not entirely serious. At heart, she was an optimist, like Richard. "That seems to be what the papers are saying."

"You know not to believe most of what you read in the papers. Anyway, we're all still here, and this isn't 1931. Bernanke has already proven that he wants to do what it takes to avoid disaster, and Obama gets it, too. They don't want half the American population on the street eating beans on toast around flaming oil barrels. Not what I would have said a few years ago, but thank goodness for the United States government."

"If it gets much worse, I suppose we could move back to China," Julie mused. After she'd graduated from UCLA in 1997, Julie had ended the only lengthy separation in their relationship by joining Richard in Beijing, where he was in the early stages of research for an economics Ph.D focusing on changes to the Chinese system under the leadership of Deng Xiaoping. Julie had not followed Richard's gradual trajectory from literature into economics and, eventually, business. She had spent her time in China learning about Zen Buddhism, which had become a lifelong interest for her. "We had a good time there, didn't we?"

Images of China had recently been returning to Richard's mind—the people, the culture, the food, including (curiously) a particular bowl of beef noodle soup that he had eaten with Julie on the day she'd come to Shanghai. The soup had been cheap, but it had seemed incredibly tasty, perhaps because of his gratitude that he could share it with his beautiful, newly-arrived girlfriend.

"Yes, we did," Richard responded. "And, honestly, it might happen—a visit, anyway. I've been thinking. China is a great opportunity for San Marino's new fund. It may not seem like it from the papers, but San Marino is in a tremendous position with the cash that we raised just before the crash. Now we need to spend it, and Chinese property looks really attractive. I already have Jasmine looking at what we can buy."

"Speaking of attractive," Julie said, "Jasmine is quite something. Why is she single? Maybe she has designs on her dashing boss?" She leaned over to wipe away porridge from Lydia's chin.

16

"I doubt it," Richard protested. "Anyhow, you know I only have eyes for my two girls." He smiled again at Julie, and made a silly face at Lydia. "Jasmine really is something, though. The hardest-working researcher I've ever had. The way she is working, I'm not surprised that she doesn't have time for men."

"So, what are the two of you going to buy in China?"

"That's what I need to figure out," Richard said. "Anyhow, we definitely should buy something. Two hundred years ago, Nathan Rothschild said, 'Buy on the sound of cannons, sell on the sound of trumpets.' He was talking about war rather than a financial crisis, but he meant that the right time to invest is when everyone is pessimistic. I'm definitely hearing the sound of cannons."

"I hope you're right," she said. A car horn honked outside. "I think *I* hear a trumpet." The horn belonged to the classic convertible Jaguar of Thomas Wilshire, the senior partner of San Marino and Richard's round-the-corner neighbor. Tom and Richard alternated sharing the short drive to work. Richard preferred the days in the Jaguar to those in his own more sedate BMW.

Richard took a last bite of the eggs and toast in front of him, stood up, and kissed Julie and Lydia, the latter responding with an enthusiastic, "Daddy work. Bye-bye!"

"Yes, honey. Daddy is going to work. You have a lovely day, and we will have a nice play before bedtime." Richard felt a usual burst of gratitude toward Julie, who had decided after Lydia was born to give up management at Modern Zen, her growing group of meditation centers, to be a full-time mom. Her very able business partner and university friend Evelyn was doing a great job running the business, in which Julie remained a half-owner. She still often visited the original center in Pasadena. Richard looked at her with an affectionate smile. "You have a good day, too. Maybe we should also have a nice play later. After bedtime."

17

Julie blushed. "Richard Gregg, there is a young girl present! Please get to work and see if you can make the most of the credit crisis."

* * *

Outside, Richard climbed into the silver XJS, a classic car that exuded good fortune. "Good morning, Tom." Like Richard, Tom was dressed casually for work in jeans and a sport jacket. Tom had silver hair and a tan, and was slim and fit—practically the Hollywood archetype of a successful, mature, southern California investor.

"Yep, another beautiful Southern California day in the middle of a global financial panic," Tom said as he backed out of Richard's driveway. "So, what's up, Doc?" The partners at San Marino liked to tease Richard gently about his Ph.D, which he didn't mind. He had never regretted his move from academia to the investment world, but he still felt proud about his doctoral work on the Chinese economic system and still wanted to find a way to make it useful.

Returning to China as an investor had been part of the plan for his career transition, but then other things got in the way, mainly the pressure to focus on the deals that could make San Marino and its investors as much money as possible. Recent events that linked China with the chance to make serious money were as exciting as anything he had encountered in a long time.

"Tom, you know I've been working on China ideas," said Richard, quickly dispensing with the small talk, as was his habit. "And it's looking good. Nowhere else in the world looks better for property investment. Chinese growth is staying strong, and this mess in the markets gives us a chance to invest at attractive valuations."

Tom nodded. "Yeah, I got that. I agree that the crisis is an opportunity, but we need to be careful. Everyone is scared. The investors in the San Marino III fund have given us a broad mandate, but we need to make sure we don't do anything that looks too crazy, or people will start asking for their money back."

"We need to invest somewhere, and I can't see anywhere better than China."

"Right. What I need from you is a solid deal, with a rock solid business case."

"I'm working on it. Give me a couple of weeks and I'll have something that the partners can discuss."

"You got it, Doc. I'm a little bored with investing in places like Orange County and London anyhow." Tom piloted the Jaguar calmly through the streets of Pasadena and then San Marino, past the stately Huntington Library, and around the corner to the small modern office building owned by San Marino Property Investments.

Inside, Richard greeted his secretary, Ellen, dropped his briefcase in his glass-fronted partner's office, and walked over to Jasmine's desk. She sat in the open-plan area where the firm's researchers worked. As usual, she was dressed immaculately in a dark suit and white blouse, and was looking intently at her computer screen, giving the distinct, and probably accurate, impression that she had already been at work for several hours.

"Good morning, Jasmine."

She looked up and smiled. "What's up, Doc?" Richard gave Jasmine credit for her cool confidence. She was the only staff member who addressed him with the same nickname as the partners used. She was polite, respectful, and diligent—very "Chinese" in most ways. But she had a daring and willingness to take risks that was not typically Chinese. He had seen it in her responses in their first interview, and it had made her a clear choice over the many other analysts—native Chinese and Westerners with Chinese experience—that he had interviewed. Richard did not want to do an expected deal. He needed someone with daring to help him spot the unexpected opportunity.

"I'm well, thanks. How's it going with the target list?" Richard asked.

"Well, you know our long list was fifteen companies. I have tried to learn everything that I can from public information. I also made preliminary calls to most of the companies, and got a lot of information that way too. Unfortunately, some of them were not very helpful."

"Don't worry about it, people are always suspicious when they get cold calls. What did you find out? I need a short list. We need to move fast."

"OK, I can give you that. To keep it simple, I have been evaluating against four criteria—private rather than government ownership, a high-quality commercial property portfolio, strong management, and big enough for San Marino to make an investment of around $50-100 million."

"That sounds right. So give it to me."

"OK." Jasmine looked for several seconds at her computer screen, and then back at Richard. "Three companies really stand out: Zhang Real Estate Trust in Beijing, China Industrial Properties in Guangzhou, and Jiangsu-Zhejiang Property Company in Shanghai."

"OK. Do you really believe in those choices? Are there other contenders for the list?"

"I don't think so," Jasmine said confidently. "I don't want to miss a good opportunity, but my feeling is that we should focus on these three."

"All right," Richard decided. "I want you and me to meet the management of those three companies next week in China. Can you set that up?"

Jasmine blinked. "I don't know if they will agree to meet us so quickly."

"You can ask. Make it clear that we will be in China next week, and that this may be their best chance to discuss an investment with us."

"Chinese people don't decide as quickly as Americans about things like that."

"Well, let's make this deal part-Chinese and part-American. See what you can do. I'm sure you'll figure something out."

"OK, I'll do my best."

"Ellen can handle the travel arrangements once the schedule firms up. Let's aim to fly out on Sunday." Richard was already backing away towards his office.

"OK, Doc, I promise to do my best."

交易

4

The New China

early March 2009

To get rich is glorious

– Deng Xiaoping

The three twenty-somethings, flatteringly seated at a table by the window, fit in well at the Crystal Jade Restaurant in Xintiandi. They were as attractive and visibly well-off as the neighborhood, a fashionable Shanghai shopping district rebuilt over the past decade in the style of a long-ago Shanghai. The new Xintiandi was certainly now cleaner and better-organized than the original had ever been, thanks to the new money.

To April's American eyes, looking out at a cool, clear February evening, Xintiandi looked like a tourist attraction, but she knew that it was equally aimed at the many Chinese *nouveaux riches*. And indeed Xu, who had become April's unofficial guide to Shanghai, had been enthusiastic about his choice of restaurant when he invited her out to dinner.

Xu had a promising job at Bank of China—although Uncle Jun was encouraging him, so far without success, to spend more time on the family business at JZP—and a flat of his own. April knew that the job and flat were the tickets to marriage for a young Chinese man, but Xu seemed determinedly uninterested in marriage. He spent almost every evening with an ever-changing circle of equally hip friends hanging out at Shanghai's restaurants, bars and night spots. This wasn't really April's scene, but joining him was a good way to experience Shanghai, and she liked it that Xu introduced her to his friends as *mèi mei* [妹妹, little sister].

The third person at the table was Annabelle, Xu's favorite date of the moment. Annabelle was Chinese but liked to use the Western name by which she was known at the Hermès shop where she worked. She was beautiful, impeccably dressed (usually wearing one of her employer's scarves), and had very little interesting to say. Xu paid little attention to her, and she barely appeared to mind. They seemed to have struck a happy bargain.

"I like this song," April said, commenting on the soulful ballad that was playing as background music.

"That's Eason Chan," Annabelle said. "*Tā shì Xiāng Gǎng rén.* [He's from Hong Kong.] My customers tell me that he is also becoming popular in the West." Annabelle liked to show off her connections. The restaurant's choice of music would have been unlikely not many years earlier. Suddenly, Chinese popular culture was blooming with a Western-styled, Asian-flavored mix of consumer goods, rock music and pretty models. Almost anything was becoming OK to keep the new urban middle class happy—at least in ways that did not challenge the dominance of the Communist Party.

"Speaking of the West, why does the Chinese press always criticize the 'Western capitalist system'?" April asked Xu quietly. "It looks to me that China has become even more capitalist than the United States."

"Why do you say that?" Xu seemed more interested in his food and in looking around at the other people in the restaurant than in April's question. They were eating *má pó dòufu*, a spicy Sichuan tofu dish, and *bái cài* [bok choy], the last course of a three-course set meal that Xu had insisted they choose.

"All that seems to matter to people our age in China is money. Buying a flat, buying nice shoes, buying whatever. That's what capitalism is about."

"Why shouldn't we buy things?" Xu continued to eat steadily, but now looked at April. "The Western financial crisis has showed that Deng Xiaoping was right when he said that 'socialism with Chinese characteristics' would beat the West at its own game. As your actor Michael Douglas said, 'Greed is good'. Now the United States has to accept that it's not the only country that can be greedy."

"I guess I agree." April felt that Xu was a little arrogant about the success of China, yet she couldn't blame him. The United States had been on top for a long time, and it was natural for him to enjoy China's resurgence. She, too, felt proud to be from a Chinese family—and didn't fail to notice that Xu referred to Michael Douglas as *her* actor. "But I really don't understand why it's all about money. Has everyone forgotten about Chinese culture? Apart from the food, that is. I really love the food here."

Xu was in the middle of eating a piece of bok choy. He finished it, put down his chopsticks, and spoke to April intently. "*Mèi mei*, I am surprised that you ask that. Of course, China has great culture, and we don't forget that. But we also know that it's always changing. This year is the fiftieth anniversary of the People's Republic of China, and look how much has happened to us in those fifty years. Our parents grew up during the Cultural Revolution and almost lost everything. Now it's our time to succeed. So of course we make money while we can. My *bà ba* seized the opportunity, and I intend to do the same thing."

"Sorry if I was too tough. Your father is great man, and I am lucky that he has given me the opportunity to work here and live with him. I really feel at home with your family."

"No need to apologize, *mèi mei*. But you're wrong about young Chinese people only being interested in money. My friend Walter, for example, is definitely interested is something else," Xu said, smiling and returning to his food.

Xu's friend Yang Jiang, like Annabelle, preferred to be called by an English name. He was a young journalist at *Shanghai Zhōumò* [*Shanghai Weekend*], a weekly newspaper that had gained a reputation for cultural and social criticism. He was pleasant, thoughtful, and slightly obsessed by Western culture—and, increasingly it seemed, by April. She liked him a lot, best among Xu's friends, but not in the way that Walter liked her.

"Yes, I know, Xu. But I am not ready for a Chinese boyfriend." This was true, but not the whole truth. She had had a Chinese-American boyfriend for a while at Harvard. He was a good guy, and her parents had approved, but it had not lasted for long.

"Why not?" asked Annabelle, apparently at last finding a topic with which she could engage. "I like having a Chinese boyfriend." She smiled primly at Xu.

What April's parents did not know, nor was she likely to admit to Xu, was that her two longer-term relationships at Harvard had been with girls. Both of them remained close friends. When the first relationship started with Lisa, who had been her friend since the day they arrived at the same dormitory in Harvard Yard, it seemed a comforting alternative to the confusing attention of the confident young men of Harvard. But with her second and more serious girlfriend, May (who was Chinese-American like her), April had come to realize that women were in her thoughts where most of her friends assumed men to be. Sometimes at night in her big bed in the Wang family house, she thought of May, or more imaginatively of somewhat older Chinese actresses like Zhang Ziyi or Chen Hao, and … well, she pursued the thoughts. No man entered her mind at those times.

"Well, at least let Walter believe he has a chance," Xu suggested. "I'm not sure what we would do with him if he thought you didn't like him. I already spend way too much time trying to convince him to relax around you."

"I do like him, but not like that, and can we please change the subject?" April answered her own question. "Why was your *bà ba* so intense at breakfast this morning? I haven't seen him like that before."

"He has a meeting today with government officials in Suzhou about JZP's new investment there. He's always tense before government meetings," Xu said. "I also think it has a lot to do with some negotiations with an American property company. *Bà* is very excited about that, but he also seems a little worried."

25

"Yes, that makes sense." April nodded. "I've been talking to the American property company for JZP. They called last week, and are coming to meet us on Saturday."

"Ah, I didn't know that *bà* had agreed to a meeting on Saturday. That's usually his day to play golf. He must be really interested in the opportunity."

"*Nǐ hǎo*, April. *Nǐ hǎo*, Annabelle." Walter in person walked up to their table, wearing a nervous smile and looking eagerly at April.

"*Nǐ hǎo*, Walter. Would you like to join us? How did you know we were here?"

"Walter called me while you were in the bathroom," Xu explained with a glint of amusement. "I guess I didn't mention that, did I?" April gave Xu a look. Walter could not help noticing—his eyes were barely leaving her face—and he frowned slightly.

"I really don't mean to interrupt. I need to … uh … get back to work anyhow to finish a story."

"No, please," April said, "please join us. I was just asking Xu why young Chinese people seem to care most about money. What do you think?"

Walter brightened and pulled up a chair. "Well, I know what Xu thinks, the little capitalist. Of course, I think that culture is more important than money. I'm actually working on a series of articles now about how important it is to preserve historical buildings as we build the new China. One of them is going to be about Xintiandi. What they have done here did preserve a lot of old houses, and it looks nice for visitors, but the full story is more complicated. A lot of houses were torn down to make room for more modern buildings. And even the old buildings that were preserved have changed use from being real homes to tourist attractions. More than three thousand families had to be relocated from their homes here," Walter said, becoming more enthusiastic as he sat down and warmed to his topic.

"So are you saying that the government should not have redeveloped Xintiandi?" April asked.

"No, I'm not saying that. I just think that people need to understand—"

As if on cue, a scene being played on the street outside the window caught their attention. A man with peasant features, of indeterminate age though plainly not young, had been searching through a garbage can opposite the restaurant, carefully selecting clear plastic bottles left by the tourists and locals, and transferring them to a handcart already piled high with similar bottles. He was just another of the ubiquitous Chinese trash "pickers" who collect any usable material, and are tolerated as an essential, barely-visible part of the economy. But not in Xintiandi. A young policeman had just grabbed the man by the shoulder and was clearly, unceremoniously instructing him to move on.

"Can you believe this?" Walter said. "That man has probably been working here for years. The government creates a situation where he could make more money, but then won't even allow him to touch the rubbish of the rich. I am going out there."

"Walter!" Xu and April spoke simultaneously, April in alarm and Xu in apparent exasperation, as Walter rose and walked towards the door regardless.

They watched as the picker initially reacted to the policeman with slight resistance, but quickly (and presumably with judgment born of experience) turned back to his cart to push it on down the street—just as Walter arrived. Walter angrily confronted the policeman, who looked at him impassively and silently. He then turned and tried to talk to the picker, who kept moving, seeming even less eager to speak with him. Walter glanced up at Xu, Annabelle and April watching him from the window, and his face relaxed from anger to resignation. He hesitated, cast one more angry look at the policeman, and re-crossed the street to the restaurant.

As Walter approached the table, red-faced from effort, anger and some embarrassment, Xu said, "So, Mr. Hero, trying to impress our friend April?"

"Shut up, Xu."

"I though a hero was supposed to be more polite than that!"

"Shut *up*, Xu."

April broke in. "Well, I'm not impressed by boys fighting, but I can see why Walter is worried about changes in Shanghai. Walter, have you discussed this with Xu's *bà ba*? From what I can see, he is an important builder of the new China."

As April had hoped, her question ended the men's argument, but not in the way she expected. Walter looked pained, and glanced at Xu, who was suddenly studying the food on his plate with intense concentration. "Of course I have known *Wáng xiānsheng* for many years, and I know what he does, but I really didn't think to ask. I don't think he would want to talk business with me."

"Why not?" April asked.

"Well, I'm a journalist. And he knows that we wouldn't see eye to eye."

"But you're a family friend. I'm sure he would discuss it with you."

"That's enough about business." Xu spoke before Walter could answer again, and April noticed that Walter looked relieved. "What else should we have to eat? Walter, are you hungry?

交易

5

Location, Location, Location

early March 2009

*It's tangible, it's solid, it's beautiful. It's artistic, from my standpoint,
and I just love real estate.*

— Donald Trump

"We own good properties because we buy at prices that are higher than the government will pay, but still low enough to make money on development." Zhang Biaoqiang, the polished, fifty-something owner of Zhang Real Estate Trust, was explaining his business model. "I worked for many years at the Ministry of Land and Resources. So I know where to find sellers, and I know how to convince them to sell to Zhang Real Estate Trust before the government forces them to sell at a lower price."

Richard and Jasmine were meeting Mr. Zhang and two of his colleagues in a drab conference room in the company's offices on the fifteenth floor of an equally drab office building near the center of Beijing. It was the second of San Marino's meetings in China—the first had been with China Industrial Properties in Guangzhou. The meeting took place only a few miles from their hotel in Wangfujing, a prosperous business and shopping district not far east of Tiananmen Square, but it had taken more than thirty minutes to travel the distance in the morning rush-hour on Beijing's wide but clogged streets.

The traffic had been just as bad in the first two cities that they had visited on their China trip—Hong Kong and Guangzhou—but the other contrasts of those cities had been stark. Looking out the window of the conference room, Richard let his mind wander over the events of the past few days.

He and Jasmine had arrived in Hong Kong on Sunday afternoon, four days earlier. Aiming to avoid jet lag by staying awake, they had taken a long pre-dinner walk, first taking the Mid-Levels Escalator part-way up Victoria Peak. From above Hong Kong's skyscrapers, they watched ships making their way slowly through Victoria Harbour between Hong Kong and Kowloon. Then they re-descended to the narrow, crowded streets near Central, soaking in the energy and decadence of the city from air that was warm even as spring was just beginning. After a late dinner, they had returned to their hotel and fallen asleep quickly, to their separate dreams of China.

On Monday, after morning meetings with two Hong Kong banks that San Marino hoped could join them in financing a China deal, Jasmine and Richard crossed the border to the Chinese mainland by train on their way to Guangzhou. This was no longer an international border, as it had been until 1997 when the British returned Hong Kong to China, but it still had passport controls and remained an important cultural divide. Guangzhou was a warm, frenetic, southern city like Hong Kong, but without the British refinement of the former colony. The capital of Guangdong province, China's biggest manufacturing region, Guangzhou was still the trading center it had been as imperial Canton, but with the old long since overshadowed by the new. It was self-evidently the embodiment of fast-growing, confident, aggressive China.

On their Tuesday in Guangzhou, Richard and Jasmine had met with the management of China Industrial Properties, the first of their target companies. The meeting in Guangzhou had been similar to the one they were now having with Zhang Real Estate Trust in Beijing, but it was overshadowed and confused in Richard's memory by a frightening encounter from later the same day. A little drunk after a lavish dinner with CIP and inspired by the walk in Hong Kong, Richard had insisted, against Jasmine's advice, that the two of them walk back to their hotel along the banks of the Pearl River. And indeed it had started as a nice walk. They had reviewed the discussion with CIP as they strolled through the heart of a rapidly changing city.

As they walked by a nearly-finished skyscraper that dominated the riverbank, Richard mused aloud. "I read that they are calling that the Canton Tower. It seems strange to use the old name of the city."

Jasmine was about to respond, when they both became aware of a group of five or six young men approaching from the other direction, walking faster than the warm evening seemed to demand. It was difficult for Richard to judge the youths' age. Perhaps seventeen or eighteen. As the group rapidly drew closer, time seemed to slow down. In Richard's memory, the events took on a dreamlike, surreal quality, perhaps because he did not understand the brief conversation that the leader of the group, thin and handsome with a cruel smile, had with Jasmine. But he could hear the tension in her voice, from more than just the effort of speaking in Cantonese, the language of the Guangdong region.

After this brief exchange—ten seconds in length?—the leader and another youth starting pulling Jasmine behind a nearby wall while the rest of the group surrounded Richard. Before the wall obstructed Jasmine's view, she saw that one of the youths was searching his pockets. For an instant, she worried about Richard, then her attention was diverted by the tall leader who was leering in her face.

"*Nǐ shì piàoliang. Nǐ xǐhuan wǒ ma?* [You are beautiful. Do you like me?]"

Jasmine did not respond, and was considering her options when she felt a hand—of the other youth, who was holding her from behind—running up her leg into her skirt. Fear closed her throat. She heard Richard shout her name as she began to struggle.

Then they were saved, miraculously it seemed later, by the appearance of a security guard, perhaps employed by the Canton Tower. He was not obviously armed, but his uniform, coupled with simultaneous yells from Richard and Jasmine, was enough to cause hesitation among their attackers. The

31

leader flashed his cruel smile and made a quick decision to marshal his troops and lead them away. He blew a sardonic kiss to Jasmine as the group of youths walked quickly but calmly away, vanishing almost as quickly as they had appeared.

They made their way back to the hotel without further incident, Richard apologetic for his insistence on the river walk and Jasmine mostly unresponsive to his questions about the incident. The next day at the airport on the way to Beijing, Richard experienced a feeling of escape. The meeting with China Industrial Properties had gone well, but he wondered whether he would be able to overcome a strong aversion to Guangzhou. For maybe the fourth time, he tried to elicit Jasmine's views of the incident. "Are you sure you are OK?"

"Richard, please stop. I am OK." Jasmine was unusually abrupt. "China can be a brutal place. We were lucky. Next time you will take my advice."

Richard decided to listen, and they spent the flight in silence, nursing their internal bruises. Richard assumed that Jasmine too felt bruised by the experience. It was hard to tell.

Beijing was very different. There was a change in temperature, from the early-summer feel of Guangzhou to late winter in Beijing. Richard also felt the chill of increased order and oppressiveness of power at the Chinese center. The feeling was familiar from his time in Beijing a decade earlier. Neither then nor now had it been unpleasant. When he was studying for his Ph.D, government control—and its gradual relaxation—were of intense, academic interest to Richard. Some of this scholarly interest remained. He now also felt distinctly safer due to the greater government presence. As a student in China, ten years ago, Richard had never thought himself unsafe, but now, after the near-disaster in Guangzhou, danger had become a new scent among China's heady mix of aromas.

Richard forced himself to concentrate again on the meeting. Mr. Zhang was explaining his company's investment strategy. "We optimize returns by pursuing two different paths to exit, that is, to selling properties. Mr. Cheng," Zhang pointed to a strongly-built, tough-looking man, also about fifty, sitting to his right, "runs our property development business. He builds on some properties that we buy. Does very good work, many years in the building trade. We make nice profit on new properties with strong demand in Beijing these days. But that takes more of my capital. So I also hired Mr. Zhao," he pointed to the handsome, smiling, thirty-something sitting to his left. "Mr. Zhao is our salesman. He sells what Mr. Cheng builds, that is easy side of his work. His more important job is reselling properties that we have bought, for an immediate profit. Not so much profit as property development, but much less risk and very capital-efficient. I let Mr. Cheng and Mr. Zhao make competing proposals for each property—I think they like it." Mr. Zhang smiled. Mr. Cheng and Mr. Zhao did not change their expressions.

"That's a good strategy," Richard said. "Some very good property development companies in the United States could learn a thing or two from you."

"*Xiè xie Gregg xiānsheng.* [Thank you, Mr. Gregg.] Actually, it was you Americans who taught me most of what I know. I was lucky to attend business school in the United States twenty-five years ago. My father was close to people around Mr. Deng, and he saw that understanding the capitalist system would be key to future success in China. So he sent me to learn about your system. Your Miss Liu had very good judgment to do likewise." He smiled at Jasmine with more interest than she liked.

"Your father's connection with Mr. Deng is very interesting," Richard said. "I spent the late 1990s here in Beijing studying the changes he made to China."

"Yes, I know," Mr. Zhang replied. "I have read your little book."

"Really! I think *Rules of the New China* only sold a few hundred copies. It read too much like a Ph.D. dissertation, people said."

"At least one copy made it to Beijing University library. And my young colleagues do excellent research."

* * *

After the meeting, Richard and Jasmine were in a taxi passing Tiananmen Square, when Richard suddenly leaned forward and spoke to the driver, "*Qǐng tíng chē.* [Please stop the car.]"

"We are not near the hotel," Jasmine said. "Why are we stopping?"

"Come on, let's walk. I love *Běihǎi gōng yuán* [Beihai Park, literally Northern Sea Park]. We can walk through it to *Hòu Hǎi* [literally, the Sea Beyond] and have dinner there."

"You're not afraid, after what happened two days ago?" Jasmine asked as he paid the driver.

"Beijing is different, and the park was always lovely when Julie and I walked there. It's safe, right?"

"Yes ... it's safe. I believe."

"OK. Let's go."

It took them an hour to walk through the large park, following the shores of its three big lakes down tree-lined walkways, past white marble statues and a tall pagoda on an island in the farthest lake. The air was cold, but the sun glinting off the water foreshadowed the warmth of the coming spring.

At first they walked in silence. Then Richard turned to the business at hand. "It makes sense, I think," he said. "We know that local governments in China finance themselves by taking properties from landowners and selling them to developers. Mr. Zhao told us today that they are getting in a little ahead of the government, and China Industrial Properties said about the same thing on Tuesday. Does it make sense to you that this works for them?"

Jasmine paused before responding. "In China, *guānxì*— connections, who you know—is the most important thing in business. Mr. Zhang told us today that he is from an important family, one that was connected to Deng Xiaoping. And Mr. Chen at China Industrial Properties gave the same impression, although he didn't say it."

"And that gives them access to deals?" Richard knew well that *guānxi*, a crucial aspect of Chinese society, translated literally to "connections" or "relationships" but went much deeper, expressing a more general notion of personal networks and influence.

"Yes. More than that. People like that can make their own rules, at least most of the time. I don't like it very much, but it's the way China works. So I believe them when they say that get good deals."

"So—which company do you like better?" Richard asked.

Again, Jasmine paused to think as they continued walking. They were passing a large statue, taller than Richard, of a fierce but stylized lion. He stopped. "Let's take a photo with this creature."

After they had recruited some passing locals to photograph them with her camera, Jasmine spoke. "Mr. Zhang is certainly very intelligent," she said, "and I like his strategy of maximizing capital efficiency by making his development and brokerage organizations compete. But his company's property portfolio is not so interesting as at China Industrial Properties."

"I agree. Why do you think Mr. Zhang hasn't found better properties? Beijing is a very big market."

"I think Beijing is the problem. At the center, close to the Communist Party leadership, it's harder for an independent businessman like Mr. Zhang to get access to favors, even with the right *guānxì*. Guangdong Province is further from central control, and industrial development there has been very fast, which means there are fewer rules. This seems to have helped CIP build a strong commercial portfolio—more like what you asked me to find when we started our research."

"You're right. Although, I confess that I'm scared of Guangzhou after what happened there. And I didn't like Mr. Zhang so much, even if he did read my book. Uh … did you see the way he looked at you?"

"Yes, I noticed. I have gotten used to men doing that."

"Well. We still need to meet Jiangsu-Zhejiang Property Company in Shanghai tomorrow afternoon, and their portfolio also looks very good. Let's not make any decisions until after that meeting." They had reached the end of the park, and crossed a busy street to another lake, *Hòu Hǎi*, surrounded by restaurants and bars, strolling Chinese couples, and a few tourists, some of them riding in pedal taxis. "So, how about dinner?"

"OK. What would you like?"

"I like all the food in China, so you choose. Let's find a place that serves yellow wine. When Julie and I were living in Beijing, that was our favorite drink."

"I love *huáng jiǔ*!" Jasmine responded, abandoning her usual reserve. "There's a very good place near here that I used to come to as a student when we had something to celebrate. It's not fancy, but I think you will like it."

* * *

Later that night, Jasmine lay on the bed in her hotel, still fully clothed. Except for a few reproductions of Chinese art on the wall, the room looked much like one in a business hotel anywhere in the world, complete with mini-bar and complimentary soaps and lotions in the bathroom. The efficiently anonymous atmosphere gave Jasmine a feeling of dislocation, as if she was not really in China. Still a little drunk from the bottle of yellow wine she had shared with Richard, and not in the mood to read a novel before falling asleep as she usually did, she reflected on the day.

The property company meetings had given her a strong feeling of continuing a family tradition. Her grandfather's family had been successful landowners in the days before the Chinese Revolution of 1949, and because of their background the family had suffered greatly during Mao's Cultural Revolution. Or so she understood. Her father refused to talk about it. From her grandfather, who had emerged from the experience a physically and emotionally broken man, she'd heard confusing bits and pieces. It was enough to give Jasmine an instinctive fear of what China could do when its people's baser instincts ran unchecked. Despite his traumas, her father's father remained a constant, gentle presence in the family house. He had a fundamental kindness that made him a good

36

friend to young Jasmine, until he died just before her sixteenth birthday.

Her own father was still a young man when the storm of the Cultural Revolution cleared in the mid-1970s and gave way eventually to the market reforms of Deng Xiaoping. He had quickly turned back to business—but rather than betting on reform, he had followed the route of the Communist Party faithful, rightly seeing the huge opportunities that would emerge for state enterprises in a rapidly-growing economy. He met Jasmine's mother while they were both promising young members of the powerful local Party committee that was remolding Tianjin into a major financial center. Now he was a senior manager at China Petroleum, as was her mother at China Construction Bank, and they seemed to know everyone who mattered in Tianjin. The family had lived extremely well by Chinese standards—but they had not used their positions, as some others had, to join the ranks of China's new super-rich.

Jasmine reached for her digital camera on the bedside table and looked at the photograph of her with Richard from that afternoon, the large stone lion crouched between them. Its blank eyes stared at the camera, with ferocity that had not abated over the centuries. Was this the same ferocity that had consumed her family in the Cultural Revolution, the ferocity of the aggressive young men who had attacked them in Guangzhou? That frightening encounter had rattled her but, even after facing the brief threat of being raped, she believed that she was less frightened than Richard had been. More than any other reaction, the incident had made her even more determined to overcome the aggression of modern China by making *jiāo yì* a success.

And yet there was something about *jiāo yì* vaguely bothering her. What was it? She repeated to herself Richard's question to her earlier about the very similar strategies of the two businesses that they had met. "Does it make sense to you that this works for them?"

Does it? she wondered, as she drifted off to sleep.

交易

6

Meeting

early March 2009

You never get a second chance to make a first impression

– Will Rogers

April looked up from her desk as Uncle Jun and "Uncle" Wu escorted two professionally-dressed people, whom she assumed to be Richard Gregg and Jasmine Liu, into JZP's glass-fronted conference room. Richard was fairly tall and thin, handsome in a conventional way, and seemed young-ish for a successful investor. He looked determined but relaxed, with the hint of a smile on his face. Jasmine was younger, almost expressionless, and beautiful. Quite beautiful.

April watched handshakes all round, and an exchange of business cards in the Chinese fashion—the card facing towards the recipient with a slight bow from the presenter. Richard, the only Westerner present, inclined his body with dignity. Uncle Jun saw April looking, and beckoned to her. She stood up and walked across the office to join the group in the conference room. Just a few steps across the industrial-grade carpet of a nondescript office, yet she felt that she was crossing a frontier.

Maybe she was over-dramatizing the situation. Or was this at last the beginning of an adventure?

"*Gregg xiānsheng, Liú xiǎojiě*, this is my niece from America, April Wang. My English is not so good, so April will help. She is very intelligent, a Harvard graduate." Jasmine gave April an inquisitive look.

"*Nǐ de Yīngyǔ hěn búcuò, Wáng xiānsheng.* [Your English is just fine, Mr. Wang.]" Richard said. "How did you end up at Harvard, Miss Wang?" he asked, smiling at April.

38

April smiled back nervously, and took a seat at the large, glass conference table. "I was born in the United States, Mr. Gregg. And I grew up in Arcadia, California—very close to your office in San Marino." She realized that her voice was shaking, and glanced at Jasmine, whose unreadable expression did nothing to calm her.

"Really? So we're practically neighbors."

"Yes, my parents moved there from China in 1980. My father has been building houses for Chinese immigrants for almost thirty years."

"Very interesting. I know there's a large Chinese community in Arcadia." He turned to Wang Jun. "I am sure that having your niece on the JZP team will make our communications much easier." And then back to April. "Did you know that my colleague Ms. Liu also attended Harvard, the business school?"

"Yes, I know," April answered after a slight pause, momentarily nonplussed by Richard's attentiveness. "My uncle asked me to learn about you and your company." She glanced hesitantly at her uncle, who smiled non-committally.

"Great! We like good research, don't we, Ms. Liu?"

Jasmine looked quickly at April and then turned to her Uncle Jun. Her tone was much more intense than Richard's. "Yes. That's why we're here. Our goal today is to understand in general terms JZP's property portfolio, how you acquired it, and how you run your business."

"Miss Liu gets right to business, I see." Uncle Jun was smiling now, too.

"I apologize," Jasmine said. April did not notice any change in her expression.

"No need, we are modern business people." Nonetheless, he paused while a shy young woman with a teapot finished her circle of the table. She poured the last cup, bowed, and left the room. "Please continue."

Richard picked up the conversation. "Thank you for meeting us today. As you know, we're investors, and I want to be clear about why we're here. We'd like to start a discussion about how San Marino and JZP could form a property-investment joint venture." He looked from Mr. Wang to Mr. Wu. "Of course, we know that there'd be many steps between this first meeting and doing a deal, but we want to make sure you're interested in heading in that direction."

"Certainly, Mr. Gregg," April's uncle answered. "We'll have a detailed discussion this morning. Then I have planned lunch at a very good duck restaurant. You must know that, in China, we like to get to know our business partners over food. Do you like Beijing duck?"

"Yes, I like it very much," Richard answered. "If Ms. Wang's research on me is as good as on Ms. Liu, you'll know that I've spent a lot of time in China."

"Yes, yes. Of course. I read your book," Mr. Wang responded casually. "Very good economic analysis, very good research. But I'll teach you some other things. I expect you understand that economics is a small part of the story in China. It's about who you know. We are going to be friends, I believe. I will show you."

"We appreciate your hospitality, Mr. Wang. And I'm certain that you have much to teach me about China. San Marino is looking for a Chinese partner because we know what we don't know. We don't want to invest in China on our own."

Over the next two hours, Mr. Wang and Mr. Wu explained the JZP business model. The essential idea was very similar to what they had heard in Guangzhou and Beijing, with the important difference that the JZP portfolio was much more impressive. JZP had accumulated, at surprisingly reasonable prices, near-prime commercial property close to substantial cities in two regions: Jiangsu province to the northwest of Shanghai, and Zhejiang province to the south. Their business model was less disciplined than the two-pronged development-and-brokerage model of Zhang Real Estate Trust, but their return on capital was significantly higher.

Some of the business language was challenging for April, and she needed to ask a few questions of Uncle Jun and Uncle Wu as they spoke. In the few gaps when she did not need to concentrate on translation, April watched Richard and Jasmine discreetly. They both paid close attention and took notes, Jasmine diligently and steadily recording information, Richard dashing off several emphatic scribbles when Mr. Wang provided details of their financial models and returns.

Richard was a fairly familiar type to April. He had elements both of the American businessmen who worked with her father and of a couple of her younger professors at college. Jasmine was more mysterious. At first glance, she showed the reserve typical of Chinese women. Deep behind that—yet still visible—was a less typical confidence and intensity.

The feeling of adventure grew on April as the meeting wore on. It was just a business meeting, yet there was something dramatic about Richard and Jasmine flying across the Pacific Ocean to talk about new buildings and large sums of money. April did not consider herself a money-focused person. But suddenly, she felt at the heart of international commerce, and surprisingly comfortable there.

"Our latest project is a major commercial office development in Suzhou," Uncle Jun was explaining, naming a city not far from Shanghai. "We've identified an opportunity to buy prime property near the city center, where we will develop a prime-quality twenty-floor office building. This will be JZP's largest project so far. We'll provide equity capital of 100 million yuan, and China Construction Bank will provide loans of 600 million yuan. This project should be very profitable."

"How profitable?" Richard asked.

"Of course, that is confidential information. But since you are not a competitor and because we are trusting each other, I will say that cashflow should be ten million yuan per year. That's *after* operating and debt service costs."

"Wow!" Richard whistled. "A ten-percent return on equity before property appreciation? In the U.S. commercial property market that's ... well, it's hard to do."

"There are big opportunities in China. And we know how to find them." Mr. Wang smiled, and paused a beat as if for a punchline. "As I told you."

"I'm impressed," Richard said. "That's the type of project in which San Marino could be very interested. How did you raise the equity?"

"As you know, Mr. Gregg, we have been successful. We recently sold a factory and warehouse property in Zhejiang, and we reinvested most of the profit. I also have many friends who are willing to invest as my partners, because I've made them a lot of money in the past." Uncle Jun's smile broadened. "But we are quite ambitious. That is why we are very happy to meet with you. I like the idea of a joint venture to bring additional capital, and I especially would like to make a connection between our two great countries."

"I like that you like the idea, Mr. Wang. Tell me ... how would you find similar properties to buy in the future? How did you find this one? We know the Chinese property market remains very strong after the global financial crisis, so there must be many buyers competing for property."

"As I said, it's important to know the right people. You have spent time in China, so you know about *guānxì*, right?" Richard nodded, and glanced at Jasmine with a slight smile.

"The people we know prefer to sell to us than to the government, because we pay a better price," Wang Jun explained. "And, Mr. Gregg, we don't think there's a global financial crisis, just a Western financial crisis. The Chinese market is very strong, and we expect it to stay that way."

Richard nodded again. "That's why we're here. We believe our investors can do better investing in China than almost anywhere else. But tell me, are the property ministries of the governments of Jiangsu and Zhejiang province concerned that JZP is buying so many high-quality properties?"

Uncle Jun laughed, although there was a tightness to his laughter. "Mr. Gregg, you must not be serious, if you know the Chinese economy so well. China is very big, JZP is still small. The government cannot buy everything. There are many private investors in property, including foreign investors. I don't think the government really notices what JZP is doing."

"That surprises me. I would have imagined that good relationships with the government were very important to your business."

"We have very good relationships with the government. But that doesn't mean they pay attention to our private business affairs. And now, will you join us for lunch? We have arranged to go to Quanjude, the famous Beijing duck restaurant." It seemed to April that Uncle Jun was a little more abrupt than usual in changing the topic.

Four months later, recalling this conversation when it had suddenly become very significant, Richard realized that the warning signs had been there from the beginning. With the benefit of hindsight, he was amazed that he had been so careless as not to see them. But now, today, he was excited by the prospect of a good deal, delighted to be back in China and speaking Mandarin, and ready for a first-rate duck lunch.

* * *

The group from the meeting—Mr. Wang, Uncle Wu, April, Richard and Jasmine—was joined by two junior colleagues from JZP for lunch at a Shanghai branch of Quanjude.

Uncle Wu, who had been quiet during the meeting, became much more animated. The group was seated at a round table in a private dining room with ornate dark wood furniture and traditional Chinese silk wall coverings featuring a dragon motif. Richard guessed that the furnishings were neither as expensive nor old as they were intended to look. After a waitress had poured red wine into small glasses, Uncle Wu stood, turned to Richard, who was seated between him and Mr. Wang, and offered the first toast. "Mr. Gregg, we are very pleased for your visit to Shanghai. We hope that our companies can enjoy successful cooperation."

43

"*Xiè xie Wú xiānsheng. Gān bēi!* [Thank you, Mr. Wu. Drink up!]" Richard responded.

Similar toasts continued during the many-course meal. Delicacies prepared with duck were a theme throughout, starting with the crisped skin from the two they had ordered. Richard showed his experience with the etiquette of Chinese business lunches, and very little effect from the alcohol that he was drinking. Jasmine and April were also invited to join several toasts, particularly by the two younger, male employees from JZP who had joined the group at lunch.

As the table became more animated, April found herself looking discreetly at Jasmine, seated directly across from her. Jasmine chatted calmly with one of the young men, seemingly oblivious to the fact that he was unable to keep his attention away from her. To her surprise, looking at his eager-to-please expression, April felt irritation. After a moment's reflection she identified her emotion more precisely as jealousy.

It must have been the glasses of red wine that brought a memory of her Harvard girlfriend May involuntarily to mind. April had known May only slightly when they met at a party at the Phoenix Club, one of Harvard's exclusive all-male "final clubs". They had spent almost the whole evening talking entirely to each other—about literature, life at Harvard, and everything under the sun—as they got tipsy and then drunk on red wine. There was a sensation of having known each other for a long time. At the end of the evening they had gone to May's and gotten to know each other well in a different way. The memory remained vivid, except that in her recollection now May's face was replaced with Jasmine's. April felt herself blushing. Then she snapped out of her reverie when she realized that Jasmine had asked her a question.

"Ms. Wang, where did you live at Harvard?"

She paused while she processed the question for what seemed like an eternity, although it was probably only ten beats of her rapidly-pumping heart. "I lived in Eliot House, just across the river from the Business School. But I don't think I ever saw you there."

"No, probably not," Jasmine agreed. "Although there are many Chinese students at Harvard. You might have seen me and not noticed."

"Yes, that could be." April's real thought was that she would certainly have noticed Jasmine.

"People have a lot of respect for Harvard here in China. You know that, I suppose," Jasmine said, raising a toast to April. "Hopefully you and I will both prove them right, Ms. Wang."

"Yes, I hope so, Ms. Liu. *Gān bēi*."

交易

7

Due Diligence

mid-March 2009

Diligence is the mother of good luck

— Benjamin Franklin

"We have built a reputation for being bold ..."

Tom Wilshire's comment made Richard proud of his China deal, and at the same time nervous about it. China was a risky place for Western investors—he often read in the *Wall Street Journal* about companies, even very experienced ones, facing problems there. Richard also knew that his time in China as an economics researcher more than a decade ago did not in any way prepare him for the risks he could face there now as a property investor. He promised himself to be careful.

It was a bright California Monday morning, and the five partners of San Marino Property Investments sat around the table in their conference room. Its floor-to-ceiling glass windows looked out on a steep, wooded arroyo, which usually produced enough natural calm to counterbalance the inherent intensity of a group of successful investors. In order of seniority, which didn't matter much in their day-to-day interactions but could matter a lot when decisions were made, the partners were Tom Wilshire, Peter Jones (San Marino's other founding partner), Jane Leeson, Richard, and François LeCroix. For the most part, they were dressed casually. None of the men wore a tie, and only François sported a jacket. Jane wore a silk dress printed with a design bold enough to make a statement in any office almost anywhere outside California.

At their regular Monday morning meeting, the partners usually disposed briskly of administrative issues, and then spent most of their time on investments—performance and any concerns of existing investments, execution issues for deals in progress, and ideas for new investments. The last area usually drew the most animated discussion, except in the fairly rare cases of serious problems with existing investments.

Tom usually chaired partners' meetings, and he did so efficiently, tolerating little small talk. The partners were friends, but the culture of the firm encouraged them to stay focused on investment, and leave personal life at home. François LeCroix, who had joined San Marino two years earlier from a Wall Street investment bank, had brought with him some challenges to the orderly San Marino ethos from that testosterone-fueled environment. The partners generally tolerated François' behavior because of his brilliance and consistent Gallic good humor, but sometimes he seemed like a dog straining at the leash, with Tom Wilshire holding the other end.

A few minutes before making his comment about San Marino being bold, Tom had turned to Richard and said, "So, Doc, it's your turn. Tell us about what you want to do in China."

"Thanks, Tom. I really think now is the time to look at China, before all the other investors realize how strongly it's going to power through the financial crisis. Jasmine Liu and I have spent the last three months looking at more than a hundred property investment companies across most Chinese provinces. Then we did detailed research on fifteen. And then we cut it down to the three strongest candidates. Last week, we went to China and met with those three."

"Poor Jasmine. Now we know what she's been working on so late every night," said François. "She wouldn't even stop to have dinner with me."

"Careful, François. Hands off the staff." Tom Wilshire was not joking. A relationship between François, the only unmarried partner, and one of San Marino's secretaries had ended with the young woman choosing unhappily to leave San Marino, but fortunately without any threat of a lawsuit against the firm.

François shrugged expressively, and leaned back in his chair.

"The three companies on our shortlist," Richard continued, "are based in three different cities, Guangzhou, Beijing and Shanghai. All of them are focused on property development and brokerage, and all seem to have sound businesses, but Jiangsu-Zhejiang Property Company in Shanghai—they call themselves JZP—is the clear leader. JZP have a more impressive commercial property portfolio and significantly higher return on invested capital than the other two."

"What about their team?" Peter asked. "Even in China, the people will still be the key asset in any investment company."

"I really like them. The founder, Wang Jun, is a self-made man, and he has a small, loyal group who have worked with him for years. And he likes the idea of working with Americans. He even has a brother who lives here in Los Angeles—right down the road in Arcadia." He paused and looked around the table.

"So, do I have the partners' approval to move forward with JZP?"

Jane leaned forward. "Not so fast, Richard. What do you mean by 'move forward'?"

"As usual, Jane asks the obvious question that needed to be asked," Tom said.

Richard looked at Tom, then out the window at the sun rising above the arroyo, then at Jane. "My plan is to proceed on two tracks. First, we would start doing financial and commercial due diligence using local consultants in China. We definitely need to know a lot more about their portfolio. Second, we would start negotiating the basic terms of the deal—and try to agree them, in heads of terms that set out the main deal points. The total budget for this phase would be a max, I think, of fifty thousand dollars, including the ten thousand we spent for our trip last week. If the preliminary due diligence checks out and we can get acceptable heads of terms, I would come back to the partners to discuss next steps."

"That sounds OK, so far as it goes. But it would help to understand—before we approve this—what you think a deal might look like." Tom was an expert chess player, and was characteristically thinking a few moves ahead. "What do you have in mind?"

"Well, it's early, but of course I have some ideas." Richard smiled slightly for the first time since he began speaking. "My initial thinking is a fifty-fifty JV, an equal joint venture between San Marino and JZP—"

"Don't we want control?" Jane interjected. "Investing in China is risky." Before joining San Marino three years before, Jane had been an emerging leader in the property investment business of Blackstein, a large private equity firm, with a stellar reputation as a smart, tough woman in the male-dominated world of private equity. Now she was San Marino's main expert on risk management.

"Yes, it is. But I don't think JZP would agree to give us control. That would be unusual in a Chinese JV with a Western company, and Mr. Wang seems to treat JZP as his baby. So I've been thinking about ways to manage our risk. At a minimum, we would insist on veto rights over buy and sell decisions, and our investment would be deferred, so we would only commit actual cash where needed to buy new properties." Jane nodded, and Richard continued. "Of course, the devil is in the details. Any other questions?" He looked around the table.

"Well, I'm sure we will all have a lot of questions if this deal moves forward, but I'm good for now," Peter said.

"It sounds like a reasonable plan," Tom agreed. "I think we should let you run with it. But next time, come back to us with a robust business case, including an analysis of the risks and how to manage them. We should also get some more background on the funnel of companies that you researched, including the long list of fifteen, and the two others on the short list. If our investors ask questions later about this, I want our process to be very clear. Does that sound OK to everyone?" Richard looked around at his partners nodding their approval.

"Thanks, everyone," Richard said. "This looks like a great opportunity to me. I think you know from experience that I'll do my best to look at it neutrally and take the risks seriously."

He had the unfamiliar feeling of making a speech to justify his convictions, which usually spoke for themselves. "How about I agree to come back by the end of April with a proposal for next steps? We could try to do this quicker, but I want to be careful, including spending a week in China with JZP. With the current instability in the market, it doesn't hurt to wait a little."

"Sounds good to me, Doc," Tom said. "But don't take too much time if you really think this is a good buying opportunity." Tom was near-legendary in the property market for his ability to take risks that turned out well, and that was why his next comment made such a strong impression on Richard.

"We have built a reputation for being bold ... and my sense is that you are onto something here. Anyone object to Richard's timetable?" Tom glanced around the table at the other partners, all of whom now appeared satisfied. "OK. What's next?"

* * *

After the meeting, Richard walked over to Jasmine's desk. She was on the telephone, and looked up and gestured for him to wait. She wrote down a few notes, and then ended a conversation in Chinese. "That was Mr. Wu at JZP. I was asking a few more questions about their business."

"Great. We just got the go-ahead for next steps with them, so there will be a lot more questions. Now is when the going will really get tough. Are you ready?"

"You know I am."

"OK. I want to travel to Shanghai for about a week in mid-April to meet with them again, and try to agree heads of terms. We won't have time before then for full due diligence, but we can make a good start. You can go ahead and hire local consultants to take a fast but careful look at their financials and property portfolio, and report back to us before we travel. We'll hire lawyers later to help us on the heads of terms."

"Sounds good, Doc. Do you know which consultants you want to use?"

"No. You figure that out. Can you get me two or three recommendations by end of the day tomorrow, and arrange telephone interviews for Wednesday morning?"

"Yes ... I will do my best." Jasmine was used to Richard moving quickly and being politely demanding, but it was obvious that the pace was increasing. She was determined to prove that she could handle it.

"And, Jasmine," Richard continued, "remember that we're hiring the consultants as smart people on the ground to check the facts. So please find a consulting firm that won't be shy in asking hard questions. But don't let them do your job. You need to know everything, too. The San Marino partners are very focused on the risks of this deal, and they're right. We need to be especially careful."

"Got it, Doc. Careful, careful, careful." The uncertainties and vague business practices of the Chinese property market—which was like a sea that could change from calm to very dangerous when the wind blew hard from the wrong direction—were one of the key risks that Richard had already asked Jasmine to investigate. It was well known that Chinese provincial and local governments controlled access to the property market, generating much of their own income by taking property away from farmers and others, and re-selling it at high prices to developers. The system provided huge opportunities for corruption. So far, JZP looked clean, but Jasmine knew that she had to peer beneath the surface.

Jasmine reflected, briefly, with pride, that she had immersed herself in *jiāo yì*. She felt a compulsion to make the deal succeed, and a lack of interest in practically everything else. The only other things for which she had made time recently were occasional phone conversations with her parents and a few friends, eating, sleeping, and a few minutes before bed most nights with a novel. She had just started reading *The Great Gatsby* in English, having first read it in Chinese several years earlier.

Her last major social activity had been a hike with a business school classmate shortly before the recent trip to China with Richard. This young American man of about her

51

age, named James—a Los Angeles native who seemed intensely interested in her, as many men did—had insisted that he show her the San Gabriel mountains above Pasadena, which he had said were beautiful. And indeed there was a spare beauty in the dry, rocky mountains. James had taken great pride in pointing out species of local vegetation, including the spiky, plentiful agave, prickly pear cactus, and quite a few other plants and trees that Jasmine could not remember. She had never really been an outdoors person, and during the hike her mind spent most of the time on the details of the property companies in China and the upcoming trip. When James dropped her off at her apartment in South Pasadena after the hike, Jasmine accepted his kiss on the cheek and decided on the spot, and with no regret, that it was an experience that she would not repeat.

As if echoing Jasmine's thoughts, Richard said, "I want you to eat and breathe JZP from now until we do a deal. Or not. Think of them as your new best friends. This is one of the main reasons that I hired you—to make sure that we really understand and connect with our Chinese partners."

"OK, Richard. I guess I better get back to work."

"Thanks, Jasmine." Richard turned abruptly, and returned to his desk.

Jasmine thought about what Richard had just said. She had not always felt comfortable with Chinese business people, although from her banking experience she was sure she could handle the interactions professionally. But "best friends"? That seemed unlikely. The only one on the JZP team who seemed remotely similar to Jasmine was the young intern, April, who had always seemed to be looking at her during the visit. Maybe that was a good place to start.

交易

8

Family Dinner

late March 2009

Anything that walks, swims, crawls, or flies with its back to heaven is edible

— Cantonese saying

Uncle Jun, Aunt Hong, Xu and April were at the dining table of the big house in the French Concession. *Mǎ tàitài* [Mrs. Ma], the family cook, who also served as maid of all works and had been with the family for decades, had just served them a delicious chicken soup. The soup was prepared with the remains of the same bird that had been used for a first course of noodles with chicken and vegetables. Mrs. Ma had bought the fowl live that morning at a local market, and its surprised head had garnished the noodles like a trophy.

Growing up with her expatriate Chinese family in California, April had understood that Chinese food is much more interesting than what is served at Westernized Chinese restaurants. But she had not truly appreciated the real variety of food in China until moving to Shanghai, where she encountered a forest of unusual vegetables, dishes that she had never really thought of as food—like the feet of pigs and chickens, and ducks' tongues—and a host of other ingredients that she never knew existed. She found herself taking to this real Chinese cuisine like a fish to water. The head of the chicken had not disconcerted her in the least. She saluted it mentally: "You are a delicious chicken."

"I love having dinner here," April enthused, wiping her mouth with her napkin and bouncing slightly in her chair. "The food is always so, so good, and it really feels like home."

"And we love having you here." Aunt Hong smiled genuinely. "Years ago, I was the one who made this food for your uncle, and your cousin as he grew up. Now Xu is a big boy, and I have become rich and lazy," she said, patting her round stomach. "But I have not forgotten how to cook. I can teach you, too, April."

"I would love that!" April said, leaning forward, her eyes widening. "I don't think my *mā* really remembers how to cook Chinese food. She was so young when she and *bà ba* left for California, and they both had to focus on work when they were trying to succeed in the United States. She never had much time for cooking big dinners—I wonder whether she missed that?" April stopped and considered. This idea had not occurred to her before, and she liked the possibility of reclaiming the culinary part of her parents' Chinese heritage. "Of course, I guess we need to see what Uncle Jun thinks before I sign up for your cooking school. He is keeping me very busy here."

Uncle Jun grunted and paid no attention to April's implicit question. He dug into his food, complaining as he ate.

"These government officials are getting greedier all the time."

"What do you mean, *bà*?" Xu asked, putting down his chopsticks. "You've always paid them well for helping us find deals."

"Now it seems that's not good enough. The officials in Suzhou who are arranging our new deal want to own part of the company that holds the property deeds. Everyone wants a piece of the action in China these days." He shook his head, and dug back into his food.

"Hmm," said Xu. "So the bastards think we weren't giving them a big enough cut."

"Yes ... or they suddenly think they can do better as property investors themselves. Rather than a fixed fee up front, they think they should share the upside if we sell the building. It changes the economics of the deal. We could keep the upfront payments ... you know ... hush, hush. Shares, though, they are something that a buyer of the building will see. So will the Americans, if they're smart. And they seem to be smart. Harvard, like you, right, April?"

"Yes, Uncle Jun. The girl Jasmine is from Harvard. And she's the one who's been calling me to gather information."

"But it's still a good deal, isn't it?" Xu asked.

"Yes, it is still a good deal," Uncle Jun said, nodding almost imperceptibly. "But details matter. And the Americans may not like what they see. Maybe we can just explain to them that this is the way we do good business in China. The way we've always done business. Hah. What do you think, April, would your friends from America understand that?"

April was sometimes not sure when Uncle Jun was joking, and this was one of those times. She responded slowly. "I don't know, Uncle Jun. Like you say, I suppose we can see what they think."

Uncle Jun grunted again, and continued drinking his soup.

Aunt Hong usually left business discussions to the men, but sometimes joined in, in her maternal way. "April, you really seem to be doing important things on this project! I suppose Uncle Jun is very lucky to have you here."

Uncle Jun continued to look distracted. Then he turned to April. "*Xiǎo zhí nü* [Little niece], I want you to make good friends with this other Harvard girl Jasmine. We really need to understand what they are thinking about a deal with us, and it seems to me that two smart young university girls ought to be able to talk to each other. Can you do that?"

April thought about this. She had already felt that she wanted to get to know Jasmine better. But to do this to help the deal seemed underhanded, and daunting. Even though she was fitting in quickly and well at JZP, April could see clearly how much she didn't know—she had barely started to learn about JZP's property business. Dealing with the more experienced Jasmine at such a disadvantage made her nervous.

Uncle Jun, Aunt Hong and Xu were looking at her.

55

"I can try, Uncle Jun. Do you really think I'm the one to do this, though? I'm glad you trust me, but … I don't understand your business very well yet."

"Don't worry, April. You've already surprised me with what you can do. And when there are questions that you can't answer, just ask me, or Xu."

"OK." April's non-committal response reflected her mixed emotions. Uncle Jun did not seem to notice any ambivalence. He nodded and returned to his soup.

* * *

After dinner, Xu invited April to join him and Walter for coffee at a Starbucks on Huahai Middle Road, one of many coffee shops that had begun sprouting up around Shanghai and other big cities in China. The Chinese seemed cheerfully oblivious to the fact that Starbucks was a cookie-cutter simulation of a traditional coffee shop experience, and flocked to it en masse—as with so many other "latest crazes" in the new China. Come to think of it, April realized, the American reaction to Starbucks had not been too different. Was Starbucks part of a new cultural bridge over the still-wide chasm between China and the West?

April tried to lay down ground rules when she accepted Xu's invitation. "Sure, Xu, I can come along. But, really, Walter needs to stop mooning over me. I'm not going to give him what he wants, and it's getting a little annoying."

"I'll try to encourage him to lower his hopes a little, but really, that's for Walter to decide. I have some other things to discuss with him that you'll find interesting, and maybe useful. I want to see what he knows about the kind of problem that *bà ba* is having on the Suzhou deal."

"What do you mean? Walter is a journalist. You can't tell him what the government officials asked for, can you?"

"Of course I would not. I'll just ask him whether he's heard about this kind of thing happening elsewhere. He has good sources on corruption. Maybe he'll guess why I'm asking, but he won't know for sure. And my family trusts him completely."

At that moment, April could not have guessed how her own loyalties would soon be divided. When Xu's trust later proved misplaced, she would be uncertain whether to take the side of her own family.

* * *

In Starbucks, Walter greeted them with a big, shy smile, and eyes only for April. "Hi, April."

"Hello, Walter." April found it impossible not to return his smile, but managed to sound exasperated at the same time. Walter looked down.

"Three large cappuccinos, OK?" As usual, Xu took command of the situation. "And Walter, don't look so sad. We have interesting things to discuss." Once the cappuccinos were in hand, he led them to a table just as it was being vacated by a twenty-something couple. The crowd in the restaurant, apart from Chinese faces, was very similar to one that might be found in a Starbucks in New York, London or elsewhere.

"So Walter, how are your articles going on preserving historical buildings?" April asked.

Walter was pleased at her interest. So pleased that he did not notice the cool, approving look Xu gave his young cousin when he realized that April had understood exactly where he wanted to lead the conversation. "I think it's going well … at least from the perspective of having something interesting to say. But not so well for the buildings. My main message is that property developers care much too little for Chinese culture, except when it is in their financial interest."

"How can you say that sitting here with the son and niece of one of Shanghai's leading property developers?" Xu feigned offense. "Seriously, though, life for a developer is tougher than you think. I've been hearing that corrupt government officials are starting to be more aggressive about getting involved directly in property deals."

Walter looked interested. "So is that what your dad is doing now? Making even better friends with the Chinese Communist Party?"

"We're all friends with the Communist Party, aren't we, Walter?" Xu paused, looked around the restaurant hastily, and brought his gaze back to Walter with now real and unconcealed annoyance. "But no, *bà ba* is not doing that kind of deal. We do need to understand what the competition is doing, though, and I thought you would be able to help."

"Well, I certainly am not going to tell you that what you're hearing is wrong. As I understand it, corruption in property deals is limited only by the creativity of Communist Party officials. Although I suppose that might be a real limit— because they're not required to be very creative most of the time." Walter smirked.

"That's not funny, Walter."

Walter suddenly looked completely serious. "Of course it's not funny, Xu." He stared at his old friend, for the first time diverting his attention completely from April. "I think that you know that I barely knew my father. He was a broken man after what the Communist Party did to him in the Cultural Revolution."

Xu drew his shoulders up slightly and lowered his voice. "Really, Walter, don't you ever worry about who might be listening?"

"I do worry, a little bit." Walter glanced back at April and spoke up. "But I worry more about a country where honesty seems to be about three steps lower in the ethical hierarchy than money and power."

Xu, now visibly shocked and angry, stared at Walter and then down at his unfinished cappuccino. "I think it may be time for me to go. April, are you coming with me, or are you going to stay here with this clever boy who wants to be your boyfriend?"

It was Walter's turn to look insulted.

April stood to leave. She was not entirely sure she wanted to go, and actually felt no particular annoyance at Xu's suggestion about Walter's feelings. She realized that she liked Walter a lot better than she liked Xu. Walking away with her cousin, she turned back to give Walter an apologetic smile, this

58

time entirely genuine. "Thanks, Walter. Sorry we have to go. See you soon?"

"Of course, April. Any time you want."

交易

9

Questions

early April 2009

Never ask a question to which you don't know the answer
– Traditional advice to lawyers

"San Marino Property Investments, may I help you?" The receptionist was California-friendly, a manner very familiar to April.

"Yes, I'm calling for Jasmine Liu."

"May I ask who's calling?"

"April Wang, from Jiangsu-Zhejiang Property Company in Shanghai."

"OK, let me see if she's in. Are you calling from China? You sound American."

"Yes, and yes. I'm calling from Shanghai, and I'm from Southern California."

"Well that's nice. You should come and visit us." The receptionist's friendliness started to seem excessive, particularly for an investment company.

"OK, sure I will," April said, laughing a little.

"OK, let me try to find Ms. Liu for you. It might take me a minute. It's only my second day on the job."

"Thank you." April felt a pang of guilt for laughing at the receptionist's friendliness. As she waited for Jasmine, she looked around at the busy, unsmiling JZP staff, and realized that in her dive into the frenetic intensity of Shanghai, she had temporarily forgotten the unaffected friendliness of busy but laid-back California. She missed it.

* * *

"Ms. Wang. Thank you for calling." Jasmine's voice was cool and professional.

April wanted to say "You can call me April," as she ordinarily would to a girl close to her age, but hesitated, confused that Jasmine seemed to be expecting her call. "Thank you, Ms. Liu," she responded, slightly nonsensically.

Jasmine seemed to sense the awkwardness. She paused, and then asked politely, "Am I correct that you are calling about our list of due diligence questions for *jiāo yì?*"

"Yes, that's right." April struggled to recover her composure. She looked down at her notes of a semi-prepared initial speech for the call, and plunged ahead. "Our team here at JZP is working on the answers, and they asked me to clarify a few of the questions with you. You'll have to forgive me. I'm not an expert on property investing like you are—I'm sort of a glorified translator. So apologies in advance if my questions don't make sense."

"I understand. Go ahead." Jasmine was consistently cool, never impolite, but never warm. Impossible to read.

"The first question is about the details that you would like on each of JZP's properties. You've asked for a full chain of title. Of course, you understand that private ownership of land, and the property registration system in China, are very new. Not long ago, much of the land which we are now building on was agricultural. So, sometimes the evidence of transition from state to private ownership, or from farmers to commercial owners, is not very clear. We do have all the proper documentation for transfer of the properties to JZP, and some back-up on former ownership. We will give you everything that we have. Is that OK?"

April worried that Jasmine would not accept this explanation. San Marino needed the documentation, she realized, both to confirm JZP ownership and to look for any tricks or corruption. And after Uncle Jun's revelations over breakfast about the demands of the Suzhou officials, corruption was very much on her mind.

Indeed, corruption in the property market seemed to be the tip of an iceberg of questionable behavior in a country that was coming loose from its ethical moorings. April had been surprised to learn from Xu that many young Chinese were meeting strangers on the Internet for *yī yè qíng* [one-night stands]. He was not ashamed to admit that he had done this several times himself, and claimed that both he and his partners had enjoyed it. April wondered. It seemed that China was straying further and further from its traditional Confucian and Buddhist values. Personally, she had begun to fear that the adventure of *jiāo yì*, which she had initially welcomed, could lead her into unfamiliar and dangerous terrain.

With these visions of a China full of corruption and driven by desire intensifying her usual insecurities, April was pleasantly relieved when Jasmine did not insist on more information. "Yes," said the older girl. "We do understand the basics of the Chinese property system, and yes, we need to learn more. But we know that we cannot ask for more information than you have. Please send what you can, and I and our lawyers will take a look. What else?" Jasmine asked, rather abruptly.

April was swallowing Jasmine's brusquely businesslike question when she was surprised by a sudden softening of tone, as if Jasmine had suddenly remembered to be friendly. "Of course, we are trying to make the due diligence process manageable for JZP. We believe we can be very successful partners in the future. I hope you understand that we need to ask some difficult questions now." April hoped the friendliness was sincere, although it occurred to her that Jasmine might be acting on the same sort of "make friends" instructions that she had received from Uncle Jun.

"Of course. May I move on to another question?" April gained confidence as the conversation progressed. Her prepared script seemed to be working, and Jasmine was cooperating.

"Certainly."

"The next area is accounting. You've asked us to provide JZP's annual accounts for the last three years, and the projections for each current project, according to international accounting standards. The JZP financial team has told me that Chinese accounting practices are very different from international ones, and that providing what you've asked for will take a lot of effort. Not that we can't do it, but we want to find out more about what you need before we spend the time doing the work."

"I think we can simplify that request, too. We've hired an accounting firm in Shanghai to help us understand your business, and they certainly know Chinese accounting standards. So please just send us the accounts and projections as you have prepared them, and we can work with our accountants to identify any follow-up questions. OK?"

"OK, great!" April swallowed as she realized her exuberance at Jasmine's cooperation might seem excessive.

April continued to ask Jasmine JZP's questions, and felt herself relaxing into the role. She did not fully understand the business issues on *jiāo yì*, but she was a quick learner, and it was not too difficult to just pass along questions from others. She managed to make good progress with Jasmine, and started to think that her understanding might be better than she supposed. Eventually, the conversation turned to logistics.

"Thank you for being so helpful today, Ms. Liu."

"Please call me Jasmine."

"Thank you, Jasmine. Please call me April."

"Thank you, April. Richard … Mr. Gregg and I will be visiting Shanghai next week. We will be doing some general research on the property market and working with our advisors, but mainly we want to spend time getting to know JZP better and visiting some of your properties. Can you help arrange that?"

"Yes, I think so. You do know that most of the properties are not in Shanghai? For example, we have a few near Suzhou. That's two hours away by train."

"Yes, of course. Don't forget that I am from China, and worked in Shanghai." Jasmine paused, seeming to realize that her response sounded condescending, and again softened her tone. April could almost hear her effort to be polite. "We'll tell you which days we're available, and hope you can organize visits to the properties that you think we should see, and the transportation to get there. There are a couple of sites that we think are most important—the big industrial park in Hangzhou and the new site in Suzhou."

"I'm sure we can arrange that."

"Excellent. San Marino will pay our own expenses, of course."

"I'll ask Mr. Wang about that. He is generous with guests. And that is the Chinese way, as you know. I believe that, at least for car journeys, our drivers will be at your disposal." April paused. "What else can we plan for you in Shanghai? I know that you lived here, but I ... we still want to be good hosts." Mindful of her "best friends" mission, April decided that if she was in for a penny, then in for a pound. "I could help take you around."

"I'm not sure that we'll have time to do much besides work, so let's figure that out when we know what our schedule is." Jasmine's response was entirely practical, but April couldn't help feeling a sting of disappointment.

"Sure, that makes sense."

"Do you have any other questions today?"

"No, none at the moment." April realized that she had many questions about what Jasmine was thinking behind her cool exterior. None likely to be answered.

"Well, then, I look forward to meeting you again next week. That will be nice." Jasmine sounded sincere, which made April feel better.

"Yes, very nice. *Zàijiàn*, Jasmine." April reflected that *zàijiàn* is usually translated into English as "goodbye", but literally is closer to "until we meet again", like the French "au revoir" or the German "auf Wiedersehen". And that was what April meant. She was very much looking forward to their next meeting.

"*Zàijiàn*, April."

交易

10

Out Together

mid-April 2009

Shanghai Beach

– title of theme song of television show 'The Bund'

April, Xu and Walter were out together at dinner again, this time on the terrace at New Heights. The restaurant perched atop Three on the Bund, an elegant, older building housing businesses and apartments, desirably situated on Shanghai's most famous street. April had found herself with less and less time to relax and enjoy Shanghai, but she had become familiar with the Bund—running along the bank of the Huangpu River, crowded with tourists and wealthy Shanghai residents, both Chinese and Western. She loved the energy and the glamour. She felt much less enthusiasm for the conspicuously excessive consumption.

Xu and Walter, in part at April's insistence, had mostly buried their disagreement of a few weeks earlier, as boys usually do. They were both too preoccupied with other things to dwell on it. Xu had started to get involved in *jiāo yì*, which, as Uncle Jun observed, was the first time that he had shown genuine interest in the JZP business. Apparently it was acceptable under the rules of the new China that he took increasing time off from his bank job to do so. And Walter's articles on historical properties were nearing completion and taking all of his time—or all except the part reserved for attention to April, who had been friendlier to him in recent weeks.

Xu seemed tense tonight, for reasons April believed she understood. Annabelle had not joined them, and April was fairly sure that she had not been invited. When Walter asked about her whereabouts, Xu gave a vague answer about an event at Hermès.

Suddenly, Xu smiled, stood and waved emphatically towards the entrance of the restaurant, and began walking in that direction. He had spotted Jasmine—who had, to April's surprise, agreed to join them at the restaurant.

Jasmine's resistance to social distractions had persisted upon her arrival in Shanghai with Richard three days earlier. She had followed each long day of meetings and site visits with evening work in her hotel room, reviewing what she had learned during the day and preparing for the next. Richard, while not explicitly insisting that she avoid socializing, had tacitly encouraged her schedule, himself spending the evenings speaking with his partners in Los Angeles about the JZP deal and other matters, catching up with Julie and Lydia each day via Skype, and joining Jasmine for discussions of their progress with JZP.

April had felt disappointment that what had seemed like the beginnings of a friendship with Jasmine, in their recent telephone calls, had stayed entirely professional in Shanghai. April's social interactions with Jasmine and Richard were limited to the long business lunches that are a regular part of Chinese dealmaking. At these lunches, April had observed that Xu was visibly entranced by cool, beautiful Jasmine, although April did not feel quite the same surge of jealousy that she had at their first lunch six weeks earlier—perhaps because she had gotten used to men's typical reactions to Jasmine, or perhaps because she sensed Jasmine's indifference to Xu. Each day, Xu had suggested that Jasmine join him and friends for dinner to "experience a different Shanghai", and each day Jasmine had refused, explaining that she already knew Shanghai well from her days working at ICBC.

Xu politely but tenaciously refused to be deterred by Jasmine's evasion. Today, Richard, Jasmine, April, Uncle Wu and Xu had left Shanghai at dawn for a visit to JZP's industrial park outside Hangzhou, the capital of Zhejiang province. Their trip had taken just over an hour on the fast train from Shanghai, followed by another ninety minutes by car out of

Hangzhou and into the rapidly industrializing but still-beautiful Zhejiang countryside. Hangzhou was one of the most prosperous cities in China, home to leading e-commerce company Alibaba and its founder, Jack Ma. Uncle Wu had explained that JZP believed second-tier cities like Suzhou and Hangzhou would be the engines of continued Chinese growth, and were a top focus of JZP's investment strategy.

They had spent the morning driving around JZP's property. Over lunch with the site manager, Xu had insisted more determinedly than before that Jasmine should join him and April for dinner on the Bund. Jasmine refused again, pointing out that the next day would be another long one. But on the train back to Shanghai after an afternoon of meetings with the site manager and his team, Jasmine surprised them (and perhaps herself) by asking April quietly if she and Xu would mind if Jasmine changed her mind and accepted the dinner invitation.

* * *

"Miss Liu, you know April, of course." Xu had escorted Jasmine to their table, trailed by the restaurant's hostess who had greeted Jasmine at the door. The hostess was a beautiful girl in traditional Chinese dress, but it looked to April as though it was Jasmine in her business suit whom several men turned to see better as she walked past their tables. "Allow me to introduce my friend Jiang."

"*Fēichang hǎo rénshi nǐ* [Extremely pleased to meet you]," Walter responded politely. April was quietly pleased that he did not seem to show the same goggle-eyed initial interest in Jasmine as most other young Chinese men.

"*Wǒ yě hen gāoxíng rénshi nǐ* [Likewise]," Jasmine responded. "I realized today that if we are going to work together as joint venture partners, I should not be so impolite to keep declining your dinner invitations. Thank you for inviting me."

"You are a sensible girl, Jasmine. There is more to life than work." Jasmine's arrival appeared to have restored Xu's usual confidence.

"I work hard, Mr. Wang. I expect we'll all need to do that to make *jiāo yì* a success. But with your friend Jiang here at the table, I assume we should not discuss the details of our project. Don't you agree, Ms. Wang?" April was disappointed that she had become "Ms. Wang" to Jasmine again.

"Yes, Ms. Liu. Perhaps Walter can tell us about his work. It's very interesting." April noticed Jasmine's confused expression, and then understood. "Jiang likes to be called Walter," she explained. "He's working in the property market, too, as a journalist." Walter looked pleased at the attention.

"So tell us, Walter, what are you writing about, or investigating?" Jasmine asked. "I am trying to learn everything I can about the Chinese property market. That's my job, as you may know from your friends."

Walter took a minute to consider his response as two young waitresses delivered part of their dinner—six or seven dishes, a selection of meat, vegetables, noodles and dim sum. The waitresses placed the dishes on the large, spinning platter that is at the center of many Chinese restaurant tables—what April would have called a "lazy Susan" at home in America—and began to help serve it. April noticed that one of the waitresses bore a striking resemblance to her ex-girlfriend May, and surprised herself, as she looked from the girl to Jasmine, at her lack of interest in the resemblance. Walter looked at the food thoughtfully, shook his head and smiled. "Well, Ms. Liu, or may I call you Jasmine?"

Jasmine smiled her assent neutrally. Xu frowned.

Walter sat up. "Unlike you and your *jiāo yì*, Jasmine, I am happy to talk about my work. Not enough people in China are paying attention to what I'm writing about, which is the destruction of Chinese culture in the name of progress … in the name of property development. I'm writing about why historical Chinese buildings—important pieces of our cultural heritage—are disappearing as our cities grow."

Xu looked annoyed, but kept his voice calm. "Walter, I think we can spare Miss Liu the details. She'll be able to read about it in the newspaper when your article is published."

"On the contrary, Mr. Wang, I would like to hear more. It is not often one gets the details from a journalist before an article is published. That is the sort of thing for which we investors are trained to look, is it not?" Jasmine looked at Xu, then back at Walter. "So, why is this happening? I've always been taught that our Chinese historical buildings are valued."

"That may be the case for *Gūgòng* [the Forbidden City] or places like Xintiandi that can be turned into tourist attractions. But most historical buildings are not valued enough. Or at least the land that they are on is so valuable to developers that it's impossible to preserve the buildings." Walter looked away, towards the corner of the terrace. "Do you see that table in the corner, with the group of middle-aged men and young girls?" Jasmine and April turned discreetly to look; Xu was stony-faced. "That is one of Shanghai's leading property developers, entertaining a couple of officials from the Ministry of Land and Resources."

April looked at the table and, remembering what Xu had told her about *yī yè qíng*, asked almost involuntarily, "But why are the girls ... ?" Her voiced trailed off as she realized that she could not ask her question in a polite way.

Walter looked at her with a raised eyebrow, and then laughed. "Perhaps not what you are thinking, April. I imagine those girls are just the most attractive young employees of the developer's company. All very proper but still ... you won't see the men's wives at this kind of dinner."

Walter turned back to Jasmine. "So, the answer to your question is: money. I'm surprised that you don't understand that from your time in banking. Chinese developers are paying corrupt Chinese government officials for the right to destroy our history."

Xu's face was flushed, his mouth drawn up into a grimace. "Shut up, Walter," he hissed, and continued in a threatening whisper. "You cannot say that to a group of property developers. We are not all the same. And you should have the good sense not to say that at all in public. You don't know who could be listening. And you know, of course, that you can never write that—your editor would never print it, and you would lose your job."

Walter looked down at his plate and said, quietly, "I will write something."

Xu seemed to realize that he had lost his composure. He paused, and smiled at Jasmine. "So you see, Miss Liu, we speak differently at dinner than we do at lunch."

Jasmine looked back at him evenly. "Yes, Mr. Wang, you do."

The rest of the evening passed less dramatically. All four of the group seemed to take an increased interest in the food, and their bowls and chopsticks clicked along in inanimate conversation. Jasmine and April made polite small talk, while Xu and Walter stewed from their earlier exchange, joining in only occasionally. After the meal had ended with a selection of fruit, Xu offered to take Jasmine home by taxi, but she demurred. "My hotel is very near, and the weather is good. I'll walk. And apologies, but I think I should go now, to get some sleep." She stood to leave.

"I cannot let you walk home alone," Xu insisted.

"Certainly, you can. I spent two years working in Shanghai, and I did just fine on my own." Jasmine turned to Walter. "Thank you for the interesting part of the conversation tonight, Walter. I hope we meet again." She turned to Xu and April. "Mr. Wang, Ms. Wang, see you tomorrow morning. We still have a lot to do." She turned and walked out of the restaurant quickly, her long hair swinging.

交易

11

Family Business

mid-April 2009

Though the bribe be small, yet the fault is great
— Sir Edward Coke

The elder Mr. Wang had excused himself from the visit to the property in Hangzhou, explaining that he had a lunch meeting in Suzhou, and would meet the San Marino and JZP teams in Suzhou the next day. It was entirely true that he had a meeting in Suzhou. But he knew that he could not tell Richard Gregg the nature of the meeting, which he was dreading.

It turned out to be worse than he expected.

In the morning, Mr. Wang had visited the new JZP project, which was located to the east of Suzhou's old city, close to *Jīnjī Hú* [金鸡湖, Golden Rooster Lake]. No matter how long he spent in the property business, it gave him pleasure to watch the construction of his buildings. He resisted the urge to supervise projects directly, aware that the people he hired knew the detail much better than he did. But he usually asked a lot of questions, and once in a while he had discovered and avoided major and potentially costly mistakes. Like the time he had caught a contractor using sub-standard steel—Mr. Wang had spotted printing on a stack of I-beams that identified them as produced by a manufacturer different from the one that JZP had agreed to pay. Today, there wasn't much to ask, because the foundations of the building were still being dug. Still, he enjoyed spending almost an hour watching the coming and going of bulldozers, backhoes and dumptrucks. But part of his mind was already considering the predictably unpleasant discussion that awaited him with the government officials.

After leaving the building site, Mr. Wang had set off on foot, walking along Jinji Hu toward the city center. The lakeshore, lined with office buildings and resort hotels, was not particularly beautiful. Yet he often walked here because he found the water extremely calming. It was at its best on this sunny day in early spring, with noon sunlight glinting off small waves blown along the water's surface by a light breeze.

From the lake to the meeting, Mr. Wang felt that he traveled from a sphere of calm to one of uncertainty. It was an increasingly common, unnerving feeling for him. A feeling that he knew, from various conversations with other businessmen, to be increasingly common for them too in the expanding bureaucratic maze of the new China.

Leaving the lakeshore, he headed into the busy chaos of Suzhou's business district. Like its larger neighbor Shanghai, Suzhou was an old city with a modern center that had sprouted up rapidly during the economic boom of recent years, frequently obliterating centuries-old buildings. Mr. Wang had no trouble finding the nondescript office block belonging to the Jiangsu provincial government. He had been there many times before. Hesitating for a few moments before entering, he crossed a large lobby and ascended in a crowded elevator, the other passengers leaving in ones and twos until he reached the top floor alone. When the elevator doors opened, a hostess in business dress greeted him immediately and led him to a private dining room, where his two lunch companions were waiting.

Li Zhiyuan was a senior official of the Jiangsu province branch of the Ministry of Land and Resources, and Yang Sicheng was a similarly senior official of the Ministry of Housing and Urban-Rural Development. The two men embodied the stereotype of senior government men. They were older than most officials—probably in their early sixties—and he knew they were both influential in the local Communist Party. They wore similar-looking navy blue suits, white shirts, and diagonal-striped ties that Mr. Wang imagined had been selected by their wives to look suitably serious for men of their importance.

73

The meeting started with pleasantries. As an introductory course of dim sum was served, a waitress poured *bái jiǔ*, a strong Chinese white spirit distilled from sorghum, popular at business meals as a sign of prosperity, power and tradition. Mr. Wang told the officials about the growth of JZP and, slightly warily, of the progress of the new project in Suzhou. He related with real pride how Xu was finally becoming involved in the JZP business. Mr. Li and Mr. Yang asked polite questions until a second round of drinks were poured. Then, they got down to business, and things quickly took an unpleasant turn.

"Your *son!*" Mr. Wang repeated.

"Yes," responded Mr. Li blandly. "It is wonderful that your son is working with you on the business of JZP. Likewise, my son is interested in property development."

Mr. Wang started to frown instinctively, then transformed his expression, he hoped, into one of polite puzzlement. "So if I understand correctly, you would like your son to own some of the equity in our Suzhou office tower. That would be highly … unusual. Hmm. How much equity did you have in mind?"

"We do not think a large interest is needed. My son would like to own merely five percent."

Mr. Yang, who had been constantly, and annoyingly, drumming a chopstick on the table, spoke for the first time. "And my sister would equally like to own five percent. She is very interested in property development too."

The two officials looked at Mr. Wang like cats that had eaten a pair of canaries.

Mr. Wang struggled to contain his shock—and his distaste for the officials' crude greed. "You understand that this ownership would have an initial equity value of ten million yuan, and that we expect it to be worth much more in the future?"

The two officials looked at each other and back at Mr. Wang. Mr. Li spoke. "Surely you are not questioning the value to you of our approval of the project? If the property had been offered on the open market, you would have paid many times that amount through a higher purchase price." Then Mr. Li smiled broadly, and Mr. Wang realized that another surprise was coming. "This project will be very profitable for JZP, particularly with your new joint venture with the American property company."

Mr. Wang felt a jolt, and wondered whether he had visibly jumped. He had understood suddenly that the officials knew much more than he had realized about the project with San Marino. Their knowledge about the Americans was probably a major reason behind the new ownership demands. Of course, the government and the Communist Party could be expected to have eyes and ears almost everywhere, but he'd thought he could trust his team to keep a secret. Who at JZP could be responsible? He made a mental note to find out and forced his mind back into the meeting, which was rapidly turning from bad to horrific. He sat quietly and looked mildly interested.

"Don't forget that you will continue to need our help," Mr. Li continued. "The investment by the Americans in your joint venture will require approval by the Development and Reform Commission and by the Commerce Department. We can help make that happen."

"I don't expect we will set up the JV in Suzhou, so … I do not think we will need too much help."

"We have friends in *many* places. And of course we will be pleased to assist you with your joint venture's investments here in Jiangsu province. We want to help you succeed, and we think that will be easier if our family members are part of your team."

The implicit message was that their assistance would turn into silent, invisible obstruction if Mr. Wang did not agree to their demands. Still, he was not willing to give in right away. "We are old friends, and we have worked together for a long time. JZP has always made sure that you are well paid for your assistance. What's wrong with keeping that arrangement?"

The group fell silent as plates were cleared, a soup was served, and wine glasses were refilled. Once the waitresses had left the room, Mr. Li spoke again. "We appreciate the arrangement that we have had, but, as you must know, such approaches are becoming more difficult in China. Rather than receiving payments, we would like to be investors."

"But you are not investors!" Mr. Wang said, angrily at last. "You are asking us to give away our equity to your families as a gift."

"*Wáng xiānsheng*, you should be more careful what you say," Mr. Yang responded equably. "Mr. Li and I have been assisting your business for years, and that means our families are assisting your business. Now our family members are generously willing to join your team at JZP. Certainly it is appropriate to give them some equity as compensation for their services. That is the way business works."

"And how I am supposed to record that in our accounts? What will I say when the Americans ask about the ownership of the business by your families?"

"We assume that you can figure that out," Mr. Li said equally agreeably. "It's your business, after all."

Mr. Wang felt his temper rise again. "You're right, it is my business." He breathed in, struggling to remain calm. "I am considering your proposal that part of it should belong to your families. I don't think you are making the best decision. These ownership records will create clear documentation of your families' involvement in the transaction. Do you really want that?"

Now it was Mr. Li's turn to be angry. "I told you that my son is interested in property development. So is Mr. Yang's sister. And we are helping you. Are you saying that you refuse to have them involved in your business? Are your business and your family too good for my son? He knows your son Wang Xu, and from what I hear, Xu spends most of his time with beautiful girls at expensive restaurants. My son will do real work."

Mr. Wang returned Mr. Li's angry stare but felt sadness. Wang was genuinely encouraged that Xu was finally showing some responsibility, but the justified criticism of his son hit home. It was embarrassing that his family could develop that kind of reputation. He felt his resistance deflate, looked away from Li and asked quietly, "Do I have a choice?"

Understanding that they had won this battle, Mr. Li and Mr. Yang smiled and said nothing.

交易
12

Field Trip

mid-April 2009

Seeing is believing

The teams from JZP and San Marino were standing near a very large hole in the ground. From where the group was standing, they could catch glimpses of late-morning sunlight glinting off the water of Jinji Hu, visible in patches between the buildings along its shores.

They had spent the past hour touring the building site where JZP's new flagship office development in Suzhou would rise, and Mr. Wang was explaining the choice of the site to Richard and Jasmine. "The strategy of JZP is to benefit from the industrial growth of China, trying to be ahead of the market. We think there are big growth opportunities in Suzhou. It's close to Shanghai, very close on the fast train that you took this morning, and as property prices continue to rise in Shanghai, we think that Suzhou will be more and more attractive. It has a big economy of its own, and we think it could even become one of the most important industrial cities in China." Mr. Wang seemed committed, almost fanatic, on this topic. Jasmine looked at him. It was if the enthusiasm in his voice masked an edge of panic.

* * *

The whole day had an odd feeling. It had started with the train ride from Shanghai. That morning, Richard and Jasmine had left their hotel at dawn in a taxi to Shanghai's Hongqiao train station, where they met JZP's Head of Business Development Mr. Wu, along with Xu and April, to catch a train to Suzhou.

Their departure for Suzhou was delayed for ninety minutes without explanation, which was unusual for the ordinarily reliable Chinese railways. On the train, Mr. Wu and Xu had sat across from Richard and Jasmine in facing seats, with Xu and Jasmine opposite each other nearest the window. April was on the other side of the aisle. Jasmine did her best to deflect a series of questions from Xu, while Richard studied a pile of documents and Mr. Wu looked detached. Xu's rude behavior the previous evening had contributed to a growing distaste in Jasmine, which she tried only halfheartedly to hide. After six or seven very brief answers from Jasmine, Xu seemed to get the picture and read a magazine while they waited for the train to leave.

Once the train finally got moving and they left the center of Shanghai, they watched as the speedometer, found in each carriage of most Chinese bullet trains, rose until it indicated over three hundred kilometers per hour. At one point Jasmine looked over at April and found the pretty younger girl apparently staring at her. Jasmine gave April a quick smile, and was surprised to see her face light up and then flush. Then April looked away, apparently embarrassed.

An explanation for the delay in Shanghai came en route. The train slowed, and then passed what appeared to be a serious train accident on a parallel track, crowded with a large number of emergency vehicles and police, in all likelihood dealing with serious injuries from two crumpled carriages. But before they really had a chance to see what happened, the still rapidly-moving train had taken them past the accident and onward to Suzhou.

The accident remained on Jasmine's mind for the rest of the journey, which passed without incident. She decided to distract herself from the possible casualties and Xu's unwanted attentions by watching attentively the views passing outside the train window. On the longer train ride to Hangzhou the previous day, and also during the drive from there to the JZP property, there had been chances to see a little of rural China, including peasant farmers working in the fields.

Jasmine knew that rural peasants remained an important segment of the Chinese society and economy—even if not the backbone it had once been—but this was not a China that Jasmine knew well. Growing up in central Tianjin, she was more in contact with the places her country was going than those where it had been. Today, the direction of development was unmistakable. There were few open fields, and she saw signs of industrialization everywhere. It seemed that the outskirts of Shanghai nearly blended with those of Suzhou.

At the Suzhou railway station, Xu managed to shepherd Richard, Mr. Wu and April into one taxi, and to accompany Jasmine in another about a minute behind them. On their way, Jasmine witnessed another accident—smaller than the rail crash but much more disturbing because she saw it happen in front of her. A young woman on a bicycle, probably about her own age, was hit by a speeding red sports car driven by a young man trying to beat a changing traffic light. Horrified, Jasmine watched the woman's body fly through the air and crunch sickeningly against the windshield of a car that had stopped at the light on the other side of the road. It seemed impossible that she could have survived.

Jasmine screamed, as their taxi slowed briefly but did not stop. "Shouldn't we do something?" she asked Xu.

He shrugged. *"Nǐ zhīdào zhèmeyàng de shì zài Zhōngguó kěyǐ fāshēng.* [You know this kind of thing can happen in China.]" He seemed curiously unmoved, and Jasmine realized that he was right. In the face of disaster, Chinese people did often exhibit a fatalism born from long experience of hardship. Still, to her, it seemed that the insensitivity had gotten worse in the few years she had been away, as Chinese society became continually more competitive and focused on personal success.

She had still not had a chance to discuss the accident with Richard by the time they arrived at the building site. Now she wondered whether the shock had contributed to her impression that there was anxiety and a little hysteria in Mr. Wang's voice. Richard did not seem to notice. Seeing her looking at him, Richard smiled briefly and gestured with his head that she should pay attention to Mr. Wang.

"Suzhou Industrial Park is just over there on Jinji Lake," Mr. Wang motioned with his hand. "That's the biggest cooperative project between China and Singapore. It began in 1994 and keeps growing fast. The location for our project is not in one of the most expensive areas of the city, but it is in one where we think property values will increase rapidly as the growth of Suzhou continues."

Richard jumped in with questions, as he had at other JZP sites. This kind of property strategy was his bread and butter. "Mr. Wang, I agree with your careful approach to site selection. But that's the first time I've heard you say it's your strategy to be ahead of the market. What is it that makes you think you can beat the market? When property prices are rising, it's easy to make money. But when there is a correction, as we have had recently in the United States with our financial crisis, investors who are over-extended with bets on rising prices can easily get hurt. That said, I don't think that China will be hit as hard—in fact, that's why we're here—but ups and downs are inevitable."

"You are right, Mr. Gregg, it is not easy to outsmart the market. But I have two good answers to your question. First, we will never make too many risky bets on rising prices. Our investments are conservative, with careful control of acquisition and build costs. Our rental yields should cover our finance and operating costs even with a big economic downturn. Second, while we cannot expect to beat everyone in the market, we think we know the property market in this part of China and the people in it better than almost anyone else. In your book, you wrote about Deng Xiaoping's reforms many years after they happened, but I was there in the early days of reform, and saw what it would mean for the Chinese property market. We have built our business slowly and surely over more than twenty-five years with the same kind of insights."

"*Wáng xiānsheng, nǐ shì yī wèi hěn cōngmíng de tóuzīzhě.* [Mr. Wang, you're a very intelligent investor.] We could be very successful partners."

"I would like to be your partner, Mr. Gregg. Shall we discuss that over lunch?"

After three years in the United States, Jasmine was getting reacquainted with the importance of meals to Chinese business. But today, the prospect of lunch, indeed the prospect of anything, felt slightly ominous. Unsure of the reason for her feelings of unease, she tried to suppress them, but without success. For the first time in a while, she caught herself in her bad habit of twirling her hair around her finger. Was she reacting to the tension that she had sensed in Mr. Wang? Or was it perhaps only that the two accidents of the morning had called to mind a saying that she had learned in the United States—that bad things come in threes?

* * *

Lunch started oddly indeed. Richard had insisted that he and Jasmine share a taxi to the restaurant that Mr. Wang had selected—Song He Lou, a two-hundred-year-old restaurant near one of Suzhou's historic canals, known for traditional local cuisine. Richard explained to the JZP team that he and Jasmine needed a few minutes alone to discuss San Marino business.

The ride to the restaurant took them through Old Suzhou, sometimes known as the "Venice of China", where they saw canals with stone bridges, traditional stone pagodas, and glimpses of manicured gardens. Although the tide of development was starting to submerge Suzhou as it was Shanghai, a greater concentration of the very old was still visible. Jasmine found herself wondering what Xu's journalist friend would say about the need to protect Old Suzhou from development. Caught in the ebb and flow of city traffic while Richard explained details of his plan for proposing a joint venture to JZP, they arrived fifteen minutes later than the other taxi carrying Mr. Wang, Mr. Wu, Xu and April.

When they arrived at the restaurant, the three men from JZP were deep in discussion outside, and did not immediately notice their arrival. Jasmine saw what appeared to be anger on Mr. Wu's face as he spoke heatedly to Wang Jun and Wang Xu, who had their backs to the arriving taxi. It was April, who had been standing off to one side, who alerted them to the arrival of Richard and Jasmine, and the discussion abruptly ended. Jasmine did not have time to ask Richard if he had seen what she had.

The food at lunch was predictably excellent. As the elder Mr. Wang explained, it featured two local specialties—*sōngshǔ guì yú* [fried sweet and sour Mandarin fish] and *xièfěn dòufu* [crab tofu]. The group also drank plenty of *bái jiǔ*, which took the edge off Jasmine's unease but did not dispel it. She was relieved, at least, that Xu's attentions over lunch were less persistent than usual—both because he seemed chastised by their interactions the previous evening, on the train, and in the taxi, and because the lunch conversation quickly turned to business discussion between Richard and the older Mr. Wang.

After a few toasts with *bái jiǔ*, Richard became the most expansive that Jasmine had seen. "*Wáng xiānsheng*, I don't think I need to hide that Ms. Liu and I really like what we have seen of the JZP business. You have excellent properties that should generate very attractive returns if your assumptions are correct. Since we are leaving for Los Angeles tomorrow, I'd like to describe what I have in mind for a deal between San Marino and JZP. Would that be OK?"

"I would be very grateful if you would do that, *Gregg xiānsheng*. We are also impressed with what we have learned about San Marino, and we would very much like to pursue a successful cooperation."

"Thank you. So here's what I'm thinking ... although my ideas will need to be approved by my partners in Los Angeles."

"Of course, we understand."

"I see an opportunity to combine existing JZP investments with capital from San Marino to create a fifty-fifty joint venture. For example, we really like the property in Suzhou that we saw this morning and the industrial park in Hangzhou. If JZP were to contribute those to the joint venture at their current market value and San Marino contributed an equal amount of cash, that would provide an immediate return to JZP." Richard paused, looking at Mr. Wang for a response.

"It is a very interesting idea. How large would you expect the joint venture to be?"

"Well, we would have to work on that, but let's assume at least $100 million—$50 million from San Marino, in cash, and $50 million from JZP, mostly in property. For example, you told us that JZP's equity investment in the Suzhou building is 100 million yuan, or just under $15 million. We accept that the market value of the equity would be higher than that, since JZP has created a lot of value by arranging the deal. If we add the Hangzhou property to that, we would be well on our way to a $50 million valuation. If San Marino provided $50 million in cash, that would provide immediate resources to do three deals of similar size to the one here in Suzhou. And if things go well, more capital could certainly be available from us and our investors."

Mr. Wang smiled. "Gregg *xiānsheng*, you began by saying that you did not want to conceal your views of our business. So I will pay you the same respect by saying that I like your proposal. It is very flattering that San Marino would consider trusting JZP with such a large investment. But I must ask you … I am very proud of my business and I still enjoy it … who would be in charge of the joint venture that you suggest?"

It was Richard's turn to smile, and continue with even greater energy. "I should have answered that question without you needing to ask it. San Marino invests in strong property management teams, and we would not want our partnership with JZP to change what you have been doing so well. We would expect the JZP team to be responsible for day-to-day operation of the joint venture, although we would expect you to hire additional staff to handle the expanded portfolio, with our involvement in the hiring process. And of course San Marino would need to be fully represented on the JV's investment committee, with veto rights over any investment decision."

Mr. Wang looked thoughtfully at Richard, then at Xu and then back at Richard. "I have built my business for my family, and I am very proud that my son is here today to learn with me about this great opportunity to do business with you—"

"—yes, thank you very much, *Gregg xiānsheng*," Xu interjected, first looking at Richard and then glancing almost shyly at Jasmine, his usual arrogance absent.

"Excellent," said Richard. He was still smiling, his hands set wide apart on the table. "I suppose we should call the lawyers to start working out the details."

"Yes, certainly. But first, let us drink to successful cooperation." Motioning to a waitress to pour another round of *bái jiǔ*, Mr. Wang seemed to harbor none of the tension that Jasmine had noticed earlier, and she wondered again if she had imagined it.

* * *

Even after the successful discussions over lunch, Jasmine was unable to shake her feeling of unease. The image of the young woman's body crunching on the windshield of the car kept repeating in her head. Later that evening, in her hotel room, Jasmine looked on television and online for any mention of the accident, and was unsurprised to find nothing. Somewhat more surprising was the absence of any mention of the railway accident that they had seen—she supposed that the Chinese government did not allow reporting on failures of its fast-growing high-speed rail network.

At least, she comforted herself, bad things *don't* always come in threes. In fact, after lunch, her own, longed-for success with *jiāo yì* suddenly seemed within reach. It took Jasmine some time to fall asleep, and as she drifted off, she had an almost-dream in which she imagined herself telling her grandfather about her success. The kind old man was animated in a way that she had always imagined he could be, but had never seen while he was alive. It was an intensely pleasant dream for now, although it would acquire the aspect of nightmare later, when the day's progress in Suzhou had taken them into uncharted territory. Jasmine would feel then that maybe their progress was the third bad event of the day.

85

交易

13

Final Issues?

late May 2009

The devil is in the details

Jasmine knew that *jiāo yì* was in reach, but the path still did not look easy. It was not that the challenges ahead were particularly dangerous, but rather grinding: a continuing tedium of seemingly endless meetings and conference calls. Since she and Richard had returned from China six weeks earlier, there had been almost constant, intensive negotiations, mostly on the telephone between Los Angeles and Shanghai. Because of the fifteen-hour time difference, these calls usually began in Jasmine's late afternoon, the morning of the following day in Shanghai. They often continued late into the evening.

The stress was considerable, and Jasmine surprised herself on the weekends by seeking relaxation in walking the paths of the San Gabriel mountains, where James had taken her a couple of months earlier. She did not invite him along. Jasmine knew that a single, beautiful woman walking alone in the mountains needed to be very careful. She made a passing mental connection to the frightening encounter with the gang of young men in Guangzhou, but it was not enough to dissuade her. Something was driving her to take the risk. So far she had been lucky, not encountering anything close to a frightening situation.

She liked the warm sunshine, the clearer air as she climbed out of the LA smog, and particularly the trees, which she had started to recognize. Her favorite was the California live oak, its twisted branches and small leaves giving a strong impression of age. She imagined that the old live oaks growing above Pasadena had to be surprised at the concrete jungle of Los Angeles that had emerged below them in recent decades.

Like the way the ancient culture of China must be surprised by the landscape of capitalist development that had emerged in every Chinese city.

On this Monday morning, she arrived at the San Marino office refreshed by a long Sunday afternoon walk during which she had ventured higher into the mountains than before, on previously unseen trails. She felt ready for the conference call between San Marino and JZP scheduled for the afternoon, to work out the final major issues on the joint venture. It was an important call, and Richard, Jasmine, the younger and older Mr. Wang, April, and lawyers for both sides would all be on the line. This was the core group that had been working on *jiāo yì*—except for Mr. Wu, who would not be on the call. He had recently, without explanation, disappeared as a visible member of the JZP team.

Richard suggested to Jasmine that they have a working lunch in the San Marino cafeteria to prepare for the call. They chose sandwiches from the wide selection ordered in every day from a local deli, and made available to the whole San Marino staff to encourage them to keep working during the lunch hour. The cafeteria was light and airy, situated immediately below the partners' conference room with the same view of the wooded arroyo, and furnished in blond wood tables and chairs. It tended to fill up at lunch, but there was enough space to accommodate at least half of the thirty or so people who worked at San Marino without feeling crowded.

Richard got right down to business. "So what are the issues we should raise on the call? And what questions should we be prepared to answer?"

"I'll start with the second question. That's the easy one," Jasmine responded. "I am fairly sure JZP won't raise any real issues, other than valuation, which is one of our issues, too. They want this deal so much, and they don't want to raise any barriers to it. Sometimes I think … they want it too much."

"Yes, I thought about that, too," Richard agreed. "But I decided a while ago that it's just the reality that this is a good opportunity for them. It's attractive for a Chinese property company to receive investment from the United States, and there aren't many other funds with the skills and guts to make this investment in the middle of the credit crunch. Also, I think they're inexperienced with this kind of deal, so they don't really know how to negotiate it hard. Does that make sense? You know the Chinese negotiating style better than I do."

"Yes, it makes sense …" Jasmine paused, about to add *but something still seems a little unusual,* and then decided not to do so. Richard's explanation did make sense. She did not have any real facts to support her concerns. And she had decided that her feeling that something was amiss was mostly linked to that odd day in Suzhou. The shock of that morning's events could easily have affected her judgment—although the odd conversation that she had witnessed before their lunch that day was still weighing on her mind.

Jasmine knew it was her job to spot problems, but she could not see enough real reason to divert *jiāo yì* from its current successful course. After all, it was Richard's pet project, and her own ticket to success at San Marino. Richard did not seem to notice her pause, and she pressed ahead. "On your first question about our issues, let's start with valuations."

"Yep. The most important place to start for any investor." Richard took a bite of his roast beef sandwich and motioned for her to proceed as he chewed.

Jasmine looked at a spreadsheet on her laptop. "I hope that JZP will agree on $22 million for the new Suzhou project, $10 million for the existing Suzhou building, $15 million for the Hangzhou industrial park, and $6 million each for the smaller buildings in Shanghai and Wuxi—$59 million total. Maybe we will need to compromise and end up around $60 million."

"That sounds right to me. The matching $60 million in cash from us is definitely something that I can sell to the San Marino partners."

"Are you sure you don't want a bigger deal?"

"Well, I did initially tell the partners that the JV might own $100 million of property to begin with, and $200 million once we are fully invested. But it's sensible not to start too big. The partners will appreciate that we're not shooting too high, and there's plenty of upside in a $120 million deal. Can you prepare some slides on the properties and valuations for me to present at the partners' meeting tomorrow?"

"Of course. I'll get that to you tonight."

"Great, what else?"

"JZP still hasn't provided title documents for the new Suzhou project. They say it's because that construction just started and there are some open government approvals. That sounds like an acceptable explanation to me, but we need to see those documents."

"Absolutely," Richard said. "We need to be super careful with due diligence. Let's press JZP, and make sure More Fish are on top of that, too." Morton & Fisher were San Marino's usual lawyers, a large, high-priced law firm based in Los Angeles that most at San Marino irreverently called "More Fish". The firm had turned out to be a natural choice for the JZP deal because of their sizable office in Shanghai. Jasmine had gotten to know the More Fish lawyers better than she would have liked. She had been speaking daily, many days more than once, with Jonathan Zhou, a polished Chinese-American partner based in Shanghai who led the firm's team on *jiāo yì*. She found him to be competent but very … boring, like most Chinese men she knew professionally.

"Will do." She paused to make a note. "The next point is our initial contribution to the JV. We want to contribute our $60 million only as and when it's needed for investments—not right away when the deal initially closes—but JZP are concerned about that. They're reluctant to turn over their properties without getting our money. If you don't mind me saying, I can understand that from their perspective."

"Well, it's standard operating procedure. An investment fund like us can't ask investors to turn over cash to be managed by another company before it's needed for a deal. And we can make sure that JZP is protected. Remember, I suggested that we give them rights over our shares in the JV until we pay in our cash. We need to educate them about that."

"OK, but you are going to need to take the lead in explaining it. More Fish say the share pledge structure doesn't work under Chinese law."

"Tell those sharks to figure something out, because this one is a deal-breaker. That's what we pay them for." Richard waited while Jasmine made another note and then took a bite of her red pepper and halloumi on focaccia. "Anyhow, we do need to decide how much cash to provide to the JV initially. What's our model say?"

The sun chose that moment to appear from beyond a rare cloud, lighting up Jasmine's face, as if to put her calculations in the spotlight. Like most junior professionals at investment firms, Jasmine was responsible for building spreadsheet models of investment deals, using the skills she had learned at business school. It wasn't her strong suit, but she tried to compensate for lack of innate numeracy with an excess of care and repeated checking of her own work. "It looks like about $2 million will be more than enough—$1 million for start-up costs including signing bonuses for new employees, and another $1 million of working capital. Plus, we think our deal execution costs will be about $1 million. So we will need to draw down $3 million from our investors."

"That may be OK, but let's start by telling JZP that they should start with $1.5 million. We can compromise at $2 million, and hopefully get them to provide at least some of the cash. That would be a nice way to get their share up from $59 to $60 million, rather than just increasing the valuation. Mr. Wang talked a lot about his wealthy investor base—I'd like to see him prove that to us."

"OK, Richard. I probably should have been tougher with my proposal to start with. Sorry about that." Jasmine tugged at her hair.

"Don't be silly. These are things you'll learn with time. What else do you have?"

"Just two small points. We need their sign-off on the deal structure, including that our investment will come through a special purpose vehicle established in the British Virgin Islands."

"Yes, that's our usual structure. Mmm. The BVI companies always make me think about sailing there." Richard was an avid sailor, although he had had less chance to get onto the water since Lydia's birth. "It's really a beautiful place—the Rocks at Virgin Gorda are amazing, and Cane Garden Bay is probably my favorite beach in the world. There's a guy called Quito Rymer who plays all kinds of music all night in a great beach bar. It makes me happy just thinking about it. You should go there."

Jasmine returned his smile. "Maybe, Doc. We Chinese were known for sailing many centuries ago, but it's not really a popular activity in China these days. It does sound like fun." Jasmine paused, looked down at her notes, and turned back to Richard. "My last point is to get an update on their progress on finding additional investment staff to hire for the JV."

"Right, make sure both of us get a chance to interview anyone they're considering seriously." Richard smiled at her. "Really good work, Jasmine. I like to think I know what I'm doing in China, but with you on our team, I feel safe that we aren't missing a trick."

"Thanks, Richard." Hearing her boss's vote of confidence, Jasmine wondered again whether she should have said more about her feeling that something was unusual about JZP's approach. Was she allowing San Marino to walk down a dangerous path, or simply striding confidently ahead to safety? Reaching the same decision that she had on the weekend as she climbed higher into the San Gabriel mountains, she resolved to stay quiet for now, and to keep her eyes open.

交易

14

Missing Documentation

early June 2009

It is almost always the cover-up rather than the event that causes trouble
— *Howard Baker*

A week later, on the other side of the Pacific, in the glass-fronted conference room at JZP, things were much worse than Jasmine could have imagined. The elder and younger Mr. Wang had their backs to the office, facing Mr. Wu across the table. The latter had tears in his eyes, in full view of the rest of JZP's staff, who were ignoring the confrontation ... or pretending to do so.

The confrontation had been set in motion two months earlier, on the morning after Mr. Wang met with the Suzhou officials, and before the meeting with San Marino on that next day of accidents and agreement. Preparing to meet the Americans over a solitary breakfast at his Suzhou hotel, Mr. Wang had considered how the officials could have found about the JV. As he supped a traditional congee and sipped a less traditional espresso—a habit he had acquired from many mornings at business hotels like this one—it did not take him long to come to the sickening realization that Mr. Wu was the only person who could have told them.

He had confronted his old friend and colleague the next day, just before lunch. It was Mr. Wu's angry denial that Jasmine had witnessed as they approached the restaurant.

Mr. Wang had at first accepted that denial, wanting to believe that he could still trust *Lǎo Wú* [老吴, Old Wu], as he had long affectionately and slightly teasingly called his slightly older friend. But trust had not returned easily, and he had decided to check his suspicions. Now he had proof. And in the conference room that proof was hitting home.

"*Lăo Wú*, why did you tell our friends in Suzhou about the JV application?" Mr. Wang asked calmly.

"How can you accuse me of this again? *Why* have you stopped trusting me? You have even kept me from working with the Americans, the most important project that JZP has ever had. I am the best person to help you make the project a success." Mr. Wu's face was clouded with apparently genuine anger. Observing that anger, Mr. Wang hesitated, wanting again to believe the denial, hoping it was genuine and wondering how, if it were not, his old friend could lie so convincingly. He prepared to deliver what he imagined would be the decisive blow.

There was nothing wrong in what he had done to find out. Still, it had caused Mr. Wang a twinge to think it was *Lăo Wú* he was testing when, a few days earlier, he had called another old and trusted friend, an official of the Development and Reform Commission in Shanghai, and asked him to look out for inquiries about a joint venture between JZP and an American company. His friend had not asked questions, and had promised to let Mr. Wang know if he heard anything.

Then Mr. Wang had casually mentioned to Mr. Wu that JZP's lawyers had just submitted the initial JV application to the Development and Reform Commission in Shanghai.

Mr. Wang was surprised how quickly his deception showed results. The day after he planted the seed Mr. Wu, Mr. Wang's friend at the DRC called to tell him that a Mr. Li from the Jiangsu Ministry of Land and Resources had been asking questions about the JZP joint venture. The friend had truthfully told Mr. Li that he knew nothing about the JV. And Mr. Wang had his proof.

Now he reluctantly passed on that proof to Mr. Wu. "*Lăo Wú*," he said gently, "let me tell you something important about the JV application to Shanghai. I am sorry, but … there was no application."

Mr. Wu looked confused. "What do you mean, no application—" Then realization dawned on his face, followed by shock. After a few seconds of silence as the color drained from his face, Mr. Wu began to cry, and buried his head in his hands.

Xu was the first to speak. "Uncle Wu, how could you be a traitor to our business and our family?" he said angrily.

"Quiet, Xu," Mr. Wang said, and then turned to Mr. Wu. "Why did you do it, *Lǎo Wú*?"

Mr. Wu gathered himself, and delivered what seemed to be a speech he had known he would someday need to give. "It started a few years ago. Mr. Li offered to help my son get into Beijing University if I would provide him some minor information about JZP, relating to the construction schedule for one of our buildings. The information did not seem important, and I convinced myself that I was helping JZP by cooperating with our friends in the Suzhou government." He paused, looking for understanding to Mr. Wang, who remained impassive. "The requests started to become more frequent and detailed, and when I started resisting, Mr. Li threatened to cause problems for my son at university and to tell you what I had been doing. I know I should have stopped then, but I was a coward. Can you ever forgive me, *Wáng lǎo bǎn*?"

Mr. Wang looked thoughtful. "I may be able to forgive you, but you have betrayed my trust. I do not know whether I can work with you any longer. Please go now, and give me some time to think."

"*Wáng lǎo bǎn*, please. Please do not destroy my life. I am no longer a young man. I cannot start again."

"It is not I who created this problem. Please, go."

Mr. Wu open his mouth to speak again, but said nothing after Mr. Wang raised a silencing hand. Then he bowed his head and left the conference room.

"Xu, please call April," Mr. Wang said when he had left. "We need to discuss what to do next on *jiāo yì*. We cannot let what *Lǎo Wú* has done ruin this opportunity."

"They really want to see those documents, Uncle Jun." After joining Mr. Wang and Xu in the conference room, April was describing her latest conversation with Jasmine.

"Xu, what do you think? What will the Americans think about the Suzhou families' ownership in the project there?"

"*Bà*, I don't think they'll like it. Of course, we can try to explain that these are some of your co-investors. They may not notice the families' government connections."

"Yes, you're right, they may not notice it." Uncle Jun looked encouraged. "And if they do notice, we can explain that dealing with investors with government connections is part of doing business in China."

"I hope that would work." Xu looked doubtful. "We have done our best to make it look like the people in Suzhou paid for their shares. But the Americans have been very careful with their financial due diligence." Xu had become very interested in the financial side of the deal, and his father was relying on him increasingly. "If they follow the cash and figure out that we gave away those shares, we have a problem."

"It's a problem whatever happens!" Mr. Wang said angrily. "Once this joint venture is in place, I hope I'll be able to kick these officials back into line." Xu gave him a skeptical look. "Anyhow, I can't see what choice we have—they'll find the documentation in the public records anyhow once it is filed. April, please go ahead and tell the Americans that our lawyers will place the Suzhou documentation in the data room tomorrow. I'll call them now."

"OK, Uncle Jun."

April left the room with a worried backward glance. Xu lingered behind. He looked at his father thoughtfully. "*Bà*, I have an idea to help deal with this problem. It may cost us some money, but it will keep the deal from falling apart."

"Tell me what it is."

"Let's not tell the Americans about the Suzhou families' ownership. If they find out later, we can pay their share out of

95

our own profits. We're already making good money on the deal from the valuation that the Americans are giving to it, and there should be a lot more profits to come. And once the JV is in place, hopefully we can convince the Suzhou officials that their families have no right to the Americans' share of the gains."

"It is a good idea, Xu. But what do we do about the documents?"

"Let's tell the lawyers not to hand over the last document transferring the ownership shares to the Suzhou families. Then the Americans will just see our ownership."

"And what about the public records?"

"If we wait a couple of weeks to file the change of ownership, the American lawyers may not notice it. And we can ask the officials in Suzhou to delay putting the documents in the public files. Maybe that traitor Wu can help us with *that*," Xu sneered.

"And how do we explain when they notice it later? That is going to happen."

Xu paused, and looked down. "Then we say it was April."

"*Nĭ shuō shénme?* [What are you saying?] What a strange idea. April has nothing to do with what happened in Suzhou. Why would the Americans believe that she does?"

Xu continued looking down. "Of course she has nothing to do with that. But she *is* in charge of the documents. If an important document is missing, it might be her fault."

Uncle Jun looked shocked. "Xu, she is your cousin. She is living in our house."

"*Bà*, I have no wish to hurt my cousin, but I do want to make sure that JZP gets this deal and to protect our investments. The worst thing that happens to April is that we have to send her home to America. I think she is planning to go back before too long anyhow."

Uncle Jun looked crushed, and then resigned. "This is a very bad thing. Those officials in Suzhou are putting me in a position to hurt my family in order to protect my business."

He paused and looked at Xu, his mouth set. "But you're right, it's a good idea, and … April will be OK. We'll make sure to take care of her."

Then Mr. Wang slowly picked up the telephone. "I'll tell our lawyers to keep those documents away from the Americans for now."

交易

15

Guys and Dolls

late June 2009

Music To Watch Girls By
– Andy Williams (song title)

"Richard, *bien sûr* you can take a break. You *need* a break."
François LeCroix was lounging on the corner of Richard's
desk, just before nine o'clock on a Friday evening.

"François, you know the China deal needs my time. I'm
planning to go home in an hour to spend some time with Julie.
I've hardly been seeing her these days. At least I've been
making it home to put Lydia to bed most nights, but then it's
been straight back to work."

"One drink won't kill you, will it? We can drive up to Mi
Piace." The popular Italian restaurant on Colorado Boulevard,
the main street of Old Pasadena, was a few miles to the north
of San Marino. It was always packed late evenings with a
trendy crowd of twenty-, thirty- and forty-somethings.

"Uh. No, I suppose it wouldn't kill me. And that's close to
home. Let's make it quick. Can you be ready to go in ten
minutes?"

"I was born ready. And very intelligent, so I don't have to
spend as much time at work as you do." François smiled.

"Get off my desk." Richard smiled too.

"Tell you what, I'll head out now and meet you there. I
might have a chance to speak to some lovely Pasadena ladies
who *appreciate* my exquisite French manners."

* * *

As soon as Richard walked into Mi Piace, François waved from the bar, where he was already in conversation with an attractive, petite brunette.

"Welcome, Richard. I was just telling Stephanie that I needed to call you and make sure you had kept your promise to take a little break from your big deal. What are you drinking?" François motioned to the bartender.

"Your China work sounds great." Stephanie seemed genuinely interested. "I'm a real estate broker, but I've always wanted to get into bigger property investment deals." She looked to Richard rather more intelligent than the butterflies François usually chased.

"And of course we must talk about that more." François handed her his business card, and turned to Richard. "So what will it be?"

"I'll have a vodka tonic with a slice of lime."

François ordered the drink and turned back to Stephanie. "You'll call me soon, OK? Now I must talk to Richard. He's very serious, and I'm lucky to have a few minutes of his time."

"Yes, OK." Stephanie gave a small frown of disappointment. "Maybe I'll call you." She turned politely and joined a group of women and men her age at the other end of the bar.

"Moving quickly as usual, I see," Richard commented once Stephanie was out of earshot.

François looked after Stephanie briefly, turned back to Richard, shrugged and changed the subject. "So tell me, Doc, how is it really going in China? That's what I want to hear. We need some excitement and innovation at San Marino, and your China deal is the best that we have."

"I thought this was supposed to be a break!" Richard smiled, but didn't hesitate to talk about *jiāo yì*. "It's going very well, I think. From a financial perspective, the deal looks incredibly good. JZP's portfolio looks better than almost anything we see elsewhere, and they're willing to share the upside by contributing their properties to the JV at valuations not too much higher than they paid."

"So are you asking yourself whether it's too good to be true?"

"Well, of course I am. I'm asking that any way I can," Richard conceded. "And it seems legit. JZP's explanation is that really good deals are available in the Chinese property market because the market is changing and growing so fast, and that they're in a great position to find deals because of their experience and connections."

"And you believe them?"

"Yes, I do. The thing I would worry about would be if they were getting the deals through special favors from the government … some sort of illegal corruption. But I don't see any evidence of that, and our lawyers are checking it out carefully. And I really like Wang Jun, the founder of JZP, and his team. It's a real compliment that Wang is willing for us to buy half of a family business that he has been building for more than twenty-five years. He knows that this is a long-term relationship, and that we need to be straight with each other. Chinese business people are really serious about the personal side of deals."

"I know you like Chinese people. You've traveled to China for many years, *n'est-ce pas?*"

"Well, it's been a while. Things are very different from when I was studying there in the nineties. So much change, and so much opportunity—this really looks like it's going to be the Chinese century. A lot of risk too. But I think if we do this deal intelligently and carefully, the opportunities should far outweigh the risks. I'm making sure that I have plenty of help to get it right—we've hired good lawyers and consultants, and Jasmine is doing great work."

"I'm sure you enjoy traveling with the lovely Jasmine."

Richard frowned, annoyed. "François, you know that's not who I am. Seriously, I think Tom, Pete and Jane—and I—are going to lose patience if you keep chasing the women around the office. There are plenty of other women around." Richard glanced over at Stephanie, who was looking their way. She smiled at him briefly before flicking her gaze to François and then turning back to her friends.

"Yes, my dear partner, I understand. But I cannot help admiring beautiful women. In France, you know, we don't think that is such a problem."

"We are not in France, François. And now it's time for me to get home to my own beautiful women."

"Are you not even going to finish your drink?"

Richard took a final sip of his vodka tonic as he stood up. "It's time for me to get home. Are you staying?"

François smiled. "As you say, there are plenty of beautiful women around. See you tomorrow, and please say hi to lovely Julie for me." The San Marino team was tight-knit, and Julie and the other spouses were very much part of their little community.

"See you tomorrow."

* * *

When Richard arrived home, a little before ten o'clock, Julie was asleep on the sofa, her hair slightly rumpled but looking as beautiful to him as she always had. Richard still thought of Julie as the girl of his dreams. He woke her with a gentle kiss.

"Hi honey," she responded sleepily. "Working late again, I see."

"Yes, although I did just have a quick drink at Mi Piace with François LeCroix. He was chasing women as usual."

"Lucky women," Julie smiled. "François may try to show a lot of French attitude, but down deep he's a sweetheart. You know, if I hadn't met you first … " Julie knew she had been a good catch for Richard, and she liked to tease him about it.

Richard kissed her again. "I suppose I'd better start coming home sooner. As soon as this China deal is over, I promise. How's our little angel?"

"She went right down tonight after you went back to the office."

"I'll have a quick look at her, and meet you in bed."

101

She smiled slyly. "Sounds like a good plan. I might even wear something nice."

交易

16

The Day Before

July 15, 2009

Learn from yesterday, live for today, hope for tomorrow.
The important thing is not to stop questioning.

– attributed to Albert Einstein

Jasmine woke up from a fitful sleep. Although the rough weather of her flight into Shanghai two days before had not dulled her excitement about *jiāo yì*, the storms had invaded her dreams during both of the nights so far in China. She was not a fearful flyer, but the flight had been genuinely awful, and during the worst turbulence, she had been frightened. In her sleeping mind, the rough jolts of the flight had morphed into other poorly-remembered nightmares, some of them involving scenarios of conflict and confusion about *jiāo yì*. Waking from this continuing turbulence, Jasmine felt disoriented and less optimistic than when she arrived in Shanghai.

She slid out of bed in her long, cotton nightgown, stretched, and looked out the window of her room on the eighth floor of The Peninsula, which gave her a panoramic view across the Bund to the Huangpu River and beyond. On the other side of the river, the skyscrapers of Pudong stood at attention, dominated by the strange, futuristic shape of the Oriental Pearl Tower with its huge spheres at bottom and top. The view raised her mood, and a long, hot shower helped some more. By the time Jasmine had donned her usual uniform for business meetings—a dark business suit with a perfectly tailored skirt and a conservative white blouse—she felt ready for what promised to be a busy day.

Jasmine and Richard had agreed to meet for breakfast before heading to the office of Morton & Fisher to prepare for completion the following day. All of the business issues on *jiāo yì* had been decided, and the concerns that Jasmine had felt six weeks earlier about JZP's approach had gradually evaporated. But there was still work to be done to make sure that completion the next day went smoothly—the completion process involved many documents, and final edits and process needed to be confirmed. "Boring lawyer stuff," Richard called it, but she understood that by calling it boring, he was not saying that it was unimportant.

When Jasmine arrived in the elegant lobby of The Peninsula, Richard was already sitting drinking coffee and reading *The Wall Street Journal Asia*. His brow was furrowed as he studied the paper intently; he appeared tightly wound, and ready for action.

"Good morning, Richard."

"Good morning, Jasmine. Big day today. Will you have any breakfast before we go?"

"Yes, I will have some tea and a little to eat." Jasmine almost always liked working with Richard, but today his intensity, combined with her remaining agitation from her disturbed sleep, put her a little on edge. "If you don't mind waiting, that is."

"No problem. I'll ask the waitress for your tea while you get breakfast. I can keep myself entertained." Richard smiled, his brow unfurrowing, and motioned towards his newspaper.

Jasmine walked across the room to the breakfast buffet—rather a fancy version of the type usually found in business hotels in China, offering various Western and Chinese dishes. She opted for the latter: some dumplings in soup and a tea-soaked egg, one of her favorite foods, practically unavailable in the United States. When she returned to the table, Richard turned to business even before she sat down. "So the plan for today is to go through each of the documents with the lawyers and make sure there are no open issues. I think we're in good shape for completion, but you can't be too careful."

"Yes, Richard, I think we're in good shape."

Richard looked at her, apparently realizing that her response was a little short, and his face relaxed. "I know I'm being intense, but you know I want to make sure everything goes right. You're a perfectionist too, Jasmine. I hope you can bear with me for another day and a half." He smiled.

Jasmine smiled back. "No problem, Doc. I think I want this deal as much as you do." She thought about what she had just said, and felt confident it was true. Jasmine had always been ambitious, always wanted to prove herself, but this was something different. The stakes were much higher than they had been at university or even at ICBC—where she had been a small cog in a large machine—and the risks greater. The combination of importance and risk was a call to action. Failure was unthinkable.

"Yes, you certainly act like you do. Everyone at San Marino is very impressed." Richard paused, and gave her some time for a few quick bites of breakfast. "Shall we go?"

* * *

The early Shanghai summer morning had not yet gotten hot, as it would in a few hours, and Richard and Jasmine decided to walk to the nearby offices of Morton & Fisher rather than taking a taxi. At first they walked quickly in silence, appearing just what they were—transnational business people hurrying to meet the pressures of business. Then Richard glanced at his watched, and slowed slightly. "We're early. I guess we don't have to run."

"Thanks. My shoes are more difficult than yours." Jasmine was not wearing the high heels that were becoming fashionable among Chinese women. She didn't need to exaggerate her looks, and hated having sore feet. But even in low heels, she had been struggling to keep up with Richard's longer stride.

"Sorry. I have been so focused on *jiāo yì*, I almost forget to look around at China. So much has changed here since I lived in Beijing with Julie. Back then, there were still some Mao suits. And a *lot* more bicycles. Now it's business suits and BMWs.

Amazing. Shanghai looks more like New York or London than it does like Beijing in 1997."

"It has changed a lot even in the three years that I have been living in the U.S."

Richard nodded, and fell silent again, his thoughts apparently returning to *jiāo yì*. Jasmine continued to look around at the city sights as they walked. She was proud of Shanghai, and believed that it was now more impressive than New York or London—although that was not a thought that she would share with Richard, for fear of seeming arrogant. Because of rapid growth, large areas of the Shanghai were completely new, and there was a feel of success in the air that the West was starting to lose, more and more quickly now since the beginning of the financial crisis.

Like its Western counterparts, Shanghai was covered with advertising, for both Chinese and Western brands, on shopfronts, buildings, billboards, taxis and almost all other available space. The most visible Western brands were those selling luxury goods to Chinese *nouveaux riches*: Tiffany, Prada, Gucci, Hermès. The Chinese brands were dominated by financial companies—banks like her own ICBC, insurers like Ping An and China Life. Jasmine still felt torn between China and the West, but she was unquestionably at home in this familiar world of commerce.

Suddenly, Jasmine was jolted out her commercial reverie by a very traditional sight, but one she would not have expected in this place. On the other side of the street, coming their way, was a class of young schoolchildren, perhaps five or six years old, dressed in uniforms with red scarves, accompanied by two teachers. Jasmine had no idea what they were doing in downtown Shanghai—an urban elementary school?—a class field trip?

The sight of the class brought to mind a conversation with her mother a few days earlier, before her departure for China. The purpose of the call was to plan a visit home to Tianjin after completion of *jiāo yì*, but her mother had taken the opportunity to ask, not as gently as Jasmine would have expected, whether Jasmine ever thought about getting married.

As a successful businesswoman herself, Jasmine's mother was very supportive of her career progression, but she was also a Chinese mother. The unspoken but not at all subtle implication of her question was that, at twenty-eight, Jasmine was rapidly approaching the age of an old maid in traditional Chinese culture—although younger attitudes were slowly changing.

Looking at the schoolchildren, Jasmine realized that when she was their age, her mother had been younger than Jasmine was now. Was her single-minded focus on career really the right thing? Maybe it was time to start looking for a man, although the prospect of doing so held absolutely no attraction for her. In any case, marriage was definitely not something that would distract her from *jiāo yì*, which was where her thoughts turned quickly when the schoolchildren had passed.

* * *

Morton & Fisher's office was in one of the many modern office towers that dominate the Shanghai skyline. The day of work with their lawyers on the JZP deal turned out to be as boring as Richard had predicted, involving careful review of several dozen documents, last-minute corrections, and calls to the JZP's lawyers—a Chinese law firm—to make sure that all of the corrections were agreed. The most important discussion centered on ownership of the JZP properties.

"So have you gotten completely comfortable with the property documents that JZP has provided?" Richard was speaking to Jonathan Zhou, who was flanked by a younger male lawyer in a conservative suit and tie that were virtually identical to the ones that Jonathan wore. Jasmine had forgotten the name of the younger lawyer, who did not speak a word during the meeting, and took copious notes. The two lawyers sat across from Richard and Jasmine, who faced the window of the tasteful glass and steel law-firm conference room, which overlooked a busy Shanghai street far below.

"Well, maybe 'completely comfortable' would be a slight overstatement, but I feel as comfortable as I can be. The documents that JZP has provided clearly establish their ownership, they match the information in official records, and we haven't identified any particular problems."

"And that's the case for their new Suzhou property, too?"

"Yes," Jonathan replied. "Those documents came a little bit late, but they check out fine. Actually clearer than for the older properties. Property records now are getting better than they were five or ten years ago."

"Sounds good. Anything else we should be worrying about?"

"I don't think so. You're right to focus on ownership issues. Corruption and fraud are real problems in Chinese property deals. But this deal looks OK to me. In fact, this is one of the best deals for a Western client that I've seen in the past couple of years. Financially it looks good—you know that better than I do—and the relationship with the Chinese partner is very balanced. Some of our clients have to make a lot of concessions to get a deal through, particularly where there is government involvement, and that has just not happened here."

"Well, Jonathan, it's good to have your vote of confidence. Your partners in California have always given San Marino good advice on our U.S. deals. Our read is that Mr. Wang at JZP is a very smart businessman, and understands that a fair deal with us provides a great platform for him to do more property deals."

"Yes," Jonathan nodded emphatically. "It's a rather ... well ... Western attitude, but we're seeing more of that in China. Publicly, the Chinese are currently blaming the Western capitalist system for the global financial crisis, but privately Chinese business is becoming more and more Westernized."

"So we all like our *jiāo yì*. You know, San Marino is here because we think—actually, mostly because I think—that China is going to get through the crisis in great shape."

"Let's hope you're right. I'm optimistic, too."

* * *

The meeting with the lawyers continued until late afternoon. When Jasmine got back to her hotel room, she had a message from April to call her.

"*Wéi.* [Hello.]"

"Hello, Ms. Wang, it's Jasmine."

"Hello, Jasmine ... I mean Ms. Liu ..." April sounded nervous.

"It's OK to call me Jasmine. May I call you April?"

"Yes." April's one-word response sounded breathless. There was a pause. "So, it was *you* who called *me.* Was there a reason for your call?"

"Yes, of course. I called you." April was obviously off balance, and Jasmine's concerns about *jiāo yì* abruptly resurfaced. Or was there some other reason for April's nervousness? "I just wanted to confirm the plan for completion tomorrow. The San Marino team should come to the office of our lawyers, Xin Lu Law Firm, at nine a.m. Is that OK?"

"Yes, it's OK. There will be four of us—Mr. Gregg, me, and two lawyers from Morton & Fisher. I just got back from their offices, and it looks like we're ready to go. Do you agree?"

"Yes, Mr. Wang said that everything is ready to go. There will be five of us tomorrow—Wang Jun, Wang Xu, two lawyers from Xin Lu, and me."

"What about Wu Zhiguo?"

There was another pause before April answered. "He is busy looking after one of our development projects tomorrow."

Jasmine wondered what could be so important that Mr. Wu would miss completion of *jiāo yì,* but she decided not to press the issue. "OK, I think that's all we need to know. So ... see you tomorrow morning. Let's hope it will be an easy day." The lawyers didn't see any problem, Richard didn't see any problem, and Jasmine decided to focus on getting the deal done.

"See you ..." April hesitated, and Jasmine stayed on the line. "If you wish, once it's done, perhaps Wang Xu and I could take you out to dinner again. Walter might like to come along

109

too—he and Xu seem to have gotten over their fight. When do you leave Shanghai?"

"Thank you for the invitation. I'm actually leaving Friday, the day after tomorrow, for Tianjin to visit my family. And of course we have the completion dinner tomorrow night. Maybe some other time—it would be good to go out with you and Walter … and Xu." Jasmine realized a beat late that it was the wrong time to be conveying her dislike for the son of the owner of their joint venture partner.

"Well then, I suppose I'll see you tomorrow morning, and at the completion dinner. My uncle has arranged a very nice dinner, I think."

"OK. See you tomorrow."

"See you tomorrow."

交易

17

Friends

July 15, 2009

Friendship … is not something you learn in school.
But if you haven't learned the meaning of friendship,
you really haven't learned anything.

– Muhammad Ali

Hanging up the phone with Jasmine, April was dismayed that her friendliness had produced a rather unenthusiastic response. She realized that Jasmine put her on an emotional roller-coaster—like no one else ever had. It did comfort her that Jasmine had made clear her dislike for Xu, a feeling that April often shared. Actually, anything that brought her closer to Jasmine felt good.

April took a deep breath, and looked around the nearly dark JZP office. It was after nine in the evening, and she was the last to leave. The familiar shapes of the desks took on a slightly threatening aspect in the dark, and contributed to her feeling of dislocation and agitation. As she had discussed with Jasmine, *jiāo yì* seemed to be in order, which should have been the most important thing. She hummed her theme song as she turned out the light at her desk, but it did not calm her down.

In her agitated mood, April did not want to be on her own. She considered heading home for a late chat with Aunt Hong. April had very little in common with her aunt, but always found it calming to talk with the older woman, whose interests in life were dominated by a simple agenda of home and family. But instead, she picked up her mobile phone again.

Walter answered on the first ring. "Hi, April. It's always nice to hear from you!"

"Hi, Walter." She paused when she realized that she did not know why she had called him.

He seemed to read her mind. "You called me. Care to tell me why?" She heard his smile.

"Tomorrow is the big day for our deal with the Americans …" She didn't fill in what was on her mind.

"And, so …? Shouldn't you be getting ready for bed?"

"Walter, would you mind meeting me for a drink?"

* * *

Outside, the streets were still busy, full of late-working business people, the young and old enjoying the warm summer evening, and a few tourists. April walked slowly towards the small bar near the JZP offices where she had agreed to meet Walter, who had much further to travel from the apartment that he shared with his mother.

She meandered, window-shopping, past stores on *Huáihǎi zhōng lù* [淮海中路, Huaihai Middle Road], then paused in a bookshop, where she lost track of time as she browsed through the fiction section, wondering whether her Mandarin was good enough to start reading Chinese novels in the original. Growing up with Chinese parents, she had learned excellent spoken Mandarin, which had served her well at JZP. Reading and especially writing were a greater challenge—although she had so far been able to manage the documents for *jiāo yì* without complaints from her colleagues.

While she browsed, a thirty-something Chinese man who had been in the shop when she entered kept eyeing her appraisingly across the stacks of books. On a few occasions, he seemed about to speak with her before she moved away. His final approach was the most determined, giving her a chance to look at his face as she said *"Bù hǎo yì sī"* ["Excuse me"], and moved past him as he began to speak and then reconsidered. The man was handsome but shy-looking, reminding her of an older version of Walter, and then quickly of the fact that she was late. Without looking back, she left the shop.

The bar was called *Xìngyùn 8 Jiǔbā* [Lucky 8 Bar], and the '8' in the sign at the top of its façade was provided by a large 8-ball. The owner had apparently wanted to attract both pool players and people wanting to benefit from the luck that Chinese ascribe to the number eight. It was a small bar, with room for only a few tables around the beaten-up pool table. The walls were covered with photographs of Chinese celebrities, mostly actors and singers. The photos were not signed—it was not the sort of bar that was likely to be frequented by celebrities. It was a simple, cosy watering hole, which had become the favorite meeting place of Walter and April as their friendship blossomed in the past few months. Today, despite the crowded streets, the few worn tables and chairs were mostly empty, perhaps because it was a Wednesday evening or because the weather was so nice outside.

When April arrived, Walter was already waiting, reading a book at a small table in a corner. He looked up when the door opened, smiled broadly at April, and stood to greet her. After confirming that April was mostly OK, Walter went to the bar to buy two glasses of red wine, and they settled back in to his table.

Being with Walter made April feel comfortable, almost immediately calming the agitation she had felt in the dark JZP office, which her walk had failed to dispel. Notwithstanding her initial reactions to Walter's romantic interest in her—and to April's pleasant surprise—the two had steadily become good friends. She found Walter to be a refreshing break from most of the young people she met in China, with their persistent focus on money, jobs, houses, possessions, and eventually marriage. It was obvious that Walter genuinely liked her beyond his attraction to her—which he had not overcome, as he occasionally reminded her. He seemed to understand and accept that April did not want a relationship.

"Thanks for meeting me, Walter. It felt like such a strange day, and I really needed to talk with a friend before the big day tomorrow."

"You know I'm always happy to meet you," he smiled wistfully, "although it would be nice to have more of you." Another reminder. He refocused. "So what's wrong? Why was it a strange day?"

"Well, nothing specific that actually happened. I think I'm worried about two things." April paused. "Can you keep a secret?"

"Sure. Of course I can."

"I mean a really important secret. One that would be interesting for you as a journalist. But you can't use it. If you did, it could be very bad for JZP. And for me."

"You have my word as your friend that I will keep your secret. I would never do anything to hurt you. JZP ... I don't know. But you are my favorite, you know."

"Enough compliments, Walter. I trust you, though. So, here's the thing. JZP was forced to give shares in JZP's new project in Suzhou to family members of two government officials there."

Walter laughed. "That's not a secret. Xu practically told me that at dinner a few months ago."

"Well, now you can be sure. But that's not the strange thing. We gave the Americans documents showing the new owners, and they didn't ask anything about the government ownership. It doesn't make any sense to me—they've been so focused on ownership issues. What do you think could be going on?"

"Well, it is hard to know for sure. Americans are usually very careful about corruption, especially because they have a law called the Foreign Corrupt Practices Act that's very strict. But maybe your American friends have gotten a private explanation from your Uncle Jun that this is the way we do business in China, and think they won't get caught."

"I don't know. That doesn't seem to be the way that they've approached *jiāo yì*. I suppose I can only wonder about it for now. Maybe I'll learn more after the completion of the deal tomorrow."

"Maybe you will, but people keep very quiet about corruption. They pretend that it's just part of business. And of course they want to protect themselves."

"You don't think it should be part of business."

"Of course I don't. That's why you see me and Xu fighting. He's more practical, and he's right that it's very hard to change these things. I am an idealist, which may be impractical, but it works for me."

"I don't know what I feel about it anymore. I wanted an adventure here in Shanghai, but this was not what I had in mind. I guess I didn't expect knights in shining armor, but somehow I thought my family would be ... better than this."

"Well, I know what I feel, and I think I have to do something about it."

"What do you mean? You just promised me that you wouldn't use what I told you."

"Don't worry. I keep my promises. Especially to you. I just mean that I am serious about the articles that I am writing on corruption. I need to write something that will make people pay attention." Walter furrowed his brow in determination, and April could see that his thoughts briefly jumped elsewhere.

"OK, I trust you, too. Just be careful." April paused. "It does really help to talk to you about it, Walter." April paused again, longer than the first time, and Walter remained silent as he watched her deciding what to say. "The other thing I wanted to tell you is personal. It's hard to say, too ... not something that I've told anyone before. Well, actually, two people know, but they are a special kind of exception."

"So I am an exception too?"

April laughed. "You are exceptional, Walter, but not the kind of exception I meant. You will see why it's funny." She paused again. "I know that you like me as more than a friend, and I wanted to explain why that's not going to happen."

"Never?" Walter looked crestfallen.

"I don't like to say never, but it's not very likely." April caught her breath. She had never really thought about "coming out" as—well, she honestly wasn't sure exactly what she wanted to call herself. But suddenly, she realized that this was what she wanted to do, and Walter was a good enough friend that the truth felt natural. "The truth is that I like girls."

"What do you mean?" Realization dawned on Walter's face as he finished the question.

"Well, I once had a boyfriend in college. But after that I had two serious girlfriends—those are the two exceptions—and it felt a lot more … right than being with a man." April rushed on, testing her thoughts, and the words. "I'm not sure whether I'm a lesbian, or bisexual, although I do know that I want to be with a woman now. That's the other thing that's been upsetting me, what I wanted to tell you."

"Well, you told me." He raised his glass for a toast and tapped hers. "Congratulations. It's disappointing for me, but on the bright side, at least it helps my confidence to know that you don't not want me … if you know what I mean … since I am wonderful, of course. Anyway, I suppose I'll get used to it. You are my friend."

"Actually, I haven't told you the main thing that has been bothering me."

"Really?" Walter's eyes widened. "More surprises! Thank goodness I'm sitting down."

"Actually, this part probably won't bother you as much as what I just said." April smiled, "In fact, I think it would probably bother Xu more. You definitely can't tell him."

"My lips are sealed."

April paused once again before giving voice for the first time to what had been bothering her for months. "I think I have fallen in love with Jasmine."

交易

18

Completion

July 16, 2009

*If I'd had some set idea of a finish line,
don't you think I would have crossed it years ago?*

– Bill Gates

When she awoke on Thursday, the day of completion, Jasmine felt much better than she had the previous morning. She had slept soundly, the turbulence of the flight finally receding into the background. A thought from the flight did return to her, though. "Today is the end of beginning," she said to herself.

She walked to the window, which had become a habit when she woke up, and looked at the flow of people walking on the Bund. From this distance, they were faceless, but mostly recognizable from their clothing, gait, and group size as tourists, business people, shoppers or other locals. The people on the Bund had become a metaphor for Jasmine of international commerce, a flow of power and money. She felt certain from her months working on *jiāo yì* that she wanted nothing more than to be an important player in that flow. Today was the day when that would start to happen. The end of beginning.

Jasmine had no way to know that, by its end, the day would feel much more like the beginning of the end. The signs would emerge slowly as the day progressed. It would be another day of bad things that came in threes, but, unlike in Suzhou, the bad things would not be destructive or upsetting. They would seem like little things, each minor and inconclusive.

* * *

The early part of the morning was a replay of the previous day—breakfast with Richard, and then a walk to Morton &

Fisher on a sunny Shanghai morning. Despite having struggled to keep up with Richard the previous day, Jasmine had chosen today her favorite pair of shoes, which, inconveniently, had higher heels. Today she was focused on success, with no room for distraction like that from the schoolchildren on the previous morning. And her choice of footwear forced her to concentrate on the walk.

Richard did not hurry as he had at first on the previous morning, and looked distracted. Jasmine assumed he was thinking about completion. They walked most of the way in silence. It was not until they approached the lawyers' building that Richard spoke. "Have you ever been to a completion meeting before, Jasmine?"

"I have not, Richard. I'm embarrassed not to have more experience."

"Don't worry about it. It sometimes takes a while for a junior investor to have that opportunity. And it's not rocket science. Completion meetings are usually really boring, just moving a lot of papers and signing most of them. The way I see it, boring is the way things should be when everyone has done their work. Like we have. So are you ready for a boring day?"

"Yes I am, Doc—" Smiling and looking at Richard as she responded, Jasmine failed to notice a wide crack in the sidewalk, which caught one of her heels and broke it off cleanly. She narrowly avoided falling by grabbing onto Richard with both hands, dropping her briefcase on the sidewalk and spilling its contents of deal documents.

"Are you OK, Jasmine?" Richard seemed unfazed by the small disaster, but Jasmine reddened as she knelt to collect the papers.

"I am so sorry, Richard."

"Don't be silly. Let's hope this is the worst thing that happens all day."

Hobbling into the building on her one broken heel, Jasmine made an effort to gather herself. The first bad event of the day had shaken her mood and her confidence. She hoped Richard was right.

* * *

Richard's prediction about the completion meeting turned out to be nearly correct. For more than two hours, the meeting in the conference room at Xin Lu—which was less expensively furnished than the one at Morton & Fisher—was predictable and boring. Junior lawyers shuffled a series of papers in front of Wang Jun, who was signing for JZP, and Richard, who was signing for San Marino. A few small issues came up, such as details of addresses and passports required for identifying the individuals involved, but overall the process was smooth. A large amount of tea was consumed.

Then suddenly a minor roadblock appeared. Mr. Wu was needed to sign one document as the sole director of a JZP entity that had developed one of the smaller properties. JZP's lawyers from the Xin Lu firm had assumed Mr. Wu would be present, and had forgotten to raise the issue when he did not arrive as part of the JZP team. They did not realize their mistake until the document appeared in front of Mr. Wang for signature.

A hasty series of telephone calls managed to track down Mr. Wu quickly, but it took another forty-five minutes for him to arrive. While they were waiting, Mr. Wang invited Richard to another conference room for a private conversation about their future joint venture, and the rest of the group waited awkwardly in the main room.

When Mr. Wu arrived, his hair and clothing were rumpled and there were dark circles under his eyes. His appearance surprised Jasmine, because Mr. Wu had always been neat and good-humored, if rather reticent. There was little time for her to observe more closely before he had signed the document, while Richard and Mr. Wang were still out of the room, and promptly disappeared. Oddly, Xu seemed to urge along Mr. Wu's departure with a hand on his elbow, leading him out of the room. When Xu noticed Jasmine looking, he removed the hand and looked away.

119

This second small problem of the day added to Jasmine's feeling of unease. April had told her that Mr. Wu would be busy at one of JZP's development projects, and whatever had kept him there and away from the completion meeting had to be important. So his evident tiredness and stress were probably a result of that important work. Or were they? And what was going on with Xu's behavior, which, notwithstanding his modern manners, seemed inconsistent with proper Chinese respect for elders?

When Richard came back into the room with Wang Jun, he looked cheerful and relaxed, and pulled Jasmine aside. "I just had a very good chat with Mr. Wang. He was telling me about other projects that they have lined up. There is *so* much opportunity in this deal."

"That's great. Mr. Wu came and signed the document, so I think we are almost done." Jasmine wondered whether she should tell Richard about Mr. Wu's appearance and the odd interaction with Xu, then decided that it was the wrong time to raise the issue. The deal was almost done.

When the last document was signed, Richard walked around the table to shake Wang Jun's hand. "*Wǒ xīwàng wǒmen hěn chénggōng hézuò.* [I hope and expect that we will cooperate very successfully.]"

"Yes, Mr. Gregg. I hope so, too." Wang Jun shook Richard's hand, as did Xu. "We have arranged a special dinner for you tonight to celebrate our future working together. So that you can relax after so much travel, dinner will be in a private dining room at the Yi Long Court restaurant in your hotel. It's a very good restaurant—the chef has a Michelin star."

"We are grateful to you for arranging that. This deal has been a lot of work for all of us, and this evening, we look forward to relaxing with you as our new friends. Of course, soon we will need to get on with the real business of making money from our joint venture." Richard never forgot about work for long.

"Yes, work always calls," Mr. Wang agreed. "I apologize that I must go speak to our accountants about the accounts for JZP, which need to change now that we are in the joint venture with San Marino. So we will not be able to share lunch with you now. I hope that you and Miss Liu won't mind finding your own lunch. We'll meet you tonight at the restaurant at seven o'clock."

Jonathan Zhou broke in. "I appreciate that you've invited me to the dinner, too, Mr. Wang. Excuse me, but I do need to keep us working for the moment. May I ask your lawyers when they will be able to provide Morton & Fisher, and San Marino of course, with copies of the documents signed today?"

His counterpart from Xin Lu responded. "It will take us a day or two to get everything organized into a proper documents bible, but we've been scanning each document as it is signed. Within the hour, we can have the documents on a CD that you can use until the bible is ready."

"We appreciate your quick work," Wang Jun thanked the lawyer. "April, please stay here until the CD is ready, and bring a copy to the celebration tonight for Mr. Gregg and Miss Liu. Then everyone will have what they need to get back to work tomorrow." Mr. Wang smiled.

"Yes, Uncle Jun."

Jasmine turned to April. "I would wait here for the CD, but—" She pointed at her stocking feet, and the broken heel of the shoes in her hand. "I think it might be easier for me to leave with Richard now." Jasmine realized that her excuse did not really make sense. But something made her want to get away.

"No problem. I am happy to wait and bring it to you." April blushed, which surprised Jasmine. Why did she seem to have such a strong effect on the younger girl?

The third small problem of the day resulted from Jasmine's decision not to wait for the CD. Later in the day, April would forget to bring the CD to the restaurant. It was a very small mishap, but the consequences for *jiāo yì* would be enormous. For the time being, though, the deal was complete.

121

* * *

Yes, the end of beginning, Jasmine thought as she rode in a taxi with Richard from the completion meeting back to their hotel. The completion had produced a strong feeling of accomplishment, but not one of closure. After all, the joint venture with JZP was now an investment that San Marino owned, and the big question in the coming years for San Marino and its investors would be how that investment was going to perform. Ensuring its good performance would be primarily the job of the JV's management team in Shanghai, but Jasmine knew she would have an important ongoing role.

There was also something else incomplete, a feeling that she had missed something, triggered by the odd visit of Mr. Wu. The attitude of Wang Jun and Wang Xu at the end of the completion meeting had also struck her strangely, contributing to her unease and reawakening earlier fears that something might be wrong with the deal. Unlike the San Marino team and their lawyers, who were full of the energy and excitement of the completed deal, Wang Jun had seemed simultaneously relieved and subdued. It was unlike him not to have arranged lunch for the San Marino team.

Wang Xu had looked like the cat who ate the canary. Jasmine realized that she might just be put off by her distaste for Xu and his arrogance, which had grown stronger as the deal had progressed. She was used to the attention of men and did not usually let it bother her, but for some reason, Xu's persistence in the face of her obvious lack of interest had started to make her feel irritated every time she thought about him.

Anyway, it was a familiar feeling for Jasmine to worry that things might go wrong, one instilled by her careful parents. Concern about the possibility of missing something was a main reason that she focused so completely on work, always aiming to get things right. So maybe this was just paranoia, and everything was OK. She was confident in the answers that she and the lawyers had given to Richard about the completeness of due diligence and the attractiveness of the deal.

Jasmine wondered whether Richard could see what she had seen in the JZP team at completion. She suspected not, both because it required a Chinese eye to fully judge the subtleties of their reactions, and because she had found that Richard's relentless focus on the financial and commercial details of investment opportunities was sometimes linked with a surprising blindness to the human dimensions of the people with whom they did business. She supposed that this usually helped Richard as an investor, since property investing success was generally driven by financial considerations—interest rates, occupancy rates, rental yields, lease terms. Deliberate focus on these nuts and bolts was often necessary to tolerate the questionable and colorful characters that one tended to meet in the property market, even the high-end commercial property market.

Jasmine hoped and believed that this focus on fundamentals was the right approach in the JZP deal. The Wang family, including arrogant, unpleasant Xu, were in fact rather polite, solid citizens compared to some people she had encountered in other business dealings, both in the United States and China. She decided that there was probably nothing that she could do about the worries that were nagging her, at least not now.

Richard cut across these musings as they approached the hotel, after ending a call on his mobile phone. He had called Julie as soon as they left the lawyers' offices, waking her in the middle of the California night. They had a brief, animated discussion of the success of *jiāo yì*, the attractions of Shanghai, his imminent return home, and—a tidbit for Julie to pass on to Lydia—the fact that he would be accompanied by a large, soft Hello Kitty doll.

"Well, Jasmine, what do you think?" Richard asked, then answered his own question. "I guess it's time to celebrate. I'll say it again. You've really done a great job getting us here."

"Thanks, Richard. Thanks a lot." Jasmine decided not to respond as usual about how they were a team, and how much she had learned. She was a little tired of the compliments, perhaps because her worry over the Wangs' behavior fed a concern that she did not deserve them.

"So, the completion dinner is at seven." They were walking into the lobby of the hotel. "Shall we meet here in the lobby at six-thirty to have a celebratory drink on our own first?"

"Sounds good, Richard. See you then. And thanks again for all your support."

交易

19

Dressing Up

July 16, 2009

The Way You Look Tonight
– Frank Sinatra (song title)

Back in her hotel room, Jasmine took a deep breath and lay down on her bed. She tried again to make sense of what she had seen at completion. But before she had considered too long, her concerns started to dissolve by reflex, by a very Chinese reflex that came naturally to Jasmine.

Like her father, who had recovered quickly from what the family experienced in the Cultural Revolution, Jasmine was culturally inclined to move on from adversity. This reaction was the *alter ego* of her instinct to worry, and was the quality that enabled her not to become submerged in uncertainties. "Life is tough and I will be tougher," she thought as she drifted into an afternoon nap.

When Jasmine opened her eyes, she felt disoriented, and then briefly concerned that she had overslept the dinner. She relaxed when she saw the sky outside was still bright, and checked the clock to confirm that she had enough time to shower and dress. The nap had refreshed her and nearly completed the process of dissolving her worries. Now, the prospect of the completion dinner excited her.

Although Jasmine had always worked hard, at university she had not hesitated to let down her hair on social occasions. Mostly this had involved dinners with friends, cooking, talking, and listening to music. And *hóng pútáojiǔ*, red wine. She loved red wine, and it had a strong effect on her. She became less intense, more the life of the party and the center of attention— and, with her looks, attention was easy for her to attract, particularly from the boys. After a couple of glasses of red wine, she had sometimes kissed a boy, although it rarely went further than that.

There had been one serious relationship, after she left university, with another banker. He had been as beautiful as Jasmine, which was the main attraction, particularly after a half bottle of red wine. Unfortunately, beyond the mutual physical attraction, there was little that provided a foundation for a solid relationship, and Jasmine had usually found it more compelling, and even more interesting, to work late than to join her boyfriend for dinner or drinks with friends. Gradually, he drifted away to the many other women available to a handsome and successful young banker, and Jasmine did not regret the loss.

Her socializing had become less and less frequent as the social memory of student life receded into the past and the demands of work became more compelling. With her move to California to join San Marino, socializing with friends her own age had stopped almost entirely. She had not sought out any friends in Los Angeles, and had politely deflected the attentions of the few who pursued her—like the boy James who had taken her walking in the mountains. Her social life had gradually contracted to occasional work dinners, and brief interludes as a tour guide for a couple of university girlfriends who had visited her from China.

Tonight, with the relief of completing *jiāo yì*, she felt ready for a good time. She enjoyed Richard's company, and also that of most of the people she had met at JZP. And she hoped that Mr. Wang intended to invite some other powerful and perhaps interesting people to celebrate his new relationship with the Americans. Of course, she did not like Xu, but she was reasonably confident of her ability to handle him, if in no other way than by simply ignoring him.

Jasmine had, just in case, packed her little black dress—a modestly alluring, silk cocktail dress with a pleated skirt to just above the knee. It suited her small-waisted, small-breasted, long-legged figure perfectly. She wore the sheerest possible black stockings underneath. Although her low heels had to substitute for the favorite shoes that had met their end earlier in the day, she knew she looked extremely good. As she left her room and took the lift down to the lobby, taking in a couple of admiring glances on the way, she felt the power that her looks gave her and wondered how she should use it.

* * *

Back at home in the Wang family house, April did not feel so confident. She usually liked returning to the house, particularly as the summer advanced. The walk from the Shanxi Nan Lu metro station first took her through some of the oldest, most charming parts of the French Concession, including buildings and shops that reflected its French heritage. There was a French bakery that she particularly liked, where she often stopped for a croissant in the morning, and sometimes a coffee in the late afternoon on the rare occasions when she found herself headed home early.

The Wang house itself was covered with flowering vines, mostly bougainvillea and jasmine. The first impression approaching it from the street was a gentle scent from the jasmine, then a riot of color as the house came into view, dominated by the red, pink and white bougainvilleas, the jasmine's perfume growing stronger and stronger as she approached the front door. But today the usual good mood produced by these sights and smells did not take hold. Like the flowers' namesake, April was pleased with completion of *jiāo yì*, but, also like Jasmine, she too felt that something was wrong. For her, the feeling was not at all easy to shake.

April's worries were more focused than those of Jasmine: concerns that she was being drawn into the sort of property market corruption that Walter was writing about. She did not really believe that Uncle Jun or Uncle Wu were corrupt—although she was less sure about Xu—but she understood the story that was told by the title documents for the Suzhou property. And she could not understand why the San Marino team and their lawyers had not paid more attention to these documents. They had pressed for ownership information throughout the due diligence process, beginning with her first call with Jasmine, and she found it hard to believe that they had missed the information. Yet she found it equally hard to believe that Richard Gregg would accept evidence of corruption. He was clearly a tough investor, but a careful, intelligent one who would recognize the risks of corruption. Was it possible that he had accepted the perspective that this was the way that business gets done in China? Just what had he discussed with Uncle Jun?

But right now, April's lack of confidence was not about these concerns. She knew that the completion dinner would be a proper event, and she was worried about looking good. Usually, April was fairly confident about her appearance—but she suspected that she would not measure up to Jasmine. The feeling had started to bother her strongly while waiting at the airport a few days earlier, and had only grown stronger over the few days of the closing process.

She decided to dress professionally for the dinner, choosing a sky-blue silk shirt and tailored, knee-length skirt with dark blue stockings. The smartly sober clothes accentuated her round breasts and hips without being provocative. She felt that she looked good. Yet she could not shake the feeling that she was not the equal of the taller, slimmer, older Jasmine.

April went downstairs to meet Uncle Jun, Aunt Hong and Xu. The men had both changed into modern Mao suits, Uncle Jun's embroidered with a dragon design. Aunt Hong wore a rose-colored *qípáo*, a traditional, fitted silk dress with a delicate embroidered flower pattern.

Xu's reactions to April's choice of clothing did not help her confidence. "*Mèi mei*, you look very nice, but don't you know that our work is done for today? You look like you're ready to go to a business meeting."

"Xu, you should be nicer to your cousin," Aunt Hong said, but then implicitly sided with Xu. "You know, April, if you like, I still have all of my old *qípáo* from when I was a girl, in a closet upstairs. They don't fit me anymore, and would look lovely on you."

April knew when to give in. "Thank you, Aunt Hong. I suppose, if it really isn't too much trouble …"

"Come on, follow me upstairs."

交易

20

Celebration and Distraction

July 16, 2009

A man hath no better thing under the sun, than to eat, and to drink, and to be merry

– Ecclesiastes 8:15

Jasmine saw April first. When the Wang family walked into the lobby of The Peninsula, Richard and Jasmine were enjoying their drinks, and—predictably—still talking mostly about *jiāo yì*, as well as what they had to do next upon their return to Los Angeles, and what Richard would do if anything requiring Jasmine's knowledge came up during her week-long absence to visit family in Tianjin.

Jasmine, looking briefly away from Richard, noticed near the door a pair of beautiful women in *qípáo*, one younger than the other. Traditional dress always put Jasmine strongly in touch with the Chinese side of her being. When she realized that the beautiful younger woman was April, she drew a sharp breath and felt momentarily disoriented. Jasmine had been thinking of April as an American, not really a part of the Chinese family that had brought her back to China to work at JZP. In fact—she suddenly realized—April was a lot like her, with strong roots in both China and the West.

Richard noticed the surprise on Jasmine's face, followed her glance, and rose to greet the Wang family. He first approached April and her Aunt Hong, and spoke to the older woman. "*Wáng tài tai, wǒ fēicháng gāoxìng rènshi nín.* [Mrs. Wang, I am extremely pleased to meet you.] Your husband is a very talented businessman, now our friend." He smiled at the elder Mr. Wang, and they shook hands. "Your son and your niece have also become good colleagues and friends." He looked in turn at Xu, who had been standing confidently next to his father and also shook his hand, and then at April.

April was feeling dazed. The decision to change into the *qípáo* had seemed a good one, until she saw Jasmine in her stunning Western cocktail dress. Standing next to similarly dressed Aunt Hong, April felt hopelessly traditional and boring compared to Jasmine's cool modernity. She also felt suddenly unsure about the reasons for the feelings of love towards Jasmine that she had confessed to Walter the previous evening. At the moment she had a powerful feeling of *want*. Were her feelings more obsessive, sexual? It was not something she had felt about anyone before.

Then April was distracted from these turbulent feelings by a familiar face on the opposite side of the lobby. Walter was sitting in a chair, casually dressed as usual, looking at the group by the door from behind a newspaper. April was tempted to laugh, because he cut a rather awkward figure with his clumsy effort to be inconspicuous. Before she could think about what she was doing, April nudged Xu and pointed discreetly across to Walter.

April instantly regretted blowing Walter's cover, not least because she felt guilty about having told her journalist friend what she knew about JZP—although she was still confident that he would not betray her trust. Xu's reaction was predictable. He politely but abruptly separated himself from the group, saying "Excuse me, I have just seen a friend and I would like to speak with him."

The remaining eyes in the group by the door followed Xu, and it was quickly apparent that this was no simple friendship. Xu's body language to Walter was aggressive, and it appeared that he was asking Walter to leave the hotel. Unintelligible scraps of their heated conversation, rapidly turning into something more like an argument, could be heard across the lobby. Other people nearby turned to look.

Clearly embarrassed, Mr. Wang turned to Richard. "I apologize for the rude behavior of my son. Shall we go upstairs to the restaurant?"

"Yes, of course, no problem."

As they walked up the stairs, Richard turned to Jasmine and asked quietly, "Do you know who that was with Wang Xu?"

"Yes, he is a journalist, a friend of Wang Xu. I met him one evening at dinner with Wang Xu and Wang April."

"It's hard to imagine why Wang Xu would be so angry at him."

"Actually, they had an argument the night we had dinner. Walter—that's the Western name that the journalist likes to use—was working on articles about improper destruction of historical Chinese buildings. Xu did not like what Walter had to say about property developers paying off corrupt Communist Party officials."

"What?" Richard paused in mid-stride. "*Xu* has been arguing with a journalist who's writing against property corruption?" He glanced back behind them and then looked hard at Jasmine. "Is there a reason you didn't tell me about that before? Is it possible Walter is pursuing something about JZP?"

"No. I mean ... I'm sorry, Richard. I actually didn't think about telling you. It seemed as though Walter was just making general comments about Chinese property developers, and Xu was just ... reacting to that." Jasmine considered whether there could in reality be a connection such as Richard was suggesting, and experienced a sudden horror. Her afternoon worries about *jiāo yì* returned like a slap.

"OK. But please tell me the next time you hear something like that."

"OK, Richard. I am really sorry. I will not forget to do that." Jasmine hoped hard that they would hear no more information about corruption soon. As she walked to the top of the ornately carpeted stairway, a strange feeling settled in the pit of her stomach. Involuntarily, she twisted a loop of hair around her finger.

* * *

132

Jasmine felt partly relieved to be climbing the stairs away from the peculiar altercation between Xu and Walter, but the next distraction from the celebration of the completion of *jiāo yì* did not take long to appear. Mr. Wu was waiting for them at the top of stairs, near a desk where a traditionally-dressed hostess was greeting guests at the hotel's Yi Long Court restaurant. Jasmine was relieved to see him there, nicely dressed in a suit and tie, a smile back on his face. She wondered again whether her reaction to his behavior at the completion meeting had been paranoia. Mr. Wu introduced his wife—a small, quiet, exceedingly polite woman—to Richard. As he turned to include Jasmine in the introduction, Mr. Wu's expression changed from cheerfulness to shock. He literally paled.

Realizing from his gaze that Mr. Wu had seen something behind her, Jasmine turned and saw a small older man in a business suit, accompanied by an even smaller woman of similar age. The man smiled and approached their group. *"Wáng xiānsheng, Wú xiānsheng, nǐmen hǎo. Shénme jīngxǐ kàn dào nǐ zài zhèlǐ!* [Hello Mr. Wang and Mr. Wu. What a surprise to see you here!]"

"Lǐ xiānsheng, nín hǎo. Wǒ yě hěn jīngxǐ kàndào nǐ. [Hello, Mr. Li. I am also very surprised to see you.]" Mr. Wang appeared to be almost uncomfortable as Mr. Wu, although his surprise bore a slight edge of anger and less obvious shock. "What brings you to Shanghai?"

"My wife and I," Mr. Li indicated the woman next to him, who was looking down at the ground without expression, "are celebrating our thirty-ninth wedding anniversary. Of course, next year will be a bigger one, but we decided to make this one special too."

"Wǒ gōngxǐ nǐ men. [I congratulate you.]"

"Thank you. We do not have so many opportunities to dine in Shanghai as a powerful businessman like you."

"Bù gǎn dāng. [I do not deserve your compliments.]" Mr. Wang used a traditional Chinese expression for responding politely to sincere flattery, but his expression was stony. He seemed eager to end the conversation, then hesitated, turned

133

and steered Richard forward to meet Mr. Li with a gentle hand on his elbow. "Let me introduce our friends from the United States, Mr. Gregg and Miss Liu from San Marino Property Investments. Mr. Li is a government leader from Jiangsu province. We sometimes encounter him in our work there."

"*Hěn hǎo rènshi nín.* [Good to meet you.]" Richard responded, his face also impassive.

"*Yě fēicháng hǎo rènshi nín.* [Also very good to meet you.]" Mr. Li answered, with greater enthusiasm.

"And now it is time for us to have dinner," Mr. Wang said. "Mr. Li, I hope that you and Mrs. Li have a very good evening. *Zàijiàn.* [Goodbye.]" Without waiting for a response, Mr. Wang turned to the hostess, who had been watching the conversation politely.

The hostess led them down a hallway past the main dining room of the restaurant, where a well-dressed mix of Chinese and Western diners were engaged in hushed conversations, and to a small private dining room decorated with modern art and featuring windows onto an immaculate kitchen where the restaurant's chefs were preparing food. On the way down the hallway, Richard dropped slightly behind with Jasmine and whispered to her, "What the hell was going on there? Did you see their faces?"

Jasmine shrugged, pulling again at her hair, unable to answer. Richard looked at her searchingly as if he could suddenly see the earlier suspicions that she had not voiced, and then walked on, seeming to accept that there was nothing more to say now.

* * *

They were a group of ten at the completion dinner. The Wang family, April, Richard, Jasmine, and Mr. Wu and his wife were joined by Jonathan Zhou and the lead lawyer from Xin Lu, without their spouses. They fit snugly around the circular table in the small private dining room. Confronted with the expense of the Michelin-starred restaurant at the Peninsula, Wang Jun had apparently decided not to spring for a larger dining room like those they had experienced at other restaurants, nor to invite any guests who were not closely connected with *jiāo yì*.

Before dinner, Wang Jun asked the waitresses to open two bottles of expensive *bái jiǔ*. Then he stood and spoke, his face more relaxed than it had been a few minutes before. "We know that Americans may prefer to drink Scotch whisky, and many people are learning to like it here in China, but tonight is a night for tradition. This brand of *bái jiǔ* is called Maotai. It is very famous. Your Mr. Kissinger once said to our Mr. Deng, 'If we drink enough Maotai we can solve anything'. Fortunately, tonight we are not looking for solutions. We are here to celebrate the deal that we have just made. So I would like to drink the first toast to you, Gregg *xiānsheng*, for having the vision to find JZP as a partner and the patience to work out *jiāo yì* with us. *Gān bēi.*"

Richard joined him in downing their small glasses of *bái jiǔ*, as Mr. Wang's *gān bēi* required him to do, and returned the toast. "*Xiè xie Wang xiānsheng*. Thank you for your hospitality, your compliments, and for bringing this excellent *bái jiǔ*. As you know, China is very important to me. I certainly prefer to drink *bái jiǔ* than Scotch here. When you visit us in Los Angeles later this year, as we have planned, we will treat you to some excellent whisky, although I regret that since we are a much newer country than China we will need to bring it in from Scotland." Most of the party laughed—not April, who had returned to her preoccupation with Jasmine. "We look forward to very successful cooperation. *Gān bēi.*"

These were the first of innumerable toasts. During dinner, the *bái jiǔ* was followed by several bottles of red wine, Jasmine's favorite. As one of only three team members from the San Marino side of the deal, Jasmine was the recipient of numerous toasts and felt the wine relaxing her. The effect dulled her earlier agitation, and fended off her usual annoyance from having to make conversation with Xu, who was seated next to her. Xu, for his part, was on his best behavior, rising to the occasion with maturity that was unexpected, at least to Jasmine.

At the start of the meal, Xu himself took the opportunity to lead a toast. "Gregg *xiānsheng*, I share my father's admiration for your work with us. I would like to offer a toast to both of you leaders in *jiāo yì*. I haven't always been such a diligent worker, but because of this *jiāo yì*, I've become an important part of our family's business for the first time, and I can see better what a great leader my father is. Now that we also have a new partner in San Marino, even greater success is surely within our reach. *Gān bēi*."

The sumptuous meal consisted of more than a dozen courses—dim sum, soups, meat dishes, vegetables, noodles, rice. The food at the Yi Long Court was prepared in the Cantonese style—from Guangdong province—which competes with the food of Sichuan province as China's most famous cuisine. Someone had selected an assortment of very traditional Cantonese dishes, including *gū lū ròu* [sweet and sour pork], *héyè zhēng tiánjī* [steamed frog legs on lotus leaf] and *fǔrǔ* [fermented tofu]. It was all delicious and—together with the copious alcohol—gradually lulled all at the table into a state of relaxation and camaraderie, taking the edge off the earlier distractions in the lobby and at the entrance to the restaurant.

Even April gradually relaxed, with the wine dimming the intensity of her feelings from before the meal. The very traditional Chinese evening also made her feel again that the choice of the *qípáo* was not so bad. She was gratified to notice Jasmine's eyes on her a few times during the evening. On the one occasion when she managed to catch and hold Jasmine's glance, the flawless older girl smiled and nodded at her, before turning to respond to a question from Xu.

After a dessert course of exotic fruit had been served, Uncle Jun rose to offer a final toast to the guests. "I hope that our guests have enjoyed this meal celebrating the beginning of our cooperation," he said. "My one regret is that we were unable to serve you *Shànghǎi máo xiè* [Shanghai hairy crabs], the specialty of Shanghai, but unfortunately it is not the season. I am comforted, though, that this is the beginning of a long cooperation. We look forward to seeing you here many more times, and in the fall we will serve you *máo xiè*."

April thought about this somewhat odd toast. Was it just ordinary Chinese modesty, or did her uncle really believe that he had left something unfinished? This train of thought prompted the anxious realization that she had left at home the copy of the completion CD meant for the San Marino team. Slightly panicked, April stood, a little unsteady from the red wine, and walked around the table to tell Uncle Jun of her omission. He smiled, told her not to worry, and spoke to Richard.

"I apologize that we have forgotten to bring to you the documents CD that we promised—it is at our home. My niece April will bring a copy back to the hotel in a taxi later this evening. I hope the delay will not be a problem."

"Of course not," Richard said. "Please feel free to send it in the morning. I'm sure we won't be doing any more work this evening."

"I insist. We keep our promises, even the small ones."

April looked doubtfully at her uncle.

"Thank you," Jasmine broke in. "When Ms. Wang returns, she can bring the CD to my room so that she does not disturb Mr. Gregg. Is that OK, Ms. Wang?"

"Yes, certainly, Ms. Liu. I should be back in about thirty minutes or so. I hope it will not disturb you too much to stay awake."

交易

21

Together and Apart

July 16, 2009

Hello Goodbye

– The Beatles (song title)

When April arrived at Jasmine's room on the eighth floor, the door was ajar. April heard soft Chinese music coming from within and knocked at the open door. She heard Jasmine call, "Come in."

Jasmine had taken off her shoes and stockings, and was standing by the large windows overlooking the Bund and the Huangpu River. She turned to face the door, and April saw that she was holding another glass of red wine. The source of the music was not clear—apparently some sound system provided by the hotel. "It is beautiful, isn't it?" Jasmine pointed behind her out the window.

"Yes, it is." April walked across the room to the window, where she handed the documents CD to Jasmine.

"Thank you. May I offer you a glass of wine?"

"Yes, OK." April's voice was a little shaky.

Jasmine set the CD down on a table near the window, near an open bottle of wine, then scanned the room calmly. Locating a second, empty glass on the dresser, she retrieved it, poured for April, and handed the glass to her.

"Thank you again for bringing the CD to me. And thank you for working so well with me on *jiāo yì*. I should have said that before."

"Of course, that's my job." April suddenly recalled Uncle Jun's request that she become friends with Jasmine. It seemed absurd now to think of it as a job. She intensely wanted

Jasmine to be her friend, to respect her. And of course she wanted more too, but that was not something that she dared to hope for. Her voice shook as she said, "I ... do you think we could be friends too? Now that JZP and San Marino have agreed on the joint venture, I suppose we will continue to work together, and ... well ... it would be nice ... but I guess I can see that you don't like my cousin Xu very much ...," April realized that she was rambling, and Jasmine's sharp glance brought her up short, sure that she had crossed a line.

Jasmine looked at her intently for a few seconds, an eternity for April, and then spoke with quiet conviction. "You're right, I don't like Xu, something about him makes me really uncomfortable." And then she was gentler. "But of course you and I can be friends. You shouldn't have to ask. That's my fault. I know that ... I can seem cold."

"No, you—"

Jasmine cut her off. "Don't say what you were about to say. I know the impression I give."

"You know, I think we might have a lot in common. Harvard, working on *jiāo yì*, and I noticed that you are reading *The Great Gatsby*." April pointed to the book on the table beside the bed. "That's a great book."

"It's my favorite. Why do you like it?"

"The best part is the excitement of Gatsby's parties. I imagine myself being the golfer, Jordan Baker. Although I'm not as cool as she is, or as thin."

Jasmine looked at April's body, started to say something, then appeared to change her mind. "I want to be like Gatsby. Rich, with a big house, doing what I choose."

"I guess you want to end up better than he did."

Jasmine surprised April by looking thoughtful. "You know, I hadn't thought about that. In China, it seems we can never predict when disaster is going to strike. When I first read *The Great Gatsby* in Chinese, the ending seemed natural. Now, I'm reading the original to understand the story better and improve my vocabulary, but it's taken me a long time with the distraction of *jiāo yì*."

"That's funny. I was in a bookstore just yesterday wondering whether to start trying to read novels in Mandarin. I may be from a Chinese family, but I have a long way to go to be really comfortable with the language."

"I like being back in China, now that my job gives me some distance from it." Jasmine turned and walked to the window. "Shanghai is so beautiful at night."

April joined the taller girl at the window, and they stood together watching, or maybe not watching, the ships on the river and the lights of Pudong. April had long felt that the elevated vantage point of the observation deck on the Oriental Pearl Tower would provide a useful perspective on Shanghai. The pressures of *jiāo yì* had gotten in the way, but the urge to visit the tower returned while she stood with Jasmine looking at it.

Then they were holding hands. April was not sure whether she took Jasmine's hand, or Jasmine took hers. It surprised her how comfortable it felt, perhaps because it was such a relief for April to finally be physically close to Jasmine. It was also exciting. The possibility that Jasmine might want more acted like a powerful drug. They stood for several minutes in silence. April's breathing quickened and she started to feel light-headed.

And then they were kissing. This time, April thought Jasmine had made the first move towards her, and she was quickly sure that Jasmine wanted her. Jasmine's lips, tasting of red wine, were soft, yielding and hungry. In a way it felt familiar to be holding a woman again, but kissing Jasmine was much more exciting than anything April had experienced with her girlfriends at Harvard. April moved one of her hands onto Jasmine's lower back, and Jasmine made a soft sound.

Then the older girl stepped back, with another intense look at her, and April thought with a sinking feeling that Jasmine was going to tell her that their kiss had been a mistake, and ask her to leave. But April was wrong. Jasmine reached behind her own back, loosened a fastening, and with a shrug and a wriggle let her dress fall to the floor. April looked at Jasmine's beautiful body—long legs, flat stomach, small but prominent breasts. Jasmine was wearing nearly identical bra and panties to the ones April had on that evening—black, slightly lacy. April decided that the only good response to Jasmine's undress was to join her. "This is the first time that I have worn a *qípáo*. I borrowed it from my Aunt Hong, and she had to help me with the last button ..." April turned to expose her side. "Maybe you could help me now ..."

After the third button was unlooped, Jasmine noticed the same thing as April had. "You have good taste in lingerie." She smiled faintly. "So, what do we do now?"

"What do you mean?" April came close and put her arms around Jasmine's waist, their stomachs nearly touching, and looked up into her face.

Jasmine seemed to blush, which surprised April. "Until tonight I didn't even know for sure that I wanted to be with another girl. Just yesterday, on the way to meeting the lawyers, I saw a class of schoolchildren, and I started thinking about whether I should be starting a family. So I guess I am confused. But when I saw you looking so beautiful in your *qípáo* ... I suddenly thought maybe I should ... we should ... I want you. You are so beautiful. I am not sure that I know what to do."

"Do you mean you don't know if we should be together?" April observed to her astonishment that she was in charge of the conversation. She felt sudden tenderness. Jasmine looked at her.

"I want you. But I don't know how to be with a girl."

Suddenly, April was confident, realizing that Jasmine really did not know what to do.

"You should touch me the way that you want to be touched."

Jasmine looked away, seemingly embarrassed. April gently took Jasmine's hand again and led her to the bed. Jasmine seemed relieved to let April take the lead.

Under the influence of the red wine and her desire, Jasmine gradually let go of her usual reserve, and became more and more excited under April's cautious caresses. By the time April's hand had slowly made its way inside Jasmine's panties, Jasmine was wet. Feeling April's finger there, she moaned, the controlled Jasmine of their business meetings completely gone. April continued to stroke her gently while kissing her nipples, watching and listening for clues, adjusting her touch. After a little while, April felt Jasmine tense, and then heard her scream briefly as she came.

They lay tangled as Jasmine's breathing slowly calmed. Eventually, Jasmine spoke. "That was the first time I have ever come. I didn't even know I could do it."

April was a little surprised, and smiled at her. "Yes, it's really nice the first time, and it keeps being nice." She waited, wanting. Jasmine snuggled and kissed her, seemingly satisfied, and April eventually realized that Jasmine didn't understand what she needed. Was Jasmine actually selfish, or had she been so consumed by her own need that she had forgotten about April?

Unable to wait, April said, "Umm, Jasmine ..." took Jasmine's hand, and put it between her legs. Finally understanding, Jasmine tried to copy what April had done to her minutes earlier, but it quickly became evident that Jasmine was too much a novice. April changed approach, taking the lead again. She slid close to Jasmine, placed both of Jasmine's hands on her breasts, and put her own hand between her legs. April saw Jasmine's surprise, and then watched Jasmine's eyes widen as she saw April become more excited.

Fortunately, Jasmine guessed what to do with April's breasts, kissing her nipples in turn as they hardened. April climbed a steep hill of excitement, wanting Jasmine and then wanting her more. Jasmine murmured, "Your breasts are so beautiful and round." April tried to respond, losing focus as she climbed higher. And then she dropped off the edge into her own, back-archingly powerful orgasm.

As April returned to herself, the two girls cuddled and then kissed. After a while, Jasmine drew back and said shyly, "Sorry that you had to show me what to do."

"*Please.* You can see how much I wanted you, how much I enjoyed that. Anyhow, next time I'm sure we will be more coordinated." April paused. "That is ... I assume you *would* like there to be a next time."

"Yes ... I would."

"I'm happy about that." The girls closed their eyes in each other's arms. After a little while, April spoke again. "So. What happens next?"

"What do you mean?"

"Well, now that *jiāo yì* is done, will you still be visiting China? I want to see you." April hoped that she did not already sound like a demanding girlfriend.

"I will probably be here often, and all of the visits will be to work with JZP. I think that Richard wants my main focus at San Marino to stay on this deal, and making sure that the JV works."

"That's good news." April paused. "There *is* one other question that I wanted to ask you about *jiāo yì.*"

"Yes, certainly."

"You paid so much attention to all the ownership documentation for JZP's properties. Why didn't San Marino ask any questions about the additional owners of the Suzhou tower?"

Jasmine sat up, suddenly serious. "What are you talking about? For Suzhou? We confirmed that JZP is the only owner of that project. Well, apart from the bank."

April was suddenly confused. "But—it was right there on the documents that the lawyers put into the data room. Two other, smaller owners based in Suzhou. Surely you could not have missed that?"

Jasmine felt the room spin. Her earlier feelings that something was wrong had now become a practical certainty, even though she did not yet know the details. "I did not miss that, April. Tell me what you think was in the documents."

April started to answer, and then had the good sense to realize that she was already far out of her depth. Although she felt very close to Jasmine from what they had just shared, she realized that her business loyalties lay with JZP and that she had probably already said too much. "Actually, I'm not sure what I was saying," April said, retreating. "Maybe I made a mistake."

"Are you sure? This is a serious matter." Jasmine was suddenly deadly serious and sober, the cold Jasmine that April had been watching for months.

April was crushed, and awed by Jasmine's self-control. She knew she would never have the same ability to turn her emotions on and off. "I don't know. I think maybe it's time for me to go home."

Jasmine watched silently as April got dressed. April began to cry as she did so, and made her way to the door while still carrying her shoes and stockings. She was about to leave without another word, then turned to Jasmine. "I guess there won't be a next time, will there?"

"*Wǒ bù zhīdào*, April. *Wǒ zhēn de bù zhīdào.* [I don't know, April. I really don't know.]"

April hesitated tearfully, then turned and walked out the door, which clicked shut loudly behind her.

Jasmine felt sick—from the wine, from the intensity of the sex, and from the shock of what April had just said. She did her best to gather her thoughts, picked up the hotel telephone, and dialed Richard's room. She was grateful that he answered on the second ring. His voice made clear that she had woken him, but she did not take the time to apologize. "Richard, I think we have a problem with *jiāo yì.*"

Damage

交易

22

Damage Control

July 17, 2009

*Omnishambles (noun)—a situation seen as shambolic from all
perspectives; compound from the Latin 'omni' for all and, the originally
Middle English, 'shambles' for a scene of complete disorder or ruin*

– Oxford English Dictionary, 2012 Word of the Year

"Explain to me how you could possibly have missed this
fucking mess," Richard practically shouted at Jonathan Zhou.
"Please excuse my language, but *how* is it possible that we
learned about a major ownership issue on a JZP project by a
chance conversation when it was your job to conduct due
diligence? How many times have I emphasized that clear
ownership was one of the most critical issues? You knew that
without me saying it anyhow." He stabbed at the document on
the conference table in Morton & Fisher's office, where
Richard and Jasmine were sitting on Friday afternoon, the day
after completion. Across from them were Jonathan, the office's
American senior partner Daniel Wilmot, and two associates
who had worked on *jiāo yì*.

Jasmine had never before seen Richard lose his temper.
Often he was demanding, but he had always been calm and
polite. His outburst, and the unfamiliar contortion of his
features that accompanied it, brought back a vivid memory of
the one time that she seen anger from her calm, quiet
grandfather. It had been in 1997, the last year of his life, when
Jasmine was fifteen. She recalled the year clearly, because her
grandfather's anger was prompted by a dinner-table discussion
of the so-called "Asian financial crisis" of that year. The crisis
had not been a bad one in China, but Jasmine's father had
worried that the loose credit policies at China Construction
Bank would eventually contribute to a similar event in China,

147

and complained that his warnings to bank management were falling on deaf ears.

As her father was explaining his decision to hold his tongue from further complaint, her grandfather, who always joined them for dinner and almost never spoke, shouted: *"Rúguǒ nǐ bàoyuàn, tāmen huì chénmò.* [If you complain, they will silence you.] That's what they did to me." Then he fell silent and refused to speak for several days. The vehemence of her grandfather's reaction—one of the few clues she had to what he had experienced in the Cultural Revolution—had shocked the younger Jasmine.

Witnessing Richard's anger, her grandfather's words suddenly came back as vividly as the day they were spoken: "If you complain, they will silence you." And hearing the words in her head, Jasmine wondered with a start whether she had unconsciously heeded her dead grandfather's advice in being so slow to mention her concerns about JZP.

Jasmine felt her mind reeling in several directions at once, tugged by strong currents of events. She was shocked by the course that *jiāo yì* had taken so soon after completion. Although she had grown to trust Richard as a friend and supporter, she was afraid that he would blame her for the emerging disaster. There was also a strong, turbulent undercurrent related to her sexual encounter with April— although she promised herself to try not to think about that until the problems with *jiāo yì* were under control.

She was struggling, too, with a smaller but more immediate concern—perhaps what had triggered the memory of her grandfather—that she had just missed her flight home to Tianjin. Richard had made clear that her involvement in initial damage control took priority over her first day of vacation, and she had readily agreed. Still, she needed to find time to call her parents, tell them not to meet her at the airport, and try to explain the reason in terms that they could accept, without breaching any confidence about the challenges that San Marino was facing in Shanghai. Thinking about family, an image of the schoolchildren that she had seen on the

148

morning of the day before completion popped unbidden to mind.

Forcing her mind back into the conference room, Jasmine listed to Jonathan, whose usually polished exterior was marred by a sweating and furrowed brow, trying to answer Richard's questions. "Well, this document is from the Suzhou Zhangjiagang Development and Reform Commission. That's the government body responsible for registering companies in Suzhou. The document states that on Monday this week— four days ago—information was provided to the government that there are two new five-percent owners of the JZP company that owns the Suzhou project. The document also shows that the change of ownership actually occurred in late May—almost two months ago—so there was a fairly long delay in submitting this information to the government."

"Is that kind of delay legal? And do we have any idea why we did not receive this information from JZP?" Wilmot asked. He was a tall, handsome man in his late fifties, with the kind of thick shock of grey hair that is supposed to give clients confidence about their lawyer's experience.

"Well, strictly speaking, yes, the company should have provided the information sooner," Jonathan answered, "but it's not a major violation. We don't know why JZP didn't tell us about this, but they had to know. It really doesn't look good. The change of ownership seems to have occurred by the time in June when they provided the documents on the Suzhou project. Those documents showed one hundred percent JZP ownership, which was confirmed by our check of the government records. At that time, the records did not yet contain the new ownership information."

"Shouldn't you have reconfirmed the government records closer to completion? That's standard procedure." Richard was still angry, but seemed to be calming down a little as he considered the implications of the apparent deception by JZP.

Jonathan looked acutely embarrassed. "Yes, we did ask on Tuesday, but Suzhou was the only government office that did not respond. We didn't think it was a big risk item—after all, both JZP and Wang Jun personally have given warranties that the information they provided is accurate—so we didn't bring it up at completion. That was a mistake."

"Yes, it was a mistake." Richard was much calmer now, a determined look in his eye. "Thank you for admitting that. I suggest that Morton & Fisher inform your insurance company that San Marino may have a malpractice claim against your firm. However, we are not going to pursue any claim for now. What we need to do is try to figure out how to fix the problem. I trust you will put your best people on that, and not bill us for the work?"

Wilmot and Jonathan both looked relieved, and the former spoke. "Absolutely, Richard, thanks for your understanding. We value our firm's relationship with San Marino and will do everything we can to fix this deal." He looked at his watch. "I apologize, if you will excuse me I have another meeting now that I really shouldn't miss. So unless you have other questions for me now, I will leave you in Jonathan's capable hands. If you need anything from me, please contact me any time. You know where to find me."

"Thanks, Daniel. I like getting free legal advice." Richard smiled briefly for the first time since Jasmine had awoken him the previous evening. Once Wilmot had left the room, Richard turned back to Jonathan and his team. "What do we know about the two new owners in Suzhou? Who the hell are they?"

"Well, there is more bad news, although not really unexpected. Li Yu appears to be the son of Li Zhiyuan, a senior official of the Ministry of Land and Resources, and Yang Zitong appears to be the sister of Yang Sicheng, a senior official of the Ministry of Housing and Urban-Rural Development. So, I'm afraid it looks a lot like some kind of corruption, with the officials' families being rewarded for assisting the project."

"What a fucking mess," Richard said, but this time without anger. "I'm impressed, though. You've learned a lot in the half-day since we discovered this problem."

"Well, this is an important problem for us. People like Mr. Wang and JZP are not the only ones with *guānxi*. We knew that we needed the information fast, and we used our connections to get it. And we're trying to learn more about them, and rule out more charitable explanations. It's a long shot, but the new owners *could* be investment contacts of JZP, although that wouldn't explain the concealment of their investments."

"Richard," Jasmine said, plucking a nagging memory from among her confused feelings, "the Jiangsu official that we met before the completion dinner was also a Mr. Li. I wonder whether it was the same person."

"Hmm. I bet you're right. That would explain why Mr. Wang and Mr. Wu looked so alarmed to see him. I wonder whether it was just a coincidence that Mr. Li was there, or was he trying to put some kind of pressure on JZP?"

"It wouldn't surprise me if he were," Jonathan said. "Corrupt officials seem to be getting bolder and more creative all the time. I wouldn't be surprised if Mr. Li or Mr. Yang were responsible for delaying the response of the Suzhou government." Jonathan shook his head with obviously genuine regret. "We should have looked behind that delay."

Richard acknowledged Jonathan's renewed apology with a quick nod, closed his eyes, and leaned back in his chair. After a few moments of silence, while the Morton & Fisher lawyers looked at each other awkwardly, Richard leaned forward again. "OK, as I see it, we have three big problems. First, the JV doesn't own as much of the Suzhou project as we thought. That may actually be the smallest problem. We valued the Suzhou property at $22 million, ten percent of that is $2.2 million, half of which is ours. So the direct financial problem is worth a few million at most. Like Jonathan said, we may have a legal claim against JZP and Mr. Wang for that, but let's see if we can figure out a way around the problem other than suing our JV partner. Second, even if we don't sue JZP, we can't trust them. That's a bigger problem, at least until we have some answers. We need to take a hard new look at every property in this deal, and see if there is any other evidence of corruption. Third, and maybe most dangerous of all, now that we suspect corruption, we need to be sure not to create bigger problems for ourselves by violating the Foreign Corrupt Practices Act back home. I think that means that the JV shouldn't start looking for new properties until we get a handle on this situation. We are going to need some advice on that from your colleagues in the United States."

"Yes, that sounds right to me," Jonathan agreed, "and we'll get started on the legal analysis. But let's also start with practical steps. We'll try to learn more about the new investors. And isn't your next step to ask Wang Jun why they didn't provide this information, and what it means?"

"Of course. I wanted to get your advice first. As soon as we finish, I'm going to call him." Richard grimaced. "It's not going to be a pleasant conversation."

交易

23

Confrontation

July 18, 2009

No good deed goes unpunished

When Richard Gregg had called the previous afternoon, Wang Jun had been in his office at JZP. He had just finished another lengthy meeting with JZP's accountants on the financial details transition to the new joint venture. Mr. Wang knew immediately that something was wrong from the tension and chill in Richard's voice—completely different from what he had learned to expect from the American, whom he had genuinely come to like.

While Richard was telling him that San Marino and their lawyers had learned about the other investors in the Suzhou project, Mr. Wang looked at the photographs of his family on his desk. He felt little surprise, which itself at first surprised him. Then, as the force of what Richard was saying struck home, Mr. Wang realized that he had been waiting for this other shoe to drop ever since the Suzhou officials had first made their ownership demands.

Richard had asked angrily for an immediate meeting, but Mr. Wang had politely but firmly insisted that they wait until the following morning. He claimed other commitments and said that he needed a chance "to look into the issue". He felt that he needed time to think, to find a solution to the looming crisis.

Until recently, Mr. Wang's confidante in such times of difficulty had always been *Lǎo Wú*. Mr. Wang did have a vaguely forming plan to bring Mr. Wu back into the JZP fold—this had started with an invitation to the completion dinner the previous evening—but he was not prepared to trust

Mr. Wu with the discussion he needed to have now. He suspected that Mr. Wu was eager to do practically anything to regain trust, yet he needed to be sure. He could not risk Mr. Wu telling the Suzhou officials what San Marino had learned. And he was still not fully over his shock at Mr. Wu's role in creating the problem. So instead, he called Xu at work at Bank of China.

Mr. Wang did not tell his son what had happened—he always assumed that what he said on the telephone was not private—but made clear that it was urgent and serious. Xu suggested that they meet at the Lucky 8 Bar on Huaihai Middle Road, the same place where April and Walter had met three days before. It was not a coincidence that Xu chose the same watering hole that Walter had selected. It had been their most regular meeting place over the course of their long friendship.

* * *

"So what are we going to do, *bà*?" It had not taken the elder Mr. Wang long to explain the predicament. They were sitting in a table in a corner, sipping glasses of Tsingtao beer, out of earshot of the other patrons, who were few in the late afternoon. They were conspicuous in their business attire— Xu's suit and tie were particularly smart—but if anyone were to ask they were just a father and son sharing a beer near home.

"*Wo zhēnde bù zhīdǎo.* [I really don't know.]" Wang Jun leaned his face into his hands, rubbed his eyes with his palms, then leaned back in his chair, took a sip of beer, and looked at Xu appraisingly. "Xu, have I told you the story of how our business started?"

"You have told me a few things, not much. It started in Suzhou, right? Where our problems are now."

"Yes. There were difficult times then too, worse than now. I do not like to talk about it, but I want you to hear it now. I hope maybe there is a lesson about what to do with the challenges we face."

"OK, *bà*."

"We are an old Shanghai family, you know. Since *Jiěfàng Zhànzhēng* [the War of Liberation, or Chinese Revolution] our family have always been good Communist Party members. But in *Wénhuà Dàgémìng* [the Cultural Revolution] we appeared to some people like … class enemies. Too rich. We destroyed all the old artwork and traditional clothing that we owned, but it was not enough. It was very dangerous for us in Shanghai.

"My *bà*, your *yè ye* [father's father], had friends in the government who gave him a job managing some government buildings in Suzhou. It got the family away from Shanghai, to a safer place—a place where my brother and I could stay with our parents, rather than being sent to the countryside like many children. It saved us, but there was a big price to be paid—money and … other things."

"What other things?"

Mr. Wang's face creased in pain. He began to speak, then stopped. "That I will tell you some other time." He took a long sip of beer. "Anyway, when *Wén Gé* [the Cultural Revolution, for short] ended, my *bà* kept working in the Suzhou property business, and I followed him. Your uncle, April's *bà*, moved to the United States to look for new opportunities, but I stayed here. Eventually, we turned our work for the government into a real business—once Mr. Deng let us do that. And I was right. Look what I have built."

"Yes, *bà*, JZP is a great company."

"And now it could all come apart. Government officials saved our family, and now they want to destroy us. For what?" He paused only briefly, looking at Xu and shaking his head, before answering his own question. "For money. Something has gone wrong with this country. We all use *guānxi* to make money. JZP is doing it too, to get advantages on our property deals. And we are paying the price." As he spoke, the door of the bar opened and a forty-ish man entered alone wearing a business suit and a loosened tie. He glanced at the elder and younger Wang at the table in the corner, then walked to the bar.

"So what are we going to do?"

Wang Jun glanced at the new customer, who was speaking with the bartender, and then looked back down at his hands. *"Wo zhēnde bù zhīdǎo."*

"Zhēn de? Wo zhīdǎo. [Really? I know.]"

"OK, tell me what we should do. That is why I wanted to speak with you. You have become a very able young businessman, Xu."

"Hǎo de. [OK.] It's very simple. Last month we made a plan about what to do with the Suzhou problem, and we should stick with it. Your story about the Cultural Revolution tells me that we need to fight for what we have, whatever the cost."

As Xu spoke, the businessman at the bar walked their way looking at them, then sat at the next table. Mr. Wang assumed that the man was probably just looking for companionship, but there was too much curiosity in the man's face for him to risk answering Xu. And anyway, he really didn't have a response.

* * *

Early the next morning, the incriminating document that had been the focus of Richard's diatribe at Morton & Fisher was on a different conference table—this time at JZP, where Richard and Jasmine were meeting with the elder and younger Mr. Wang.

"You knew about this." Richard was staring intensely at Wang Jun. When the older man failed to respond, Richard pressed more aggressively. "That was meant to be a question. You knew about this, didn't you? You knew that there are investors other than JZP in the new Suzhou project." The polite Richard had entirely vanished at this meeting, replaced by an aggrieved and aggressive American businessman. Mr. Wang had seen the type before, but had not expected Richard to become its personification.

Mr. Wang steeled himself for the chosen course. He looked up, keeping his face expressionless, or so he thought. "Yes, of course we knew that. And we thought you did too. We certainly were not trying to hide it. This document on the table is a public record."

Richard looked as though he was going to explode. "You submitted the information to the government five days ago!" he shouted, slamming his hand on the table. "The transfer of ownership took place two months ago. You didn't include it in the documents in the data room for *jiāo yì*. You waited to file the information with the government until you hoped it was too late for us to find out before completion. And that turned out to be right—because the Suzhou government was then so slow in responding to our lawyers!" A light appeared to go on in Richard's head. "In fact, for all we know, *you* asked your collaborators in the Suzhou government to delay the response to us."

"Yes, we understand how this looks. It is our mistake. Please allow me to explain."

"Yes, absolutely, please explain. I really need a fucking explanation." Richard's expletive shocked the room into silence. Xu looked alarmed, his eyes guarded. Mr. Wang, calling upon Buddhist practice that he had followed since childhood, forced himself to breathe slowly and stay calm. Taking in the silence, Richard seem to realize that he had lost his temper, and said more calmly, "I really need something that I can take to my partners in California so they will continue to believe in this deal."

This was a challenge to which Mr. Wang had a genuine response, and he spoke with sudden passion. "Why should they not believe in this deal? JZP has joined you as partners, trusted you to share our business. We have put more at risk than you have. San Marino does not even need to risk much money until the joint venture finds new properties."

"I understand the deal," Richard said quietly. "Now please tell me what is happening with the Suzhou property."

"As I said, until yesterday afternoon, we thought you knew all the details. I was very surprised to receive your call, which is why I asked for time to investigate. I am ashamed to tell you that we have learned there was a mistake made by my staff, by my niece April. She is intelligent, but very inexperienced. April was in charge of delivering documents to our lawyers for *jiāo yì*. When she sent the Suzhou project documents, she forgot to

157

include the documents that had just arrived about our new investors. A simple mistake, but a bad one. Her job at JZP will be terminated today."

Having played the cards that he had agreed with Xu, Mr. Wang studied the reactions of the San Marino team. Jasmine looked ill. Richard looked skeptical. He asked, "You expect me to believe that something so crucial to this deal was the mistake of a twenty year-old? Why did JZP wait to submit the documents to the government until this week?"

"I expect you to believe it because it is the truth. April is twenty-four, graduated from Harvard. We thought we could trust her with handling documents. And submitting the documents this week is not an unusual delay in China. Please ask your lawyers."

"Yes, we already asked." Richard looked down, drumming his fingers on the table for a few seconds, then back at Mr. Wang. "OK, let's say I believe you. What are you going to do to fix your mistake? We and our lawyers think that both you personally and JZP have a legal obligation to ensure that the change in ownership does not disadvantage San Marino."

Mr. Wang was relieved to be back on familiar ground, negotiating a property deal. "Let us not talk about legal obligations. We're your partners, and we have made a mistake. We've given you a very good valuation for the Suzhou property—$22 million. Let us say we reduce that valuation to $20 million because of the new ownership."

"*Xiè xie.* [Thank you.] We appreciate that proposal," Richard responded, recovering his usual politeness. "But ten percent of $22 million is $2.2 million, so we think the new valuation should be $19.8 million. San Marino's obligation to contribute capital for its fifty-percent share of the JV will need to be reduced by the same amount. And we need to understand more about these new owners, Li Yu and Yang Zitong. Who are they?"

Mr. Wang felt the ground begin to shift under his chair. "Your financial proposal seems reasonable, but we must check it with our lawyers and investors. We will get back to you on that. As to Mr. Li and Ms. Yang, they are typical investors in our projects, from wealthy families in Suzhou. I have told you about our network of investors long ago."

"Yes, you have. But it seems odd to us that these two investors are close relatives of senior government officials. Officials who would be in a position to have assisted JZP with the acquisition of the Suzhou property."

Mr. Wang felt as if the room had moved into slow motion as he realized with shock that San Marino already fully understood what was going on. He opened his mouth, but no words came out. He continued to look at Richard while he attempted to regain his composure. "How did ... ?" He paused. "How did you learn that? This is not something we knew about Mr. Li and Ms. Yang. Of course, in China many wealthy people are related to government officials, so you should not conclude very much from that."

Richard looked at him levelly, and spoke slowly. "You expect us to believe that you knew nothing about this?"

Mr. Wang saw no choice but to press ahead. "Yes, I do. Have we not been open with you all the time?"

Richard did not answer. "OK, we'll have to do more research, and I really need to discuss this with my partners in Los Angeles. And you need to confirm that you agree to the financial approach that we just discussed. Thank you at least for not fighting us over that. Until we have resolved these issues, San Marino does not want the JV to do anything other than manage the initial properties. No new hires, no expenses beyond the essentials. Is that clear?"

"Mr. Gregg these are JZP properties—our business alone until two days ago. I do not think you can tell us—"

"Mr. Wang, these properties are owned by the JV now, and the JV agreement is clear that San Marino has veto power over all major decisions. Under the circumstances, I think it is clear that you should listen to us about a minimal operational approach. Is that clear?"

"Mr. Gregg, I think—"

"Is that clear?" Richard's voice was sharp, angry again.

Mr. Wang looked down at the table silently for several seconds. When he looked back at Richard, his eyes were defiant but his answer was not. "Yes, it is clear."

"OK. We'll be in touch with you as soon as we get back to Los Angeles. In the meantime, I would appreciate if you could learn what you can about the relatives of your investors—that is, assuming you really don't know about them already." Richard looked down at his notebook. "We understand that Mr. Li's father is Li Zhiyuan, a senior land official, and Ms. Yang's brother is Yang Sicheng, a senior housing official."

Mr. Wang silently gave up hope that he could keep any secrets from Richard Gregg and San Marino. At the same time, his admiration for his new partners increased. He glanced briefly at his son beside him. "OK, we will see what we can learn."

* * *

After Richard and Jasmine had left, the two Wangs returned to the conference room. Xu spoke first.

"*Bà*, how can you let them treat us like that?" he said angrily. "Those are our properties."

"*Wang Xu, nǐ zhīdào wèi shénme.* [You know why.] We got caught in our dangerous game. And *Gregg xiānsheng* is right—the properties belong to the JV now. We need to get used to that." He paused. "And now we need to continue with your clever plan. Let's go home and speak with April." Mr. Wang felt that he was on a runaway train that he had no hope of stopping.

* * *

Arriving home, they met April on her way out the door. She looked sunny and casual in blue jeans and a lightweight taffeta blouse with a flower print.

"Hello, Uncle Jun. Hello, Xu. I'm on my way out to meet Walter for lunch. Would you like to come along, Xu?"

"Who is this Walter?" Uncle Jun asked. "A Chinese boyfriend?"

160

"My friend Jiang likes to be called Walter," Xu explained. "He'd like to be April's boyfriend, but April doesn't seem to want that. Anyway, I don't think I can come along with you today to meet Walter." He looked questioningly at his father.

"Good to choose a boy carefully, April," Uncle Jun said. "Don't move too fast. But before you go out, Xu and I would like to discuss some work issues with you. It's related to *jiāo yì*."

"Sure, Uncle Jun. I hope there isn't any problem. Is there something that I have done?" April's breathing quickened and she frowned unconsciously, as if she had recalled something.

"Actually, there is a problem. Come inside and sit down."

They sat at the dining room table and asked the cook to bring tea. Mr. Wang looked at the paintings on the wall and the dark, polished wood of the table, and wondered what was going to become of all of the expensive things he had worked so hard to accumulate. At least this time he would not have to destroy them himself. He looked at a nervous April and continued. "April, I need to tell you some bad news. There has been a problem on *jiāo yì*, and the team from San Marino believes it is your fault." The color drained from April's face. "So I am going to ask you to leave JZP and go home to your family in Los Angeles. I am sorry."

"What … ?" April looked stunned. "What mistake did I make?"

"The documents in the data room did not show the new investors in our Suzhou project. Now, San Marino knows about it and they are very angry. They know that you were responsible for managing the data room documents—"

"But didn't you tell them this wasn't my fault? You said *you* would tell the lawyers to put those documents in the data room." April's dark eyes seemed huge in her pale face.

Mr. Wang forced himself to look at her coolly, surprising himself that he could be so cold-hearted to his brother's daughter. He felt transported back to the bad days after the Cultural Revolution, when he had watched his father make the same kind of hard decisions. "April, after our family's hospitality to you I am surprised that you would question me

161

on this. I will protect you from San Marino's anger. But I cannot protect your job. We have enjoyed having you with us here in Shanghai, at home and at work. Now it is time to go home."

"But Uncle Jun ... " Her voice was still full of protest. She looked imploringly at Xu. But getting no response at all from either the elder or the younger Wang, April fell silent and looked down at the wooden parquet floor of the dining room. For what seemed like a very long time, no one spoke. "May I go to lunch now?" she finally asked in a quiet voice, fighting back tears. When Mr. Wang nodded, his face grim, she stood and walked out the door.

交易

24

Out of Control

July 20, 2009

Things fall apart; the centre cannot hold;
Mere anarchy is loosed upon the world

– William Butler Yeats, 'The Second Coming'

"In over thirty years of property investing, I've never had a deal go bad this fast." Tom Wilshire was speaking to a meeting of the San Marino partners late on the morning that Richard returned, alone, from Shanghai. Richard had allowed Jasmine to continue on to visit her parents in Tianjin, two days late. He had considered asking her to skip the vacation entirely, but when it came down to it there was no immediate work that he absolutely needed from her—or at least nothing that she couldn't do from Tianjin—and he wasn't the vindictive kind of boss.

Richard had flown overnight, and came direct to the office from the airport. Although the flight had been smooth and he had slept a few hours, he felt exhausted and stressed. Outside the window of the partner's conference room, it was a perfect Southern California day, a little cooler than usual for July. But Richard felt as if a dark cloud had descended over Los Angeles. Over his life.

Tom was much less relaxed than usual. "I'm not saying this is your fault, Doc, but … really … were you trying to set some kind of record? You discovered this problem less than twelve hours after completion, right? Shouldn't someone have seen this coming? Our investors could have a field day with this one. We said we would be super careful going to China, and now look what we've done."

Richard had invested a lot in convincing his partners that China was the next big opportunity for San Marino. Now, his dream of combining China with property investing, which had seemed to be turning into reality, was instead transforming to nightmare with startling speed. He felt the beginnings of panic, and quelled them carefully.

"First of all, Tom, I apologize. You know that I'm a very careful investor. This is my deal, and I have to take responsibility for the problems. This was a difficult one for me to catch—there seems to have been deception by JZP, and our lawyers made a mistake that allowed that to happen—but, yes, there were signals that I could have seen. I could have watched the due diligence process and the lawyers more closely."

"What about your star Chinese analyst? Wasn't this her job?" Peter Thomas was known for being very demanding of performance from the firm's junior staff.

"Yes, Jasmine saw some warning signals that I missed, but, well, she screwed up too. She told me that she thought the behavior of JZP's owners was odd for Chinese business people, but didn't mention it because she wasn't sure she could support the concerns and didn't want to derail the deal."

"Shit," Peter said. "That's her job. To derail a bad deal. Shouldn't we fire her? That's a pretty elementary mistake."

"No. I don't think we should fire her. I need her to help me sort this out, and I'll take responsibility for getting her back on track. I'm sure my enthusiasm for the deal contributed to her staying quiet about her concerns, and I definitely should have questioned her more closely before completion about this kind of thing. Of course, I've made it crystal clear to her now that she has to bring any concerns like this to me immediately."

"Maybe a little too late, Doc," Tom observed blandly. "What do you think you can do to fix this?"

"I have already agreed in principle with JZP to adjust the JV pricing so there is no loss to San Marino from the new ownership. And we have only contributed $1.5 million to the JV so far for initial operating expenses, and JZP have put in another half a million. That money will go a long way, because

I have insisted that the JV not work on any investment projects until we sort out our problems. So our financial risk is limited."

"You don't really think that addresses the problem, Richard, do you?" Jane Leeson was not the most active participant in partners' meetings, but when she had something to say it was usually incisive. "You have heard of the Foreign Corrupt Practices Act, right? It's an old law, but the U.S. government has recently gotten very aggressive enforcing it."

"Yes, I know that."

"We can't invest in a business that succeeds by bribing government officials," Jane continued. "We think that is what happened on the Suzhou deal. And until we have some very good proof, we probably have to assume that JZP has been doing something like this on all of their deals."

"It looks like we have acquired a small problem, n'est-ce pas?"

Peter Thomas ignored François' deliberately misplaced light-heartedness. "Jane is right," he said. "My suggestion is that we ask Jane to lead an internal investigation of this deal, working with our lawyers. Richard can work to fix this, but we don't change anything without a sign-off by the partners based on Jane's recommendation."

"Jane, we would really appreciate if you could do that," Tom agreed. "Do you have time? We know you're busy on a couple of your own deals."

"I'll do it. None of us wants the firm to break the law."

* * *

After the meeting, Richard trailed to his office and stared out the window. He felt helpless. He had achieved the goal of completing *jiāo yì*, his golden dream, and it was rapidly looking like a poisoned chalice. Worse than the Suzhou disaster itself was the feeling that there was little he could do now to try to fix the deal. Until the lawyers at Morton & Fisher made progress in gathering information, and until Jane Leeson decided how to run her investigation, Richard knew that his only sensible course of action was to keep his hands off.

165

He wondered whether he could handle it.

The situation had sickening echoes of a previous failure—one about which Richard had never told anyone but Julie. The story he gave out for public consumption about why he had moved from academia to property investment was that he had wanted to get involved in real business, that academia was too abstract, too … academic. But this was not the whole truth. When Richard had completed the Ph.D thesis that eventually became his book *Rules of the New China*, the faculty review committee had told Richard that his work was too practically oriented, not strong enough on theory. They awarded him a Ph.D, but rejected his application for a tenure-track teaching position at UCLA. He had a similar lack of success during the following year with other universities that he considered good enough for him. When his best offer for a tenure-track role turned out to be teaching modern Chinese history at Iowa State University, Richard decided that the writing was on the wall for a career change. The cornfields of Iowa weren't for him.

Eventually, he had gotten his thesis accepted by a small academic publishing house, and the predictions in the book about the growth of China had turned out to be startlingly accurate over the almost-decade since it had been published. The book continued to sell a few copies, but never attracted widespread attention. Richard consoled himself with the explanation that he was before his time. Yet, by the measures of the ivory tower on which he had originally set his sights, his academic career had not been a success.

He wondered now whether the outcome was going to be the same in property investing. His years of competent work and partnership at San Marino might be sufficient to overcome the damage that a true disaster on *jiāo yì* would cause, and he would limp on into unendurable mediocrity, given only idiot-proof deals. He was too practical for an academic career, and lacked enough practical skill to be successful as an investor—in short, a failure.

Richard took these gloomy thoughts to lunch in the San Marino cafeteria, where he lingered over the *Wall Street Journal* and a toasted ham and cheese sandwich, followed by two double espressos. His poor spirits did not yield to either the comfort food or the caffeine. The latter was in part an effort to cut through his jet-lag fatigue, which he knew was one of the elements adversely affecting his mood, as it usually did. Still, he did not head home yet for a proper sleep. He wanted his colleagues to see him on the job dealing with the consequences of the mess he had created. It had been years since he'd had to put in face time.

He returned to his office in this miserable mood around two-thirty, and decided that he needed to snap out of it and start thinking about solutions. But he found himself staring out the window without generating anything remotely useful. Just after three, as early as seemed reasonable, Richard called Jasmine on her mobile. It took her until the fourth ring to answer.

"*Wéi* [Hello]," she answered in a sleepy voice.

"Jasmine, it's Richard. Sorry I woke you."

"What time is it?"

"Six in the morning, your time. Sorry to interrupt your holiday again."

"That's OK. You don't sound well, Doc."

"Tom Wilshire asked Jane Leeson to look over my shoulder while I try to fix the JZP deal. Peter Thomas asked me if I should fire you. And, to be honest, I'm not sure they feel so certain about keeping me around, with the mess that I have caused for the firm. You might ask, aside from that, Mrs. Lincoln, how was the play?"

"What …?" Jasmine sounded confused.

"Never mind, it's about U.S. history."

"So … what are you going to do? Do you need me to come back now?"

"No. I don't think there's anything you can't do from there. What I need you to do is start thinking about anything we could do to fix this mess. I have to admit that I'm short on ideas. I need help." Richard abruptly realized, with mild shock,

167

that there was a note of pleading in his voice. He'd hardly remembered that this side of him existed.

"Of course." Jasmine sounded suddenly awake. Had she heard his incipient panic? "I'll get to work right away. And don't worry. You always figure out the tough problems."

"Thanks, I wish I believed that now. *You* sound calm. Aren't you worried about losing your job?"

"Richard, I am Chinese."

"What do you mean?"

"Well, you can start with the U.S. history expression you just used. I think I understand it. It's about your President Lincoln who was shot, right?"

"Yes, right. Well done."

"My grandfather was shot during the Cultural Revolution, and barely survived. That's recent history—less than forty years ago. In China, we know that everything can change very fast. So, yes, I am worried about losing my job. But I must accept that can happen."

"Fair enough. You're right that there could be worse things than a busted deal. Family is more important. I should have asked, how are your parents?"

"Thanks for asking. They are the same as always. Actually, I told my father a little about what is happening on *jiāo yì*."

"What did he think?"

"He wasn't surprised. He said that corruption is everywhere in China. He asked why we were so worried about it."

"It's not that simple, Jasmine. It's illegal for a U.S. company to pay foreign bribes. There is no way San Marino can look the other way. That's why the firm asked Jane Leeson to investigate the deal."

"So what do you plan to do next?"

"I don't know, Jasmine. I don't know."

"Do I definitely still have a job … now?"

"Yes, of course you do."

"Well then, I am going to try to find out as much as I can about what JZP has been doing to get these property deals. OK?"

"Thanks, Jasmine." Richard smiled to himself at Jasmine's persistence, but he still felt sick to his stomach. "Remind me when you will be back in L.A."

"The plan was for me to stay until next weekend. Is that still OK?"

"Yes, no problem. You have plenty of family and work to keep you busy there this week. Please call me as soon as you learn anything useful."

* * *

Later that evening, Richard sat at the kitchen table with Julie after putting Lydia to bed. She was still dressed for her visit that day to Modern Zen, in tight black leggings and a pale yellow t-shirt bearing the company's slogan, "Don't Think. Meditate." Easier said than done, thought Richard.

"This morning Tom Wilshire asked me in disbelief how the China deal could go so bad so fast, and I realized that he was describing exactly how I felt. Four days ago I thought I had pulled off the deal of a lifetime, and now the whole thing is a mess." Elbows propped on the table, he lowered his head into his hands.

"Richard Gregg, I am surprised at you. You have always solved every problem that you have encountered, and this one is not even your fault."

"I don't know. I should have seen this coming. You know, if this mess gets bad enough, I'm not sure that I'll keep my job at San Marino. Then, who knows—we might not be able to keep this house. I want Lydia to have a good life. And forget about our plans to buy a sailboat and sail around the world."

"Richard, we were almost poor when we met, and we stayed that way for a long time. I don't want to go back to that either, but we were happy then. We have plenty of money in the bank, and we'll find a way through the rest of it. Lydia is doing great, and she's going to have a good life because she has two parents who love her."

"You are right. Lydia is doing really well, and we'll make sure that continues. But her father is having serious problems."

"What is really going on here, Richard? You don't sound like you."

He looked at Julie, his eyes moist. "I don't want to fail again."

"Honey, you have never been a failure at anything. Those idiots in the Chinese history department at UCLA just didn't recognize brilliance when they saw it. But you do need to get a grip. I watched you make the university problem a lot worse than it had to be, and I don't think any of us want to see that happen again. For Lydia's sake, please be the Richard Gregg I know."

Richard looked at Julie admiringly and recognized the sense of her words, but they did not fully lift the pressure of despair and failure. "OK. I'll do my best." He forced a smile.

"I know you don't always agree with my Zen philosophy, but maybe you should try some meditation. A lot of our clients at Modern Zen are skeptical at first." Richard raised his eyebrows. "At least you have to recognize that problems become bigger if you let them grow in your head."

"Maybe … I don't know."

"Look. Let's get your mind off of this for tonight at least. We have a couple of good movies from Netflix, and I intend to take advantage of you on the sofa while we watch one of them."

Richard looked at her non-commitally. "I really need to spend some time figuring out what to do with the China deal."

"Richard Gregg, I spent the last week by myself with our daughter, while you have been in China with your beautiful assistant getting yourself into a mess. If you don't spend some time on my needs tonight, you will definitely have bigger problems then you do now. Zen philosophy has never been able to keep me from needing a proper shag." She smiled.

Richard smiled too, genuinely this time. "I am lucky you love me, Julie. You're right, I *am* going to figure out a way to fix this situation. And I suppose that can wait until tomorrow."

交易

25

Farewell

late July 2009

Parting is such sweet sorrow

– William Shakespeare, 'Romeo and Juliet'

April decided that she would spend her last full day in
Shanghai being a tourist, and the prospect—a welcome relief
from the stress of recent weeks—made her feel more cheerful.
After breakfast, she dressed in an old favorite: a knee-length,
navy, pleated synthetic skirt with white polka dots, and a white
t-shirt printed with flowers. She spent the morning shopping
on Nanjing Road, choosing gifts for her parents, and then
strolling along the Bund. She had agreed to meet Walter at
two o'clock in the afternoon on the top observation deck of the
Oriental Pearl Tower. Her late evening with Jasmine had
given the lofty TV tower a special significance, and it felt
important to visit before she left.

April had spent almost all of her time in Shanghai on the
west side of the river, and decided to take the Huangpu River
Ferry to cross to Pudong. Seeing the Bund recede over the
water as she crossed, along with business people, bicyclists and
tourists, provided a new perspective. It suddenly looked like a
place to be visited, no longer home.

After reaching the other bank, April had lunch in a noodle
shop, crowded in among local workers and a few Chinese
tourists. She chose a Japanese udon noodle dish and buried
herself in a book, successfully deflecting any unwanted
attention she might have received alone. Emerging back into
the unfamiliar streets of Pudong after lunch, April briefly got
lost, and then found her bearings by looking up for the spire of
the Oriental Pearl Tower. She negotiated the entrance to the

tower and ticket desk, and found herself at the back of an elevator filled with German tourists. When the elevator doors opened at the observation platform, she spotted Walter almost immediately, waiting for her with a large bouquet of red roses. As soon as she freed herself from the screen of tourists, she ran over and gave him a big hug.

"Wow, I should have started buying you flowers sooner!"

"Flowers are a good way to a girl's heart. These are lovely. But really, it's just nice to see you."

"I'm going to miss you, April."

"I'll miss you too, Walter." She looked toward the edge of the observation deck. "Shall we have a look?"

"Yes, sure. I'm excited. I grew up in Shanghai and I've never been up here."

They walked to the full-length glass windows, which were bordered at their base with more than a meter of glass floor, giving them the impression of being suspended in space. "I'm glad that I'm not afraid of heights," April said.

Walter nodded, and was slow to respond as he looked at the incomparable view. "This is incredible. How did I not think to come here before? I can't imagine any better way to get to know Shanghai."

"I don't feel that I have had long enough to get to know Shanghai."

"Then stay."

"I can't challenge my Uncle Jun. It's really a shame. My parents often told me how different it is to be Chinese in China than in America. They like their life in California, but I think they miss China. I was just starting to understand how they feel."

"You are getting a very bad final lesson on China. It really isn't fair what your uncle has done. Protecting the family is very important in our country, and he is turning his back on you."

"I don't understand it either. If I had really made a mistake then I would understand why I should lose my job. They are blaming me for something that I didn't do, and that they know I didn't do. Even Aunt Hong has stopped being friendly to me."

"They must be very afraid of something. I have seen this many times working on my articles. No one can talk about corruption because they are afraid. But few businessmen can resist the urge to make more money by joining the corrupt system. It's all around us."

"Well, I suppose there is nothing I can do about it now. I guess I'll just go home to my family in Los Angeles and look for another job." She looked gloomily down at her hands on the rail by the window.

"Things could be worse. I would *love* to visit Los Angeles—Hollywood, Sunset Boulevard, Malibu. Since you are going to miss me so much, how about inviting me to visit you?"

"You have a standing invitation!" April smiled at Walter. "Come on. Let's have a look at the view. I may as well enjoy my last day here."

They spent the next half hour walking around the outside of the observation deck. It was an unusually clear day. There were stunning views to the east across Pudong to the East China Sea, and to the north across the Yangtse River to Chongming Island. Walter was most interested in the nearer sights of Shanghai, and he animatedly pointed out a number of the building projects that he had been investigating for his articles. He got particularly excited when he thought he noticed a new construction project across the river in the older part of Shanghai. Then, in the middle of an explanation, he suddenly stopped and turned to April. "Maybe I can help."

"What do you mean? Help with what?"

"With your problems at JZP."

"How?"

"I am learning a lot about corruption in the property market, including how to put pressure on corrupt officials and business people. You heard Xu say that no one would publish my articles, but he's not right. Times are changing. My newspaper is willing to publish stories about corruption if I really have the facts. There are limits of course about what we can write ..." Walter looked thoughtful. "I think a story about corruption at a medium-sized company like JZP that is dealing with foreign investors is just what they might like. Would you like to help me write it?" Walter smiled.

"Please, Walter. Why would you suggest that? Even with what they have done, I could never do that to my family. I'm surprised that you would consider doing something like that to Xu. He's your friend."

"I don't think we are really friends any more. We still act like friends because we've known each other since we were children. Now we are very different. I don't think I like who Xu has become, and I am fairly sure he doesn't like me very much either."

"Well, you should still treat him like a friend. Anyway, I am not going to help you write about JZP."

"OK. But if you change your mind, you know where to find me."

"It won't be so easy to find you from Los Angeles. But I suppose I can call." April paused and looked down at her hands again.

"Of course you can—"

"Walter?"

"Yes?"

"I did make a mistake."

"What do you mean?"

"I didn't make the mistake that Uncle Jun says I did, but I did make a mistake. I don't think he knows."

"What did you do?"

April spoke quietly, still looking down at her hands. "I had sex with Jasmine."

There was a long pause.

175

"OK, *now* I'm jealous. But why was that a mistake? Did you both enjoy it?"

April felt relief. Of course Walter would not judge her. "Don't be *too* curious, Walter. It was a mistake because I said something after we had sex that helped Jasmine figure out there was something wrong with *jiāo yì*. I think that's what started the problems. So I suppose I deserve it that I lost my job. I'm ashamed to admit it, but the worst part is that I seem to have lost Jasmine. I haven't spoken with her since that night." April turned and looked out over Shanghai, and hesitated to turn back to Walter as her eyes filled with tears. "I love her."

"Well, maybe you should call her."

"And say what?"

"Tell her that you love her."

"I don't think I can do that yet."

"OK, then talk about *jiāo yì*. Maybe she wants to talk to me about my article."

"You never stop thinking about work, do you Walter?"

"I only stop when I am thinking about you, April. I am really going to miss you. Even if you don't love *me*, you have become my best friend. Shanghai will not be the same without you." He looked up at April, blinking hard.

"Don't start crying too, Walter. I had better go home. Uncle Jun and Aunt Hong have planned a dinner before I leave for Los Angeles tomorrow."

"It sounds like they are embarrassed about their behavior."

"I don't know. I really don't want to go to dinner, but I don't think I have a choice."

"OK. If you don't mind, I am going to stay here. I never realized how much I could learn about Shanghai development by looking at it from above."

"No problem. I would rather leave you here than in the metro."

"May I kiss you goodbye?"

April kissed Walter lightly on the lips. "Let's not say goodbye. I have the feeling that we will meet again soon. See you later, OK?"

"OK." Walter stayed glued to the spot as he watched April leave. As the elevator doors shut, she could see him waving at her from a distance. Then she was descending, down towards Shanghai—heading towards the big house in the French Concession for what she imagined might be the last time.

* * *

Where the farewell with Walter had been sad but comfortable, April's final family dinner at the Wang's big house in the French Concession was awkward and strange. Mrs. Ma laid out a particularly nice dinner, beginning with several types of dim sum and soup, then a series of meat, vegetable and noodle dishes, including a whole roasted Beijing duck. The good food did nothing to lighten the atmosphere.

Uncle Jun, Aunt Hong and Xu had dressed rather formally, similarly to the way they had dressed for the completion dinner two weeks earlier. Not expecting such a ceremonial send-off, April had stayed in her cheerful tourist outfit for dinner. She hastily excused herself to change, choosing the businesslike outfit that she had originally planned to wear to the completion dinner.

Once they were all seated at the table and eating the first course of dim sum and soup, awkwardness settled in with a vengeance. They all seemed to be wondering whether they should mention the elephant in the corner of the room. After her conversation with Walter, although she still couldn't quite feel responsible for what had happened, April wanted to acknowledge her role in events, somehow to make it better. "Uncle Jun, Aunt Hong, Xu, thank you so much for your hospitality in Shanghai, and thank you for this nice dinner. It will be very sad for me to leave Shanghai tomorrow. I am *so* sorry that it is not ending well."

No one spoke, for what seemed to April like minutes, although it was probably about twenty seconds. Uncle Jun continued eating his soup, seemingly oblivious to what April had said. Xu looked at April distantly and coldly, then at his father, then back at April. Aunt Hong, apparently realizing that the men of the family were not going to speak, broke the silence. "We have enjoyed having you here too, April. Maybe it has not ended so well ... We know life can be difficult. Your Uncle Jun and I were poor when we met, and we have been lucky. Now it may be a hard time again, but I believe we will be OK."

"Thank you, Aunt Hong." April was surprised that Aunt Hong, who usually spoke about domestic affairs and trivialities, had jumped rather directly into the heart of the matter. "I am sorry if I have contributed to the difficulties. I really don't understand what is happening."

Xu's eyes flashed. "You don't understand, *mèi mei*?" His use of the term of endearment was now laced with sarcasm. "Which part of our situation do you not understand? Since your *bà* ran off to America, my *bà* has been working in China to build a business. Now you come back as a tourist, and in a few months you and your American friends may have destroyed all that we have built."

"I am not working with the Americans, Wang Xu." April addressed Xu formally, trying to show respect.

"Oh, no?" Xu sneered. "How else did they find out about our friends in Suzhou? I know you became friends with that arrogant Liu Mo Li, and you went to see her the night after completion. What did you tell her? Were the Americans paying you to help them?"

April realized that Xu had guessed something near the truth, but she also knew that he was just guessing and had no idea of what had happened between her and Jasmine. She desperately wanted to tell the truth, with the hope that it would redeem her in the eyes of her Chinese family. But she knew that hope was foolish. Even if she could put to rest Xu's suspicions that she had intentionally hurt JZP, the revelation that she had passed on clues about the investors in Suzhou could not help. And she had no idea how to tell the story without revealing her sexual encounter with Jasmine, which she knew would be incomprehensible, at best, to Uncle Jun and Aunt Hong, and would make Xu angry and jealous. So she held her tongue, and decided to defend herself. "Cousin Xu, I am surprised that you would suggest that. You have blamed me for mistakes with the documents on *jiāo yì* that I did not make. Isn't that enough?"

Xu did not answer, but to April's surprise Uncle Jun came to her defense. "Xu, April is right. We have not been fair to her. Now it is time to be kind as we wish her safe travels back to America."

"Thank you, Uncle Jun."

Uncle Jun was suddenly attentive and focused. "Please do not thank me, April. I cannot imagine what my *dìdi*, my little brother, will think about the way that I have treated his daughter. The best I can do is wish you safe travels, which is not enough."

"Thank you again, Uncle Jun."

"Safe travels, April."

交易

26

Reflection and Progress

early August 2009

From each according to his abilities, to each according to his needs

– Karl Marx

Tom Wilshire's Jaguar convertible smoothly negotiated the curves of Mulholland Drive, along the spine of the Hollywood end of the Santa Monica mountains. From Richard's side of the car, the urban patchwork of the San Fernando Valley spread out below, with the studios near Ventura Boulevard in the foreground. A few minutes later the expansive concrete jungle of the Los Angeles basin came into sight from the driver's side. Under a cloudless blue sky, the bright late morning sunlight was quickly warming the air blowing their hair. It was the kind of day that made Los Angeles feel like a sub-tropical paradise.

They were on their way to participate in a San Marino Property Investments tradition—the annual lunch at Gladstone's in Malibu. Tom Wilshire and Peter Thomas had first built their reputations and fortunes with a series of spectacularly successful investments during the 1980s in beach-front properties in Malibu. Gladstone's—a popular bar and restaurant on the beach at the intersection of the Pacific Coast Highway and Sunset Boulevard—became their local watering hole. And although they decided to move, to build an investment fund business in more sedate San Marino in the 1990s, the laid-back energy of Malibu remained close to their hearts. The most regular manifestation of this was an annual invitation to their entire staff to join them for a boozy Friday lunch to celebrate the lazy days of August.

The previous evening, Tom had surprised Richard by calling to suggest that Tom drive the two of them to the lunch, and that they leave an hour earlier than necessary for the drive to Malibu, even taking account of unpredictable Los Angeles traffic. Hearing a note of alarm in Richard's acceptance, Tom had assured him cryptically, "Don't worry, it's all good, Doc."

As they set out south from Pasadena on the 110 Freeway that morning, Richard decided to enjoy the day and stop wondering what Tom had in store for him. The reason for the early departure had become clear when they reached downtown Los Angeles, and Tom headed northwest on the 101 Freeway towards Hollywood rather than west on the 10 Freeway towards Malibu.

"Where are we going?" Richard asked.

"We're taking the long way around, Doc. I'm going to take Mulholland Drive, then across on the Ventura Freeway and down Topanga Canyon to Malibu."

"It's a nice day for that drive." Richard paused, but Tom did not jump into the gap. "But why?"

"I do some of my best thinking while driving. Thought it would be a good way for us to think through this China thing together."

Richard glanced, gauging his senior partner's mood. Tom's tone was relaxed, but Richard knew that Tom deeply disliked the possibility of losing money on *jiāo yì*. Tom and San Marino had an admirable track record of virtually never losing money on a deal, and certainly never so spectacularly and quickly as it seemed might happen with the JZP JV. Cautiously, he tested the water. "Sure, tell me what you're thinking."

"No!" Tom's tone was sharp. "Tell me what *you're* thinking first. This is your deal."

Richard was taken aback, but answered candidly. "Well, Tom, to be honest, I've been wondering what I *can* do while Jane is investigating and the lawyers are analyzing our options. So I haven't made much progress in figuring out a solution."

"Yeah, I noticed that. The Richard I know would be doing something creative and bold. Hell, the whole China deal was creative and bold. Show me some more of that."

"But look where it got us. Do the partners still have confidence in me to drive this deal?"

Tom had been driving quickly round the curves of Mulholland Drive, and he slowed down and looked over at Richard as he spoke. "Doc, I can't speak for everyone, but I have as much confidence in you as in anyone at the firm. Some bad things happened in China that you couldn't control, and you made some mistakes. So you're human. Now go fix it. The only way this is going to turn into a disaster for *you* is if you let that happen."

Richard considered this. He recalled Julie's similar request: *be* Richard Gregg. Something seemed to loosen up. Yes. He damn well would.

"Thanks a lot, Tom. I *have* been worried, you know. I know we are friends, but, well, thanks … It means a lot what you just said."

"Don't mention it. You see that big house there?" Tom slowed the car some more, and pointed to a house ahead and up a hill, visible behind a fence.

"Yeah, sure."

"That used to belong to one of my best friends, Jay Wilkinson. Knew him since college. We used to play tennis every week, at a court at that house. About five years ago, he died of a heart attack while we were playing. Biggest shock of my life." Tom paused, and Richard thought he saw tears in his eyes. "Life is short, Richard. Don't waste it doubting yourself."

"Wow, Tom, I'm sorry. Is that why you brought us this way? To show me that house?"

"Maybe. I think I did it for me too. I haven't been up here since the day Jay died. So now, please, tell me what you are going to do with the China deal."

"Alright. I've been giving it some thought. I guess I've just been scared to move."

"Let's hear it."

"Well, it seems to me that there are two key points. The first one is that the deal is still very attractive on the numbers, particularly with some confidence coming back into the markets over the summer. There's no reason that San Marino should lose money, even if we just take the properties that the JV already owns, clean up the mess, and sell them on. That would be a disappointing result, but at worst we should be able to avoid disaster and at best we might still make some decent money."

"I agree. This isn't the first legal mess that I have encountered, and focusing on the assets has always been the way out. So what's the second point?"

"It's just the obvious problem. JZP's investments definitely involved corruption of government officials—at least the Suzhou deal, and probably most or even all of the others. I really should have seen this. There were definitely some clues. I guess I wanted the deal too—"

"Water under the bridge, Doc. What are we going to do now?"

"So. There are three main options. First, we could try to fix the deal. The Foreign Corrupt Practices Act prevents us from running with an investment involving corruption, but we could try to clean up the JV and stick with it. Basically, we would have to get the other shareholders out of the Suzhou property, and try to confirm there are no similar problems with the other properties. Unfortunately, much as I would like to do that, I don't think it's realistic. The process would be messy, and it would be hard for us to know if we had really fixed the problem. We would probably end up spending a fortune on lawyers trying to protect ourselves."

"Yes, I agree."

"So the second option would be to unwind the deal and give the properties back to JZP. I'm fairly sure JZP would be willing to do that. But at best San Marino would lose all of the upside in property value, and we'd be stuck with the deal expenses and wasted time. Our investors would hate it. That's the outcome that has been keeping me awake at night."

"Yep. We'll do that if we have to do it, but no one would like it. Should I be excited about your third option?"

"Maybe. It's not rocket science. We need to find a new buyer for our share of the JZP JV. Someone who would pay enough to cover our expenses and maybe give us some return."

"Wouldn't any other buyer face just the same problem that we have?"

"Maybe not. Particularly if the buyer is Chinese. Corruption is sort of a way of life in China, and the right buyer might not look too hard. We would still have to clean up the government ownership on the Suzhou deal, and be careful that people don't start to talk about our problems. Like I said, the first key point is that these properties are worth a lot of money." Richard pressed his lips together, considering. "I think it's doable to find a willing buyer."

"Sounds plausible. So, are you going to run with that?"

"OK ... but what about Jane's investigation?"

"Just keep her informed of what you're doing. Nothing prevents you looking for a new deal while Jane sorts through the mess you made." Tom smiled at Richard to take the sting out of his comment.

"Yes, sir! I'm on it." Richard felt his mood lift to match the blue skies above. Tom was still on his side. And fixing *jiāo yì* with what he had already begun to think of as *xīn jiāo yì* [the new deal] fit with his instincts as a deal-maker.

The rest of the ride to Malibu was uneventful, neither Tom nor Richard speaking much. As they descended Topanga Canyon toward the Pacific, Richard felt a sense of excitement and anticipation for the first time since the completion dinner a few weeks before. They arrived early at Gladstone's, and were sharing a beer when everyone else arrived on two small buses that the firm had provided.

The lunch at Gladstone's was as excellent and relaxing as ever. It was California summer paradise—drinking beer and eating lobster and Dungeness crab, next to a beach where light breaking waves were shared among a few surfers, windsurfers and swimmers, and a crowd of seagulls looking for scraps.

Halfway through the lunch, François LeCroix came over to Richard and Jasmine, who were sitting together. "Richard, Richard, I see you down the table talking the whole lunchtime to Jasmine, and I know you are talking about work. This is very naughty. This is her first time at our Gladstone's lunch. You must allow her to enjoy the California sun." He turned to Jasmine. "I am correct, *non?*"

Jasmine smiled at François. "Yes, you are correct. Richard has cheered up and is telling me what we are going to do in China."

"Yes, but François is right. Let's enjoy the day. So, François, what's new with you?"

"Well, life is good, of course. We have the lovely California weather. We have all the lovely girls, like these on the beach. And then sometimes we do some investing and we make some money. There are so many reasons to be happy."

It was hard not to be infected by François' relentless Gallic-infused optimism. But Richard found himself irresistibly eager to get back to work, to start work on *xīn jiāo yì*. After lunch, Richard confirmed that Tom intended to stay around for a while, and thanked him for the ride through the hills and his support. Then, Richard made sure to be on the first of the two buses headed back to San Marino, with Jasmine in tow.

* * *

As soon as they got back to the San Marino office, early in the Shanghai morning, Richard picked up the telephone and called Wang Jun's mobile phone. Mr. Wang picked up on the first ring.

"*Nǐ hǎo Wáng xiānsheng, zhè shì Richard Gregg.*"

"Hello, Mr. Gregg. I am pleased to hear from you directly." Mr. Wang answered in English. "There has been too much talking by the lawyers recently."

"Yes, I agree. I would like to propose a way to solve the problems we're facing, and I thought it would be best for just the two of us to speak. I will try to speak Mandarin but may use some English too. I think we can communicate. *Hǎo ba?* [OK?]"

"*Hǎo de.* [OK.] What is your proposal, Mr. Gregg?"

"I would like to be your partner, Mr. Wang, but with what we have learned about the Suzhou deal I fear that there is no way that San Marino can stay in the JV. I don't want to accuse you of corruption, but you must admit it doesn't look good."

"I understand. You must draw your own conclusions, Mr. Gregg."

"I could ask you to take back full control of the properties, but that would be very embarrassing for me, and I would need you to pay at least the valuations that we agreed, which would be expensive for JZP."

"Yes, I agree that would be difficult."

"What I would like to do is find another buyer for San Marino's share of the JV, one who is also acceptable to you."

"But would not any American buyer have the same problems with this deal that you do?"

"Yes, probably. So I want to look for a Chinese investor." Mr. Wang was silent for some time. "Did you understand? *Wǒ yào zhǎodào zhōngguó de tóuzīrén.*" Richard repeated himself in Mandarin.

"Yes, Mr. Gregg, I understand. You want me to share the company I have built for my family with another Chinese family. Why would I do that? There are no opportunities for me in such a deal. Like there are … like I thought there were … working with American investors."

"You might do it because it is the best choice that you have."

"I do not know if that is correct, Mr. Gregg. I will need to think about your proposal. Please let me call you in a few days."

"OK. But please realize that if we cannot figure out a solution together, I will need to find one on my own."

"I understand, Mr. Gregg. For now, thank you for your call. *Zaìjiàn.* [Goodbye.]"

"Before you say goodbye, let me say the rest of what I wanted to say. To make this *xīn jiāo yì* happen, I would need two things from you. First, we need to settle the financial arrangements for the Suzhou property on the basis that we discussed. Second, I need you to give me confidence that there aren't any more hidden investors in any of the properties that the JV owns. OK?"

"OK, I understand, Mr. Gregg. *Zaìjiàn.*"

"*Zaìjiàn, Wáng xiānsheng.*"

* * *

When Mr. Wang put down the telephone, he looked thoughtfully at his wife, with whom he had been eating breakfast when Richard called. "I have made bad mistakes for our family, and I do not know how to fix them."

"You have always tried to do the best thing for this family. You should not blame yourself. What can you do?"

"These problems started when I agreed to the requests of those bastards in Suzhou. I thought that I had no choice. But I was wrong. Maybe I would have made a little less money, but our family business would still be safe. Then I tried to fix that first mistake by blaming my brother's daughter for it. That was certainly wrong."

"Do you mean that April did not make the mistake that you said?"

"No she did not. We just told that to the Americans. It was the idea of our son." Mr. Wang registered the brief shock on his wife's face.

"You may have made some mistakes, but you are a good man. A family man. You are not the type of person who would hurt the daughter of your brother ... who lived in your house, and worked for your business. You must fix this."

Mr. Wang looked at her seriously for a few seconds before responding. "Yes, I know. I must fix it."

交易

27

Cultural Revolution

early August 2009

If you want to know the taste of a pear, you must change the pear by eating it yourself. If you want to know the theory and methods of revolution, you must take part in revolution. All genuine knowledge originates in direct experience.

– Mao Zedong

Just a few miles away from San Marino, April was *hors de combat* at her family home in Arcadia. It felt both familiar and strange. The flight back from Shanghai had been smooth, foreshadowing the uneventful days that followed. Her parents were the same as she had left them, her room in her parents' home was the same, her U.S. friends were the same, bar a few minor changes to jobs and relationships. Yet, after the excitement of Shanghai, it all felt different, more of a culture shock than she had felt upon arrival in China. Despite the unpleasant ending to her time in Shanghai, April could not shake the feeling that she was missing out now on some continuing adventure, on excitement that she still wanted to share. That excitement was definitely not to be found on the quiet streets of Arcadia.

To blunt the edge of incipient boredom, April tried to return to some semblance of earlier routine. Her parents helped with this by not asking too many questions about Shanghai. Her father understood from a conversation with his brother, Uncle Jun, that something unpleasant had happened, but he refrained from quizzing her about it. Like most Chinese parents, April's were very attentive to the life and choices of their only daughter. But, thankfully, they had also learned to give her space—perhaps both because of long years learning the customs of the United States, and out of necessity over the more than four years that she had spent at Harvard and then in Shanghai, home only for the summers.

Yet April herself found it impossible not to think about Shanghai, especially about Walter and Jasmine. Her feelings about Walter were clear: she was missing a friend. Those about Jasmine were a lot more complicated. One afternoon, shopping with her mother at the Westfield mall in Arcadia, looking in the display window of the Victoria's Secret shop, April started fantasizing about wearing the latest lingerie fashion for Jasmine to undress her. Turning away from the display and her fantasies, April felt a sudden jolt as she saw Jasmine and Walter walking hand in hand through the crowds in the mall, about forty feet away and coming towards her.

"April, what is it?" April's mother was surprised as her daughter suddenly stopped walking and her expression froze.

April quickly realized that her eyes had deceived her. "Nothing, Ma. I thought I saw some people I knew in Shanghai. But it's not." The couple did slightly resemble their Shanghai alter egos, particularly the young man. The girl looked less like Jasmine, but enough to pull a very sensitive trigger. April had been seeing Jasmine everywhere. She wasn't crazy, she assured herself. It was perfectly possible for her to run into Jasmine here—San Marino's offices were less than five miles to the west of Arcadia, and Jasmine must live somewhere not far away.

April decided on the spot that she needed to face her worries about what had happened with Jasmine, and call her. After all, they had said they would be friends before their encounter in the hotel room. There were also things to discuss about *jiāo yì*. This decision sent her further into the state of agitation she had felt when she thought she saw Walter and Jasmine, and her mother couldn't help but notice in the car on the way home. "April, what *is* it? Are you all right? You have been in a strange mood since you came back from China." This was the first time either of her parents had raised the issue.

"I'm OK, Ma. It is just taking me a little while to adjust to being home. And today I am feeling a little sick."

"Really? We need to take good care of you. Your father and I are worried."

"Thanks, Ma. Don't worry. I am fine."

"Well, you just said you are sick. I want you to stay home for the rest of the day and get some rest. And when you are feeling better, maybe you should go out and look for a job? You are a smart girl. No use wasting time."

"You're right, Ma. I need to do that. I already looked at a few job listings on the Internet, but I haven't applied for anything. If it's OK, I'll start doing that seriously tomorrow."

"Of course, April. Today you need to rest."

Once April was back in her room at home, she lay down on her bed, on top of the duvet covered with faded images of Hello Kitty that had been a prized gift on her eleventh birthday. The duvet cover had somehow never been retired—partly because of April's own nostalgic childhood attachment and partly because her mother seemed to like keeping her room furnished as it had been when she was a child. She did not close her eyes. Instead, laying on her back and looking at the ceiling, she picked up her cell phone and called the familiar number of San Marino Property Investments.

"Good afternoon, San Marino Property Investments!" The familiar receptionist answered, now doubtless more experienced than when April had first spoken with her, but just as enthusiastic.

"Hello, this is April Wang. May I speak with Jasmine Liu?" April felt that her voice was shaking, as it had the fateful night in the hotel room with Jasmine.

"Of course, April. It's been a few weeks since we have heard from you. Are you doing OK?"

The question seemed more friendly than concerned. But April found herself wondering whether everything was OK, and being completely unsure of the answer. "Yes, I am fine. Is Jasmine in?"

"Certainly, she is. I will put you through to her now. You have a nice day."

"Yes, you too."

April's nervousness increased as she waited for Jasmine to come to the phone, long enough to make her wonder whether something was wrong, whether Jasmine was trying to avoid her. Her worries vanished when she heard Jasmine's voice.

"*Nĭ hăo*, April. Sorry I kept you waiting. It took me a minute to transfer the call to a conference room where I can speak privately." Jasmine's voice was gentle, the business Jasmine again replaced by the friend that April had known so briefly. "*Nĭ zěnmeyàng?* [How are you?]"

"I'm OK, Jasmine. I'm back in Los Angeles, just down the road from you. I'm living with my parents in Arcadia."

"I was worried about you. You lost your job because of me."

"I lost my job because of what JZP did. That's not your fault. I know they blamed me for it. I hope you understand that it was not true."

"Yes, I do. We are still trying to figure out what happened, but it's obvious that this was not a paperwork mistake by you like your uncle said."

"Thanks, Jasmine. Actually, I know someone who might be able to help you solve the problems with JZP. Do you remember Walter, the journalist who joined us for dinner with Xu in the spring?"

"Of course I do. He is a nice boy."

"Yes, I didn't know him so well then, but he has become my good friend. He is writing articles about property corruption, and wanted me to help him write about JZP. Of course I can't do that to my family, but I am very upset about what happened. I don't mind if you talk to Walter about it."

"Thanks, April. I may do that. How do I contact him?"

"I will email you his email address and mobile number." April paused, wanting to change the subject to more personal matters, but Jasmine got there first.

"I have been thinking about you a lot, April. I miss you."

"I miss you too. Can I see you?" Receiving a confirmation that Jasmine missed her, particularly while April was laying in bed, made her feel warm, a pleasant glow spreading from below her waist quickly to the rest of her body.

Jasmine was silent for several seconds. "I want to see you. What happened between us in Shanghai really shocked me, especially because of what you told me afterwards about *jiāo yì*. I think I confused the two things for a while. Now I know that I really liked what happened with us, and I had wanted it for a long time … and I want it to happen again. But I don't think I am ready to see you yet. My job also is in danger, and I am spending all my time trying to fix that. And I am still a little unsure what I want from you. And what I can give. Can you understand that?"

"Yes, I understand. I felt some of the same things after the first time I was with a girl in college." Suddenly, April felt relaxed and confident, sure that things with Jasmine would be OK. "I have never felt nearly so strongly about anyone as I do about you. Please think about seeing me. Arcadia is very close, and I need something to keep me busy—sorry, that sounded wrong. I just want to see you." Amazed that her earlier fantasies of seeing Jasmine seeming to be converging with reality, April allowed her left hand, the one not holding her mobile phone, to wander to the source of the warmth that she had felt a moments earlier and rest there gently.

"OK, well, I will think about it. Thank you very much for calling me. Can we talk again soon?"

"Any time. I will send you my mobile number in the email about Walter."

"Thanks a lot, April. I am so glad to hear that you are OK—you really do sound well. See you soon."

"Yes, as soon as possible!"

As soon as the call ended, April sent the promised email. Having accomplished this task, she decided she was unable to resist what had begun during the call, and spent the next ten minutes taking herself to a place where she had already gone several times, while thinking about Jasmine, since their late-night hotel meeting in Shanghai. It was nothing like actually being with Jasmine, but it was somewhat satisfying, much more so now than on the other recent occasions. Soon after she finished, April fell into a deep sleep.

* * *

Jasmine picked up the telephone on her desk as soon as she received April's email. Although it was early morning in Shanghai, Walter was quick to answer the telephone.

"Walter, this is Jasmine Liu. *Nǐ jì de wǒ ma?* [Do you remember me?]"

"*Dāngrán jì de.* [Of course I remember.]"

"Is this a good time to talk?"

"Sure, I am just walking on my way to the metro. And I'm alone."

"That's good. I understand from Wang April that you may be able to help me."

"Yes, I hope so. What did you have in mind?"

"You know that April lost her job because of corruption on JZP's deal with my company San Marino, right?" After Walter murmured assent, Jasmine continued. "Well, we have learned some things about the corruption, but we need to know more. If I tell you what I know, can you help me learn more?"

"*Dāngrán kěyǐ.* [Absolutely.]"

"*Fēicháng hǎo.* [Excellent.] April told me that you are a good friend and would help."

"She's a very good friend. But ... well ... the only thing I ask is that I be allowed to use what you tell me in my articles for *Shanghai Weekend*." Hearing Jasmine's sharp intake of breath, Walter added hastily, "Of course, it would all be on background. No one would know that the information is from you."

"Yes, but this is confidential information that I learned at work. I don't think I can do it. My boss would not be happy." Or would he? Jasmine considered. Richard had been rather explicit that she should do what she could to find solutions to the problems with *jiāo yì*.

"OK, have it your way. But I don't work for free. If you decide you can provide information that I can use, then give me a call and I will think about helping you."

"So you want me to be an informer? That strikes too close to home. This is not the Cultural Revolution."

"Why?"

"Why is it not the Cultural Revolution?! That is a very silly question." Jasmine was beginning to question April's wisdom in suggesting that she go to Walter for help.

"No. Why does it strike close to home?" There was an edge in Walter's voice.

Jasmine wavered, then decided she had nothing to lose by telling a little family history. After all, it was a common story in China. "The Cultural Revolution almost destroyed my grandfather. He was a very important person to me, yet I feel that I never really knew him." Walter conspicuously failed to respond. "Did you hear me? I don't like feeling like an informer."

After another silence, Walter spoke, his voice almost cracking with emotion. "That was my family too. My grandfather was killed, and my father barely survived. He never got a chance to tell me what happened to him, because he shot himself in the head when I was five years old. So you might say that I don't like a reminder of the Cultural Revolution either."

"I am sorry. You have suffered more than I have."

"Don't apologize. You could not have known. Listen, tell me what you know about the corruption at JZP, and I will find out what I can. I won't use the information for an article unless you tell me it's OK."

Jasmine hesitated, then decided to jump in with both feet. "It's OK. If you write something, maybe it will help. These corrupt officials are the same kind of people that hurt our families. They are only out for themselves, and they shouldn't be able to get away with it. Let me tell you what I know."

As Jasmine started to tell Walter about the Suzhou officials, she looked across to Richard's office. Later, when she contemplated the chain of consequences that her disclosure to Walter would set in motion, she would wonder why she hadn't just walked a few steps and asked Richard first. Maybe she was trying to live up to her parents' expectations that she would be a confident and successful businesswoman in a man's world. Or maybe she had just been afraid that he would say "No".

交易

28

Turning the Tables

early August 2009

A gentleman is conciliatory but not accommodating;
the common man is accommodating but not conciliatory

— *Confucius*

Wang Jun looked at the sun sparkling off *Jīnjī Hú* as he walked and thought. He had spent the morning checking the progress of the Suzhou development, working through construction issues with JZP's site manager and the project manager of the construction company, East China Office Construction (ECOC). The biggest issue they discussed involved the windows—the building plans called for custom-sized windows, and the supplier had shipped a standard size about two centimeters narrower, apparently hoping that no one would notice, or at least that no one would care. It had been the JZP site manager who noticed, and who then learned that ECOC intended to install the wrong-sized windows with extra-wide border fittings. Mr. Wang insisted in no uncertain terms that the windows be replaced. He had the impression that ECOC was hoping to share in the cost saving with the window supplier.

The work at the site was extremely enjoyable and relaxing for Mr. Wang compared with his recent stress over *jiāo yì*. The attempted deception over the windows was a typical problem in China—minor fraud and corruption was everywhere. It would not have ruined the building to be built with the standard windows, but he was proud that JZP had discovered the problem. That kind of attention to detail was what had made them successful over the years. He told the site manager so, complimenting him for his vigilance.

196

Mr. Wang still had to remind himself that the Suzhou development was no longer owned by JZP, but by the joint venture with San Marino. As that change of circumstances nagged him over the course of the morning, he found himself wishing intensely that he had stuck with owning his own business. It was a good business that had made his family rich.

What had possessed him to feel so strongly that he needed more through *jiāo yì*? That need had led to give in too easily to the much nastier corruption proposed by the Suzhou officials—surely he should have had better judgment than that. And then, worst of all, he had betrayed the trust of his own brother's daughter to try to protect that mistake. If he was a gentleman, as he liked to believe, then a sort of temporary insanity seemed the only explanation for his actions.

After leaving the building site, he set out along the lake to a restaurant where he had agreed to meet the two officials, Li Zhiyuan and Yang Sicheng. It was a beautiful afternoon. Suzhou was developing quickly, but it still had a much calmer feeling than Shanghai, and remained more Chinese—still mostly free of the expatriate bankers and Western brands that were increasingly visible in Shanghai.

The walk gave him another chance to reflect on his conversations with Richard and then his wife two days earlier. Since then, Mr. Wang had felt simultaneously calmer and more combative about the challenges facing the JV, him and his family. While he felt deeply conflicted about Richard Gregg's proposal of selling San Marino's half of the JV to a Chinese company, Richard was certainly correct that the problems in Suzhou needed to be cleaned up. And he felt no conflict at all about what his wife had said. His feelings about both conversations led him in the same direction, towards today's meeting with the two Suzhou officials. Mr. Wang was determined to do better than Richard had requested, and cleanse the Suzhou project entirely of the officials and their families.

Mr. Wang had insisted on meeting at the restaurant on *Jīnjī Hú* rather than in government offices. He wanted to be on neutral ground. It was an ordinary business restaurant, but he saw no reason to choose a more expensive place to confront his enemies.

Mr. Wang had confirmed in advance that the restaurant could offer *chá dào* [茶道, traditional tea ceremony, literally "way of tea"] to begin lunch, which he intended to convey a point of Confucian right behavior. Arriving early, he arranged with the hostess to be seated in a corner of the main dining room next to a fountain, far enough away from other guests that they would not be overheard if they spoke softly.

When Mr. Li and Mr. Yang arrived, they both seemed annoyed, put upon to be summoned to a meeting, uninterested in the formalities of the way of tea. Slightly surprised at first by their indifference, Mr. Wang remembered that the two officials had been peasants who used the Cultural Revolution as a route to power. They were unlikely to know the ways of gentlemen. He felt momentarily divided as to whether he should be ashamed of his feelings of superiority, or vindicated in his contempt at the officials' behavior. Then he dove into the heart of the matter.

"*Lǐ xiānsheng, Yáng xiānsheng.* Thank you very much for joining me for lunch today."

"Of course, Mr. Wang. We trust that your project here in Suzhou is going well. My son is very pleased to be involved." Mr. Li smiled without warmth.

"Yes, my sister is very grateful as well. She is already interested in joining other projects, and we are speaking to other investors about that."

"Thank you for your consideration. Actually it is not going so well. My American investors have learned about your families' shares in our project and they are very upset. They understand that these shares are payments to government officials … to you. They say that American law requires them to suspend their investment because of this. It is a very big problem."

"Mr. Wang, are you trying to insult us?" Mr. Yang was first to respond. "Those shares are payments for the work that our family members are doing for your business."

"Yes, and your problems with American law are not our problems," Mr. Li added. "We are in China, a socialist country, not the capitalist society of your American friends."

Mr. Wang wondered whether Mr. Li realized that his answer made no sense at all, but he decided to let it go. "Whatever you say, we all know why JZP gave those shares to your families. I do not think the Americans will stay quiet about this. Do you not think it is safer for you to give back the shares?"

"Mr. Wang, now you are threatening us, and asking us to give you something for nothing." Mr. Yang turned from Mr. Wang to Mr. Li. "I do not know if we should stay to listen to this."

"This is not good for your business to say this to us," Mr. Li said. "We have always been good to JZP. Why are you suddenly making things so difficult for yourself?"

Mr. Wang took a slow sip of tea, set his teacup down slowly, and paused before he spoke. "I am not asking to receive something for nothing, any more than you did when you asked for the shares in the first place. Neither am I threatening you. If you want me to be clearer, what I was thinking is that certain kinds of behavior by Communist Party officials are not so accepted in our socialist Chinese country as they used to be. I assume that you have heard about the campaign against corruption by Bo Xilai in Chongqing?" Mr. Wang knew that linking the project to an anti-corruption campaign would be dropping a bomb, but he was no longer frightened of the effect.

Mr. Li spoke quietly when he responded. "Mr. Wang, if you had spoken any less clearly I would assume I had misunderstood, but since you have been clear to me I will be clear to you. We are not in Chongqing. You are speaking to two of the most senior Communist Party officials of Jiangsu province. This will not happen here. Even in Chongqing, Mr. Bo is finding corruption only among junior officials. The behavior of the Communist Party leadership is not in question."

Mr. Yang was more visibly angry. He stood up before Mr. Li had finished speaking and hissed at Mr. Wang, "I will leave you now and I believe that Mr. Li will accompany me. If you wish to do *any* property business in Jiangsu, I suggest that you reconsider what you have said."

"I am sorry that you will not stay for lunch." Mr. Wang spoke calmly. "I will consider what you say, but I am simply telling you the real problems for my business that you and your families have caused. I do not know what else I can do."

The two officials left without a further word, leaving Mr. Wang to finish the tea on his own. A Communist Party member himself, he had just aggressively challenged a senior party member—the first time in his life he had dared to do anything of the kind. Yet he felt strangely calm about it. He doubted that Mr. Yang or Mr. Li would follow through on the threat to disrupt his investments in Jiangsu, particularly while their families still owned shares in the Suzhou project. Of course, assistance from them on new property deals was now unlikely, but there were other directions for him to go for new business, and things might change. In China, things changed often.

* * *

"Who is your source for this story?" Huang Siyu was sitting at his desk in his tiny office at *Shanghai Weekend*, where he was managing editor. Walter was sitting on a stool squeezed among the piles of paper that took up most of the limited available space in the office. Mr. Huang was smoking a cigarette, the full ashtray wedged in among the papers. It looked as if a stray ash could easily start a fire.

"Mr. Huang, if you promise me that we will not publish information that identifies her, I will describe who she is. I won't give you her name. If that's OK." Walter's biggest journalistic heroes were Bob Woodward and Carl Bernstein, who had broken the Watergate scandal in the United States using information from 'Deep Throat'. He had always admired the protection that they had given their source, and promised himself to do the same for Jasmine. The JZP corruption might not involve the President of the United States, but it was a very good story, and Walter had little trouble imagining himself as Bob Woodward.

Walter expected that he had a large enough store of credit with Mr. Huang to pursuade him to accept some secrecy about his source. Walter had written a series of articles for *Shanghai Weekend* that had been very popular with readers, and Mr. Huang had praised the articles for their accessible writing style and careful research. The two had almost become friends, which was unusual in China for a junior reporter and his experienced boss.

"OK, we can do that. Of course, people may guess the source of the information once we publish an article about it. It does not sound like very many people know about this corruption."

"Yes, maybe that is true, but the identity of my source may be difficult to guess. Anyhow, the source is willing to take that risk."

"OK, fine, and no names. But tell me some more."

"I can tell you that the source is one of the key people who worked on the deal."

"That sounds reliable. Why does this person want to talk? Doesn't he want to protect the deal?"

Both Walter Mr. Huang had referred to the source as *tā*—which can mean either "he" [他] or "she" [她]—and Walter could almost hear the question in Mr. Huang's voice. Walter had no intention of resolving the ambiguity. In fact, he intended to cultivate the impression that the source was a man. "Yes, perhaps, but he also wants to fix the problems on the deal. I guess he thinks that some publicity could help fix the situation. And we made a strong personal connection too."

"OK, it sounds like your source is a risk-taker."

"Yes, I suppose so. Does that bother you?"

"No, not really. It's not up to us to question the behavior of our sources. We often learn the truth for strange reasons. But it tells me to be careful, because we may be in a volatile situation. So tell me again what you will be able to write from what he has told you."

"It is a typical story of property corruption, unfortunately not related to the work I have been doing on destruction of historical buildings. The American investment company discovered that family members of senior officials of the two Jiangsu province ministries—the Ministry of Land and Resources and Ministry of Housing and Urban-Rural Development—are shareholders in the latest JZP development in Suzhou. I have done research, and it appears that the family members have no experience with property development. There is not one-hundred-percent proof, but it seems obvious that the family members' shares are payments for assistance by the officials. We don't have to prove it anyhow. My story will just print the facts and not claim corruption. Our readers can draw their own conclusions."

"Do you know the names of the officials and their family members?"

"Yes, I do."

Mr. Huang was quiet for a short while, while he shuffled some papers from one pile on his desk to another, without looking at them. "OK, I want to run the story. But first you should spend your next week checking all the facts as well as you can, from other sources. I want to see five hundred words by the end of next week. We'll plan to run it in the August twenty-first issue. And we won't print the names of the officials and their families."

Walter protested. "Why such a short story, and why not print their names? My source is very trustworthy. If I find more evidence to support him, can we say more?"

"I don't think so, *Xiǎo Yáng* [Little Yang]." Mr. Huang used a common, affectionate way of addressing a junior co-worker. "This is a dangerous kind of story. Let's start carefully and see what happens. If it attracts the right kind of attention, there will be a chance to say more later."

交易

29

Mending Bridges

mid-August 2009

Hǎo Jiǔ Bú Jiàn [好久不见, Long Time No See]
—*Eason Chan (song title)*

When her mobile rang, April was feeling bored. It was an unfamiliar number. She guessed that the call was from a potential employer or recruitment company—one of the many that she had been writing and calling—and the prospect did not excite her. April had begun looking for work the previous week, as she had promised her mother, but the process had so far been uninspiring and frustrating.

In the depth of the financial crisis, entry-level jobs were thin on the ground—even for a Harvard graduate with good work experience in China, a key market for many California companies. Financial markets seemed to have turned the corner from the panic of late 2008 and early 2009, but companies remained unsure of how bad the economy would get, and no one seemed to be hiring. She had responded to a few promising postings on Monster.com, and had one interview the following week for a job as a documents paralegal at a large law firm. It sounded extremely dull, but was advertised as reasonably well-paid and would give her something to do.

It was early Saturday afternoon. She had slept late, had lunch with her parents, and was half reading the latest Kathy Reichs novel and half daydreaming in the sunny back yard when the call came.

"Hello?"

"Hello, April."

She recognized the voice instantly—Jasmine, but not the soft Jasmine of their call ten days earlier. Yet there was something in Jasmine's voice, even in just the two words, that immediately threw her off balance, and she was slow to respond.

"Hello? April?" Jasmine repeated, when April failed to speak. "It's Jasmine."

"Yes, I know. I didn't recognize your number. It was a surprise to hear your voice."

"Is it OK that I called? This is my mobile phone. I guess I have always called you from work before."

"Of course it's OK that you called. I am really happy to hear from you. To be honest, I am a little bored and it would have been nice to hear from anyone … Actually, that's not what I mean. I am especially happy to hear—"

"April, can you come to San Marino to meet me and Richard?" There was a note of urgency in Jasmine's question.

April was pleased at the prospect of seeing Jasmine, but disappointed that it sounded like the purpose was work. Why Richard? "OK, I guess. I was hoping that you were calling to ask me on a date."

"I want to see you, and this is a good excuse. Sorry, I don't really mean an excuse. It's just that there is still a lot of pressure at work. I told Richard that you are here, and he asked if you could help him understand what is going on at JZP."

"I told you that I cannot tell any more secrets from my family … from JZP. Are you trying to use our friendship for information?" April wondered if her confidence in Jasmine's feelings for her was justified after their last call.

"That's not fair. I am sorry that you think I could be that kind of person." Jasmine's voice rose in mild anger. April wondered how the long-awaited call could be going wrong so quickly—was their relationship cursed? Get real, she told herself, it's not a relationship at all. Jasmine continued evenly, "I don't think you should worry about Richard's questions. I

204

told him that you are an honorable person and loyal to JZP, even if they didn't treat you well. He knows that he cannot ask you for confidential information."

"OK, I guess it doesn't hurt to listen to what he has to say. When did you want to meet?"

"How about around six p.m. today? Or when would be convenient?"

"OK. I don't have any plans," April lied. She had made plans with one of her high school friends, Ellen Wong, to see *Julie & Julia* that evening. Ellen was not an especially close friend, but the prospect of dinner and a movie with her had sounded like a nice break—until Jasmine called. Even the disappointment of a business meaning with Jasmine and Richard was more enticing than more Arcadia boredom. At the very least, it was a connection back to the adventure of Shanghai. "Where shall we meet?"

"Do you mind coming to San Marino? Richard thought that maybe we could meet outside the office, at the tea room at the Huntington Botanical Gardens. Do you know it? It's walking distance from our office."

"Yes, that's a nice place. You're lucky to work near there. And your boss has good taste."

"Yes, he is a good boss. Maybe better than I am an employee. I talked to your friend Walter about *jiāo yì*, and I haven't mentioned that to Richard yet. So please don't bring that up, OK?"

"Right, got it."

"And ... April, I am sorry if I insulted you before. I really do want to see you."

"It's OK. I'll need to ask my mother if I can borrow the car. If you don't hear from me, I'll see you at Huntington Gardens at six."

"I look forward to it." The softer Jasmine was back. Was she one person, or two? "*Zàijiàn*, April. See you soon."

205

"*Zàijiàn*, beautiful Jasmine." It was not until after April had ended the call that she realized that she had spoken aloud the adjective that always described Jasmine in her head.

* * *

The roses in bloom outside the Huntington Gardens tea room matched those on April's dress. She had chosen a floaty summer dress, just above the knee. She knew it wasn't a usual choice for a business meeting, but she didn't work for San Marino and, after what had happened in Shanghai, she didn't feel that she had to be the one always playing by the rules. She wanted to look good for Jasmine.

It had taken April longer than she expected to negotiate use of the car with her mother—who was pleased to hear that April had a work-related meeting, but had to rearrange a long-scheduled hair appointment—and then to shower, and wash and dry her hair, choose her dress (after some deliberation), get dressed, and negotiate the route to San Marino and the Huntington Gardens, which the GPS in her mother's car chose to make unexpectedly circuitous. Despite running from the entry of the gardens to the tea room, she was ten minutes late—and slightly glowing with sweat from the run. She hoped it did not spoil the effect of her freshly-washed hair, although in her good mood it did not worry her much.

Jasmine and Richard were already waiting at a table in the tea room, and rose to greet her, both smiling—Richard's smile open and welcoming, Jasmine's unreadable.

"Ms. Wang, thank you so much for coming."

"Please, call me April, Mr. Gregg."

"OK, please call me Richard. Can I get you something to drink?—we are having iced tea."

"Sounds perfect. But I can get it."

"I wouldn't think of it."

April and Jasmine sat mostly in awkward silence, punctuated by small talk, while Richard bought a third iced tea. Soft Jasmine was gone, and business Jasmine was back. Had she reacted adversely to the way April had ended their telephone call? Mercifully, Richard returned to the table quickly.

"So, April, thanks again for coming. I hope you don't mind if I ask you a few questions about JZP and your uncle."

"I told Richard that you are worried about confidential information," Jasmine said.

"And I promise that I won't ask for any. What I really want to try to understand is your uncle's personality. I sensed that I could trust him, and then it turned out that he was hiding corrupt government payments. It doesn't make sense to me. I thought I was a better judge of character."

"That makes two of us. My uncle and aunt were very good to me in Shanghai. Then the problems came up on *jiāo yì*, and everything changed."

"Hmm. It's hard to say for sure, but I see two likely possibilities that would produce that kind of reaction. He may have been corrupt for a long time—got in the habit of the corruption—and panicked when it finally came back to bite him. Or," Richard paused speculatively, "something happened that shocked him as much as it shocked us. Does either of those stories sound right to you April?"

"I really don't know ... I wish I did."

"Maybe both stories are true."

"What do you mean, Jasmine?" Richard asked.

"Well, corruption is everywhere in China. Maybe Mr. Wang was doing the same petty corruption as everyone else, and it somehow got out of control."

April thought about this. "You know, that has the ring of truth. Before I left Shanghai, Uncle Jun seemed to regret what he had done. He must have had a really strong reason to turn against me like he did. Our family has always been very close."

"Well, do you want to help us figure that out?"

April looked at Jasmine. Richard's question offered an ideal opportunity for Jasmine to explain how April had already helped by making the connection to Walter, but Jasmine failed to seize it. April felt oddly reassured—it was nice to have a secret with Jasmine. "OK, I'll think about it."

* * *

About thirty minutes later, when the conversation at the tea room had clearly run its course, April asked Richard and Jasmine if they needed a ride anywhere. Richard's response was exactly what she hoped for. He told Jasmine that he would walk back to the office to finish some work and suggested that she accept April's offer of a lift home.

In the car, April was unsure which Jasmine was in the passenger seat. It was not soft Jasmine, but neither did it seem to be business Jasmine. She was pensive and inscrutable. April decided to give up trying to figure her out. Anyhow, it was a pleasant distraction from Jasmine's behavior to look at her beautiful legs so nearby, in sheer black pantyhose with a freckle visible near the hem of her short business skirt. "So, where do you live?" she asked.

"Near the 110 Freeway in South Pasadena. Grevelia Street. Do you know it?"

"No, but I can find it on the GPS. How do you spell it?" April typed in the name that Jasmine provided.

As they pulled up to the curb at Jasmine's building, she turned to April and seemed to make a prepared speech. "Thanks for the ride. I have gotten in the habit of hiking in the San Gabriel mountains. It's really nice, and kind of surprising since I have always been a city person. Would you like to come along for a walk with me this weekend?"

"That sounds very nice," April said cautiously.

"Or you could come over to my apartment to watch a movie," Jasmine sped ahead. April noticed that Jasmine was pulling at a lock of hair, and wondered if she was just imagining that Jasmine sounded nervous. "I have been learning about the history of Los Angeles from the movies. I saw *Chinatown* and *L.A. Confidential,* and I really want to see *Sunset Boulevard.*"

"That would be good too. We could also see something like *Swingers*. You should learn about modern L.A.—"

"April," Jasmine cut her off. "How about I make you dinner in my apartment now?"

"I didn't know that you know how to cook."

"There are probably a lot of things that we don't know about each other. Shall we try to start learning?"

"OK." April felt light-headed. She realized she'd stopped breathing briefly.

Jasmine lived in a typical, small, two-story Los Angeles apartment building, built around a central courtyard featuring a modestly-maintained swimming pool. In any other city in the world, a courtyard with a swimming pool would be a sign of luxury, but in Los Angeles it was simply a universal architectural impulse, particularly in the many mid-market apartment buildings built in the 1960s and 1970s. "You live in a nice place."

"It is simple, but I like it. In the spring, the street is very beautiful because all of these plain-looking trees put on a beautiful coat of purple."

"They must be jacaranda trees. It's a big memory of my childhood seeing them bloom every year. It's been a few years since I have been here for that." They had paused on the doorstep, as Jasmine unlocked her door.

"Please come in."

Thinking later about what happened next, April decided that she felt as though Jasmine inhaled her. As soon as she walked into the small living room with its connected kitchen and breakfast counter, and set down her purse on the table, Jasmine came near and gave her a long, passionate, hungry kiss, pressing her body against April's. Then Jasmine took her hand and led her to the bedroom, where she took off her shoes, skirt and blouse, and then urgently stripped April out of her dress.

In the hotel in Shanghai, April had very much been the leader of a hesitant but willing Jasmine. Now Jasmine was still very willing, but this time she was the leader, with a definite plan in mind. She pushed April down gently but firmly onto the bed and began to explore.

Jasmine first ran her hands gently over April's breasts, concentrating on them, looking occasionally at April's face but mostly at her body. "I have been thinking about touching you, April. You have such beautiful breasts."

April was nearly overcome by the surprise of Jasmine's enthusiasm and physical presence, and found herself unable to respond verbally. She understood that Jasmine did not need an answer from her, wanted to explore, wanted to be the leader.

By the time Jasmine started kissing April's stomach, April was very turned on, unable to concentrate much beyond the sensation of each new touch of Jasmine's hands and lips. She noticed with distant surprise that Jasmine, obviously very excited herself, had slipped her left hand inside her own sheer black panties, just as April had done that night in Shanghai.

Jasmine's kisses moved slowly downward, and April's consciousness dissolved almost entirely in sensation. When Jasmine removed April's plain white cotton panties—or almost removed them, leaving them hanging on one of her ankles— the anticipation of what was next was so strong it seemed to have color. Feeling Jasmine's lips and then tongue on her sex was indescribable pleasure.

April simultaneously wanted more and knew she would be unable to bear it for long. As she hovered on the edge, her theme song "April, come she will …" began playing in her head. It occurred to her briefly that this was a surprising time for a silly pun, before she came in a slow, crashing diminuendo. As if from a distance, April thought she heard herself scream as it happened, until she began to return slowly to herself and realized that it had been Jasmine screaming, coming right after April, still touching herself.

When Jasmine too had passed through her orgasm, she fell on top of April. April spoke first. "That was different from our first time. Very different, and better. At least, it was for me."

Jasmine leaned up on her elbows and looked at April intently, with some evident pride. "I was ashamed after being with you in Shanghai that I was so inexperienced. Not just about being with a woman, but about sex. So I have done some studying and practicing. That was not the first time I touched myself." She paused, smiling shyly. "Actually, it has been many times, thinking of you. I certainly have never wanted anything so much in my life."

"You kept me waiting. I wanted it too."

"Yes, sorry. I did not know what to do. So, are we still friends?"

"I hope we are going to be more than friends."

Jasmine smiled again and rolled onto one side. "I have a lot to tell you." She paused and tugged at her hair with a forefinger. "Things have not been easy with *jiāo yì*. I should also tell you more about my conversation with your friend Walter—we have a lot in common. I have told him about the problems with your uncle's company, and I think he may be able to help."

"I see … but you haven't told your boss about that, have you?" April looked at Jasmine seriously.

"No. I haven't."

"Why not?" Jasmine did not respond quickly, and April realized that her question was rather direct. "If you don't mind me asking."

An unusual crease appeared in Jasmine's forehead. "Honestly, I don't know. Maybe it was a mistake."

"Well, you should certainly be careful. Cover-ups can get people into trouble. Like my family in Shanghai with *jiāo yì*. Like that man in Singapore years ago—Nicholas Leeson."

"April! I am not a rogue trader!" Jasmine shoved April gently.

"OK, *OK*. Fair enough. But *please* be careful." April smiled, brightened and changed the subject. "I have to admit that fantastic sex has made me really hungry. Did you mean it when you said you would cook me dinner, or was that just a plan to get me into bed?"

"Well," Jasmine said, suddenly a little shy, her native reticence seeming to get the better of her earlier boldness, "asking you in was definitely part of a plan to get you into bed. But I do also have food to make dinner. I am planning to cook Chinese, because that's what I know how to do. That's not too boring for you?"

"You must be joking. One of the things I miss most about Shanghai is the food. Can I help you cook?"

"Sure. I have a bottle of nice red wine that we can start drinking while we work."

"Thank goodness for red wine."

"What *is* 'thank goodness'? I have never really understood what that means in English. I guess in this case it means you like red wine?"

"Yes, it means that I am grateful for red wine. To be honest, I was worried after our night in Shanghai that it was the red wine, that you being drunk was the only thing that brought us together. I feel better about that now, definitely after this afternoon, but I still think the wine helped."

"It may have helped." Jasmine ran her hand through April's hair, smoothing it back. "Thank goodness for red wine."

交易

30

Another Deal

mid-August 2009

If at first you don't succeed …

"How about we go to Mi Piace for a drink?" This time it was Richard at François' desk.

"So, *mon ami*, in your hardship you are becoming a little bit social, *non?* Of course I will join you for a drink. But we cannot go to Mi Piace."

"Why not? I thought that was your favorite place to meet Pasadena girls."

"Well …" François pulled at his nose. "Do you remember Stephanie?"

"Stephanie." Richard tried to recall where he had heard the name.

"She is the real estate girl we met last time we were at Mi Piace."

"Ah, right. What happened?"

"We … uh … shall I say that she is not very happy with me, and she knows a lot of people who come to Mi Piace. I am not very popular there right now."

"Disaster!" Richard smiled. "What will you do without Mi Piace?"

"Ah, Richard, Richard. You should not tease me. You know it is but a small problem. The world is very big. Even Los Angeles is quite large." François indicated the great expanse of Los Angeles by spreading his arms almost fully. "More than one quarter of the population of France. There are so many places to go. And so many girls. Tell me—what is the occasion for your kind invitation?"

"I have an idea that I want to discuss with you."

"Oh, no. I suppose it must be about work."

"Yes, but I think you will be interested in what I have to say. And I really need to discuss it over a drink, after the stress of the past few weeks. If we aren't going to Mi Piace, how about a little further away? Do you know the Dresden Restaurant in Hollywood?"

"*Mais non*. It is a nice place?"

"I think you will like it. Not a good place to meet girls, but I think you have enough of that anyway." François nodded with a guilty smile. "Can you be ready to go in ten minutes?"

* * *

When they arrived at The Dresden, the well-known house band Marty & Elayne were already performing from their list of covers and jazz. Richard and François were lucky to find an empty booth quickly, and slid into seats upholstered in red leather. François looked around and took to The Dresden's eclectic vibe like a fish to water. He waved for a waitress.

"So what are you drinking? Vodka tonic with a slice of lime again?" François asked Richard.

"Yes. Good memory."

"I may sometimes seem a little carefree, but I pay attention." François ordered for Richard, and the same for himself.

"So tell me about how you got into trouble with Stephanie."

"Bof. We went out a few times, had some drinks, a few laughs. Then we got a bit friendlier. You know how it goes."

"I hardly remember. I've been with Julie for almost fifteen years. And I imagine things have changed."

"Men and women together: it is always the same. We Frenchmen know that. It is one of our advantages."

"I guess you stopped calling her."

"There are so many girls, Richard. They all seem to want to know me. I am a rich investor—a good, how do you say, catch. And of course it helps that I am French, and good-looking."

"And modest."

"I know, not very modest. I get bored very quickly. I want to find someone who is just as immodest as me." He took a long sip of his drink. "And she should not be too interested in me being an investor. And very beautiful, of course. It is quite a difficult challenge, you see."

"Thank goodness it will be quite a few years until I need to warn my daughter Lydia about men like you."

"That is not fair, Richard. I treat women very nicely. I cannot help it that I am handsome, intelligent, rich and a little bit demanding. But this is so boring talking about me. Tell me what you wanted to discuss."

"Yes. Right. You know about the mess with my China joint venture. I've been spending most of my time trying to figure out what to do next. Jane is being fair with her internal investigation of the deal, but very tough. She tells me that the lawyers say we have very little room to maneuver if there is government corruption involved in the deal. And I'm now sure there is corruption—not just what we discovered after closing, but probably other things too. There is no way that JZP built its business without some corruption, and with what we know now there is no way we can move forward without trying to get to the bottom of every bit of it—which JZP would probably never let us do." Richard hesitated, and shook his head. "I still can't believe how blind I was to this risk."

"It does sound like a mess. So what are you planning to do?"

"There's only one answer. Sell it."

"That makes sense. How painful is that going to be for the firm?"

"The interesting thing is that it doesn't have to be very painful. We could make a nice little return. On the numbers, this was a good investment. The deal valuation for the JV was $60 million, or $30 million for our fifty-percent share. But I think our share is easily worth $40 million to the right buyer. There's some confidence coming back into the markets, and the Chinese property market is particularly strong. So far we have only invested $1.5 million and spent half a million executing the transaction. If we spend another half a million on the sale transaction, our total cash investment would be $2.5 million. If I'm right about the sale price, we could get back our $1.5 million investment plus $10 million profit, about four and a half times what we would have invested. Of course, $10 million is nothing like what we hoped to take out of this transaction, but it's a lot better than a black eye." Richard was very enthusiastic when talking about doing a good deal.

"It sounds like you have a plan. But of course it is not so very simple. So I suppose you want to ask me to help you find your buyer?"

"Yeah, you got it. The buyer almost certainly can't be American, because of the corruption problems, and other Western countries are probably out for the same reason. I figured a Chinese company would work, since they would know the market and probably would take some corruption as a matter of course. But JZP doesn't want a Chinese JV partner, and we need their agreement to get out of the deal."

"Of course they don't want a Chinese partner, because they are a family business, and they don't want to share with another Chinese family."

"Now I *am* impressed. How did you know that?"

"Richard, please, I am French. We are very intuitive about emotions." François glanced slyly sideways at his friend.

"OK, great. So what should I do about these emotions that are blocking my plan to save this deal?"

"I have two words for you."

"Two words?"

"*Deux mots*. Two words." François looked around as if for eavesdroppers, put a finger to his lips, leaned in to Richard, and spoke softly. "Hong Kong."

"Hong Kong? I don't know it very well. Jasmine and I stopped through on one of our visits to China."

"Some of the world's great property investors are from Hong Kong. We all know about Li Ka-shing, but there are so many more. When I was working in New York, we did quite a lot of Hong Kong deals."

"So how does that solve my problem? Hong Kong is still part of China."

"Richard, Richard. You know so much about China. I am surprised that I need to educate you about this. The Chinese still regard Hong Kong as something like a different country, almost part of the West. I don't think your friends at JZP would react too badly to the right kind of Hong Kong investor. It might even give them better connections than they thought they were getting in the deal with us."

"Huh. That's good thinking, François. I had the feeling that you were the right person to ask for ideas. So will you help me with a Hong Kong deal?"

"I suppose I would. I am very busy, yet it would be nice to visit Hong Kong again. Will your lovely Jasmine be coming along?"

Richard narrowed his eyes. "Seriously, François, you know how our partners feel about you and the staff. Jasmine does need to come along on any trip to China. Besides understanding the country, and translating, she has turned out to be a super researcher and analyst ... even if she did fall down like I did on identifying the risks at JZP. But in any case, you will keep your hands off her, right?"

"Of course, of course. But she is very nice to watch, *non?*"

"Yes, she is a pretty girl. That seems to help a lot in China. Anyway, she is tough enough to handle you, I think. So ... how do we proceed?"

"Let me make a few calls to some old contacts. I think I should be able to get you meetings at some of the top Hong Kong property companies."

"That sounds great, please go ahead. Let me buy you another drink as a small thanks in advance." Richard looked over François' shoulder and motioned for the waitress.

交易

31

In the News

August 22, 2009

There is no such thing as bad publicity

– P.T. Barnum

In 1997, after JZP had started to achieve major success, Mr. Wang had bought a new BMW 328i for the family. Not so many Chinese owned automobiles at the time, particularly high-end German automobiles, and Mr. Wang was proud to show it off by taking the family on frequent weekend trips around Shanghai and into the surrounding countryside.

Xu had never loved the weekend trips, regarding them as a family obligation that took him away from much more interesting time with his friends. The trips had become less frequent once he had started university, and recently had ceased almost entirely. Since Mr. Wang found it much easier to travel to work on the Shanghai metro, and otherwise used a JZP driver for work, the BMW was now rarely used other than for some of Mr. Wang's Saturday golf outings. It remained in excellent condition, in a garage near the family home.

As the crisis at JZP wore on, Mr. Wang had repeatedly lamented to his wife and to Xu his conviction that the crisis was caused by his own poor judgment in sacrificing principles of sensible Confucian behavior. The same sentiments seemed to be producing a nostalgia for earlier years. So on this Saturday in late August, he had asked Aunt Hong and Xu to join him for their first weekend drive in nearly two years. He seemed to have the feeling that returning to old activities would bring back better times.

Xu had initially objected that he had important all-day plans with friends. When his father insisted, though, he was actually relieved to call Annabelle with a suitable excuse for cancelling the main plan, which was to accompany her shopping near Nanjing Road. After Jasmine had disappeared from the scene, Xu had somewhat rekindled his on-again, off-again affair with Annabelle, but he felt only moderate enthusiasm about it, and certainly not for shopping with her.

The family set out in mid-morning, with Mr. Wang driving and his wife beside him. Both had dressed up more than necessary for the day, in Western-style clothes. Xu was in the back seat, slightly sullen, in blue jeans and a t-shirt. He felt self-righteous pride that he had refrained from complaining aloud during the drive. Mr. Wang had decided that they were bound for Zhujiajiaozhen, an ancient town on the canals to the west of Shanghai, not far from *Diànshān Hú* [定山湖], a large lake further to the west.

The journey of a half hour or so was mainly on nondescript highways that first wove through urban sprawl, which was gradually interspersed with increasing greenery. Reaching their destination without event, and less traffic than usual, the Wang family found what seemed to be a safe place to park the car, near a main road. They set out walking along the old streets and canals looking for a place to have lunch. Wang Jun was contemplative, responding tersely to his wife's chirpy comments about how quickly the old town was changing since previous visits. Xu paid little attention to either the surroundings or his parents, his mobile phone glued to his ear as he complained to friends about being away from the action of Shanghai.

Just before noon, it was Mr. Wang's mobile phone that rang. Aunt Hong and Xu watched as he first listened, then stopped walking, then began to ask a rapid series of questions. By the time the call finished, the color had drained from his face.

"*Bà, shénme shìr?* [Dad, what is it?]" Xu demanded.

"That was *Lǎo Wú*. We need to find a copy of *Shanghai Weekend*. There is an article about JZP."

There was a newsstand at the end of the street where they were walking, with *Shanghai Weekend* on sale. Mr. Wang bought

219

two copies and handed one to his son. Xu knew that his mother would not be insulted to be left out of the men's business, but he could see that she was concerned, and unsure what to do. Her usual approach in times of crisis was to act the mother-hen to either her husband or son, or both, as needed. She usually had some good sense to offer. Yet the latest events had taken her out of her depth. She seemed to realize that comforting her husband would not help.

Xu read the article quickly, and it hit him like a blow to the stomach. Walter! His father read more slowly and carefully while standing beside the newsstand. The older man took a few unsteady steps forward, looked around, and sat down on a nearby bench to finish reading. When he had finished he put his elbows on his knees and his head in his hands. Then he looked up at Xu. "*Xiǎo Xù*, please tell me that this Yang Jiang is not your friend."

"He is not my friend anymore, *bà*. But I know what you are asking. This is the same Yang Jiang that we know. He has betrayed us."

A strange, pained expression passed across the elder Mr. Wang's face. Xu had seen it only once before, in the bar the day his father talked about what had happened in the Cultural Revolution. "How did he learn this information about our business?"

"I don't know, *bà*, but I have an idea. I must admit to you that I am probably involved. I mentioned to Jiang that I had heard about officials trying to get more involved in property deals. I trusted him, and that was a mistake. I didn't confirm that JZP had been involved in this kind of thing—although I believe he guessed that—and I certainly did not give him any of the details in the article. But I introduced Jiang to April, and they became very good friends. I think that she may have given him most of the information."

"How could you tell your friends about the family business?" Aunt Hong found a way to join the conversation, using one of the oldest Chinese-mother tricks of criticizing a child's behavior.

"Xu, your *mà* is correct that you should be more careful. Much more careful. Your life has been easy." Mr. Wang looked around to confirm that no one was near enough to overhear, and spoke softly. "You did not live through what we have seen, the Cultural Revolution and the hard times that followed. You do not understand that our enemies are always out to take advantage of our success, that everything can change in an instant."

"I am sorry, *bà*. I am ashamed, and I know that I have much to learn. Even though you must be very angry at me, I would still like to try to help to fix what I have done."

"I am not angry at you. I *cannot* be angry at you, and not just because you do not yet know all the dangers of business. I should know these things, and it is I who have created the problems that we are facing. I cannot even be angry at April if she is responsible for telling this information. We did not treat her properly, and we deserve no less."

"We do not deserve her betrayal of the family."

"Enough about betrayal, *Xiǎo Xù*. We should not decide what has happened until we know more. Things are very bad, but I have not given up on fixing things, or at least saving our family. I want you to help me with this. First I want to find out whether it is true that April is the source of the information, before we ask her directly. Can you do that?"

"I think so, *bà*. I will do my best."

Despite his father's admonition about lack of experience, Xu had begun to share many of his father's business instincts, and realized that what few advantages he might still have over Walter would be increased by surprise. On the ride home to Shanghai—which took place immediately, all thoughts of a relaxed lunch in Zhujiajiaozhen quickly abandoned—Xu decided to try to confront Walter immediately, at the office of *Shanghai Weekend* in Jing'An. He knew Walter could often be found working there even on weekends.

* * *

Xu began his investigations by calling Mr. Wu, who told him that the article in *Shanghai Weekend* had appeared the previous afternoon, both in print and online. Mr. Wu had learned about it, to his embarrassment, from a long-time friend in the property market who had called to ask if it was about JZP. The pain in the voice of his father's oldest colleague was distinctly audible over the telephone line. Xu felt little sympathy for him after his treason to the family—betrayal seemed to be everywhere.

The article itself described a medium-sized Shanghai property company with investments in Suzhou, Hangzhou and elsewhere. The company had just agreed a joint venture with an American property investment company. The core of the article related a story of corruption involving a new office development in Suzhou, in which family members of government officials held investment interests. It explained that *Shanghai Weekend* had confirmed that the family members had no property investing experience and had never worked for the Shanghai property company.

It was cold comfort that the article had not mentioned JZP or the individuals involved by name. It was impossible for those in the know to draw any other conclusion about the identity of the property company. And Xu knew that it was all too likely that names might be released later. Walter was nothing if not determined. He had not yet been able to uncover real evidence of corruption in his series of articles on property development and historical buildings, and this latest article suggested that the corruption in Suzhou was the same type of behavior that was to blame for taking away his treasured old buildings. The article hinted that the reason for not revealing names was because the paper could not prove corruption, but Xu suspected something else was at work. *Shanghai Weekend* was playing a dangerous political game, waiting for first reactions before challenging senior government officials or a well-connected company too directly. Walter, and his editor, had more guts than he had thought.

Xu thought about the possible next moves in the game with some apprehension, but also with a little hope. In a dangerous game, many things could happen. And *Shanghai Weekend* and Walter were not the only ones with pieces on the board. There was still a chance that he and his family could be among the winners.

Unfortunately, though, his plan to surprise Walter turned out to be unrealistic. The office building housing *Shanghai Weekend* was not one of the newer ones in Jing'An, but security there was extremely tight nonetheless. The article about JZP was far from the most controversial that the paper had published, and they had plainly planned for unwanted visitors. After an effort to go directly to the paper's office on the ninth floor was firmly rebuffed, Xu was forced to resort to a mobile call to Walter.

Walter knew Xu's number, and cut past any initial pleasantries when he answered. "I thought you might call."

"*Might* call? I guess you thought maybe I would just ignore my friend who betrayed me? Well, no such luck for you. Where are you?"

"I am at work."

"Great. I am outside your office now, and I have some questions. Can we take a walk?"

"Oh." From the tone of Walter's voice, Xu realized that he had managed an element of surprise after all. "OK. As I guess you know, we just published yesterday, so I don't have a deadline at the moment. See you downstairs in ten minutes?"

While Xu waited for Walter to emerge from the building, he reflected on their relationship. He could not understand why his old friend had chosen to write the article—even if things between them had recently been difficult. Surely there were thousands of equally good corruption stories floating around Shanghai. This one had fallen into Walter's lap, but it wasn't like him to unthinkingly pick low-hanging fruit. His friend had always had a clear sense of right and wrong. Even if those sensibilities and his crusade against property development had led Walter to be disgusted by evidence of corruption at JZP, Xu found it hard to imagine that Walter would intentionally hurt him, his childhood friend, and completely without advance warning. Xu wanted to know why, just as much as he wanted to find out about the role that April had played.

When Walter appeared, and greeted him with a brusque, "*Wǒmen zǒu nǎr?* [Where are we walking?]," Xu realized instantly that something important had changed, more than just the article. Walter had always been calmer than Xu, and Xu had expected him to show some contrition for writing the article. Instead, Walter met him with a defiant stare.

"Let's walk towards *Jìng'ān Sì* [静安寺, Temple of Peace and Tranquility]?"

"OK." They walked for a short while in silence, which was broken by Walter. "How could you do it, Xu?"

"What are you talking about? I am the one who should be asking that question. *You* published that article—without even warning me about it first."

"You deserve it, Xu. What I am talking about is April. How could your family treat her like that?"

"So that's what this is about. Is she the one who gave you the information for the story?"

"Of course she didn't give me the fucking information. I did try to get it out of her, but April is too honorable to betray her family—even if it's a family that betrayed her."

Walter stormed along, tight-lipped. Xu was partly stung by the rebuke, partly intrigued. If not April …? "Then where *did* you find out?"

"Do you really think I am going to tell you that? A reporter does not disclose his sources, and certainly not to someone untrustworthy like you."

"Walter! Remember to whom you are speaking. We have been friends for twenty years."

Walter checked his pace. "Xu, we are not friends anymore because of what you have done to my friend April!" He paused, and looked thoughtful and a little less angry. "I suppose it sounds a little extreme for me to side with a new friend over an old one like that. The truth is that I am in love with April. She does not love me the same way, and I don't think she ever will, but at least I feel lucky to have her as a friend."

Xu felt his anger slowly melting away. Like his father, he was finding that a deep sadness lay at the heart of the mess they were all making. "Walter. While we are being frank, my father told me today that I am inexperienced, not careful enough, not realizing that I must look out for enemies. And he was right. And … you are right, too. We should have been kinder to April, and we should have run JZP more honestly."

"Thank you at least for admitting that."

Xu acknowledged Walter's response with a nod, as they approached the Buddhist Temple of Peace and Tranquility. The huge, ancient temple, moved to Jing'An nearly eight centuries before from an original site a thousand years older, seemed to command a feeling of calm. They stopped talking as they approached it and entered the central courtyard. They had climbed the steps to the Precious Hall of the Great Hero, and were looking at the huge Buddha, when Xu broke the silence in a whisper. "We are all wrong, my father too. We are not enemies. It is not you who is our family's enemy in this battle with corruption. And you are wrong to try to make me your enemy over the love of a girl, my cousin. Anger and love can both make us do very stupid things. We all need to stick together before we create a massive tide of problems that sweeps away everything we have built together."

"I don't know, Xu. In any case, I have made my choices. This story is bigger than me now, and probably bigger than you and your family. We just need to wait and see what happens." Walter turned and walked out of the hall and down the steps.

Leaving the temple, they headed east along West Nanjing Road, towards the Bund. As they walked past the high-end stores and boutiques, Xu reflected that he was now in the same place where he had originally planned to spend the day with Annabelle. Life changed fast.

Although his feelings were much more charitable towards Walter than they had been an hour earlier, Xu decided to make one more effort to do what he had promised his father. "You really won't tell me who gave you the information?"

"I won't."

"Will you agree not to write another story about us?"

"I can't promise that. If my editor wants to do another story on this, it is going to happen. Either I will write it or another reporter will. Better me than someone else."

"Will you at least agree to warn me before another story is published."

"I don't know if I can do that. Maybe. I'll think about it."

"OK." Xu realized that the conversation was not leading them in any particular direction. "Let's go back."

"Yes."

Whatever slight rapprochement might have occurred on their walk, both Xu and Walter sensed that things had happened that could not be repaired. They walked back to the *Shanghai Weekend* offices in silence.

When they arrived, Walter again broke the silence, less angrily but very briefly. "Goodbye, Xu."

"Goodbye, Walter." Xu reached to shake Walter's hand, and left his arm extended when Walter responded with the same defiant look with which he had greeted him thirty minutes earlier. Eventually, though, Walter raised his hand too, shook Xu's quickly, and turned abruptly to re-enter the building.

交易

32

Hong Kong

August 30-31, 2009

If you're too free, you're like the way Hong Kong is now [2009]. It's very chaotic.

— Jackie Chan

Richard, Jasmine and François took a direct flight from Los Angeles to Hong Kong, arriving on the evening of the last Sunday in August. They checked into The Mercer, a boutique hotel that François had chosen in Sheung Wan, a slightly unpolished district, but not far from Central where the offices of Hong Kong's banks and investment firms are clustered.

As on Richard and Jasmine's last visit, they quickly changed clothes and headed up Victoria Peak—this time with François, and not as tourists. Their destination was a stylish penthouse apartment in one of the towers of the Mid-Levels. The apartment belonged to Edouard Boucher, an old friend of François' father who had left France in his early twenties, in frustration during the turmoil of 1968. The wealthy, conservative Boucher family, even its young scion Edouard, had had no sympathy with the students who took to the streets of Paris that year. In Hong Kong, he had married a Chinese woman, and made his own fortune to add to the already substantial inheritance that later came to him from his family.

Edouard had seemed delighted in equal measure, François said in their taxi on the way to dinner, to offer a welcoming dinner to his old friend's son and to hear about the deal that brought him to Hong Kong. He cautioned Richard and Jasmine not to ask Edouard and his wife about children—they had had one son who died suddenly of meningitis in his teens. He added that the couple "knew everyone in Hong Kong".

227

Although Edouard and François spoke to each other partly in French, the dominant flavors of the evening were British and Hong Kong Chinese. The Boucher apartment was furnished in the style of the British Empire which had built Hong Kong. The wood-paneled walls and brocaded curtains would not have looked out of place in Mayfair. Oil portraits and paintings of clipper ships competed for space on the walls. It appeared that the Bouchers wanted to advertise a connection to British culture instead of their own backgrounds—perhaps the reason lay in the absence of evidence of the Bouchers' son on the crowded walls.

Edouard's wife May—a beautiful, poised Chinese woman who had become a successful property investor in her own right, and a fixture on the Hong Kong charity circuit—joined them for drinks before dinner in the formal sitting room. Looking around the room as she settled on a nicely-upholstered sofa, Jasmine was interested by a large picture on the wall that seemed out of place with the rest of the décor. It was a large black and white photograph of an older man with a priest's collar and neatly combed grey hair, looking seriously but genially at the camera. After accepting a second glass of red wine, Jasmine decided to ask about it.

"Ah, Miss Liu, you have noticed something very important to us. That is Pierre Teilhard de Chardin. He is a French philosopher and priest who spent many years in China. He wrote about the Omega Point, the direction toward which the universe evolves in complexity and consciousness. I was very interested in his ideas when I came to Hong Kong, and they became the reason that May and I are together." Edouard looked at his wife.

"Yes." May took up the explanation as if rehearsed. It was evidently a story that the two had related in the same way many times before. "My family lived on the mainland until the Chinese Revolution, and my grandmother worked with Teilhard de Chardin in Beijing in the 1930s. It was a point of pride for her when I was a child. Although I didn't know very much about his ideas, the connection was enough for me to start a conversation one day with a young man sitting across from me in a crowded noodle shop, reading a book by Teilhard de Chardin. That was in 1972, when I was eighteen years old. The young man, of course, was Edouard."

"Yes, it was rather bold for a young Chinese woman to speak to a foreigner in the Hong Kong of 1972. Of course, I fell in love immediately." Edouard look at May with genuine affection, and she nodded modestly.

Jasmine had sometimes heard from her parents and colleagues that Hong Kong Chinese were very different, and seeing May Boucher made her realize what they meant. Jasmine had never seen a woman sit so perfectly between East and West. The tension that Jasmine had felt between her roots and her current life suddenly felt light rather than heavy—as though it might be an opportunity. Was she clever enough to seize it, she wondered? If she did, would she be lucky enough to build a beautiful life like the one that the Bouchers had, one that could remain successful, perhaps even happy, through tragedy?

The meal was a magnificent display of Cantonese cuisine, served by two young Chinese women who were, in a memorable display of old-fashioned standards, dressed in the uniforms of traditional English maids, and discreetly managed by May. Edouard wasted little time in steering the dinner conversation to business.

Much of the discussion centered on the three potential investment firms whom the San Marino team would be meeting the next day. The firms had been selected from a longer list of about a dozen that François had recommended. Jasmine had approached the investors on the long list to gauge their interest in buying out San Marino's from the JZP joint venture—just as she had done in her initial search for potential partners for *jiāo yì*. With the issues facing the JV, this work required considerable delicacy, and Jasmine had once again impressed Richard with her effectiveness, and gone some way to redeeming her earlier errors.

François discussed his past dealings with the three firms, and Edouard and May contributed a wealth of detail, surprising even François with the depth of their knowledge of the Hong Kong investment community. The firms were very different. One was the property investment subsidiary of Jensen Michaels, a century-old conglomerate that had been set up by British traders in the early years after the British lease of Hong Kong. The second was the family investment office that pooled capital from three wealthy Hong Kong families. The third was a medium-sized investment fund with the very generic name Asia Capital Partners, established by a group of experienced Hong Kong Chinese investors who had previously worked at global investment banks.

"What we hope," Richard said, as a course of *gūlū ròu* [sweet and sour pork] with white rice was being cleared, "is that we can generate some competition between these firms, and get as good a price as possible. And if we need to speak with others to generate the right degree of interest, we'll do that."

"Yes, but?" Edouard asked.

"But what?" said Richard ingenuously. Jasmine wondered if he was playing dumb. It seemed fairly obvious to her where Boucher was going.

"Come now. Every selling investor wants to generate competition and get a good price. Why are you stating the obvious? And why do you want to sell so soon after you have done this deal? It is obvious to me that you have some problem. So what is it?"

Richard looked at François, who gave a sort of I-told-you-so shrug, then back at Edouard.

"Are we so obvious, Edouard?" Richard explained the small firestorm that had been brewing over the *Shanghai Weekend* article, also relating a few recent conversations with Mr. Wang about the article. There had been no more serious shocks since it was published, but the Shanghai property market was full of whispers about the article and *jiāo yì*. Mr. Wang had reported that the Suzhou officials had refused to meet to discuss the article, and that he was unsure whether to interpret their refusal as continued unwillingness to change their families' participation, paralysis in the face of indecision, or something else.

"Well, that is certainly a problem." Edouard looked disappointed, and then started to tell an intricate story regarding a recent society scandal in Hong Kong. Perhaps dulled by the wine and food, Richard did not think too much of this change of topic at the time, assuming that Edouard had seen a connection between their problems and the scandal closer to home. But from the perspective of the following afternoon, he wondered whether Edouard had simply concluded that their *xīn jiāo yì* was doomed to failure, and not worth any more of his valuable attention.

* * *

The next morning, Richard, François and Jasmine took the short walk along Queen's Road from Sheung Wan to Central, where their first meeting was with Jensen Michaels. The tall office buildings ahead of them were not too different from those in Shanghai, but everything else was entirely different—the landscape, the people, the excitement that was mixed with a feeling of greater permanence. The buildings on the street were mostly older than those in Shanghai, and the crowded alleys climbing from it still had the unselfconscious busy-ness of a former British trading post.

"This place is so different from mainland China," Richard observed. "I always assumed that Hong Kong would feel familiar to someone who knew even a little of China, but it doesn't. A mix of China with the West, perhaps some of London and New York, and who knows where else. I saw some of that when Jasmine and I were here briefly a few months ago, but last night really opened my eyes."

"*Mais oui!* That is what I told you when we had drinks at that funny bar in Hollywood, *n'est-ce pas?* Jasmine, you should have shown this to your boss last time you were here. He could have been more prepared for his little disaster."

"Sorry, I should have been a better tour guide." Jasmine was smiling because she knew François was mostly joking. She and François had quickly developed a good, relaxed relationship on the trip, based heavily on her playing along with François' gentle teasing of her and Richard.

231

Jensen Michaels' offices were on the top floors of one of the taller buildings in Central. As he looked up at the tower, Richard spoke energetically, "OK, team. Let's let them know how good this deal is. If they ask the tough questions about our Suzhou problems and the *Shanghai Weekend* article, we just answer them clearly, and then bring them back to the investment case. François, you know these guys, so you can take the initial lead and then let me run with our presentation. OK?"

"Yes, Doc. That's the plan I assumed." Richard registered that François seemed a little nervous. He hadn't realized that François was capable of being nervous, but decided not to ask.

After a fast ride up accompanied by noticeably uninspiring elevator music, they were ushered from the traditionally furnished reception into a modern conference room with excellent views across the water to Kowloon. The receptionist offered tea or coffee—which they all declined, choosing sparkling water. They did not have to wait long until their host arrived. Miles Lancaster was a tall, ruddy, English expat in a pinstripe suit, suspenders and a bold yellow tie. A younger Chinese man and woman followed him closely, the differences in their heights momentarily giving Richard the odd, and clearly wrong, impression that they were hiding behind him.

"François! So nice to see you again."

"Yes, Miles. It has been quite a long time since the Paris deal, *non*?"

"It has. That was a good deal. We'll always have Paris, won't we?"

"Ah, your English sense of humor has not been blunted by all this time in Asia."

"I suppose not. So you must be Richard Gregg and Jasmine Liu."

"Good to meet you in person, Miles." Richard and Miles shook hands. "I am looking forward to our discussion."

"Good to meet you, Mr. Lancaster." Jasmine too shook hands with Miles.

"Let me introduce my colleagues," Miles said after they had arranged themselves around the conference table. "Thomas Li is our lead portfolio manager. Jane Cheung manages our eastern China commercial property portfolio. If you don't mind, let's get right down to business." For a British investor in China, Miles had an unusual directness, almost like an American.

"Certainly, we have a lot to tell you," Richard responded.

"Well, to be honest, this may be a short meeting." Miles leaned back in his chair, as if trying to distance himself from the impact of what he was about to say. "Things have changed since I last spoke with you, Richard, and I think you probably know what I mean." He leaned back in and looked at Richard, and then François.

"I assume you're talking about the article in *Shanghai Weekend*," François said. "So let's talk about it, Miles. That is one of the reasons that we are here."

"OK. That article wasn't news in Hong Kong, but it turned up immediately when we started our research this week. Thomas and Jane," he motioned towards his colleagues, "tell me that it's the talk of the Shanghai property market. Put simply, we cannot even think about this investment until you clean up that mess. We can be bold in taking on an investment risk, but we are a rather conservative institution, and nothing makes us run faster than the scent of scandal."

"Shall we tell you more about the joint venture and its investments?" Richard asked.

"Can you give us an explanation of how the Suzhou problem happened, and how you are planning to fix it?"

"We're working on that. I can't tell you that we have all the answers yet. But we still think there is a strong investment case, with the understanding that any deal would be conditional on satisfying your concerns."

"Let me be blunt, Richard, and I'll give you credit by assuming that you are not trying to trick me into buying a lemon. You are an experienced investor, so you know that people like us have many places to invest our money. I know

233

you have come all the way to Hong Kong, but I am not going to waste my team's time on your deal if it's impossible. Frankly, I am surprised that we didn't hear about the article from you before you came here. That could have saved us all some time."

Miles had gotten more vehement as his little speech continued. Richard understood that defensiveness would not help in the difficult uphill battle that he suddenly faced, yet he saw no choice but to try to explain himself. "I told you the reason we are talking to you is that there are ownership problems with one of the JV's investments, and that we are looking for a Chinese partner to help manage them. That's what the article is about."

"It's not the same thing, Richard." Miles was looking even ruddier than when he entered. "Quiet problems with a deal are not unusual in China. A *public* scandal is."

"OK, maybe we made a mistake not to tell you about it. So you said you can't talk about the deal until we clean up the mess. What do you mean by 'clean up'? And are you saying that you might still be interested if we do clean it up?"

"I don't know, and I don't know. You just told me that you don't even fully understand the problem. So do that first, then figure out how to fix it. Once you think you have done so, tell us about it, and we will decide whether we are interested."

"OK, that's clear enough. We won't waste any more of your time now."

"Apologies, but that's the way it has to be. We appreciate you thinking of us as investors, and we appreciate you flying to Hong Kong to visit us. How about I take the three of you to lunch later, and we can get to know each other better?"

"Thanks, Miles. We'd like that, as long as it's an early lunch. We have two other investor meetings this afternoon."

"Sure, we can have lunch at noon." Miles smiled. "Hopefully we'll still have time to share a bottle of wine."

"I usually try not to drink with lunch," Richard said seriously, as François raised his eyebrows.

"Your choice, of course," Miles said, "but I think you may need it. If your other investor meetings are about the same deal as this one, I think you will find a similar reaction. Everyone seems to know about that article."

* * *

Miles was correct. The teams at the family office and Asia Capital Partners were not quite as blunt as Jensen Michaels had been, but the bottom line was the same. No one would touch the San Marino-JZP joint venture until the scandal created by the *Shanghai Weekend* article had abated.

Leaving the last meeting and walking back towards their hotel, the mood of the San Marino team was funereal. Richard and François discussed what to do next. They had allowed another day in Hong Kong for follow-up meetings, which were now not needed, and possible meetings with other investors, which now seemed not worth pursuing.

Asking for a restaurant recommendation at the front desk of The Mercer, François learned that there had been a cancellation that evening at Sushi Yoshitake, a tiny restaurant on the ground floor of the hotel. It was one of Asia's best and most expensive sushi restaurants, featuring a chef who had earned three Michelin stars at his restaurant in Tokyo's Ginza district. Offered a good (but still expensive) deal to take three open places at the sushi bar, they decided to forego a planned evening at a popular Cantonese restaurant, and instead to lick their wounds and plan a way forward in the restaurant's austere Japanese environment.

"That was not a good day," Richard said after they were seated at the sushi bar. He was not in the habit of stating the obvious, but was unsure where else to start.

"No, Richard, it was not. I thought that my good contacts in Hong Kong would be able to help us, but I am not a magician."

"Did you expect such a negative reaction to the article?"

"Not so much before we arrived in Hong Kong, but last night before we left Edouard Boucher pulled me aside and said that he thought we should expect serious problems. I didn't

235

mention it because I didn't want to upset our little team based on an opinion. But Edouard is usually correct about Hong Kong business."

"Damn it!" Richard said quietly. "We were so close to a solution. I wish I knew how *Shanghai Weekend* learned so much about our problems. Jasmine, what do you think? Could someone at JZP have spoken up to give them more leverage?"

Jasmine was feeling sick to her stomach, and hoped that Richard and François did not notice her distress. She was glad that she was wearing make-up—otherwise, she imagined that she would have been white as a sheet. The best that she could manage in response was, "No, I don't think so." She was grateful that Richard did not ask her why she doubted JZP's involvement.

When Jasmine had spoken to Walter, she had not expected the article to have much of an impact, much less create a major scandal. She wondered again why she had not asked Richard before speaking to Walter. Although she was unsure how much of the article came from her information, she knew that she was an important source.

Jasmine liked to think of herself as an honest person, and wrestled with the possibility of admitting now to Richard and François that she had been the key source for the article. It felt like her last chance to do so. But they might fire her immediately, and surely they would completely lose trust in her, particularly given her earlier mistake of not revealing her suspicions about JZP to Richard. That first mistake had led to the mess that they were in, and now she seemed to have made another mistake that was preventing them from getting out of it. Nothing would be gained by honesty now.

"My plan for *xīn jiāo yì* is not working," Richard said despondently as he contemplated the chunk of abalone on a small plate in front of him. "What can we do? I am starting to think we should just cut our losses and walk away from this deal completely."

"*Mon ami*, you must not give up. We must think about what it means to clean up this deal. Surely it is JZP who know how

236

best to do that, and they have more incentive to do that even than we do. They won't be able to walk away from thirty million dollars of properties, nor from the Chinese banks who are financing those projects. What leverage do we have with JZP?"

"I don't know. Mr. Wang has not been saying much." Jasmine's decision to keep her secret made her think of April, as she did frequently. April was the only person with whom she had ever really been open, which had been a tremendous relief. She realized that her reserve had long been a significant burden. As if reading her thoughts, Richard asked, "Jasmine, do you have any ideas? What about Mr. Wang's niece? Didn't you become friends with her?"

Jasmine felt herself blush, a very unusual reaction for her, and hoped again that Richard and François did not notice her strange behavior. "She lost her job because of what happened, Richard. Don't you remember?"

"Yes, I remember what Mr. Wang said. But I thought you might know more."

"Actually, I do. She moved back to Los Angeles and has been in touch with me."

"What has she told you?"

"Nothing, really. She just suggested that we get together, since we had started to be friends in Shanghai." Jasmine wondered why she was lying again. Surely she could have passed on part of what April had told her without revealing her role in the article. Her narrative of herself as an honest person seemed to be developing serious holes. "I will contact her and see whether there is anything she can tell me."

"Thanks, Jasmine. At this point, anything you can think of is worth trying."

交易

33

In Danger

September 4, 2009

Never was anything great achieved without danger
– Niccolo Machiavelli, 'The Prince'

The offices of *Shanghai Weekend* were quiet—despite the recent excitement, it felt like any other Friday. After the interest generated by the first article on the JZP deal, and the absence of any overt political reaction to it, the paper was considering a more detailed article, likely naming names, and Walter had been working on it. Even though there was not going to be any article this week, and Walter was freed from the usual Friday article deadline, he stayed at the office until nine p.m. working on research.

After he left work in the early evening, Walter took the Shanghai Metro home as usual to the flat where he had grown up and where he now still lived with his mother. Unlike Xu, Walter, as a modestly paid journalist, had not yet moved into a place of his own, and was saving money for it. Getting married was not his immediate priority—indeed he had not thought much about it until he met April. He knew that in today's China, he would be unlikely to attract a desirable wife without owning a flat. Certainly his mother impressed this idea upon him. It was hard to escape the social demands of modern Chinese society, even for an iconoclast like Walter.

Walter and his mother lived in Jiading, a northwestern suburb of Shanghai at the end of line 11, one of the newer lines of the Metro. The walk from West Jiading Station to his flat passed initially through a commercial area that was nearly empty when Walter left the station at ten p.m. His mind was full of his research on JZP as he walked the familiar route home.

The hard blow to his head was totally unexpected. He found himself lying on the ground in a pool of shadow next to a building, and wondered why he was there. Then he registered the pain on the side of his head. Then he felt the sharp pain of a hard kick in his ribs, and one that glanced off his arm and caught him in the stomach, doubling him up.

Walter had never been beat up before. Muggings were very rare in Shanghai, even in a suburb like Jiading. Not knowing what to expect, he tensed for further blows, closing his eyes. When nothing came for a few seconds, he opened them and saw two men standing close to him. Both were medium height, wearing identical grey hooded sweatshirts, and face masks of the kind used to protect against pollution, covering their mouths and noses. Nearly impossible to identify.

While Walter was deciding whether it was wise to try to stand up, one of the men bent down close to him and whispered in his ear. "*Wŏmen bù yào hái dú wén zhāng.* [We don't want to read any more articles.]" When Walter did not respond, the speaker repeated himself, louder and more insistent. "*Wŏmen bù yào hái dú wén zhāng. Míng bái le ma?* [Did you understand?]"

"*Wŏ tīng le.* [I heard you]." Walter responded with effort, hardly able to breathe from the kick in the stomach. He realized with shock not only that this was not a random mugging, but that his assailants had taken great care to plan the attack. They knew where he lived, and where he could be attacked without attracting attention. Someone had probably watched him at work today so that they knew when he would be home, or else these men had been very patient. They were not patient now.

The man who had not yet spoken delivered another hard kick in his ribs, and Walter cried out in pain.

"*Míng bái le ma?*" The speaker asked again.

"*Hăo de. Wŏ míng bái.* [OK. I understand.]"

"*Xiè xie.* [Thank you.]" There was a sneer in the assailant's voice. He leant down close again and repeated his earlier statement: no more articles. The two attackers got on a motorcycle and roared away. With effort, Walter turned his head slightly and looked after them. Not surprisingly the motorcycle had no number plate.

Walter lay on the ground after the men had disappeared, and took stock of his injuries. After deciding that none were too serious, he struggled to his feet and considered what to do. The obvious decision was to continue home. But he did not want his mother to see his bruises, at least not until he had some time to think about what had happened. So he turned around and limped back towards the Metro station. He decided to head back towards Shanghai, to the Lucky 8 Bar. He needed the comfort of the place where he had spent so much time with April. And he really needed a drink.

* * *

At eleven on a Friday night, the Lucky 8 Bar was crowded. Walter managed to find a space at the end of the bar and asked the bartender, whom he had known for years, for a double vodka. He settled in to drown himself in a pool either of liquor or of sorrow.

Things looked bleak. There seemed two likely groups of people who could be responsible for the beating—both groups that he had attacked in his article, although not yet by name. It had to be either the corrupt officials from Suzhou, or JZP and the Wang family. Did it really matter either way? The corrupt rich of China always seemed to win, and he had little doubt that there would be no punishment for those who had attacked him.

Walter also realized that the loss of April's presence had hit him harder than he had yet admitted. He had convinced himself that he had accepted that April liked girls … and that she was in love with Jasmine. The truth, though, was that he was still in love with April. The memory of her soft kiss on the day of their farewell was frequently on his lips, and his mind.

240

He asked himself where his life was going. He was pining after a girl who would never love him, working in a low-paid job, tilting at windmills ... worse than that. Fighting with forces that were stronger than him, and that had proven that they were willing to do him harm without scruples. And, really, what was he trying to accomplish? These forces of corruption were the same people who were building the new China, lifting millions of people out of poverty, creating a new consumer economy.

What was the use?

Walter was finishing his third vodka, well on his way to being drunk, when he felt a hand on his shoulder. He recoiled as he turned, still jumpy from the attack.

"Hello, Walter."

Walter rubbed his eyes. "Xu? What the hell are you doing here?" Xu was with Annabelle, who looked distinctly out of place in her Ann Taylor dress, Hermès scarf and Jimmy Choo heels. To Walter's mildly inebriated stare, she looked like a model who had been parachuted into the Lucky 8 Bar from the pages of *China Vogue*.

"Are you drunk, Walter? Why shouldn't I be here? Lucky 8 Bar is our place. Although, to be honest, I'm not entirely sure why I'm here tonight. Annabelle didn't want to come. We were out at a late dinner at a boring restaurant, and I was thinking about how everything has gone crazy with my family. This seemed like a good place to start getting back to basics."

"Go 'way," Walter said. He realized that he was slurring his speech and drew himself up. "Why the hell are you talking to me? Do you want to tell me again to leave your family alone? You don't think those thugs this evening were enough of a message?"

"You *are* drunk. What are you talking about?"

"I was just got beat up. By two thugs, on a motorcycle."

"What? Round here?" Xu's surprise seemed genuine. Through the fog of alcohol, that message was important. Walter knew that Xu was too arrogant to be a good liar. "Are you OK?" Xu and Annabelle asked at the same time. Annabelle was looking increasingly alarmed at the direction that the conversation was taking. She glanced around the bar, as if she thought Xu's attackers might have followed him.

"Yeah. Mostly. Just a few bruises. I think they just wanted to scare me."

"*Gǒupì!* [Shit!] These people you are writing about are powerful, Walter. It is risky to challenge them. I am sorry that you got hurt."

"Actually, now I'm relieved. I thought your family might have something to do it."

Xu stared at him. "I'm disappointed that you would think that. Anyhow, at least it's obvious now that you need to stop writing things that make the situation worse."

"No!" Walter shouted. Seeing Xu had jolted him out of his downward emotional spiral. He suddenly felt very sure that he needed to keep to the course that he had been following. "I won't give in, Xu. And you shouldn't want me to. If your family is as honorable as you claim that it is, then you should be fighting right alongside me. If we give in, the corrupt officials win."

A shadow of anger flickered across Xu's mouth and then vanished. "So what are you going to do?"

"Ah, I don't know yet. I need to talk to some people, make a few calls. But, don't worry, I will do what you asked, give you some warning before anything important happens. You were right, we need to work together."

"Thank you, Walter. And if you decide to do something crazy, will you let me try to convince you to change your mind?"

"Don't worry, Xu. I won't do anything *really* crazy. At least not by my standards." For the first time in weeks, Walter allowed a smile onto his face. "Would you and your beautiful friend care to join me for another drink?"

Xu looked at Annabelle, who nodded with slightly pursed lips. "Annabelle was very brave to come to a place like this."

Xu was gently teasing, but not entirely—several men had been leering at Annabelle as they spoke, and Xu had kept her close with his arm around her waist. It was the first time that Walter had seen him be visibly affectionate to her. "So what are you drinking? *I'm* buying."

交易

34

On the Edge

September 5, 2009

We live on the edge of the miraculous every minute of our lives

– Henry Miller

At around the same time that Xu and Annabelle found Walter at the Lucky 8 Bar, Jasmine and April were waking up together in Jasmine's apartment. Jasmine had arrived back from Hong Kong late on Tuesday, and had put off seeing April until Friday night, saying that she needed to work full-time on the a deal and catch up on sleep.

On Friday, April had been distracted all day, eager to see Jasmine. They had met twice more after the Huntington Gardens day, before Jasmine left for Hong Kong, and it had felt to April that they were on the edge of a real relationship. But there had been something odd in Jasmine's voice when she called on Wednesday morning. Was the girl's mood never stable for more than a day or so? April knew that she might have to get used to this. The cool Jasmine whom she had first met was clearly a veneer laid over seething emotions, ones that Jasmine herself did not seem to understand.

April had finally found a job, working as an analyst at a small investment advisory firm in downtown Los Angeles. She was to start on the following Tuesday, after Labor Day. So on Friday, on the last weekday of her chaotic summer, she found herself at loose ends, waiting for Jasmine. They had agreed that she would pick Jasmine up at work, for a cheap and cheerful Mexican dinner in downtown Pasadena. April had again borrowed her mother's car. She'd mooched about, not getting anything much done, and finally the hour for departure had rolled round.

The evening that followed had been pleasant—Jasmine was distant but friendly—and when they returned to Jasmine's apartment she had invited April in for tea without hesitation. The girls had cuddled in bed, but Jasmine did not seem interested in greater intimacy, and April had not pushed the issue. April slept soundly, and awoke with a new determination to make things work, which was reinforced by the sight of Jasmine's face inches away from her, peaceful in sleep.

"Good morning, beautiful!" April enthused when Jasmine opened her eyes. "It's another beautiful Southern California day!"

"Good morning, April." Jasmine's tone was guarded, distant like the previous evening and less friendly. April's spirits fell immediately.

"Is everything OK?" When Jasmine did not respond, she knew that it was not. After waiting a full thirty seconds for a response, April said, "Please tell me about it. I'm having a little trouble riding the Jasmine Liu emotional roller-coaster. It would help me to understand what is going on inside your head."

"Sorry, April. I am confused."

"Confused about … whether you want to be with me?"

"No. I know I want to be with you so much, and I am confused what that means. Well … Richard and François and I met a beautiful older married couple in Hong Kong, and it got me thinking whether that's what I should be seeking. I can't imagine what my parents would think about me being with a girl. They already think that it is time for me to get married …" Jasmine shook her head, and closed her eyes as if in pain.

"Look, Jasmine, just to be clear, I am not asking you to marry me and I am not even asking for a long-term commitment … yet. What I want is to find out what a normal relationship with you is like. Do you think you can do that?"

Jasmine opened her eyes and looked luminously into April's. "April, I want to have sex with you."

April's physical reaction to this declaration was sufficient to distract her from the fact that Jasmine had performed another emotional somersault without offering any answer to April's question. But how was she expected to resist Jasmine? She was moving toward this beautiful woman who wanted her when her mobile rang.

"Don't answer it," Jasmine said.

April surprised herself with an impressive act of will, supported by the desire to show some slight independence from Jasmine's whims. She turned away from Jasmine and picked up the mobile from the night table. "It's Walter!" She quickly calculated. "It's one in the morning in Shanghai. I think I should at least find out why he is calling. Then you can have me." She smiled at Jasmine, feeling satisfied to have exercised some self-control, and answered the call.

"Hi, Walter!" April tried her best to suppress her most recent emotions, and to sound bright and cheerful as she had felt when she woke up.

"Hi, April. It's great to hear your voice. I needed that."

"Yes, great to hear your voice too." April wondered why Walter needed to hear her voice. That did not sound like him.

"Is this an OK time to talk? It doesn't sound like I woke you up. I know it's Saturday morning and you like to sleep on the weekends, but it's already ten o'clock there, right?"

"I'm wide awake. But, well, actually, I am not at home. I am at … um … I am at Jasmine's apartment. She's here with me, actually."

"Wow, April! Congratulations, no wonder you sound so happy." April was pleased that she had hidden her bleaker emotions from Walter.

"I think she can hear you, Walter."

"I want to hear all about it later. I really need your advice now, though. Uh, I got beat up, over the article—"

"—What! Are you OK?"

"Yes, just a few bruises."

"Oh my god, Walter! What happened?"

"A couple of thugs on a motorcycle jumped on me near my mother's house last night. In a dark spot. Someone planned carefully."

"That's really awful and frightening. Do you mind if I put on the speaker phone so Jasmine can listen? This is her problem too."

"OK. I guess we are all in this together."

April pushed the speaker button, and laid the mobile down on the bed between her and Jasmine. "OK, we are all here."

"*Nǐ hǎo, Jiāng,*" Jasmine offered, without any of the emotion in April's voice.

"*Nǐ hǎo,* Jasmine.*"*

"OK, so what advice do you want, Walter?" April asked. "How can we help?"

"Well, the guys who beat me up said 'no more articles'. Xu thinks I should listen to them. But I really don't want to give up this fight. Getting beat up actually makes me feel all the more determined to do the right thing. But what do you think I should do? I think I want to publish another article, this time naming JZP and the officials in Suzhou. I have been working on it and I think my editor will agree to publish it next week."

Jasmine gasped and sat up. "Your first article has already gotten me into trouble too. I mean, you have to do what you think is right, of course, but because of the publicity, San Marino can't sell its share of the JV to a new buyer." Then, she seemed to realize that she was digging herself a deeper hole. She pulled at her hair. "You won't publish *that* information, will you?"

"Not if you tell me not to."

"Have you totally made up your mind to publish the second article, Walter?" April was torn between protecting Jasmine and protecting Walter.

"I don't know."

April felt that she needed to do something. The situation was out of control. "OK, it was me who started this mess that night when Jasmine and I ... well, you know ..." She blushed.

"This is not your fault, April. This is about corruption in China. It does a lot of damage. It is what I am fighting against."

"Whatever, Walter. I played a role in making this mess, and so far I've just been sitting around watching it happen. Now I'm going to do something to fix it. I'm the only one who really knows everyone involved—except those government officials, of course. Can you give me a few days to figure some things out? I need to talk to my Uncle Jun."

"My publication deadline for the article is next Friday. That gives you six days."

"OK, I'll call you in a day or two. Please try not to get beat up again. Be careful!"

"I'll certainly do my best. Bye, April."

"OK, *please* be careful. Bye, Walter." April hung up. "Poor Walter!"

"Poor Walter. I hope he will look after himself OK. And I guess we should look after each other, too."

Jasmine came closer, intending to continue what they had started, but April gently held her away. "Sorry, Jasmine, but I want to think about where I am going with this mess, and with you. It's a beautiful day. Shall we go to the beach? I always think more clearly there—it feels like you can see to the edge of the world."

* * *

On the coast of Los Angeles, just north of the main public beach in Santa Monica, the 10 Freeway from downtown hits the coast and turns northwest to become the Pacific Coast Highway. From that point, the beach is separated from the town of Santa Monica by cliffs that rise up from the road. Between the top of the cliffs and Ocean Avenue lies Palisades Park, a long, thin, manicured park with paths running among palm trees, plants and benches.

After calling her mother to confirm that she could keep the car for the day, April drove with Jasmine to Santa Monica. Walking from the car and through Palisades Park, they drew a few stares, from both men and women. When Jasmine asked her about this, April thought about whether it was because they were two beautiful young women or because they were walking hand-in-hand. She told Jasmine that it was probably both. They chose a bench in the park, and sat with the Pacific Ocean laid out before them at its best, glittering blue on the sunny, almost windless, September Saturday afternoon.

"It all looks so peaceful from here—but it's not!" Jasmine's latest mood seemed resentful. "A long way across that water is China, where it is not peaceful. Not just not peaceful for us now. It's always true in China. People are always struggling for something. The more time I spend in America, the less I want to live in China."

"I think you are being too negative. China is doing great things. I'm an American, but I'm proud to be Chinese. And people are struggling here, as well."

"I'm very proud too to be Chinese, but I don't like what China has become. The great Chinese culture has turned into a society that is all about money."

"That's funny. I said the same thing to Xu not long after I arrived in China. But even if that's right, I'm not so negative about it any more. Maybe this is a natural cost of the changes that have made China great again. As Paul McCartney and Stevie Wonder said: there is good and bad in everyone."

"I know that song. *Ebony and Ivory*, right?"

"Yes, my parents used to play a lot of music from The Beatles and Paul McCartney. You know a lot about American music." April smiled at Jasmine, who visibly brightened as the topic moved away from the problems across the water. Aware of this, April was still determined to steer the conversation back in that direction. "Anyway, let's stop talking philosophy and pop music. Right now, we need a plan."

"Yes, that's what I have been thinking about at work. But rather than solving things, I seem to be making them worse.

The information I gave to Walter for his article has made our *xīn jiāo yì* impossible. And the article caused Walter to be attacked." Jasmine looked rueful.

"Yes, it's not good. I've been blaming myself too, for telling you about the problem in the first place. But the corruption itself isn't our fault. San Marino would certainly have found out about it later, and maybe the newspapers would too. And Walter already knew about the problem before he spoke with you."

"You're right. That doesn't help us with a plan, though. These officials are very powerful, and they seem determined to stick to their position, from what your uncle is telling my boss."

"I can't believe that the Chinese central government tolerates this kind of corruption."

"The Chinese people like to believe that our central leaders are honest. I don't know about that. There have apparently started to be some strong anti-corruption efforts, like the one that Bo Xilai is leading in Chongqing. But I think that's mainly just a show to hang onto power."

"Well, no one seems to be doing anything about the corruption in Jiangsu province. We seem to be on our own to fix that." April suddenly stood up, and turned to Jasmine. "Before we get too depressed, how about we take a walk down to Venice Beach? I'm starting to get hungry, and there are a lot of nice little places there to have lunch. My favorite is the Sidewalk Café. It's next to a really nice bookstore."

"Sure, let's go."

They set out towards the beach, walking in silence. A couple of young men their age walked by them the other direction, wearing swim suits and no shirts. They looked at the girls, who were no longer holding hands.

"What are you thinking about?" April asked after the boys had passed. "You didn't like it when people were looking at us holding hands, did you? You're still worrying about what we discussed this morning when we woke up."

"No, that's not it at all." Jasmine reached over and took April's hand, and continued walking in silence.

"OK, what?"

"It's the last thing that you said before you stood up, about central leaders doing something about the corruption in *jiāo yì*. What if ... they found out?"

"What do you mean?"

"Well, what if somehow more senior officials got involved? The beating of Walter is an unusual thing to happen in China. Those officials in Suzhou must be getting frightened after the article."

"You know China much better than I do. But yes, if there *are* anti-corruption efforts, it does seem like it could help a lot for senior officials to get involved. Do you think it is likely to happen? In time to help us?"

"I was thinking that maybe we could help make it happen. My family is very connected in Tianjin, which is the home town of our premier Wen Jiabao. I think my father knows some people who are very close to Mr. Wen."

"Do you think your father would do that? In the U.S., I don't think people can just use their friends to ask the President for a favor."

"You might be surprised. I think that's the way that powerful people do things everywhere. Anyhow, that's the way *guānxi* works in China. A couple of connections can get you to some very senior people, if the connections have the right motivation. Doing a favor for the family of a friend can be a strong motivation—I've seen it many times. I can ask my father, I think."

They continued walking in silence, both thinking, still holding hands, until they reached the beach, where they took off their shoes and resumed walking in the sand.

"The beach is very beautiful," Jasmine said. "We used to go to the beach near Tianjin, but it's not so nice as here. And there are not as many interesting people to watch."

251

"Yes, I love it here. My parents used to bring me here when I was small. One time we came when my Uncle Jun and Aunt Hong and Xu were visting from Shanghai. I think I was about seven, and Xu was about eleven. Xu was a very bold kid even then." April stopped walking, and turned toward Jasmine. "Actually, that gives me an idea, maybe Uncle Jun can use his *guānxi* too, to help our plan. He seems to know a lot of people, and he certainly has a very strong motivation to fix things."

"This is starting to sound like a plan. You know, we have some interesting information to pass along too. Walter told us this morning that *Shanghai Weekend* is about to publish another article that names the officials in Suzhou. Whatever happens in secret, the Chinese government doesn't like noisy public information on corruption."

"If we do this, don't you need to talk to Mr. Gregg and your other colleagues first?"

"That's a big question. Richard has been very good to me, and I've let him down twice now by not telling him things. But I don't think I should tell him about it yet. The San Marino partners are taking a really close look at this deal with their lawyers. I don't think they would easily approve a political approach like this."

"OK, I guess. But isn't that risky? You could lose your job."

"I guess I'm developing a habit of keeping things secret. Anyhow, I would probably lose my job if I told him about what I've already done. Better to try to fix the situation first. As the British say, 'In for a penny, in for a pound'." April shot her a sideways glance. "We learned that in English class at university."

"Well, if that's how you feel, maybe it's better for everyone if I just go ahead with the plan now. You can blame the idea on me. I already lost my job." She paused and considered. "I've really been wanting to call my Uncle Jun anyway. When I left Shanghai, we didn't discuss the problems with *jiāo yì*."

"I think you're right. But how about we have lunch first? It's still early morning in Shanghai. We can decide over lunch whether we should really do this."

"That sounds great."

Over lunch at the Sidewalk Café, the women made desultory efforts to talk about other things. But they kept coming back to their bold plan, and each time they did it became clearer that they should go ahead.

After lunch they spent half an hour browsing at Small World Books, where April bought Jasmine a copy of *Tender Is the Night*. Handing it to her outside the shop, April said, "This is one of my favorite books. Since you like *The Great Gatsby*, I think you will like this one too."

"That's amazing. Thank you so much. It will be the next book that I read."

"The intensity of the emotions between Dick and Nicole Diver has always attracted me." April studied the cover of the book. "Perhaps I should be worried about what that says about me, with the disaster that they created as a couple. Our relationship sometimes seems to be heading that direction." She smiled wryly.

"Hopefully we can do better." Jasmine looked down and shook her head slowly. "I'm sorry that I am so emotional."

"Well, I guess I can handle it for the time being." April decided to change the subject, and it occurred to her that this was becoming a habit in her conversations with Jasmine. "So … shall we go ahead with our plan?"

"Yes, let's do it."

Standing on the shore looking out at the Pacific, looking over the edge of the horizon in the direction of Shanghai six and a half thousand miles away, April called Uncle Jun from her mobile phone. Jasmine waited a distance away, giving her privacy, walking in slow circles and looking at the sea and the sand.

He answered quickly. "*Wèi?* [Hello?]"

"*Bó bo.* [Uncle.]"

"April! I am so happy that you called. We did not treat you properly when you left, and I've been wanting to talk with you about that."

"Thank you, Uncle Jun. I've been wanting to talk with you too. I am so sorry about what happened."

"Yes, we have created some problems. Now I am trying to fix them … but it is hard."

"Actually, that's why I am calling. I have an idea." April explained their plan, that they could trap the officials in Suzhou with pressure from two directions—a new article from *Shanghai Weekend* that named the officials, and intervention by senior Communist Party officials with a strong aversion to publicity about high-level corruption.

"*Nà ge bànfǎ hěn yǒu yìsi.* [That is a very interesting approach.] But how do you propose to get senior Party officials involved?"

Before mentioning Jasmine's role she hesitated. "Uncle Jun, I want to apologize first for my question, but can I trust you with some very sensitive information? Can you try not to be angry at me?"

"Of course, April. I have made some mistakes, but now I know that our family must stick together. I trust whatever you propose."

"OK. I am here with Jasmine Liu from San Marino. We have become very good friends. I introduced Jasmine to Yang Jiang, and Jasmine is the one who provided him a lot of the information for the first *Shanghai Weekend* story, from what she had learned at San Marino. Now she wants to help. She thinks her family can possibly get in contact with the office of Mr. Wen."

"I understand, April. And I am certainly not angry. We expected that the information in the article had come from San Marino."

"*Xiè xie, bó bo.* The sensitive thing is that Jasmine has not told her boss at San Marino, Mr. Gregg, about any of this— because she does not know what to say to him. But she does want to help San Marino and JZP. Can you keep all of this a secret for now?"

"Jasmine is a bold and independent girl. I could see that when I met her. Yes, I will keep her secret."

"Thank you."

"So how shall we organize this plan?"

"Jasmine will speak with her parents today. We will call you back and let you know whether they can help. Could you think about who could help us in Shanghai?"

"*Hǎo de.* Thank you again for calling, April. We hope to see you again in Shanghai before too long."

"Thank you, Uncle Jun. Please say hello to Aunt Hong for me ... and to Xu. Tell them that I am sorry what has happened to our family because of me."

"April, Xu knows that this was not your fault. We all do. *Zàijiàn*, April."

"*Zàijiàn, bó bo.*"

After the call ended, April was full of warmth at the reconnection with Uncle Jun, as she turned to rejoin Jasmine, who was facing out to sea, the light wind blowing her hair and her summer dress. Looking at Jasmine's beautiful features in profile, April felt an almost electrical jolt that intruded into her Shanghai family reverie. It was a powerful mix of emotions, and she was surprised that worry about how things would work out with Jasmine was not a major ingredient. Mostly, she felt passion, and the conviction that her adventure had arrived.

Repair

交易

35

On the Offensive

week of September 6, 2009

Invincibility lies in the defence; the possibility of victory in the attack

– Sun Tzu

"*Bà ba.*"

"*Xiăo Mò Lì! Nǐ hǎo ma?* [Little Jasmine! How are you?]"

"*Wǒ hěn búcuò.* [I'm not bad at all]."

"Are you sure? You sound worried." Jasmine had a somewhat formal relationship with her father, like many Chinese children, but he knew her well, and could usually read her emotions even over the telephone.

"You always know what I am thinking, *bà.*"

"*Shénme shìr?* [What's up?]"

"Well, I was calling to ask your help with the problems in Suzhou that I told you about when I was home. What the officials have done is making it impossible to proceed with our joint venture, and impossible to get out of it. It is a bad situation for my company." Jasmine had decided not to tell her father about how she had concealed her role in the article from Richard. He was a disciplined Communist Party official, and she knew that he would not approve.

"I have been saying for many years that corruption is going to hurt the Party badly. I used to discuss this with your grandfather all the time—he felt the same way. You may not remember."

"*Wǒ jì de.* [I remember.]" The memory of her grandfather saying "*Rúguǒ nǐ bàoyuàn, tāmen huì chénmò* [If you complain, they will silence you]" came back with more force than ever.

"You said that you were calling for help. Unfortunately, I do not know what I can do. This is happening in Suzhou, in Jiangsu province. That is a long way from Tianjin."

"Yes, *bà*. But I think this may soon be national news. I believe that *Shanghai Weekend* will publish an article on Friday that names the senior officials in Suzhou who are involved."

"*Zhēn de ma!* [Really!]"

"*Zhēn de.* [Really.] I was thinking that maybe you know some people who could tell Wen Jiabao, or people who work for him."

Jasmine's father was silent for a few seconds. "Yes, I could try to do that. It would mean calling in a few old favors."

"*Bù hǎo yìsi. Nǐ kěyǐ ma?* [I am sorry. Can you do it?]"

He was briefly silent again, considering. "*Wǒ kěyǐ.* [I can do it.] This is important. It is time that I try to do something about corruption. And it is for my only child … and for my father."

"*Xiè xie, bà.* Who will you call?"

"I think that it is better that you not know that. *Hǎo de?*"

"OK. That reminds me that it is better that the people you call not know any details about the article that is coming. A friend could get hurt."

"*Wǒ yǐjīng míng bái le.* [I already understood.] I will call my friends now, and let you know as soon I make progress."

"*Xiè xie, bà. Wǒ aì nǐ.*" It was the first time in many years that Jasmine had said "I love you" to either of her parents.

She could see his benevolent smile over the telephone, and could hear the emotion in his scratchy voice. "*Wǒ yě aì nǐ, Xiǎo Mò Lì.* [I love you too, Little Jasmine.]"

* * *

Once Jasmine's father had agreed on Sunday to attempt the key piece of their plan, April and Jasmine put the two other elements of the plan into motion on Monday. First, they called Walter and told him about the hope for political pressure on the officials in Suzhou. They assured him that they were now

OK with the plan to identify JZP and the officials. And they asked if they could have a copy of the article on the Thursday evening—before it was published on Friday afternoon—so that Mr. Wang could use it to apply pressure. Walter told them that he would do his best.

Then they called Mr. Wang and told him what was happening. After reflexive concern that JZP would be mentioned in the new article, he quickly realized that this was already an open secret, and that the article could be turned into much more of an opportunity than a problem. With energy and excitement in his voice, he told the girls that he was working on his own plan to deliver the message to the officials with maximum impact.

And then there were two days of nail-biting wait—likely the calm before the storm, they realized.

* * *

"Yes, we should do it. Don't worry about me." Walter was again in Mr. Huang's tiny office at *Shanghai Weekend*. They were both tired, and looked it.

As usual, Mr. Huang was smoking a cigarette. He took a drag, and shook his head as he exhaled, adding smoke to the haze in the office. "You are a brave boy, *Xiǎo Yáng*. It will be your name on the article."

"Not so brave, *Huáng xiānsheng*. If those criminals had any real power, they wouldn't need to beat me up to try to scare me. My bruises are already healing, and I don't think they dare to do more when so much is known. It's you who are taking the real risk with our newspaper. Publishing the names of those officials is the type of action that could get *Shanghai Weekend* the wrong kind of attention from the government."

"Well, they have not reacted yet. I am willing to take the risk. I want to show that we are one newspaper that will not let criminal behavior get in the way of the truth. Corruption in China is a rising tide, and there are not many people who are willing to do something about it, or even talk loudly."

It was a Wednesday afternoon, time for final decisions on which articles would be in the Friday issue of *Shanghai Weekend*.

"I agree ... Um ..." Walter hesitated, wondering whether now was the time to ask an important question about the plan with April and Jasmine, or indeed whether he should ask at all. He decided that honesty was the best policy, not least because he knew about the mess that Jasmine had created for herself by keeping secrets from her boss. Mr. Huang was staring at him as he fumbled for words. "Mr. Huang, I have a favor to ask."

"*Hǎo, shénme shìr?* [OK, what's up?]"

"My source wants to receive a copy of the article a day early, on Thursday evening."

"*Wèi shénme?* [Why?]"

Walter knew that he couldn't reveal the plan that April and Jasmine were developing, and he had prepared an answer that was truthful without providing any details. "He knows this article could have a big effect on the deal between JZP and the Americans, and he wants to prepare."

Mr. Huang compressed his lips. "*Xiǎo Yáng*, we protect our sources, but you know it's against journalistic principles to help them with their problems. I don't think we can do what you ask."

Walter felt a sinking feeling, having told April that he thought he could deliver the article early. He knew it was a vital piece of her plan. "OK, Mr. Huang. As you say." His face must have betrayed his dismay, because Mr. Huang raised his eyebrows.

"Here's what I can offer. You can send the article to your source at the same time that our printers release the paper to distributors. That ought to give your source about an hour before the papers hit the streets, and three hours before the article is available on the Internet. Will that be enough time for your source to prepare?"

Walter smiled and nodded. "*Xiè xie, Huáng xiānsheng.* It will have to be enough." He wasn't sure that this was right, but at least he could tell April that this was the best that he could do.

* * *

262

When April heard about the timing imposed by Mr. Huang, she felt panic. Her adventurous plan seemed to be spinning out of control, like *jiāo yì* had in the first place. She made two telephone calls in quick succession.

First, she called Jasmine at work. This time, instead of her usual effect on April of producing various sorts of agitation, Jasmine managed to calm her, pointing out that the only way was forward. After all, she suggested, an hour could be a lot of time. Great battles had been won in less.

Jasmine was correct, it seemed. When April called Uncle Jun, he took the revised schedule in stride, apparently confident that his plan would work as long as the article appeared an hour in advance. He explained that the plan required help from *Lǎo Wú*. Cryptically, he resisted providing further details, saying that he would know more on the next day, Thursday.

* * *

The golf course at Shanghai Country Club, one of the oldest courses near Shanghai, wanders near the edge of Dianshan Lake. Mr. Wang had been a member of the club for many years, and before the rupture with *Lǎo Wú* the two had played there at least once a month. He had asked Mr. Wu to meet him at the club for an early nine holes on Thursday morning, and his old friend had accepted with gratitude.

Mr. Wang drove to the golf course in the BMW, on the same route past Zhujiajiaozhen that he had taken almost three weeks earlier with Aunt Hong and Xu on the day they had learned about the first article. The despair of that day was now a rapidly fading memory. The problems the article had created were still very much at the top of his mind, but now it was he who was on the offensive. He had often used Sun Tzu's *The Art of War* as inspiration for his business strategy. The ancient general said that the possibility of victory lay in the attack.

He did not immediately tell Mr. Wu why he had asked to meet, although he sensed that his friend knew that something important was afoot. They headed to the first tee of the golf course as they had many times before. Another pair teed off right behind them—they were excellent golfers, which pressed Mr. Wang and Mr. Wu to play quickly, speaking only a few words to compliment each other's play or to discuss club selection.

On the fifth tee, Mr. Wang paused, and allowed the pair behind them to catch up and play through. Once the other golfers were safely out of earshot down the fairway, he turned to Mr. Wu. "*Lǎo Wú*, I asked you here today because I want us to be friends again, and because I need your help."

"Of course I will help, *Wáng lǎo bǎn*. And I have always been your friend."

"You have not heard yet the help that I need. If you do what I ask, you will prove tomorrow that I again can trust you, and you will do so by burning your bridges to those bastards in Suzhou. Can you do that?"

Mr. Wang was pleased to note that his old friend did not hesitate. "*Wáng lǎo bǎn*, I was only waiting for you to ask. Please tell me what I need to do."

"I will tell you when we finish this round of golf. But first," he said with a smile, "I want to make sure that you still don't think you have to let me win. That is another important test!"

* * *

At the same time that Mr. Wang and Mr. Wu were on the golf course, Jasmine's father called her and reported that his *guānxi* with old friends had delivered better results than he had hoped. It appeared that someone from Mr. Wen's office would contact the Suzhou officials immediately to inquire about the earlier article, perhaps as early as today. He told her that he had done all that he could do. There would be no way of finding out when or whether the call was actually made.

Soon after Jasmine passed on this promising news, April received a call from Uncle Jun—late Wednesday evening Los Angeles time, early afternoon Thursday in Shanghai. He explained the details of what he had agreed with Mr. Wu, and asked April to arrange for Walter to email his new article to Mr. Wu on Friday afternoon, as early as he was able. Once

April had called Walter and relayed this message, the plan was in place. There seemed to be nothing more that she or Jasmine could do except hope, and try to keep from worrying.

April and Jasmine had made plans to meet at Jasmine's flat for dinner on the following evening. By the time they woke up on Friday in Los Angeles, assuming they could sleep at all, they expected that the plan would have succeeded or failed. In the meantime, they both hoped, they could find some way to distract each other from their worries with other activities.

* * *

Mr. Wang scheduled a meeting with the Suzhou officials for five o'clock on Friday afternoon, the same time that *Shanghai Weekend* was due to hit the streets. They agreed to meet after he told them that he had important new information on the Suzhou project that could only be conveyed in person. By suggesting that they meet where the officials had already previously walked out on lunch, Mr. Wang intended to remind them of that impoliteness. Indeed, he had been insistent when Mr. Li suggested a different location, and the two officials had only reluctantly agreed.

Before the meeting, Mr. Wang again took the opportunity to visit the Suzhou development, which was making smooth and excellent progress, already rising several floors above its completed foundations. Despite the difficulties that had emerged from the project, he still could not help but feel proud that his once-small company was engaged in such a significant development.

As Mr. Wang walked to the restaurant, the sky, in place of the warm sunshine of the previous meeting, showed a uniform grey. There was a light mist rising off the surface of the lake, partially shrouding the buildings around it and giving them an ominous, hulking appearance. Mr. Wang hoped that this did not forebode the outcome of the meeting. He was certain that it would be a difficult meeting, but he felt confident that he was finally in a stronger position than the officials, for the first time since their request for ownership in the Suzhou project.

When he arrived at the restaurant, Mr. Li and Mr. Yang were not there. This time, he had arranged a private dining room. The room was functional rather than ornate—the only decorations were patterned wallpaper, two reproductions of traditional nature paintings and utilitarian dark wood furniture. The carpet was industrial, a nondescript grey-green. But he did not need ornament. The room would serve well enough as a theatre for the performance that he planned.

Unfortunately, his audience did not arrive on time. After waiting in the nearly empty room for fifteen minutes past their agreed meeting time, Mr. Wang began to imagine scenarios that had disrupted his plans. He wondered whether the officials might somehow have learned of the forthcoming article—whether they might have devised some kind of official reprisal against JZP or the joint venture—or whether something even worse and unexpected had happened. Life had recently brought a series of unpleasant surprises, and Mr. Wang had been feeling almost constantly apprehensive of the next one. As the minutes passed, his earlier confidence eroded. He watched the waitresses pad in and out of the room, attending to him and wondering, he assumed, when the other guests would arrive.

Fortunately, he did not have to wait much longer. Mr. Li and Mr. Yang arrived at twenty past five. This time there were no pleasantries at all. Indeed, the two officials did not even sit down—a clear snub to Mr. Wang's hospitality. Mr. Li took the lead in speaking, as he usually did.

"*Wáng xiānsheng*, we apologize for being late. We were discussing the most unnecessary difficulties that you have been creating for us, and we have decided that we have nothing more to discuss with you today. Under the circumstances, we have decided that we will not be able to join you for dinner."

"Please explain what you mean by 'most unnecessary difficulties', Mr. Li. This is not a situation that I or my company created."

Mr. Li looked at Mr. Yang, who nodded, and then turned back to Mr. Wang. "We were contacted by the office of Premier Wen in Beijing with concerns about the article in

266

Shanghai Weekend." The men had apparently not imagined that he could have known anything about the contact from Mr. Wen's office, or they would not have mentioned it. So far, so good—maybe the plan would actually work. "We know that the source of that article must be associated with your *jiāo yì*. It is unacceptable that men like us should be challenged by the Premier's office in this way—"

"How could it be unacceptable, if it is true?"

Mr. Li shook his head angrily and declined to respond to Mr. Wang's interrupting question. "Mr. Wen's office has asked us to make sure that this does not go any further. We have assured the official that we will not allow any more lies like this to be published. We have taken steps before to punish this kind of libel, and we will not hesitate to do more if necessary."

"I suppose you are talking about sending your gang to beat up the journalist. Your behavior is criminal." Mr. Wang saw surprise register on the two men's faces at his knowledge of the beating of Walter.

"We cannot control the behavior of people who react strongly, as they ought to, to the publication of lies about their local Party officials. And now you are accusing us of being criminals. Is this what you brought us here to say?" He did not wait for Mr. Wang to answer. "We will leave now." Mr. Li seemed to realize the weakness of his denials, and he stood to leave with his eyes on the door, as if looking for an escape route. His words expressed indignation and insult, but his ferocity was that of a cornered animal. Mr. Wang could almost smell his fear.

Mr. Wang glanced at his watch. Mr. Wu should have been here fifteen minutes ago. More doubts: had Walter failed to deliver the article?—had Mr. Wu lost his nerve? There was no choice but to delay a little more.

"Please sit down."

"What?"

"Please sit down. This is not over."

"What do you mean?" Mr. Yang spoke for the first time, as, to Mr. Wang's enormous relief, Mr. Wu was ushered into the room by a hostess, as if on cue. Mr. Wu was wearing his best suit and what appeared to be a new tie. Mr. Wang thought that it had been a very long time since he had seen his old friend look better. The hostess, who had been hovering over the other men until just before Mr. Wu's arrival, asked if they were ready for dinner to be served, or drinks. Mr. Wang waved her away, eager to begin the performance before the officials decided to leave.

"*Nǐ hǎo, Lǎo Wú.* I believe that you know Mr. Li and Mr. Yang quite well." The two officials were staring at Mr. Wu.

"I do, *Wáng lǎo bǎn.* I have even brought them each a gift, as you asked. Shall I present their gifts?"

"Please do."

Mr. Wu handed two sheets of paper stapled together to each official.

"What is this?" asked Mr. Yang.

"*Lǎo Wú,* may I tell the gentlemen what you have so kindly brought them?"

"Please do."

Mr. Wang smiled, showing his teeth, not afraid to communicate his relish at delivering a likely death sentence for the two officials' careers. "This is another article by Yang Jiang, the same journalist at *Shanghai Weekend* who wrote the article that you mentioned earlier. It's an interesting coincidence that he has the same surname as you, Mr. Yang, because he is certainly not writing very nice things about you. There are quite a few details about you and your families." He paused before delivering the coup de grace. "The article is appearing in *Shanghai Weekend* today. In fact, I believe you could buy a copy of the newspaper on the street now, or read the article on the Internet this evening. But I would suggest you read it now."

Mr. Li and Mr. Yang both sat down as bidden, and began to read. As they did so, two young waitresses came in and began serving the first course of lunch, *suān là tāng* [hot and sour soup]. None of the men lifted their spoons. The two officials seemed oblivious to the food, but Mr. Wang struggled to refrain. He suddenly felt very hungry.

After a minute or two of watching the two officials reading and the steam rising from the soup, Mr. Wang noticed with surprise that Mr. Yang was crying. Thinking about the pain that he and his family had recently experienced, Mr. Wang felt a momentary pang of sympathy. But this evaporated quickly. The men would have to live with the consequences of their actions.

A few seconds later, Mr. Li looked up at Mr. Wang, not even glancing at Mr. Yang. "*Wáng xiānsheng*, this could ruin us. Please go now. We must discuss how to respond." He seemed to have turned from a cornered wolf into a cowering dog, knowing that he was beaten.

"We will wait outside while you discuss."

"No, go back to Shanghai," he snapped. "We will call you later."

"Thank you, *Lǐ xiānsheng*. I hope you understand that we will be expecting a constructive response. I don't think it will be so easy for you to tell Premier Wen's office that these are lies." When there was no further answer from Mr. Li or Mr. Yang, Mr. Wang led Mr. Wu out of the room, leaving the officials with the food—as they had done to him a month earlier.

As soon as they were outside, Mr. Wang turned to his old friend and shook his hand warmly. The weather had improved, with sunlight now coming through a gap in the clouds and illuminating the ripples on the lake. The lifting clouds that Mr. Wang saw over Mr. Wu's shoulder matched his lifting mood. Against the odds, he thought, it seemed that he and his family might yet come out as winners.

交易

36

Victory?

September 14, 2009

When the gods wish to punish us they answer our prayers

– Oscar Wilde, 'An Ideal Husband'

"She did *what!*" Peter Thomas was visibly angry, notwithstanding the good news that Richard had just delivered at the Monday morning partners' meeting.

On the previous day, Sunday, Mr. Wang had called Richard and reported that the Suzhou officials had agreed that their family members would surrender their shares in the Suzhou development, leaving the JV in the same ownership position that San Marino had expected at completion. Richard had pressed Mr. Wang for details on why the officials had surrendered their position, but he had only said cryptically, to Richard's surprise, that "*Xiǎo Liú* has some things to tell you".

Richard called Jasmine immediately to pass on the good news, and to ask her about what Mr. Wang had said. She was quick to confess her role, both in the initial article and in the scheme to fix the problem. She explained that she knew that she had made mistakes, but had the best interests of San Marino at heart. Sensing Richard's evident shock, she offered to quit her job to save him the trouble of firing her. By the time of the partners' meeting, Richard was still considering whether to take her up on that offer, although he was, as yet, inclined not to do so—mainly out of admiration both of the risks that she had taken and, crucially, the results that she had achieved.

Responding to Peter's question, Richard was still unsure whether he had the whole story. "As far as I can understand it, Jasmine was the key source behind the newspaper story that caused us so much difficulty in Hong Kong when we were trying to sell on the China deal. Then she cooperated with JZP and the reporter who wrote the story to encourage the Chinese central government to put pressure on the Jiangsu province officials who were involved in the Suzhou corruption." Richard shook his head. "And it seems to have worked, or at least it has eliminated the ownership problem."

All of the other San Marino partners, except François, began speaking at the same time. Tom Wilshire held up a hand. "One at a time. Peter?"

"This is the most outrageous behavior ever, by far, by a member of our firm. I asked whether she should be fired after she withheld her concerns about the original deal, and now I insist that we do it. As a matter of basic risk management, whatever Jasmine's intention, we cannot employ someone who has done things like this behind our back on one of our deals. High political intrigue, for God's sake! You couldn't make it up." He shook his head, more angrily than Richard had.

"OK, Peter, noted. We'll discuss Ms. Liu's ongoing employment in a moment. Jane?"

"I agree with Peter. But what I really want to say is that I disagree with Richard's implication that this somehow solves the problem. Based on what our lawyers say, there is no way we can make any new investments through this China JV without a much more thorough investigation of corruption. I seriously doubt we could get comfortable with it in any case. Apart from the legal issues, it would really worry me for us to keep an investment in the portfolio after it had been the subject of widely read corruption stories in the Chinese press. Our investors hate this kind of attention, and we need to put it behind us."

Tom Wilshire nodded approvingly. "You have my strong sympathy on that, Jane. François, do you have anything to add?"

"Well, I agree that we probably cannot keep this investment, but let's not be too hard on Richard. We have been working together to try to sell it, and I think this change helps a lot.

271

That's what he meant, I think." François looked at Richard, who nodded slightly, and continued. "As to our Jasmine, she is quite a brave girl, *non*? Of course, she needs to be more careful, but in all honesty we probably would have approved what she did if she asked us. I think we should take a careful look before we say *au revoir* to her."

"You must be kidding," Peter said. "She has to go. Now."

"OK, thanks, everybody." Tom looked around the table. "In a few minutes, I am going to ask all of you to vote on whether we should fire Jasmine. But first let's discuss next steps on this investment. Doc, this is still your deal. What should we do?"

"Like François says, I want to sell. If we can get out with a clean sale, it will be much better for the firm than just walking away. And if we do that, I doubt we will lose money. All of our potential buyers in Hong Kong told us to come back if we could clean up the mess in Suzhou. I don't know if what has happened is enough, but I think we have to try. We owe that to our investors. François has been a big help to me dealing with the Hong Kong buyers, and I think we should keep pursuing them." He looked at François, who nodded fractionally as Richard had two minutes earlier, and then around the table.

"As to Jasmine, I agree that what she has done justifies firing her, and in fact she has offered to quit. But even with François helping, I really need Jasmine working on this to have the best chance to make a sale happen in Hong Kong. She has been doing most of the talking to the buyers there. Please let me keep working with her until that deal is done, or until we know it isn't going to work, and we can make a decision then." He looked at Peter deferentially. "That's my vote."

"OK," Tom continued, "as to the deal, I propose that we give Richard another month to try to solve this problem. We do need to turn over every stone to get value for our investors for the money we have spent, and the time. We can decide after a month whether to change course on the deal. I am also OK for François to work on it, so long as he believes that this isn't going to be a major distraction from other deals." He looked at François, who nodded, and continued. "Any objections so far?" He looked around the table, and no one spoke. "As to Jasmine, we need a vote. Peter and Richard have already said what they want to do. Jane?"

"I understand why Richard wants to keep her for the Hong Kong work, but I agree with Peter. We cannot condone what she has done, and it's too risky to keep her around."

"François?"

"I agree with Doctor Richard."

"That leaves me to break the tie. I agree with Peter and Jane that Jasmine should be fired for what she has done, and I think we need to tell her that. But I am going to give Richard the benefit of the doubt on the China deal. She can stay around for a month and work with Richard on that deal, but nothing else. As soon as the deal is done, unless something major changes, she is out. Richard, will you communicate that decision?"

"Yes, I—"

Peter broke in. "I still think this is a crazy decision. She kept secrets from us. She took big risks without asking. This is the kind of thing that underlies every major financial scandal. If our investors found out about this decision, they would be livid."

"Fair enough, Peter. It's a close call. The thing that makes me willing to take the risk is that nothing I can see suggests that Jasmine was acting for her own benefit. We can't have her acting like this, but she seems to have had our interests at heart and she was lucky that she achieved a good result. I like people who are clever enough to attract good luck. But, Richard, you must keep Jasmine under very strict control. If there is even a whiff of behavior like what we heard about today, she will be fired immediately."

* * *

When the partners' meeting ended, François took Richard by the elbow, steered him to François' office and shut the door.

"Our little Jasmine has been rather naughty, *non*? What are you going to tell her?"

Richard suspected that the partners, especially Tom Wilshire, might well moderate their views on Jasmine if there was a good result in Hong Kong. They were investors above all, and results were their yardstick. But he did not want to tell her this. He did not want to raise Jasmine's hopes, and had not even decided himself whether he still wanted her working for him. He had difficulty voicing his conflicting views. "I don't know, François. I want to encourage her to do good work finding a deal in Hong Kong, but she needs to understand—"

"I think we need to frighten her a little."

Richard stared at him. "That's not my style, François."

"Then I will help you. Like I said in the partner's meeting, I admire what Jasmine achieved. But she has to learn that there are rules. I should know. I have sometimes been a bad boy because I know that I am so clever, but sometimes my cleverness gets me into trouble."

"What do you suggest?"

"Come, let's take her to lunch and give her a proper lecture." François steered Richard back out the door of his office and towards Jasmine's desk. As they approached, Richard looked at François questioningly, and he motioned Richard into the lead.

"Jasmine, could you join François and me for lunch at the Daily Grill. We can leave around twelve-thirty."

"OK, Richard." Jasmine looked at their faces. "Are you going to tell me what happened at the partners' meeting?"

"We'll discuss that at lunch."

"So … it's my farewell lunch?"

"We'll discuss that at lunch."

Jasmine looked crestfallen. As they walked away from her desk, François leaned over the Richard and whispered in his ear. "Well done, *mon ami*." Richard knew that Jasmine must be watching them walk away, and assuming that François was whispering about her downfall.

* * *

It was a day on which Richard had ridden to work with Tom Wilshire, so François drove the little team to lunch in his convertible Porsche Boxster – Richard and Jasmine squeezed into the passenger seat together for the short drive to the Daily Grill. The restaurant was part of a chain that sought to reproduce the experience of elegant grill restaurants found in U.S. cities before World War II. It had started up during the 1980s in Beverly Hills, and the Pasadena branch followed a formula of dark wood, 1930s fixtures, and traditionally-dressed wait staff.

Richard, François and Jasmine settled into a booth. Richard looked at Jasmine. She suddenly looked like a little girl, her natural poise submerged by the despair of personal failure. Once the waitress had taken their drinks order, he found himself unable to prolong the punishment.

"Jasmine, let me start by saying that you still have a job for the next month if you want it." Jasmine looked up cautiously, her face showing the beginnings of relief. "But before we discuss that, we have to talk about what you did—"

"—You are toast, young lady. Serious punishment." François acted the disciplinarian, but could not keep a slight smile off of his face.

Richard remained serious. "François can tease if he wants, but the point is important. I need to be able to trust you, and I'm not sure if I can any more. No more keeping things from me, no more making big decisions on your own. Do you understand?" Jasmine started to nod. "The partners made clear today that you will be fired immediately if that continues, and I agree with them. Got it?"

Jasmine looked down. "Got it, Doc … Richard."

Richard picked up his menu and studied it briefly. "Well, I'm glad we got that out of the way. You certainly did get one hell of a result Jasmine, and I suggest that we celebrate. What's everyone having for lunch? White wine, I think?"

275

Once they had ordered lunch, the discussion turned to Hong Kong. The mood at the table turned extravagant, because the trio had learned to enjoy each others' company on their trip to Hong Kong, and because they realized that they had a chance to reverse the near-disaster of that trip.

"So, Jasmine, the decision that the partners took is that you can help me and François for the next month on *xīn jiāo yì*. You aren't allowed to work on anything else, and you are likely to lose your job after the month even if we don't do a deal. Can you live with that?"

Jasmine's reaction did not surprise Richard. "Of course I want to help in Hong Kong, Doc," she said with a rapidly repairing confidence. He realized that, more than self-confidence, Jasmine possessed a kind of resilient self-belief, which was a tremendous asset even if it sometimes led her in dangerous directions. "I know I don't necessarily deserve this opportunity, and I am grateful the partners have given it to me. So what do we do next?"

"How about you tell me what you suggest? You seem to be very confident about making decisions."

"Well … the obvious path is to start with the same three potential buyers that we met in Hong Kong. I will also think about less obvious options, but those three firms all said that we should come back if we could clean up the problems in Suzhou. I think that they will be impressed how much we have accomplished in two weeks."

"You accomplished it, for better or worse." Richard shook his head. "I agree with your plan. Please get on the telephone to them this afternoon—first thing in the morning Hong Kong time. How do you think our buyers will react, François?"

"Well, I don't think we will get any immediate answers. They're all likely to remain interested in the properties, but they will need some time to investigate the changes in Suzhou. They will be able to see the second article in *Shanghai Weekend*, but won't have heard what Mr. Wang told us about the change of ownership. News doesn't usually travel that fast, even in China."

"So you think we still will have problems doing a deal?"

"*Au contraire*, once they think about it I believe they will jump in. And if they will not, there are many other investors in Hong Kong. I think we could have an auction on our hands."

"Let's not get ahead of ourselves, François." Richard smiled. "It does feel promising, though, doesn't it? Alright, we should spend the rest of this week getting the details from JZP, revising our presentations and arranging new meetings in Hong Kong. If things move quickly, we might even fly to Hong Kong on the weekend and start the meetings early next week." He looked from François to Jasmine, and lifted his wine glass. "I propose a toast to a great team. Shall we just celebrate and take a break from *jiāo yì* for the rest of lunch?"

"Hear, hear."

"Thanks, Doc."

"So, a lunch with Richard and Jasmine with no more talk of work! I will believe it when I see it ... Miss Jasmine, are you blushing? Surely it is not embarrassing to just enjoy yourself."

Jasmine, prompted by Richard's mention of celebration, had been thinking that she wanted to meet April as soon as possible for a different kind of business-free celebration. Blushing redder, she decided not to respond to François.

交易

37

New Beginnings

December 2009

From the end spring new beginnings

– Pliny the Elder

François watched the sailboats bobbing gently in front of a flaming orange setting sun, as he contemplated the successful day behind him. He was sitting on the terrace of Quito's Gazebo in Cane Garden Bay, on the western coast of Tortola in the British Virgin Islands. In front of him was a small, perfect, oval harbor, boasting a long crescent of beach covered with nearly white sand. Behind him, the local legend Quito Rymer himself was playing guitar, at the moment covering Bob Marley's 'No Woman, No Cry'.

François sipped a Red Stripe beer as he listened. His usual style back home would have been to choose stronger stuff, Caribbean rum perhaps, another local favorite. But as with many visitors to the islands, the relaxed pace of local life had taken him outside his usual persona, and he was a little less the urbane, French investor—although he was still wearing a business suit, albeit without a tie. He was just swallowing a sip of beer when he started coughing.

The reason for his fit was the woman who had just walked up the steps that led from the beach to the bar. She was a thin, petite blonde, perhaps in her late twenties, wearing a blue bikini top with no tan lines that François could discern, a short denim skirt that he assumed was hiding the rest of the bikini— but almost none of her thin, muscular legs—and no shoes on her sandy feet. She was strikingly pretty, in an ethereal sort of way. François, who had the habit of saying that he fell in love at first sight several times per month, realized that he had never truly fallen in love at first sight. *This* time he was sure. Or so he believed.

The woman looked around the room as if searching for someone, and then, apparently not finding what she was looking for, walked toward the bar. As she passed François' table, she paused and said, "Sorry if I surprised you," winked at him with a smile, and kept walking. Realizing that she must have comprehended the reason for his coughing, François took another sip of beer and immediately began coughing again, more loudly this time. The girl did not turn around, but he could see from the slight shake of her shoulders that she was laughing.

For the first time in his memory, François felt—what was the word?— *intimidated* by a woman, but after a brief internal pep talk, he pulled himself together, stood up, and approached her at the bar. "May I please apologize for my silly behavior? And may I buy you a drink?"

She looked at him appraisingly, and smiled wryly. "I just ordered a glass of water. Maybe you need the same? That beer seems a little much for you."

"Actually, it was you who were a little much for me." She frowned. "Of course, you have heard that before," he added hurriedly. "May I invite you to join me at my table for a glass of water? That is, if you don't have any other plans."

"OK. I don't have any other plans."

As they were sitting down, he said, "My name is François. Yours is?"

"Emily. Are you going to be as entertaining to talk to as you have been so far? I needed a good laugh after a long day."

"I will do my best. Perhaps I will not cough so much. But I do have a few other entertainments to offer."

"So I am guessing that you are French."

"*Très bien.* She is both beautiful and intelligent. I am from France, but I live in Los Angeles."

"Hah," she exclaimed. "That's a coincidence. I'm from Los Angeles originally, but I live here on Tortola. Well actually, I live on one of those sailboats out there." She seemed a little apologetic as she explained, "I work as the cook and first mate on a charter yacht."

"Excuse me for asking personal questions, but why? I am sure you are an excellent cook, but, if you don't mind me saying so, you seem too intelligent for that job."

She smiled brightly. "That is the nicest thing anyone has said to me in a long time. The truth is that I *am* too intelligent for this job, and I'm a little tired of it. But I love the islands and I love sailing, and I needed to get away from San Francisco, where I was living before. So here I am." She swept her arm, indicating the bay and the sailboats and the sun just dipping below the horizon. "So what brings you to Tortola?"

"Hmm, here we are. I came here because of a little deal."

"A little deal?"

"Yes, selling an investment in China."

"Why are you in Cane Garden Bay to sell an investment in China?"

"I am in Cane Garden Bay to enjoy the drinks at Quito's. My colleague Richard likes to sail, and he told me to come here."

"And China?"

"My firm usually sets up its investments with a holding company in the British Virgin Islands. So today I had a meeting in Road Town to complete the selling of the China investment to a company from Hong Kong. It is a long story, but it has a happy ending."

Emily looked around. "To tell you the truth, I could use a long story. Can I take you up on that drink you offered to buy? That is, if you think you can handle another beer." She smiled conspiratorially.

When they had settled back in to two more bottles of Red Stripe, François gave her a brief summary of *jiāo yì*—the first deal, the corruption problem, the Hong Kong trips, and ultimately the sale to the Hong Kong family office. It had been a satisfying exit from a messy transaction, at close to the price that Richard had predicted when they had started to discuss *xīn jiāo yì*. Their intuition to "buy low" had been right—rising markets during 2009 had provided a tailwind for the second transaction. The partners at San Marino had breathed a collective sigh of relief.

Emily remained attentive as he spoke, and when he finished, she said solemnly, almost wistfully, "You live a very interesting life."

François shrugged. "I am a businessman. I am not so fortunate as to live on a sailboat. So why is it that you ran away from San Francisco? And why did you want to hear my long story today? Are you sad?"

"Those are three different questions." She looked down at her hands, and considered them for a long moment. "Actually, maybe they are related." She looked at François earnestly. "So ... you want to hear the life story?"

"As you say in America, I have all my ears."

"I think you mean 'I am all ears.'"

"Yes, *bien sûr*. The lady is so intelligent."

"You flatterer, you. Well, I won't tell you the whole life story. We'll save that for next time." Emily smiled at François again, and he felt a powerful gratitude at the promise of a next time. "Skipping the first twenty-six years, I got a Ph.D in philosophy from UC Berkeley. Mixed with religion ... Zen Buddhism is the main thing I studied. But jobs in philosophy and Zen are not easy to come by, unless I wanted to be a Buddhist nun—"

"*Mon dieu*, what a waste!"

Emily dismissed his flirtation with a wave, and continued. "So I took a job at the *San Francisco Chronicle* as an arts reporter. That was OK, until I had a bad relationship with a rich engineer from Google who left me for someone prettier, and stupider, and the job got boring, and I decided to run away from it all for an easy job in the islands."

"I can believe stupider, but not prettier."

"Huh?" Emily looked momentarily puzzled, then smiled when she realized what he meant. "Oh, thanks. Anyway, life in the islands is not perfect either. Today I had a big argument with the captain of my yacht. I was looking for him when I met you."

"I'm glad that you did not find him."

"Yes, me too. So was your meeting today very interesting?"

"Actually, it was quite boring. The exciting part was the deal. We signed that last month. Completion was boring, as usual. Except—there was *one* thing that was remarkable, a big surprise. Funny that you mentioned the rich engineer ..."

"What?"

"I recognized someone." He hesitated. "I shouldn't tell you."

"Why not?"

"Maybe next time." He looked at her, started to speak, and stopped.

"What?"

"You ask a lot of questions. I was thinking that I'm leaving tomorrow, and was wondering what your plans are for the rest of the night. I am staying at a very nice hotel in Road Town."

She gave him a regretful but firm look. "I don't think that would be a good idea. Anyhow, I need to be back on the boat. I have guests to look after. They are out for dinner here on the island, but they'll want drinks later."

Quito Rymer had started to play *I'm a Believer* by The Monkees, and he seemed to be looking at François and Emily. When he sang "I'm in love, I'm a believer, I couldn't leave her if I tried," he winked at Emily and motioned almost imperceptibly with his head towards François. She stuck out her tongue slightly at Rymer, and smiled sheepishly.

François, who had been looking at his beer and thinking, missing the little exchange, asked "What if I miss my plane? Can I see you tomorrow?"

"We sail to Jost van Dyke at dawn. That's a different island ... a long swim, no airport."

"Then you must visit me in Los Angeles."

"I must?" She smiled.

"You must, or I will come back here and find you. Anyway, L.A. is your home, right? You should do it for your parents."

"OK, I'll do it for my parents." She smiled again. "You have a pen in that expensive suit of yours?" He took one out of his pocket, and as he handed it to her she held onto his hand, turned it over, and wrote on his palm. "My email address."

"Bold girl. I don't think anyone has dared to write on my hand since … well, since I don't know when."

"I think you will survive the shock."

"Yes, probably. My heart is beating rather quickly, though." This was the truth.

After they finished their drinks, he walked her to the water's edge. After looking around briefly, she said, "Well, my friend the captain took the dinghy, so I'll be swimming out to the boat." She slipped out of her skirt, revealing the blue bikini bottom that François had imagined, slipped the skirt into a plastic ziplock bag from her pocket, and waded into the water.

"Wait, come back."

Emily walked back, knowing what he wanted. They kissed gently, and then she waved goodbye as she slid into the water, and swam away towards the lights of the nearby yachts. François stood and watched until she was no longer visible in the dark water.

交易

38

Termination

December 2009

Rules must be obeyed

"Jasmine, I'm sorry. You're fired."

Jasmine was in the conference room at San Marino Property Investments. Across the table, with their backs to the window, were Tom Wilshire, Peter Jones and Richard. It was Peter who had just spoken.

"We're all impressed with what you managed to pull off in China," Tom said, "but Peter has convinced us that we need to enforce the principle that staff members can't make major decisions on a transaction without consulting a partner. The partners are unanimous on that." He glanced at Richard. Jasmine was surprised to see Richard nod, and knew that her luck had run out. She was also surprised and confused to see a slight smile on Richard's face. Surely, he had not abandoned her happily to the wolves?

Peter spoke again, as if on cue. "So, Jasmine, I'm the prime advocate for firing you, because rules must be obeyed. But I know talent when I see it, so I'm also first in line to try to give you a second chance. I've lined up an interview for you with a friend at HSBC, who's building their China investment group in Los Angeles. I think Tom and Richard have some ideas too."

Jasmine looked at Peter coolly. "Thank you." Then she looked at Richard, who now was smiling broadly. This felt familiar, like in China—powerful men using *guānxi* to make things happen.

交易

39

Gratitude, and Apology

January 2010

At fifteen I set my heart upon learning.
At thirty, I had planted my feet upon the ground.
At forty, I no longer suffered from perplexities.
At fifty, I knew what were the biddings of Heaven.
At sixty, I heard them with a docile ear.
At seventy, I could follow the dictates of my own heart,
for what I desired no longer overstepped the boundaries of right.

– Confucius

"Please ask *Mǎ tàitài* to set four places for dinner tonight."

"Yes? Who is coming?"

"Well, *Wáng tàitài*," Mr. Wang smiled as he addressed his wife this affectionate way, "I'm having tea with young Yang Jiang this afternoon. We have important things to discuss, and I'm planning to invite him to dinner after. Could you ask our son to be there too?"

"*Hǎo de.* What are you planning to discuss with *Xiǎo Yáng*?"

Mr. Wang considered the huge import of the planned conversation, and decided that he needed to let it take its own course. "I will tell you … *we* will tell you about that over dinner. *Hǎo de?*"

"*Hǎo.* I hope it is a good day."

"Yes. I think it will be a very good day. One that should have come some time ago."

* * *

Walter looked at Xu's number on his mobile phone, and answered quickly. "*Nǐ hǎo*, Xu. *Nǐ hǎo ma?* [How are you?]"

Since the worst turbulence of *jiāo yì* had subsided, Walter and Xu had started to get closer again. They both seemed to understand that their deep childhood friendship would not return. They had become too different. Xu was fundamentally a believer in the economic opportunities of the new China, and Walter was fundamentally a critic of what his country was becoming. Yet they both had forgiven each other, and even started to develop a grudging respect for each other's divergent paths.

"I'm very well, Walter. Sorry that I have not called for a few weeks. I've been spending a lot of time in Hong Kong working with our new joint venture partners. I don't know why we thought it was the best idea to work with the Americans. There are so many more opportunities for Chinese people working together."

"I still like the Americans, Xu."

"Or at least you like one American. How is April? I have not spoken to her in a long time. I don't think she likes me."

"April is OK. But she loves someone else. I have to accept that and not get too emotional about her. You were right."

"See, journalists are not the only people who can be right. I am glad April found a boy so soon after going home. I knew that she would bounce back."

Walter suppressed a grin. "Xu, April is in love with Jasmine."

"*What?*"

"Maybe I should have let her tell you."

"Wow. Oh. That's interesting. I guess I never had a chance with Jasmine either. Wow!" Xu fell silent as he considered the implications of what Walter had told him.

Walter picked up the conversation again. "Did you know that your *bà* has invited me to have tea this afternoon?"

"Yes, that's actually what made me think of calling you. My *mā* called and invited me to dinner, and said that you might be there too."

"I don't know anything about dinner."

"Hmm. *Mā* said that *bà* was acting a little strange."

"So you don't know what he wants to say to me?"

"No, I don't. I hope I will see you tonight to hear about it."

* * *

Mr. Wang had invited Walter to meet him at the *Hú Xīn Tíng* [湖心亭, Mid-Lake Pavilion], a teahouse located in a large pavilion in the middle of the lake at *Yù Yuán* [豫园, the Garden of Happiness] in Shanghai's Old City. It is Shanghai's oldest tea house, now rather touristy but still conveying a powerful atmosphere of tradition. Mr. Wang wanted to make the same point to Walter that he had tried to make to the two Suzhou officials in their penultimate meeting almost half a year earlier.

Walter thought he understood Mr. Wang's point, and had dressed as traditionally as he could from his limited journalist's wardrobe, wearing a lightly embroidered silk tunic over his nicest pair of trousers. When he arrived, Mr. Wang was already at a table overlooking the lake. He had chosen a modern version of classic dress, wearing a new silk blazer and trousers from Shanghai Tang, a Hong Kong clothing chain exploiting a market niche by reinterpreting Chinese clothing of the 1920s and 1930s.

The older man and younger man spoke little and politely during an elegant but somewhat abbreviated tea ceremony. The traditionally-dressed waitress who served them first washed the tea leaves before brewing them. Walter got the timing almost right with her gentle guidance, offering tea first to Mr. Wang as a sign of respect for his elder. Once the tea had been poured and the waitress had left them alone, they sat for a minute or so in silence, sipping and enjoying the fragrance of the green tea, before Mr. Wang spoke.

"*Xiǎo Yáng*, you do not know why I have invited you here today."

"I assumed that it had something to do with my articles about your deal."

"Well, yes. That was one reason. I am grateful that your articles allowed me to save my business."

"I didn't write them for you. I wrote them to do the right thing, and for your niece April. You did not treat her well."

"Yes, you are correct. I am trying to fix that." Mr. Wang looked down, and then squarely at Walter. "*Xiǎo Yáng*, I have made other mistakes too. Did you know that I knew your father before the Cultural Revolution?"

Walter sat up a little straighter and looked at Mr. Wang intently before responding. "*Méi yǒu.* [I didn't]."

"We were separated when my family moved to Suzhou. Your grandfather was my father's best friend, and your father was my best friend. My father managed to get us to safety in Suzhou—it was risky, and expensive, and we left your family behind. I do not know if we could have helped or not."

"Did you try to help?"

Mr. Wang's brow creased with pain. "*Méi yǒu.* I asked my father about it at the time, and he said it was too dangerous. Those were hard times. But it was a mistake to do nothing. I don't know how your grandfather died, or what happened to your father that led him to kill himself, but I have always felt that it was partly our family's responsibility. Since your father died we have tried to help your mother and you—that is how you and Xu got to know each other as children." There were tears in Mr. Wang's eyes.

"Why are you telling me this? Do you want my forgiveness?" Walter's tone was defiant, but his voice was shaky and his eyes were also wet.

"Your forgiveness is not mine to ask. I wanted you to know."

"How can this be true? My mother has never said anything to me."

"I believe that your mother has never mentioned this out of kindness to our family. Perhaps to help forget your father. Perhaps so that you would not hate us, so that you could be friends with Xu. But it is time for the truth. I spoke with her this morning, and she gave me permission to tell you. Will you come to our house tonight and share dinner with our family?"

Walter did not respond, and both men looked out the window—at the lake, and the bridge that brought visitors to the tea house. The bridge zig-zagged to protect the establishment from the approach of evil spirits. The waitress brought fresh tea and refilled the pot.

After several minutes, Walter spoke. "Tell me …" he said. "Xu said today that JZP is doing well with its new Hong Kong investors. Tell me—are you still paying bribes to government officials to make your business succeed?"

"If I answer your question, can I trust you that I am not going to read about it in your newspaper?"

"Yes, you can trust me."

"*Hǎo de, Xiǎo Yáng*. You know of course that there is much corruption in the Chinese property market. You helped us fix the problems in Suzhou, but we cannot avoid all corruption in our business. But to answer your question, now that we have a joint venture with a family in Hong Kong who are property investors like us, we no longer have to pay officials to give us access to good properties in Jiangsu and Zhejiang. Do you understand why that is so?"

Walter failed to see the connection. "No, I—" Then the answer was suddenly obvious to him from his research on official corruption. He said with a frown, "You are helping the officials instead to transfer their money out of China through Hong Kong."

"You are a smart boy, Jiang." Mr. Wang also frowned, and shook his head. "But you are not quite right, and I am disappointed that you would think that JZP would violate the law in that way. You are close, though. Our Hong Kong partners can help the families of these officials to buy properties in Hong Kong, or in London, or even in America. We are following the law because we do not get involved in buying the foreign properties, or in getting the money there. Yet we are still involved in a system that helps government officials benefit from their position."

"I hate that system."

"I do not like it either, *Xiǎo Yáng*, but I accept those things that I cannot change. This was a difference between me and your father. I respected him for who he was and I respect you, but that is not me. If I was not getting rich from this system, someone else would do it."

"So you have brought me here today to tell me that you did not prevent the Chinese system from killing my father. Meanwhile, you continue to get rich off that system." Walter was angry and let his voice rise. The guests at the next table turned to look.

"What would you have me do?"

"You do not need to be a saint, but you should look for ways to make the world a better place. I have been spending a lot of time learning how property developers like you are destroying the historical buildings of Shanghai. Maybe you should do something about that. I don't know ... you figure it out. I cannot tell you how to do good."

Mr. Wang looked thoughtful. "It is a good idea. I agree that preserving our culture is very important—that is why I asked you to come to this place today. What if I establish a small foundation to work on preserving historical buildings—and ask you to manage it? I think that my property connections could help such a foundation to do very effective work."

Walter's mouth opened. He shut it with a snap. "I don't want to accept charity because you feel guilty about your business."

"*Xiǎo Yáng*, you can't have it both ways. You told me what you think I should do, and I have tried to say yes. Although you are right that I feel guilty ... but not about my business." Mr. Wang paused, tears again moistening his eyes. "Your father was a very good man, and I was not able to help him, or perhaps I was just not brave enough. I was afraid like many other people during the Cultural Revolution, and I had a young family to protect."

"*Xiè xie, Wáng xiānsheng.* I apologize if I was unkind in my first reaction, and thank you for your offer. But I am happy with my job at *Shanghai Weekend*."

"Yes, you are a good and honest journalist. If you wish, you could start by working for the foundation part time and still write for *Shanghai Weekend*."

Walter gave Mr. Wang a long, interested, respectful look. "That is a very generous proposal, Mr. Wang. I can't accept it now, but I shall certainly think about it. And I will accept your invitation to dinner tonight, if it still stands."

交易

40

Foundations
January 2010

You either love or you hate.
You live in the middle, you get nothing.

— *Charlie Sheen*

April struggled up the rocky dirt path. She breathed heavily, distracted from the striking view to her right, of Altadena and Pasadena spreading out more than a thousand feet below. The reason for the effort was about forty feet ahead of her. It was not easy for April to keep up with Jasmine, who was fitter, more used to the paths of the San Gabriel mountains, and longer-legged. April very much wanted to keep those beautiful legs in sight, but Jasmine was hiking with a vengeance.

On this sunny Sunday in January, Jasmine had offered to show April one of her favorite trails. They had set out after breakfast. At Jasmine's suggestion, April wore shorts, a t-shirt and a sweater against the winter morning chill. Jasmine was dressed about the same, with the advantage of good hiking shoes. April's tennis shoes were another reason she was falling behind. But the biggest reason was a conversation that had taken place fifteen minutes earlier.

After about forty-five minutes of brisk hiking, Jasmine had paused, to allow April to catch her breath and so they could admire the view together. April was feeling off-balance, and not just from the exercise. Jasmine's behavior in their relationship had not become any more predictable in the four months since they pulled off their plan to rescue *jiāo yì*.

April had hoped that things would settle down once Jasmine had a new job, but the offer Jasmine had received from HSBC the previous week had led to celebration with no increase in stability. Jasmine seemed unable to commit, unable to pull away, unable to explain well why she kept wavering. April was at her wits' end, and this morning, something about the fresh air and beautiful surroundings had convinced her that now was a good time to say something about it.

"Jasmine, why are we here?"

"What do you mean? I told you that I love this hike, and you agreed to come along."

"I mean, what are we doing in this relationship? I never know how you are feeling. I don't think I can take it anymore."

Jasmine stared at her. "You know that a relationship with you is not something that my parents would accept. I have told you many times that I am having a hard time working out what to do."

"That's bullshit." Jasmine's eyes widened. "You can't treat a lover like that."

"Well, it seems I can." Jasmine's attitude became the cold, calculating one that April had not seen in some time. "I think you want me so much that you will follow me while I figure it out."

"Fuck you, Jasmine."

Jasmine did not respond, and after looking at April expressionlessly for about two seconds, turned and resumed hiking, much faster than before. She did not seem to care that April started falling well behind, although in the few instances when Jasmine disappeared around a corner, the distance between them shortened considerably. April realized that Jasmine must have been waiting, not ignoring her completely.

After thirty minutes or so of this chase up the path, April saw Jasmine stop up ahead in a large flat area on a bluff, and sit down on a low wall among what appeared to be the ruins of a building. As April drew near, Jasmine asked, "Do you know what this is?"

"I guess it's a fight," April said. "I hope you aren't going to tell me that it's the end of us."

"No," Jasmine said, sweeping her arm to indicate the scene in front of them. "I mean, do you know what these ruins are?"

April looked around more carefully. On the slope past the edge of the bluff she could see some rusted machinery, including several vertical, toothed wheels at least five feet in diameter. "No. What is it?"

"These are the foundations of Echo Mountain Resort. There were hotels up here, and a railway ran all the way up that slope from Altadena until the 1930s. I was amazed when I first found it."

"What happened to it?"

Jasmine shrugged. "Time, I guess. I think of Los Angeles as a young city in a young country, with development always moving forward. But you have some ruins, just like in China." She fell silent, looking out at the view.

April looked at her, angry at herself as she realized that Jasmine was right about what she had said. She loved Jasmine too much to give her up, and was frightened that her language in their earlier conversation might have driven her away. "Jasmine?" The older girl did not respond. After a minute or so, April sat down beside her and tried again. "Jasmine, what are you thinking?" Again, no response. Then, Jasmine stood up, walked away to the edge of the bluff, and looked out over the view. April remained sitting, and began to cry quietly.

The sound of April crying finally produced a reaction, and Jasmine turned around a walked back to April. "April, I didn't mean to—"

"Jasmine, I am so sorry what I said to—"

"No. Let me speak." Cool, tough Jasmine was certainly back. Except that when April looked up into Jasmine's eyes, she saw tenderness. At least it seemed to be tenderness. It was not an expression that April could recall seeing on her face before. "You were right what you said to me. I have not been fair to you."

"I shouldn't have—"

"*Let me speak.*" Now that she knew Jasmine did not want to leave her, April found Jasmine's command both reassuring and a little thrilling. April had realized over the past months that fulfillment of a desire for a stronger partner was one of the things that had been missing in her relationships with Lisa and May. "For a long time I have felt caught in between China and the West. I have been treating you badly because I have been trying to resolve the conflict between what I feel for you and my Chinese expectations for a traditional life. Those are my parents' expectations."

"I understand——" Jasmine cut her off this time with a firm shake of the head.

"I need to be my own person. Not Chinese. Not American. Just me." She looked around. "Look at these ruins. If I keep bouncing back and forth, I will be dead like the people who played at these hotels, without ever having the chance to enjoy life." She looked at April, who now felt certain that what she saw on Jasmine's face was tenderness. It was nice, even if it looked a little out of place. "I am going to be my own person, me. And I would like to be me with you. Will you give me a kiss?"

"Do you think that I could say no?"

交易

41

Blue Skies and Big Waves

late March 2010

If one does not know to which port one is sailing,
no wind is favorable

– Lucius Annaeus Seneca

"Jibe, ho!" Richard called, telling the crew of the sixty-foot, two-masted ketch *Catalina Lady* to turn the boat from a southwest to a northwest heading, past the northern end of Santa Catalina Island. Emily was at the wheel, wearing the same blue bikini that had impressed François in Cane Garden Bay, this time partially covered by a waterproof windbreaker. She spun the wheel on Richard's command to make the turn.

Richard, who looked an extremely comfortable sailor in his shorts, t-shirt and baseball cap, was handling the mizzen sheet at the rear of boat. François, who managed to look slightly uncomfortable in clothing that imitated Richard's, was standing by on the main port winch in case the partially-furled headsail needed adjustment once the boat was on its new heading.

The skies were blue, but the crew was struggling with a strengthening wind that was blowing across more than twenty miles of open water from the coast of Los Angeles, producing a swell about six feet high and growing. Although they had lowered the sailboat's large mainsail an hour before, the boat continued to surge ahead strongly under the reduced sail, rolling as it headed diagonally across muscular waves.

The other four people on board were now sitting on the cockpit benches, also wearing lifejackets like the three who were managing the sails. Jasmine and April were next to each other holding hands. April looked nervous, Jasmine impassively interested. Julie was sitting calmly opposite them with Lydia in her lap. Lydia, who had recently celebrated her third birthday, seemed least concerned of those aboard, contributing emphatic comments and questions: "Another sailboat!" and "Mommy, are there fish in the water?"

* * *

The sailing trip had started that morning at Marina Del Rey in Los Angeles, where Richard had rented *Catalina Lady* for a two-day trip. He had decided to combine Lydia's first sailing trip with a celebration for the San Marino team from *jiāo yì*.

Richard made it clear to Jasmine that he still thought of her as part of the team, even after her enforced move to HSBC. And when Jasmine had asked to bring along April, Richard readily agreed, observing that April felt like part of the team too now. Although the two girls had not advertised their relationship, it had become an open secret. Jasmine had done her best to keep the implicit promise of stability that she made on top of Echo Mountain, and April had happily enjoyed the smoother ride.

At the last moment, François had invited Emily, who had arrived two days earlier for a week "visting her parents" in Los Angeles. She had declined François' repeated invitations to stay at his chic bachelor's apartment in Pasadena. The previous evening, though, after a dinner at which she and François had picked up their conversation where they had left off in Cane Garden Bay, she had not resisted his suggestion to see the apartment. Once they had discovered that they got along as well in bed as they did over beer in the islands, François did not have too hard a time convincing her to join the sailing trip.

Catalina Lady was heading across the twenty-five-mile-wide channel between Los Angeles and Santa Catalina Island. Richard had made the sail many times before, although never as skipper of quite so large a boat. Still, he was confident that he could handle the passage even with an inexperienced crew.

The day had begun with perfect sailing weather—clear blue skies and a light morning sea breeze. April and Jasmine, neither of whom had ever sailed before, headed for the bow of the boat to begin with, after some initial nervousness. They sat with their legs dangling over the side, looking out to sea, holding hands, and chatting quietly. The rest of the crew kept busy in the cockpit. Julie, despite plenty of experience on boats with Richard, played with Lydia and left the sailing mostly to Richard and Emily. After a while, Jasmine reappeared to ask questions about how the boat was sailed, which Richard and Emily answered with evident pleasure and some demonstrations. François also tried hard to learn. Emily had gently teased him that she could never live with a man who didn't know how to sail, and he seemed to have taken her comment to heart with an uncharacteristic earnestness.

Things first started to get challenging when the sea breeze died, and then was replaced by a strengthening wind off the land. Richard was perplexed, but the forecast had been for moderate winds and sunny skies, and he was not worried. As the wind and waves grew, he started to feel anxious, but reassured the crew—particularly François and April, who had started to ask a lot of questions about safety—that a big boat like *Catalina Lady* could easily handle the stronger wind. By the time Richard thought to re-check the weather forecast, and learned that there was an unexpected Santa Ana condition, it was too late to turn back to Marina del Rey. They had to press on to Catalina.

* * *

"Jibe, ho!" Richard shouted again over the noise of the wind. The rocky northern tip of Catalina lay about half a mile to port. As the boat turned towards the island, the mizzen slammed across with a bang, despite Richard's efforts to control it. April gave an involuntary squeak.

"I think it will be OK," Jasmine said, hugging April with a comforting smile. She returned to watching Richard's moves intently, and studying the boat. It was a simple machine, she thought, yet it could so efficiently use moving wind and water—turbulent, fluid elements—to send people racing across the sea. Jasmine considered the zig-zag of their course, taking them to their chosen destination. She could do this too—on a sailboat, and in life? Why not?

"Hey, Doc, are you *sure* this is safe? Why are we aiming so close to the island? Look at those waves." François sounded nervous as he pointed to the explosive sprays of foam kicked up by the heavy swell as it broke on the shore. Jasmine shot him an angry glance, which he didn't notice.

"You're right," Richard called. "That's a lee shore over there with the wind and waves blowing onto it—extremely dangerous and we've given it a wide berth. But past that point is the western side of the island, which is protected from the wind. It's very safe. You'll see in a few minutes."

"My friends in France tell me about *le Mistral* in the Mediterranean. I wonder whether it's like this."

"François, you do have hope as a sailor," Emily said. "The Santa Ana is a mountain wind a lot like the Mistral."

"Yep," Richard said, "and it wasn't supposed to happen today. Sorry, gang. But really, don't worry, I've been in much worse conditions and survived." He smiled. François, April and Jasmine didn't look as though they appreciated the humor. But, as Richard predicted, the big waves nearly disappeared soon after they passed the tip of the island, and the wind weakened noticeably. The mood of the crew improved dramatically.

An hour later, around five in the afternoon, they pulled into Catalina Harbor, which was crowded with boats seeking shelter from the waves battering the harbor at Avalon, the main town of Catalina on the other side of the island. Avalon had been their original destination, too. Richard anchored between two other big boats, waving to their new neighbors as they approached. He announced that dinner would feature fish cooked on the deck barbecue, with drinks beginning around six-thirty, giving everyone time to clean off the salt from the day of sailing.

Jasmine and April were the first to emerge from below after their showers. April took the opportunity to phone Walter, while the couple were standing together at the bow, looking out at the harbor, the boats and the sea. The sun was dipping low outside the harbor's narrow entrance, promising a spectacular sunset through a few rose-tinted clouds.

"Good morning, Walter. Guess where Jasmine and I are."

"I don't know. In California somewhere?"

"That's why I like you, Walter, you're so intelligent. We're on a sailboat near an island called Catalina."

"I'm jealous. You sailed there? How was the sailing?"

"It was scary at times, but I liked it, I think. Jasmine wants to learn how, I can tell. You'll have to come sailing with us some day. How are you doing?"

"I'm very well. I've been working on your uncle's foundation. I think this is what I was born to do. I can fight for what I believe, and really accomplish something. Believe it or not, keeping old, beautiful buildings is something that I seem to be able to convince the government to support, particularly with the connections that your uncle has."

"That's great, Walter. We have good news too. Although Jasmine lost her job at San Marino because of the mess with *jiāo yì*, the partners helped her get a new one at HSBC. She's still in a trial period, but it looks like it will be OK."

"Tell Walter that I don't blame him that his articles got me fired," Jasmine said, with her arms around April and her head close to the phone.

"I heard that," Walter said. "Thanks Jasmine."

"And Jasmine's boss Richard also helped me get a job at another investment company in Los Angeles that's doing deals in China. So there's a good chance I'll be visiting you soon."

"That's great, April. I still love you, you know."

"Shut up, Walter," April said gently.

"I heard that, too," Jasmine said.

Walter's smile could also be heard in his voice. "OK. Listen, I need to go to work now, but let's talk soon."

"Yes, definitely."

The girls spent another ten minutes watching the sun sink lower towards sea. When they returned to the cockpit, Julie and Emily were sitting and chatting about their mutual interest in Zen, while Lydia played with dolls on the floor. They invited Jasmine and April to join them.

Richard and François were below in the galley, where Richard was mixing drinks while François chopped vegetables for dinner. Richard made no effort to avoid being overheard as he chatted with François. "This girl you found is quite something. She talks about Zen with my wife, and she speaks Mandarin almost as well as I do." Emily had learned good Mandarin for her studies. "And best of all she is making you domestic. I didn't even know that you knew how to chop vegetables."

Emily called down from above. "I had to show him how to use a knife, but he's a quick learner."

"She also seems to be good with Lydia's dolls," Julie added.

François said quietly to Richard, "Do you remember that girl I told you I was looking for? I didn't think she existed. But here she is."

Richard patted François on the shoulder. "Congratulations, *mon ami.*"

* * *

After dinner, Julie put Lydia to sleep in their cabin, and the six adults continued drinking in the cockpit. The post-sunset glow in the west had mostly faded, and stars were appearing quickly in a clear sky. The boat continued to bob gently in the wind, which was still insistent even after crossing the island, although it produced only small waves in the protected harbor. Richard offered a toast. "To good friends and colleagues, and to our success."

"Hear, hear," Julie agreed. "It's particularly nice to have new friends join us. Thanks for coming along, Emily, April."

"Thank you so much, Mr. Gregg," April said. "Sorry I was nervous during the big waves. I hope I can learn to like the adventure of sailing. You're a good captain."

301

"Thanks, April. I propose another toast to big waves. Life is full of them, and mostly we seem to get through. We certainly had some big waves in China, and we didn't accomplish everything we intended, but we learned a lot and lived to fight another day. I count my blessings." He raised his glass.

"Richard Gregg, you sound optimistic again!" Julie said, turning to kiss him on the cheek.

Richard turned too and neatly intercepted her kiss on his lips. "Yes, I suppose I need to practice what I preach and learn to ride the waves a little more calmly. Maybe it *is* time for me to try meditation."

"Speaking of China," Emily said, "François told me on the night that we met that he had seen something interesting at the completion of your *jiāo yì*, but then he wouldn't say any more. You promised to tell me later, François."

Richard sat up and turned to François, clearly interested. "What's that? You didn't say anything about that to me."

François frowned at Emily in mock exasperation, turned to Richard, and hesitated, considering. "OK ... I'll tell you, but not the name."

"The name?" Richard asked.

"We thought that we sold our investment in *jiāo yì* to a Hong Kong family, but I don't think they invested alone. At the completion, there were also some representatives of a co-investor, who happens to be a, let's say, a well-known American software billionaire. I knew them from a deal a long time ago in Paris. I'm sure that the representatives didn't expect to be recognized, and I don't think they knew that I did."

"And you think this U.S. investor, whose name you won't tell us, knew that he was investing in a Chinese property deal involving evidence of corruption? Just what our lawyers told us that we couldn't do under U.S. law?"

François shrugged. "I have no idea what he knows. These ultra-rich people have so much money offshore, and sometimes even they don't know what it's doing."

Jasmine, who had been quiet for most of the day, spoke up. "Our journalist friend Walter who wrote the articles in *Shanghai Weekend* likes to say that corruption is everywhere, that so many people are trying to get ahead any way they can. I think he's right, but that maybe it's a little worse in China. I almost wrecked *jiāo yì* by trying to fight the corruption there on my own."

"Well, you also saved *jiāo yì*," Richard said. Jasmine took April's hand without looking at her. He smiled. "Yes, of course, April made it happen too … and Walter."

"And Walter's editor … and Richard, supporting it to the partners," added Jasmine. "And François' contacts, and my father, and April's uncle, and …" She trailed off, as if wondering where interlocking causes and effects ceased.

"When I think about corruption, the interesting thing for me is that we humans are the ones who get to choose right from wrong," Emily said. "Buddhist philosophy says that in a world that does not have meaning, right living is the only choice we have."

"*Mon dieu*, too much philosophy for me," François said to her. "Please just give me a kiss. That is right living."

Acknowledgements

Many people helped me to write this book, my first novel. At the head of the line is my lovely, super-intelligent partner Katharine, who helped me conceive the original idea, served as an intellectual sparring partner throughout the process, and edited the final draft. And second must be my cousin Erica Ashton, also an editor, whose detailed comments and edits on the first draft helped turn a plot into a novel.

I also greatly appreciate the time and useful suggestions of others who read and commented on my drafts, including my father and mother, Winnie Chang, Michelle Clifton Davila, Paula Prynn, Jenny Scarfe Beckett, Justine Solomons and Magnhild Viste.

And thanks to the people who helped me produce the publication version of *The Deal*: Sarah Juckes and the team at CompletelyNovel, and my cover designer Jan Marshall.

Thanks also, always, to my beautiful daughter Lily, for being my sunshine every day.